Camp Colorblind

&

JC Conrad-Ellis

For information about Provision Press please
visit our website at www.blackdiamondseries.com.

Library of Congress Cataloging-in-Publication Data

Conrad-Ellis, JC.

CAMP COLORBLIND/ JC Conrad-Ellis
ISBN 13: 978-1-957593-01-2
Fiction Based on True Events

Copyright Registered: 2022
Published by Provision Press in the USA

January 2022

10 9 8 7 6 5 4 3 2

Printed in the USA

To: My Exhibit B pit crew

With love, Exhibit A
Vroom, vroom

ACKNOWLEDGEMENTS

Once again, I humbly thank God for allowing me to share my love of writing and gracing me with the ability to use my time and talent (you'll be the judge of that) to pen another tale for readers everywhere to treasure and enjoy.

Please indulge me as I pause (ever so briefly this go round) to again express my sincere gratitude by thanking the patchwork quilt of folks that I recognized in my first novel, <u>Boys, Beauty and Betrayal</u>. A list that is far too long to duplicate a second time, but miraculously, the overwhelming majority of those listed remain sparkling gems in my life. Their support, encouragement and love fueled me to continue on this sometimes lonely and risk filled journey to publish <u>Camp Colorblind</u>, a trek that has been filled with exhilarating thrills, as well as a few potholes and disappointments. But fortunately, the thrills outweighed the potholes tenfold! While the brilliance of some of the gems in my life may have dimmed or outright vanished, their season in my life produced fruit when I needed it, and for that I am grateful. Sadly, even though some of the patches in my life quilt have been removed, I have been blessed to add more patches to the beautifully woven, perfectly tattered quilt that blankets the roots of my tree.

To my patchwork quilt posse: I thank you for reading the book, buying multiple copies, writing reviews, giving copies as gifts, choosing the book as a book club selection, hosting book signings for me, working the table and selling books at book signings, buying more books at my signings to help motivate me, encouraging your friends to request the book in book stores and online, telling your vast network circles about the book, inviting me to speak at schools and other civic and social venues, rolling up your sleeves and writing marketing plans, brochures and press releases for me, praying for the book's (and my) success, helping me spread the buzz, and nudging me to publish Camp Colorblind sooner than later! You know who you are, you know what you did, and you know that I love you for it!

A special shout out to the following patches who belong on the JC Conrad-Ellis Marketing/Public Relations Extra Mile Wall of Fame: Brian Ellis, Sharon Ruff, Kelly West, Nicole Roberts Jones, John Conrad, Shari O'Bryant, Michael "MC" Coburn, Michelle & James Richardson, Angela Hall, Kim & Alex du Buclet, Necole Merritt, Jillonda Reed Washington, Maurice Markey, Karyn Roelke, Sandra Townsend & The mothers of Jack and Jill of America, Inc., Mid-Western Region, The women of Delta Sigma Theta Sorority, Inc., Chicago Alumnae Chapter, Milwaukee Alumnae Chapter, The Bible study ladies of Bristlecone Pines, Molly Fay and the crew at The Morning Blend - NBC Affiliate/TMJ4, my publisher, Valerie Connelley and the team at Nightengale Press for their guidance, faith, nurturing, patience and tutelage.

To my readers: Welcome back and thank you for your continued support! A few things to remember: Open your minds to embrace different things. Try not to judge others or you'll be judged by the same measure with which you judge. Try to live your life so that it's a meaningful one. Be a help or a blessing to someone every day. Forgive quickly because life is short. Forgive yourself when you blunder. Release negative stereotypes one enriching experience at a time. If something takes you out of your happy place for a moment or two, put yourself back in your happy place by doing something nice for someone else. Build a bridge and begin to get over the drama in your life. Reduce, reuse & recycle. You don't need anyone's permission to be joyful and happy.

Remember, I write for you. Thank you for giving me a reason to indulge my pleasure. Keep reading!

CONTENTS

*Matthew 7: 1-4   {1}"Judge not, that you be
not judged. {2}For with the judgment you
pronounce you will be judged, and the measure
you give will be the measure you get. {3}Why do
you see the speck that is in your brother's eye,
but do not notice the log that is in your own eye?
{4}Or how can you say to your brother,
'Let me take the speck out of your eye,'
when there is a log in your own eye?*

The Holy Bible
The New Oxford Annoted Bible
Revised Standard Version
NY Oxford University Press
1973

Chapter 1

It's A Boy!

She stood frozen in her tracks. Her eyes roamed left, neurotically counting ten hangers in the closet. Forcing her arm to move, she methodically hung her jacket, stacking her sneakers directly below. Tanisha watched as the light jacket slid slowly down the wire hanger, twisting and twirling like a circus acrobat suspended on a silk cord. The powder blue jacket now swaddled her shoes like a newborn son. As she raced out the door to join Maria's family for ice cream, Tanisha was glad that she'd remembered to grab the jacket. Against the ice cream parlor's arctic chill, it had provided just enough armor for her thin frame. She counted the hangers a second time, rhythmically listening to the sound of her brother's statement, savoring every word like a gourmet meal. "Some – boy – called – but – he – didn't – leave – his – name," she repeated robotically, the words bouncing off the hangers creating an imaginary echo that only she could hear. A pregnant pause inserted after each word, her mind's way of giving itself time. She needed time to comprehend the meaning of each precious syllable. Tanisha hung her jacket a second time. *Had she heard her brother correctly? Had he really said that a boy called her tonight?*

"A boy called, but he didn't leave his name?" Tanisha repeated. The sound of those words brought a rush of adrenaline to her heart. "Did you even bother to **ask** him his name?" she asked indignantly, the irritation dripping from her sharp tongue as she resisted every urge to end the question with "moron."

Byron's scowl was intense yet fleeting. The brief cutting of his eyes toward her would have been missed had she blinked at that moment. Without uttering a word, she knew his thoughts. His look said, 'of course I did. I know how to take a phone message. I'm thirteen years old now, stop badgering me, stupid!'

"What did his voice sound like, Byron?" Tanisha asked. Her voice now dripped with honey instead of vinegar.

Byron was focused on his soccer game and stared intently at the television ignoring Tanisha's question.

"Byron! What did his voice sound like?" Tanisha repeated much louder.

Her brother had a slight hearing problem, and was forced to sit in the front of the class in school. But at home, Tanisha suspected that he suffered from selective hearing loss and used his hearing trouble to conveniently ignore people as he chose. This was one of those times.

She decided to change her strategy. "Who's playing?" she asked.

"Huh?" Byron groaned.

"Who's playing?" she repeated louder.

His eyes glued to the game, he mumbled a reply. "Nigeria against Columbia," he offered gruffly. "Now, shush, Tanisha! I'm trying to focus."

Byron groaned as a goal was scored. She wondered which soccer team he was rooting for and decided that he must be rooting for the Nigerian team because the team that had scored the upsetting goal didn't have any afro haircuts on the field. Tanisha wanted to ask him why he chose to root for the Nigerian team, but knew that she would not be able to talk with him until a commercial came on. She plopped on the sofa to plan her next barrage of questions and stared blankly at the television, wondering how many calories the players burned running up and down the field at a breathtaking pace. Observing how engrossed in the game her brother was, her mind drifted back to his initial introduction to the sport of soccer.

൚൘

A large Laotian family moved into the Cedar Grove complex shortly after the Carlson family arrived. The family consisted of five boys, their parents and one set of grandparents. Tanisha marveled at how that many people fit in the three bedroom town home that she felt was barely large enough for the Carlson family of six. Byron befriended a boy his age named Lou. It was Lou who introduced Byron to the game of soccer.

"In my country we call it futbol. But here you call it soccer," Lou explained. Although Lou spoke broken English, he and Byron quickly became inseparable. Byron spent most of his time kicking around a soccer ball and surfing the television stations for a soccer game to watch. It didn't matter to Byron if the game was televised in Spanish, Byron watched anyway. He studied the players' moves intent on mimicking some of the intricate maneuvers with Lou and his brothers. Their friendship a perfect example of the barter system at work, Byron helped Lou with his English and Lou helped Byron with his soccer.

Tanisha was curious about the new family and questioned her brother on their lifestyle.

"Byron, where do all of them sleep?" Tanisha quizzed one day.

"The parents sleep in the small bedroom like yours. The grandparents sleep in the big bedroom, and Lou and two of his brothers sleep in the bedroom like the one that Jack and Allen and I share," Byron explained.

"But there are five kids, where do the other two sleep?" Tanisha tested.

"Oh. The older two brothers sleep in the basement. They have these mats that they roll out," Byron continued. "Why do you care?" he groaned.

"I was just wondering. Why do the grandparents sleep in the biggest bedroom?" Tanisha continued.

"I have no idea," Byron stated before walking away. "And I could care less."

Tanisha was far too curious to let it rest. She went to the library and checked out a book on Asian cultures. She read that in Asian cultures it's common for generations of families to live together in one house. And the elders are always shown the most respect and given the best of everything.

When Lou's family moved to the Cedar Grove complex, Tanisha's dad Jackie referred to them as refugees explaining that the country of Laos was under siege and their government was in turmoil, so many Laotians sought political asylum in the United States to escape the political warfare and poverty in Laos. Another Laotian family had recently moved to the Cedar Grove subdivision and Tanisha wondered if they were related somehow. She asked Byron.

"Is the new family related to Lou's family?" she asked.

"No. Just because they're from the same country, it doesn't mean they're related, stupid," Byron replied. "Are you related to every black person in Cedar Grove?" he asked.

"They look alike," she defended. "They could be related."

"They look nothing alike," Byron replied. "They just look alike to ignorant people like you, thunder thighs," he laughed.

৪৩

At school, Tanisha noticed that the Laotian boys were able to assimilate into the Battle Creek Junior High culture fairly quickly. The school had just formed a soccer team and the Laotian boys' superior soccer skills were much appreciated by the coaches and other players. She marveled at how a sport was able to bridge a language and cultural gap so quickly. Tanisha thought it odd that of the two families that lived in Cedar Grove, none of the families had daughters. She wished that there was a Laotian girl that she could get to know to understand their culture better. She made a note to research that later or to talk to her dad about it. He would probably know. Jackie knew everything.

Now that her parents were officially divorced and Jackie had moved out, Tanisha found that she missed her dad's opinion on current events and how he tried to use every moment as a teaching moment for his children. She missed how he would grumble and talk to himself as he read the <u>Chicago Tribune</u> newspaper or watched the local news. He never deliberately engaged the children in his mutterings, but Tanisha and her brothers were able to glean his opinion as he yelled at the television screen or muttered his thoughts aloud as he read the paper. Tanisha loved to run to the paper box near the Cedar Grove community center to buy the Sunday paper for Jackie because the one who ran to the store to get the paper usually got a fifty cent tip for the errand.

೮ა೮ჳ

"Tanisha, now if they don't have any more Tribs, bring my money back. Don't buy a <u>Sun Globe</u> even if they don't have a Trib, I can't read that paper." Jackie would remind his children every Sunday without fail.

"Why don't you like the <u>Sun Globe</u>, Daddy?" Tanisha asked once.

"I just don't like that paper. Never did," Jackie responded as he shuffled into his porcelain office.

The Carlson children knew Jackie's Sunday paper reading ritual and knew that it was wise to brush their teeth and shower before Jackie summoned for his paper and retreated into his "office" for his meeting. It was unwise to enter for at least twenty minutes after the meeting, which usually lasted an hour. The suggestion to turn on the ceiling fan to circulate air during the meeting was always summarily ignored.

Before the Carlson family moved to Newberry East, Illinois, the family lived in a small three bedroom bungalow on Chicago's south side. The bungalow had one small bathroom that the family shared. A scrawny first grader, one day Tanisha banged on the bathroom door screaming. "Daddy, I have to use it bad!" Jackie reluctantly exited the bathroom mumbling that he wasn't finished. Tanisha brushed by him to prevent wetting herself and plopped on the toilet to relieve her bladder. As she peed, she exhaled deeply with relief. On the inhale, she was overcome by the sickening smell of rotten eggs. Tanisha thought she would vomit and held her breath. But as she held her breath she realized that she'd sucked in the polluted rotten egg air and blew the air out of her lungs, but then the smell came back in full force. She pressed her tongue into the roof of her mouth and held her breath again until she finished using the bathroom. She flushed the toilet and bolted out of the bathroom without washing her hands, a mortal sin in the Carlson family, as Jackie stood in the hallway waiting to reenter the bathroom. Tanisha remembered running outside to breathe in fresh air in gulps.

⁎⁎⁎

Years later, the thought of the smell that she encountered when she interrupted Jackie's bathroom meeting made her laugh. Fortunately, the family now had a small powder room on the first floor of their town house, so the children didn't have to interrupt Jackie to use the toilet. Not that it mattered, Jackie was gone. She missed hearing him hum in the bathroom and longed to see him splash aftershave lotion on his freshly shaved cheeks.

Almost one year later, her parent's break up still felt like a bad dream. Unlike the dramatic break up scenes on television or in the movies, there had been no big fight or argument. Her dad had just taken the children out to breakfast and told them that he was moving out for awhile until he and Billie Mae could work through a few issues. He moved out almost a week later. Billie filed for a legal separation immediately and then filed for divorce. The children saw Jackie on the weekends or during the week if there was a school event that he came out to attend. Now that Jackie was gone, the family seldom purchased a newspaper. The few times that Billie bought a paper, she bought the <u>Sun Globe.</u> Missing her current events' secret weapon, Tanisha found herself calling her dad daily in order to engage him in a current events discussion, but mostly just to hear his voice.

Tanisha stared at her watch. She couldn't believe that a commercial had not aired yet. She sighed loudly, hoping that her brother would look up from the television set, but his eyes stayed glued to the soccer game. In the corner of the small room, she saw her youngest brother Allen asleep on the sectional sofa. She hadn't noticed him before. As Tanisha studied her sleeping younger brother she wondered how he could sleep with his head almost hanging off the side of the sofa.

"Byron, how long has Allen been asleep?" she asked sweetly. "Did you see him take his allergy medicine?" Byron sat silent.

"Byron! I know you heard me!" Tanisha's tone changed to a deep authoritative one.

Byron responded without looking at Tanisha. "He fell asleep about an hour ago, and I saw him take his allergy medicine right before he nodded off. Now chill, I'm trying to watch this match."

Byron's obsession with soccer created interesting knock down drag out fights with Allen who was not the slightest bit interested in soccer. A stocky nine year old, Allen was especially verbal about Byron's new soccer pastime and his monopoly of the television. Allen believed that, as the youngest, he had television seniority to watch whatever he wanted since his older siblings had watched television for more years than he. It was a compelling argument that never worked with Byron who always challenged Allen to a wrestling match with the winner choosing the evening's program. Although four years his junior, Allen was almost as tall as Byron but not as muscular so his attempts to wrestle Byron for television rights always amused Tanisha who sometimes served as the wrestling match referee. Allen usually lost the duels but occasionally Byron would strike a compromise and allow Allen to watch a preferred program before switching to the soccer game. Tonight Allen lay sprawled across the sofa snoring softly and hugging the tattered baby blanket that he'd slept with since infancy.

Tanisha chuckled as she imagined the wrestling match that had probably ensued, ending in Byron's victory.

She stared at the soccer game hoping that her presence would spark a recollection and Byron would miraculously remember a name, any name. Just as she was beginning to think that the game was running without commercial interruptions, a commercial appeared, so she tried again.

"Think, Byron. Are you sure the person who called didn't leave a name?" Tanisha pleaded. This time her tone was as soft as cotton.

Byron looked up from the television and shrugged his shoulders before responding. "Like I told you, he didn't leave a name. When I asked him if he wanted to leave a message he just said no thanks, I'll call her back."

"Did he say, 'no thanks' or 'naw, no thanks?'" Tanisha asked.

"What difference does it make, Tanisha? He didn't leave a name!" Byron groaned.

Tanisha sighed loudly as she realized that Byron was incapable of providing a voice analysis. Besides, if the person hadn't left his name then there was no reason to badger Byron for more information. Tanisha decided to abandon the mission and retreat to her room to call Lori. She tucked the tattered baby blanket under Allen's chin and mumbled a soft goodnight to Byron who was engrossed in his soccer match once again.

Her thoughts spun back to who the male caller could have been. The only boys who had her new telephone number were Darrell Hunter and David Barton who'd gotten her number to give to Byron Bird. Darrell had not spoken to her since her driveway dump after the Turnabout dance a few weeks ago and he had no reason to call her so Tanisha concluded that the call must have been from Byron Bird.

Tanisha ran up the stairs to her bedroom two at a time to call Lori.

Lori answered the phone on the first ring.

"Hey, girl! I think Byron Bird finally called me." Tanisha was slightly winded from her sprint up the stairs and sat on the floor in her bedroom to catch her breath.

"Good. It's about time, but why did you say you "think" he called you?" Lori asked.

"Well, my brother answered my phone and said it was a boy but he didn't leave his name." Tanisha could hear the doubt in Lori's voice. "And he's the only person that it could be. I mean Darrell has my number but why would he call me?" she asked. "He hates me after I dumped him on his driveway," she reminded. "Besides, he's dating Tracy Jones now."

"Good point. So what are you going to do?" Lori asked.

"I don't know. That's why I called you. What should I do?"

"Do you still have his number?" Lori asked.

Tanisha had Byron's number memorized but didn't want to admit that to Lori. After memorizing the seven digits, she had tucked his number away in an old purse hanging in her bedroom closet just in case her memory failed her.

"I think I kept his number," Tanisha offered coyly. "Let me check my old purse." Tanisha retrieved the number and confirmed that she still had it. "Do you think I should call him?"

"Well, who else could have called you?"

"I have no idea. The only other boy besides Byron Bird who has my number is David Barton. But why would he call me? He told Rashanda that he needed my number to give to Byron Bird," Tanisha explained.

"Maybe David Barton likes you. Have you ever thought of that?" Lori suggested.

"Not really," she offered unconvincingly. "I'm not his type. Besides, he told Rashanda he wanted my number to give to Byron," she shrugged.

"Girl, he may have just said that. And how do you know that you're not his type? Have you seen his type?" Lori quizzed. "You never know what someone's type is."

"I guess that's true. But you've never seen him. He's one of those pretty boys that Maria is always fawning over when we walk through the mall," she explained. "Don't tell her I said this, but he's cuter than Todd," she shared. "Or at least in that obvious pretty boy way that she likes," Tanisha clarified. "He's so much more Maria's type than mine," she continued. "He just looks like he'd be a jerk."

"You are so judgmental," Lori laughed. "You said he was nice," she reminded. "And even Rashanda said that he was really nice when she met him at the skating rink."

Tanisha kicked her feet in the air and stared at the ceiling in her room. "He is nice," she agreed. "And I had fun talking to him on the John & Judy ski trip, but I think he was just being nice to me so I wouldn't feel out of place since everyone else knew someone at his party," Tanisha said. "He was just being a good host."

"I'm just saying, it could be him reaching out to you," Lori offered confidently.

"What should I do?" Tanisha asked.

"You should call Byron. Just tell him that your brother left a message that someone called. And if it wasn't him, he'll just think that you have so many boys calling you that you can't keep track," Lori giggled. "You better call before it gets too late. It's almost 10:00."

"Good point. I wish you lived closer so you could come over and call him with me. I'm so nervous. I need some courage," Tanisha sighed.

"You'll be fine. Girl, Charlotte is waiting to use the phone again. She says it'll just take five minutes. You're so lucky to have your own line," Lori groaned.

"Okay, I'll call him, and then I'll call you back. By the way, Maria and I are cool again. She apologized in the kitchen for treating me like dog poop on the John & Judy ski trip. We'll see how long this mood lasts," she finished.

"I figured that you and Maria must have made up when she invited you to get ice cream with her family. I'm glad that everybody's on speaking terms again! Hallelujah!" Lori squealed.

"Lori, call CJ and find out if Darrell called me would you?" Tanisha pleaded.

"Okay. I'll sneak and call CJ right now before I give the phone to Charlotte. I'm sure CJ will know because they talk about everything," she whispered. "If Darrell called you, I'll call you right back in five minutes, but if he didn't call you I won't call you back, okay?"

The girls hung up and Tanisha studied Byron's number: 555-9137. She knew she wanted to call him, but her heart raced. She pressed the receiver down with her thumb finger and twirled the squiggly cord of the pink princess telephone. As she waited for the five minutes to pass, she decided to do a few sit-ups to work off some of the pizza that she'd eaten. She hung up the receiver and grunted through fifty crunches as she watched her alarm clock. Five minutes later, the phone still hadn't rung.

Tanisha took several deep breaths. She put the phone up to her ear, took another deep breath and dialed 555-91 before quickly hanging up the receiver. *What if his mother answers? It's almost 10:00 at night! What will his mother think of me if I call this late? I don't want his mother to think that I'm fast. At least Darrell's mom knows me from school so when I say hello to her, she knows who I am. If Byron's mom answers, I'll just say hello Mrs. Bird. This is Tanisha Carlson. May I speak to Byron, please?*

Tanisha repeated her greeting three or four times in her most proper tone, the one she used when she answered the service desk phone at Save Mart. She stood in front of her bedroom mirror with the receiver next to her ear, practicing her greeting with a smile in her voice.

Her voice exercises complete, she exhaled deeply and dialed the number, her nerves jockeying for position. The phone rang three times and Tanisha was prepared to hang up when a deep male voice answered.

"Hello," the voice said.

"Hi. Um, this is Tanisha Carlson? May I speak with Byron, please?" Tanisha asked nervously, her phone script rehearsal failing her. She curled her toes and squeezed her eyes shut, bracing herself for the response. She remembered to breathe and realized that the person on the other end of the phone couldn't see her. She opened her eyes. Tanisha heard the person bellow in a deep voice. "Hold on, please. Byron, you have a telephone call." She could hear maturity in the person's voice and assumed it must be Byron's father.

A few seconds later, a younger male voice picked up another receiver.

"I got it, Dad. Hello," Byron coughed into the receiver.

"Hi, Byron. This is Tanisha Carlson," she said nervously.

"Hey! How you doing, Tanisha?"

"I'm fine. Did I catch you at a bad time?" Tanisha asked.

"Naw! I was just chilling and watching the Bulls game with my brother."

"Oh, I won't keep you then. By the way, did you call me earlier tonight? My brother Byron told me that someone called, and I thought it might have been you." Tanisha held her breath again awaiting his response.

"You have a brother named Byron? That's funny. Naw, I didn't call you. I lost your number and I was going to have my boy Todd get it from his girlfriend but I forgot. So how you doing?" Byron's voice trailed.

Didn't he just ask me that? She exhaled and responded again that she was fine but her thoughts were swimming. *If Darrell and Byron didn't call me, then who did? And why didn't David Barton give Byron my number?*

"So how was your day?" Tanisha asked.

"Oh, it was cool."

Are the Bulls winning?" she asked.

"Huh? Uh, yeah, they're winning," Byron replied distractedly.

"Well, you should get back to your game," Tanisha suggested.

"Naw, don't hang up. I want to talk to you," Byron replied.

"Actually my brother needs to use the phone, so I need to let you go," Tanisha lied. She had wanted to talk to Byron Bird on the phone for months. Now he was ignoring her to watch a basketball game. Tanisha was suddenly very annoyed with Byron Bird.

"Since I have you on the phone, let me go ahead and get your number," Byron said. "Hold on while I get a pen."

Tanisha quickly rattled off her number. *I hope he doesn't call me back. He's lame.* Her Byron Bird crush had crashed and burned. She considered dialing Lori to give her an update, but remembered that Charlotte would probably be on the phone. Tanisha decided to go to bed and worry about who her mystery caller was in the morning.

‘’

He felt like a stalker. All that was missing was a trench coat, a fedora and dark sun glasses. On a whim, he'd gone to the skating rink hoping that he would see her. If questioned as to why he was there, he was prepared to tell her that he skated to strengthen his ankles for ice hockey, a sport he hadn't played since he was twelve, but she didn't need to know that. He paid his admission fee and rented skates, casually skating around the crowded rink, one eye glancing toward the main doorway on every rotation. Thirty minutes later, sweat beading on his brow, he needed a beverage. In the concession area, he was careful to position himself facing the door, sipping on his lemonade and studying the skaters for any sign of her. He nursed his lemonade for twenty minutes. By 8:00, he knew that Tanisha and her girls were not coming. The teen skate night ended at 9:00 so that the rink could be cleaned in preparation for the adult skating party that started at 10:00.

As he turned in his rented skates, he noticed a pay phone by the bathroom.

He peeled his car out of the parking lot and stopped at a gas station. As he filled up his tank, he noticed a payphone illuminated under a street light. He walked inside to purchase a pack of gum and pay for his gas. Another pay phone was mounted on the wall next to the bathroom. Jiggling the change in his hand, he walked out of the gas station and toward the illuminated pay phone that beckoned him like a magnet. He had memorized Tanisha's number and decided that he had to talk to her. He knew that she lived in Newberry East which was five minutes away from the roller skating rink and thought that maybe if she wasn't doing anything he could stop by her house and they could go for a walk. Without thinking, he dropped a quarter into the payphone and dialed her number. As the phone rang, he thought of what he would say. The words scrambled in his head like a word search puzzle. *I need a reason to call her. Hang up, man! What are you going to say to her? She'll think you're psycho. How are you going to explain having her number?* The phone rang five times. *Lucky for you, there's no answer or you'd sound like an idiot. Have a script ready next time, chucklehead.*

"Hello," a young boy answered.

"Uh, hello? Hello! May I speak to Tanisha?" David stammered quickly, his thoughts racing for an opening statement like a lawyer preparing to address the jury.

"She's not here. May I tell her who's calling?"

"No that's okay. I'll call her back later." David hung up, his hand resting momentarily on the cradled receiver. *Why didn't you leave your name and number, idiot?* He exhaled and slowly walked back to his car before peeling away and flooring the Corvette all the way to his house. Ten minutes later he pulled the car into the driveway and stared at the family's English Tudor style home. His parents were attending a hospital benefit, and his two siblings were away at college. The dark house loomed eerie and uninviting, he dreaded going inside.

Parking his car at the end of the long driveway, he clicked the garage door opener and sauntered toward the garage. *We're the only house in the subdivision that doesn't have a three car garage. I am so tired of scraping snow off my ride. I hope my old man makes good on his promise to have the third garage bay added on before winter hits.*

Clicking on every light switch in his path, he stopped in the kitchen and helped himself to one of his dad's beers, being so bold as to grab a frosty mug chilling in the freezer. His parents didn't approve of him drinking beer, but after his parents came home early and caught him with a beer in hand, he received a long lecture on under age drinking and David was told to never drive his car if he's even had one beer or the car would be sold. He tilted the mug to the side and filled his glass over the sink, allowing the foam head to settle before taking a swig of the cold beverage.

His eyes panning the room for the wandering remote control, David plopped on the sofa and watched the Michael Jackson Thriller video, his thoughts racing.

Should I call her again tonight? She's probably home now, it's after ten o'clock. But what if she can't have calls this late? I'll call her tomorrow. What am I going to say when I finally talk to her? She's already told me that she can't date yet. Plus, she thinks that Todd is too old for Maria, and I'm older than Todd. What will your opening statement be, moron? When you call her you need a reason to call her, genius. I can't believe I'm tripping about a fourteen year old girl that I barely know!

His gait heavy, he trudged into the kitchen for a snack, haphazardly washed his beer mug and placed it back in the freezer. *Hide the evidence, David. No need for them to come home and you have exhibit A in your hand. You're just asking for a lecture.* Once in the garage, he flicked on the light to toss his beer bottle in the family's new blue recycling bin in an effort to avoid a tongue lashing from his mother about the importance of doing his part to help the environment and the world by recycling. This time, the laundry room light awakened the sleeping Belvedere who'd ignored him when he first arrived home, preferring to continue his twelfth nap of the day. Lured by the bag of chips in David's hand, Belvedere stretched out of his doggie bed and followed David into the family room, plopping at his feet as Michael Jackson mooned walked across the screen.

Chapter 2

The Working Girl

The April showers had indeed brought May flowers, and the insects and worms that also signaled the arrival of warm weather and sunshine. It had been several weeks since her mystery caller. That morning, she lay in bed still wondering who the mystery caller could have been and why he hadn't left his name. *Lori still thinks it was David Barton, and I'm beginning to agree with her. But why did he call me? Why didn't he leave a name, and why hasn't he called back?* She pulled her new comforter up to her chin and snuggled under its warmth.

The alarm clock buzzed loudly. She turned it off quickly. Already awake, she stretched and yawned. She had to be at Save Mart at 9:00. Work wasn't as much fun anymore since she didn't like her new responsibilities. The personnel manager's voice rang through her sleepy head.

"Tanisha, we're promoting you to checkout supervisor!" Deanna said. *"You've been doing such a great job on your register that I know you will keep up the good work. Congratulations!"*

It hadn't been a promotion. Tanisha was assigned as the supervisor by default since she was the only part-time cashier whose register usually balanced at the end of her shift. She hated supervising the other cashiers. They were usually whining and complaining about something or another and now they viewed Tanisha as the enemy, a member of management. The other cashiers stopped talking whenever she came around and treated her like a company spy. If they only knew the truth; she was not a member of management. Her pay had not been increased, and the only perk she got was the honor of making change. She also wore the master register key and was responsible for correcting voids when the cashiers rang the same item twice or a customer changed her mind about a purchase. Tanisha preferred working on the cash register and studying the purchases that people made. Whenever she could, she volunteered to bag merchandise for the cashiers so that she could study customer purchases. Studying the buying habits of strangers made her feel like she was inside of their heads.

Sometimes she was scheduled to fill in at the service desk where she answered the store's main telephone line and handled refunds and returns. Tanisha enjoyed changing her voice when she answered the store's telephone and would sometimes answer the phone using a deep sultry adult voice or a high pitched cheerleader voice.

"Thank you for calling Save Mart, may I help you?"

It was a silly game that she played to amuse herself to make the time pass faster. Tanisha preferred to work at the service desk because she could bring her notebooks to the desk and study her school work during slow evenings.

Tanisha's friend, Vicky Mildred, also worked at Save Mart in the ladies' apparel department. Vicky was sixteen and had worked at Save Mart for almost two years. Vicky had encouraged Tanisha to apply at Save Mart, and coached her to lie on her employment application by stating that she was fifteen instead of fourteen and lived in a low income household.

At first, Tanisha was reluctant to lie about her age, but she really wanted the job so she did it. She'd brought along a copy of the family's rent subsidy letter as well as her most recent report card that showed that she had straight A's. Her interview with Deanna Lemkel the personnel manager had lasted ten minutes, and she'd been hired a few days later. Tanisha thought that the personnel manager was on to her lie when she noticed that Tanisha was fifteen but only in eighth grade. Tanisha had anticipated that she might notice that, so she'd already crafted a plausible lie and explained that her family had moved to Newberry East from Chicago and that the Newberry East school district had held her back one grade when she transferred. Deanna believed her lie and did not ask to see her birth certificate to verify her age.

Tanisha was paid the minimum wage, and she was usually scheduled to work at least twenty hours each week. She most enjoyed working when she knew that Vicky was also scheduled to work the same shift. Tanisha and Vicky would sometimes take their evening breaks together. When they worked on Thursdays, they coordinated their fifteen minute break so that they could watch *Cheers* and sing the theme song.

Tanisha loved the *Cheers* sitcom but always marveled at how few minorities ever managed to wander into the *Cheers* bar.

Vicky's mom sometimes gave Tanisha a ride home at night. If Tanisha knew that Vicky was working, she would take a cab to work and Mrs. Mildred would give her a ride home, saving her a bike ride in the dark.

Tanisha stretched again and quickly checked her schedule. She saw that she was circled S.D. which meant service desk. She raised both thumbs up. Saturday morning at the service desk was always the busiest time for returns and exchanges. She knew the day would fly by quickly.

She grabbed her phone and called Vicky to see if she was working.

Vicky answered the phone on the first ring.

"Hello." Vicky's voice was gruff and raspy and Tanisha could tell that Vicky was still asleep.

"Hey, Vicky, I didn't wake you did I?" Tanisha asked.

"Yeah, but that's okay. What time is it?" Vicky wore contact lenses and couldn't see her large LCD clock without her glasses.

"It's eight fifteen. Do you have to work today?" Tanisha decided to get to the point so Vicky could get back to sleep.

"Yeah, but I work one to nine fifteen tonight, so I'm closing," Vicky yawned into the phone.

"I work nine to five tonight, so we'll miss each other," she said. "But I'll be at the service desk, so I'll see you when you come in."

"Okay, girlfriend. I was out late last night, and I need to get some more sleep. If I get there early," Vicky yawned. "We can chat for a few minutes before I punch in."

"That's cool. Sorry I woke you, Vicky." Tanisha hung up the phone.

She would have to ride her bike to work. She glanced at her clock. It was 8:16.

She raced downstairs and poured a bowl of raisin bran and covered it with milk. Tanisha preferred to eat her raisin bran soggy and liked it to sit in the milk for at least ten minutes. The longer it sat, the better it tasted to her. She only ate Kellogg's Raisin Bran and wouldn't eat the Post or generic raisin bran that Billie Mae sometimes bought. It didn't produce the right consistency after sitting in the ten minute milk bath. Attacking the stairs two at a time, she scurried into the bathroom and washed her face as the shower warmed. Lathering quickly, she rubbed baby oil over her wet body, wrapped herself in her towel and tiptoed the eight steps back to her bedroom. Tanisha sprinkled baby powder between her legs and on her chest. She always perspired after riding her bike to work and the baby powder absorbed the moisture. She hung the damp towel on the hook in her closet and pulled on her navy blue corduroy pants and white cotton sweater, a necessity against the Save Mart air conditioning. It was early May, and the temperature was expected to be in the low seventies. She knew that she looked like a fashion mistake wearing corduroy in the spring, but the last time she'd worn her khakis to ride her bike to work, she'd gotten oil from the chain on her pants leg that had left a stain that she couldn't get out. With Save Mart's no jeans policy, she needed to wear dark colored pants whenever she rode her bike. It was now 8:23.

She pulled out her pink sponge rollers and stuffed her hair under a baseball cap. From past experience, she'd learned not to brush out her curls until she got to the store because the wind and baseball cap would soften the curls during the bike ride to work. Racing back down the stairs she quickly ate her bowl of raisin bran. Disappointed with the cereal's crunchy consistency, she didn't have time to let the cereal get any mushier. It was 8:29. She raced back upstairs one more time and quickly brushed her teeth rinsing several times to get the sticky raisins out of her teeth. 8:33.

The bike ride took exactly thirteen minutes which gave her a little over ten minutes to put on her smock and brush out her hair. She raced past Byron and Allen who were sprawled across the living room floor watching Saturday morning cartoons and singing along as the *Conjunction Junction School House Rock* jingle played.

She grabbed her special work backpack. "Bye guys! I'm heading to work. I'll see you later today," she shouted. They mumbled soft goodbyes. She unlocked her bike from the window grating on the front of the family's town home and jumped on her maroon bicycle. She checked her watch. It was 8:35.

There was only one way to get to the Save Mart from the Cedar Grove complex. Tanisha had to ride down a narrow two lane street that was bordered by a cemetery for one half mile on one side and well appointed homes on the other side. The first three quarters of a mile were not lit by street lights and there were no sidewalks, so Tanisha learned to ride very close to the gravel side roads. At that hour of the morning, there weren't that many cars on the road, so Tanisha didn't have to pull in to the gravel side roads before reaching the sidewalk portion of the journey. She'd gotten accustomed to the road kill that she sometimes saw on the side of the road. The nocturnal raccoons and possums would wander along the street and freeze at the approaching lights of cars traveling at forty five miles per hour. Tanisha always looked away when she saw the large bumps in the middle of the road or the circle of crows picking at the furry carcasses. The sight of the birds feasting on the road kill always made Tanisha queasy, but today there were no dead critters littering the street.

Tanisha made good time and pulled into the Save Mart parking lot three minutes ahead of schedule at 8:45. She coasted over to the bike rack in the front of the store and mopped the sweat beads from her brow with a red bandana that she kept tucked in her backpack. She locked her bike and smoothed her clothes, squinting as the sun beamed on the black asphalt.

She smiled at Bob the security guard who held the door open for her.

"Hey, Bob! How's it hanging?"

"It's hanging low, Miss Tanisha, hanging low." Bob tipped his invisible cap and bowed at Tanisha.

Bob was Save Mart's head of security. He was twenty two years old and took his role very seriously. Bob often involved Tanisha in the store's surveillance activities. Sometimes he would call the service desk and ask her to call the Steiffer police department to have them place patrol cars in the parking lot at the store's two exits in case a shoplifting sting turned into a parking lot chase.

Tanisha was glad that Bob was on duty today and hoped that it would help the time go fast. Since she had to work, she was missing the Saturday afternoon mall trip with her friends, but they were planning to go to the movie theatre that evening at 7:00. The girls weren't going to see a movie but wanted to hang out in the arcade area, play video games and check out boys.

Tanisha slipped on her teal smock, stuffed her backpack in her locker, and swiped her time card at 8:50. She raced to the cash cage to pick up her money bag for the service desk and speed walked to the front of the store to set up her register. There were several Save Mart customers waiting by the main door. *How sad that these people have nothing better to do but wait for Save Mart to open. I'd be home in bed!*

She knew that the service desk traffic was often sporadic on a Saturday morning, and generally didn't get really busy until after 11:00, but you could never predict how busy it was going to be. She hoped that she would have time to sneak in a quick call to her brother to coordinate the car pool. She also wanted to review her notes for her algebra test on Monday.

Tanisha had planned to ask her brother Jack to chauffeur her and her friends to the movies, but when she woke up, he'd already left for his teller job at the Newberry East Bank. She would have to try to catch him later that afternoon when he came home, since Billie had flatly refused to take them. Tanisha had been surprised by her mother's terse response.

"Mom, can you give me and my friends a ride to the movie theatre tomorrow?" Tanisha asked cheerfully.

"It's my friends and me, Tanisha. You always end with yourself, you know that. You never say me and anyone. It's always, anyone and me," she corrected. "And no, I can't take you. I have other plans," Billie replied.

"Well, are you going near the mall at least?" she pleaded. "Maybe you could just drop us off on your way!"

"No! I said I can't take you. Now stop asking!" Billie shouted. Her tone startled Tanisha, and she almost dropped the glass that she was holding. She stared blankly at her mother, not knowing what to say.

"I'm sorry I yelled at you, Tanisha. But I can't take you," Billie repeated softly.

Tanisha stared at her mother before sulking to her bedroom and closing her door. She plopped on her bed and let herself slide to the floor, flipping to her knees, her hands in the prayer posture. 'God, why is Billie Mae being mean again? Is that what the mental illness does to her? Will she be like this forever? Please make her better. Amen.'

Tanisha quickly counted her service desk money bag and signed the slip confirming that the bag contained nine hundred dollars. *Why were Billie's moods so unpredictable?*

She closed the register as a senior citizen approached the service desk. Tanisha smiled and processed her first return of the day.

Chapter 3

How crazy is crazy?

The warmer weather brought green grass, pastel colored tulips and honey bees. It also brought out a change in seasons for Billie Mae. Deciding that she was feeling better, she'd stopped taking her medication on the fourth of April, the anniversary of Rev. Dr. Martin Luther King Jr.'s death. She'd deliberately chosen that date as a way to bury the old, mentally ill Billie Mae. She placed the medicine in a shoebox in her closet and sealed it shut with duct tape. Her own private funeral for the dreaded lithium pills. Besides, the pills had caused her to gain almost fifteen pounds. She'd had enough. It was now the fifth of May. Cinco de Mayo. She decided that she would celebrate her thirty day independence from mental medication on the day the Mexicans celebrated their independence.

As the medication slowly worked its way out of Billie's system, Jack and Tanisha watched in silence as Billie's behavior slowly regressed. Every day that passed, her behavior became more and more erratic. She stopped cooking meals and cleaning her room and once again started drinking and hanging out with her sister, Aunt Shanay. Billie was now regularly complaining that she hated her new job at the cable company.

When Tanisha left for work that morning Billie Mae was snoring loudly in her bedroom lying in the clothes that she'd worn the day before. *Did she sleep in her clothes? She must have.* Tanisha paused in the doorway and quietly watched her mother, the previous night's eruption fresh on her mind. *It's hard to believe that this is the same woman who was being so nice and helped me host my Thriller party a few weeks ago.* Tanisha shook her head and tiptoed down the stairs.

After finding her lithium prescription and talking briefly to their dad about their discovery, Tanisha and Jack waited, expecting Billie to share her mental health issues. Several weeks had passed, with no word from Billie Mae. Tanisha was growing accustomed to the kinder, gentler Billie and warming up to the idea of getting to know her mother when her mood shifted, seemingly overnight.

Tanisha waited for her next service desk customer, a smile plastered on her face as she robotically wiped the service desk counter with cleaning solution. Her thoughts drifted to her latest Billie Mae sparring match.

୫୦୯୫

Ready to shepherd her brothers through their Saturday morning household cleaning duties, Tanisha bounded down the stairs to assume her role. Byron was responsible for cleaning the downstairs powder room every Saturday and Allen's chores consisted of dusting the living room and hall bookshelf.

"Okay, Byron and Allen, Scooby Doo is over now, so it's time to clean up," she reminded tying a pink bandana around her hair.

Byron and Allen obediently rose from the sofa to start their chores.

"You're not their mother, Tanisha. They're watching television. Leave them alone," Billie Mae barked. She casually took a long pull from her cigarette, carefully placing it in the gold ashtray on the white plastic patio table that served

as an end table. Billie shuffled through the magazines scattered on the floor and picked up Cosmopolitan and flipped through the pages.

Byron and Allen stood frozen in their tracks. Tanisha was shocked speechless for a moment. She'd heard Billie Mae come home at seven o'clock that morning after an all night partying session with Aunt Shanay. When she heard a car door slam, Tanisha peeked through her bedroom curtains and saw Billie Mae walking up to the house with a cigarette in one hand and a cup of gas station coffee in the other hand. She watched as Billie Mae placed the coffee cup on the hood of the car and went to the trunk to retrieve something. Tanisha raced to the bathroom so that she could pee and slip back into her bedroom before Billie came in the door. The last time Billie Mae came home in the wee hours of the morning and found Tanisha awake, she'd insisted that Tanisha make her breakfast. Tanisha was in no mood to serve Billie Mae so she peed quickly and flushed the toilet just as Billie Mae's key was turning in the lock. Tanisha crawled back into her bed and picked up her Teen magazine and quietly flipped the pages listening for Billie Mae to come up the stairs to crawl into bed. At least an hour had passed and Tanisha still hadn't heard Billie Mae enter her room. Tanisha's stomach was growling with hunger. She glanced at her alarm clock. It was after eight o'clock. Tanisha was starving and wanted a bowl of cereal. She peeked through her door and saw Allen bounding down the stairs.

"Whew!" she thought. "If Allen is up, then Billie Mae is less likely to go off on me or pick an argument." She walked downstairs and saw Billie sprawled across the living room sofa asleep. Allen was perched on the living room floor watching cartoons and munching on a bowl of dry Cheerios and drinking a glass of milk. Tanisha went into the kitchen and made herself a bowl of cereal. She really wanted grits, but she knew that if Billie awoke and smelled grits, then she would request eggs and sausage too and Tanisha was not in the mood to cook breakfast for Billie Mae.

"But we always do our chores after Scooby Doo is over so that we're finished before Soul Train comes on," Tanisha explained.

"Well, I'm their mother and I said that they don't have to do what you say," Billie spat. "I'm tired of you bossing everybody around in this house. You're too damn grown, little girl. This is my house and I said that they don't have to clean up. If you want something cleaned, then you clean it yourself!" Billie barked gruffly, her eyes boring through her daughter like fire on steel.

Tanisha didn't know how to respond. Just a few weeks before, Billie Mae had taken her to the Turnabout Dance and picked her and her friends up. She'd been on time and been the model of politeness. Shortly after that, Billie Mae had actually thanked Tanisha for making sure that the house stayed tidy while she worked. Was this the same woman who had hosted her recent Michael Jackson Thriller party and picked up pizza for her friends? Tanisha stared at Billie Mae as Byron and Allen looked on, paralyzed with fear. Byron shrugged his shoulders at Tanisha as though to suggest, "I don't mind cleaning up now, but I don't want to disobey Mom."

Defeated, Tanisha retreated and went to her room to finish her homework. Twenty minutes later, she heard Billie stomping up the stairs. Tanisha sat up in her bed and stared at her door, bracing herself for round two. She exhaled only when she heard Billie Mae's bedroom door slam loudly. She finished her algebra homework and read her social studies report before tiptoeing to listen at Billie Mae's door. Her mother's snores confirmed that she was asleep. Tanisha walked sullenly downstairs and joined Byron and Allen in front of the television.

"Hey, Tanisha, I don't mind cleaning up. I'll help you now," Byron offered. "Come on Allen, let's do our chores," he ordered.

"I don't want her to wake up and see you guys doing chores and go off on me again," Tanisha whispered.

"I'll just tell her that it was my idea. Come on Allen, turn off that television!" Byron ordered again.

Tanisha cleaned the kitchen while Byron quickly cleaned the powder room and Allen dusted. Although the carpet was in desperate need of vacuuming, Tanisha didn't want to risk waking Billie Mae with the noise from the vacuum cleaner.

"Byron, why don't you go and get your laundry basket and I'll start sorting our laundry if you agree to help me fold it when it's done," she suggested.

Billie Mae believed that the children should do their own laundry so Tanisha and Byron agreed to take turns doing their laundry with Allen's laundry. Jack didn't want anyone to ruin his clothes, so he did his own laundry. It was Byron's turn to do the laundry, but Tanisha wanted to reciprocate his kindness by helping with his regular chores. Although he hadn't said anything, Byron was now starting to notice Billie Mae's moodiness.

On Saturday mornings, Jack worked the 7:00 shift at the drive-up window at the bank and got home just after one thirty. He usually grabbed a quick sandwich before taking a nap to rejuvenate for his Saturday evening activities. Tanisha had decided not to go to the mall with her girls that afternoon because she needed to talk to Jack about Billie's behavior and her run in with their mother that morning. When he walked in the door, Tanisha followed him into the kitchen and told him what happened in whispered tones. Byron and Allen stood in the dining room watching out for signs of Billie Mae and adding animated color commentary to Tanisha's tale.

"Wow! It sounds like she went off. How did she look?" Jack smeared a liberal slathering of mayonnaise on his bread.

Tanisha shrugged her shoulders. "She looked like she'd been out all night. As Dad would say, she looked like ten miles of bad road," she added. "I didn't really make eye contact with her, but she had her usual mean mommy look on her face when she talked to me and then she softened up her face when she talked to Byron and Allen." Byron and Allen stood in the doorway listening intently and nodding their head in agreement.

"You guys, go back in there and watch television so I can talk to Tanisha," Jack ordered.

The boys disappeared quickly as Jack munched on his bologna and cheese sandwich.

"What do you think we should do?" Jack asked.

"I don't know. But I think we need to do something. She's back to her old tricks again, Jack," Tanisha whined. "First she's nice. Then she's mean. I'm tired of it. I feel like I'm walking on egg shells all the time."

Jack stared at his sister sympathetically. "I know Dad had to work today, but let's call and see if he's home yet, sis. We better call from your room in case Billie picks up the extension in her bedroom," Jack suggested.

Jack grabbed his sandwich and they quietly walked up the stairs. As they tiptoed past Billie Mae's room, they could hear her snoring loudly. Walking into Tanisha's room, they closed the door and turned on Tanisha's clock radio to create background noise.

Tanisha dialed the number and Jackie answered on the third ring.

"Hello." Jackie's voice always sounded irritated on the telephone. Tanisha envisioned his forehead creasing together as he answered the phone and the large mole centered between his bushy eyebrows shifting slightly as though running from one eyebrow to the next. Jackie's eyebrows were almost close enough to be considered a uni - brow.

Jackie's skin tone was very pale, his complexion almost translucent, the blue green veins easily visible through his light skin. His features were slight and Tanisha once teased that his nose looked like the butt of a chicken sitting in the middle of his face. Jackie was five feet eleven inches tall and his weight fluctuated between one hundred seventy and one hundred and eighty pounds. By all standards, he was a very handsome man, but lacked taste in fashion. Jackie often wore clothes stained with barbecue sauce or motor oil and wore plaid pants with striped shirts. Tanisha suspected that he might be color blind.

A chain smoker, Jackie didn't believe in dry cleaning, so his clothes always smelled of Kool menthol and motor oil. Jackie was also a social drinker and sometimes smelled of whiskey or rum. His signature scent was menthol, motor oil and rum with an occasional splash of Old Spice. When they were married, Jackie and Billie Mae went out on the town for their anniversary and New Year's Eve and occasionally Valentine's Day. Tanisha thought it was corny for her parents to only go out on those three nights and dubbed these dates "Amateur Night" when rookies like her parents who never went out on the town, went out on the town. Every now and then Jackie and Billie Mae would surprise Tanisha and attend an adult only birthday party. Whenever Jackie got dressed to go out on the town, Tanisha would sit in the bathroom and talk to him while he shaved. He would usually turn on his favorite Chi-lites or Stylistics album, and walk around the house with Magic Shave cream on his face as he sang along to the soulful tunes and sipped on a cocktail. He had all of the songs memorized and Tanisha loved to hear him sing in a voice that fluctuated between tenor and baritone in perfect harmony with the record. Once dressed, Jackie would splash Old Spice cologne on his face and neck and Tanisha would giggle as Jackie winced when the cologne stung his freshly shaved skin.

"Hey, Daddy, how was work today?" Tanisha sang.

Jackie was an electrician with the Amtrak Railroad Company. He worked at their plant in Hammond, Indiana. He hated his job with an intense passion.

"Oh hey, Booger! Work was the same old same old. You know how it is. But I'm really getting tired of working with these racist jerks who don't want you to work with them no way," he coughed. "They think that because they're white, they're smarter than I am, and don't think that I know what I'm doing," he ranted. "And then when I correct them on something that they did wrong, they don't believe what I'm saying until somebody that looks like them tells them the same thing that I just told them! It makes me sick!" he barked. "But of course they pretend like they're hearing it for the first time. Half of the

idiots that I work with live in trailer parks and are dumb as a stump. The truth is that most of them only got the job because of somebody that they know, and then they want to make me feel like I don't know what I'm talking about. I'm so tired of needing a co-signer for them to trust that I can do my job!" he said. "I'm smarter than all of them put together, and they know it," he ranted. "It gets on my nerves, but what am I gonna do?" he ended. "The money's good, so you gotta take the good with the bad."

Tanisha could hear him take a pull from his cigarette and exhale as his tone softened and he continued, "You didn't have to work today, Booger?" her dad asked.

Jackie had called Tanisha Booger her entire life. When she questioned him on the origins of the nickname he would just laugh. "That's just what I call you, Booger. I don't remember why." Now that Tanisha was fourteen, Jackie was careful not to call her by her pet name around her friends, which she appreciated.

"No. I have to work tomorrow. They don't usually make you work Saturday and Sunday because on Sunday they pay double time at Save Mart. I wish I did have to work today though, I need the money to buy these jeans that I want."

"I know that's right. Ain't nothing like time and a half on Saturday and double time on Sunday. Those are my favorite days to work." Jackie had received an Associates degree in chemistry and was one of the smartest people that Tanisha knew, but he often spoke using improper English to emphasize a point.

Jack tapped on his watch to hurry his sister along. "Hey, Dad, Jack is on the phone with me and we need to talk to you about Mom," Tanisha said quickly.

"Oh, yeah? What's going on?" Jackie asked.

Jack and Tanisha spoke softly into the phone and shared how Billie's behavior had changed over the past three weeks. Tanisha ended the story by replaying what happened when she tried to get Byron and Allen to help her clean up that morning.

"Well, you can be bossy, Tanisha. You know that." Jackie took another pull from his cigarette.

"But Dad, why should I have to clean up everything around here? She doesn't do anything around the house anymore and I don't think it's fair that she doesn't make Byron and Allen do anything. They never complain when I ask them to help me, they just do their chores and then go back to whatever they want to do. Like this morning when Billie, I mean Mom, finally went upstairs to lay down, Byron offered to do his chores and made Allen do his too," she whined.

"I guess you're right. As long as you're cleaning up with them, then I don't see why that would bother your mother. It sounds like she's off her medication again." Jackie sighed loudly. "She still hasn't told you about her mental illness?" he asked.

"No, Dad," Jack replied. "Why don't you just tell us what's going on," he suggested.

Tanisha could hear Jackie take another pull from his cigarette, a habit she prayed he would break soon. Exhaling loudly, he reluctantly explained the history of Billie's bipolar disorder.

Jack and Tanisha learned that Billie had suffered severe psychoses after childbirth after three of her pregnancies. He used the term "nervous breakdown episodes" stating that the episodes were so severe that she'd had to be hospitalized. He also explained that Billie needed to take maintenance medications for the rest of her life in order to manage the chemical imbalance in her brain.

As Jackie shared Billie's mental health history, Tanisha had a flashback of Billie being taken away in a police car.

At five years old, Tanisha hadn't understood why the police had handcuffed Billie and taken her away. The police car brought out the curious neighbors, and she'd felt like a celebrity that afternoon when many of the older children and adults on their block quizzed Tanisha about why her mom went away in the police car. Tanisha was a precocious five-year old and proudly retold the story to anyone who would listen.

"My daddy was walking around the house with Magic Shave cream on his face and my mom grabbed Jack's hand and ran out of the house. My new baby brother Allen was in his crib napping and me and Byron were playing on the front stoop when my mom ran down the stairs with Jack and ran down the block screaming that my daddy was possessed. I don't know what possessed is, but that's what she said. And then my daddy came outside naked. He only had a towel on his butt. And he asked me where my mom went so I told him that she ran down the block with Jack. Then my daddy went back into the house and then two police cars came and went into my house. And then my mom came up and hid behind a tree with Jack. He was crying. I ran into the house to get my daddy and told him that my mom was hiding behind the tree. Then the police came out and took my mom away in the police car because she said some bad words to my daddy and to the police officers. And then my grandma Bootsy came over to my house and she's at my house now frying chicken."

Grandma Bootsy moved in with them and stayed for two months. Tanisha didn't see Billie again until she came home a few weeks before Tanisha started kindergarten. No one had explained where Billie was during that time. Jackie just explained that "Your mom is sick right now, and she'll be back when she's better. The police took her to the hospital, and children aren't allowed to visit at the hospital where she's going."

Tanisha snapped out of her flashback as Jackie finished his story.

"And that's what happened. She hasn't had an episode since Allen was born," he continued. "When I was living there I used to make sure that she took her pills every day. Hell, I watched her take her pills, but even then I think she hid them under her tongue sometimes and spit them out. She says the pills don't make her feel like herself and they make her gain weight," he offered.

"But all I know is that the doctor said that she should be taking medication for the rest of her life, and when she's on the medication, she functions better."

"I remember that, Daddy. I remember Mom running around the block with Jack and the police taking her away," Tanisha said.

"You remember that, Booger? Well, you would have been about five when it happened. I guess you might remember that. I never said anything about any of this because I was trying to wait for you guys to grow up, but I guess you're growing up now and you need to know. Jack, do you remember any of this?"

Jack was sobbing quietly. He shook his head and softly mumbled yes. Tanisha stared at her brother with a furrowed brow.

"You would have been almost seven years old. It was a tough time for our family, a really tough time. I was hoping that she would keep taking her medication, but this is typical of what she's done her whole life. She'll take it for a while, start feeling better and then she decides to stop taking it," Jackie coughed into the receiver. "But I'm glad you've told me that her behavior has changed, maybe I'll say something to her about her medication," he continued.

"Thanks, Daddy," Tanisha replied.

"I'm worried about you guys out there with her not on her medication. There's no telling what could happen. I want you both to look out for Byron and Allen too, okay?"

"We will, Daddy. I need to let you go, I have to use the bathroom," Tanisha lied.

She hung up the receiver and stared at her older brother. "What's wrong with you? What's with the tears?" Tanisha asked. She continued without waiting for Jack's response. "So Billie Mae really is crazy. At least now I understand why I feel so close to Grandma Bootsy, she practically raised me."

"She's not crazy, Tanisha, she's sick. Mom has a mental illness," Jack explained. He reached for a tissue on Tanisha's dresser and wiped his nose and eyes. "She needs our help, Tanisha. I feel sorry for her."

Staring at her brother, hearing the whole story from Jackie, a wave of anger erupted. "How can we possibly help her Jack? If she's not willing to take her medication, what are we supposed to do?" she barked. "I'm going to stay away from her crazy tale, that's what I'm going to do! You can feel sorry for her if you want to," she added. "But I feel sorry for myself. I feel sorry that I got her for a mother," Tanisha barked. "I need to finish my homework, Jack," she said. She closed her door behind him and leaned against it.

Tanisha spoke through clenched teeth, "As if my life wasn't screwed up enough, now I have proof that my mother is a mental case, and she's too mean and self-centered to take her medication so that she can function like a normal person! If my friends find out that my mother is psycho, my social life is doomed." Tanisha slumped to the floor, her weight against the door. "God, please tell me what to do," she sobbed.

৪০০৪

Tanisha felt her forehead creasing intensely with hatred as she thought about Billie Mae. Her thoughts were interrupted by her first service desk telephone call. She cleared her throat and forced herself to smile.

"Thank you for calling Save Mart. This is Tanisha speaking. How may I help you?" Tanisha sang into the receiver, her peppy cheerleader spirit masking the Billie Mae rage that she felt.

Chapter 4

Customer Profiling

The drab, round clock above the main entrance seemed to be frozen. Irritated, Tanisha glared at the clock and frowned. The time appeared to move even slower under her gaze, the seconds ticking by like minutes, and the minutes like hours. She stared at the clock and yawned, imagining ways to make the boring clock face more appealing. *The numbers on the clock could be insects or flowers or past presidents or donuts. Donuts?* She was hungry. Her eyes roamed the area for something to straighten, dust or read - anything to make the time go faster. She'd only processed four returns all morning. Even the phone lines had been slow. On days like this, she missed being on a register. At least on a register, there was a steady stream of customers to profile. Vicky raced by the service desk on her way to punch in.

"Hey Tanisha, I'm late as usual!" Vicky panted. "I'll come back up to chat after I punch in," she promised as she bolted to the time clock. "One more red circle on my time card, and I'm going to get written up," she yelled over her shoulder as she whizzed down the aisle to the back of the store.

It was 12:55, and Tanisha was glad that it was almost time for lunch because her stomach was growling. Spiking her metabolism, her bike ride had consumed her soggy raisin bran breakfast and she was more than ready for lunch.

Tanisha usually brought a sandwich for lunch, but today she had been running too late for work and hadn't had time to make one so she'd have to buy a lunch from the Save Mart cafeteria. She'd already reviewed the algebra notes that she tucked into her smock pocket and felt more than ready to ace her exam. She doodled on a pad of paper and day dreamed about what she would have for lunch. *Should I have a cheeseburger or a basket of chicken fingers and fries?*

Tanisha's eyes lifted as two well dressed customers walked into the store. The male customer wore a suit and tie. The female customer had long wavy brown hair and was wearing a skirt cut above the knee and a long sleeved pink silk blouse. She carried a large purse emblazoned with the Gucci logo.

They're dressed well to be shopping at Save Mart. They're probably running in here to get a last minute wedding or birthday card or batteries on their way to a wedding reception or party. I bet his name is Bob and her name is Kate.

She giggled to herself. Tanisha loved profiling the customers. She studied their clothes and jewelry and tried to determine what they did for a living and where they lived by the things that they bought or returned and how they were dressed. When she worked on a register, she especially enjoyed it when the customers paid by check so she could see their address and confirm her customer profiling talent. The Steiffer Save Mart was the only Save Mart within a thirty mile radius and attracted customers from all of the nearby cities and villages. If the customer lived in Glen or Morning Side, the two most exclusive suburbs in the area, Tanisha would always follow the customer out of the store with her eyes to see the type of car that they drove. She was always amazed that customers who lived in the more exclusive areas of Glen or Morning Side bought the most interesting products from Save Mart and often came in with coupons.

Customers had no choice but to breeze by the service desk on their way to start their shopping so Tanisha came to view the service desk as her own invisible customer profiling perch. Not as much fun as studying their purchases, the service desk profiling was better than staring at the drab wall clock, willing it to move faster.

The female customer breezed by the service desk without so much as a glance in her direction, but the male customer made eye contact with Tanisha and smiled. She was shocked. No one ever smiled at the service desk. She quickly smiled back and continued her doodling, smirking at her own silliness. Her eyes followed the well dressed couple down the main aisle, and to her surprise, the male customer looked back over his left shoulder, made eye contact with Tanisha, smiled and waved. Flushed and embarrassed, she waved back meekly. The male customer then stopped his female companion, whispered something to her and she too turned around and looked at Tanisha. Tanisha quickly looked down and started scribbling on her note pad once again. When she looked up, the couple was nowhere in sight.

Whew! That was close. I have to be more careful when I'm playing my customer profile game and not stare at the customers so obviously. I wonder where they live and why they're all dressed up on a Saturday morning. They look like Barbie and Ken.

She was glad when a customer approached with a return for the ladies apparel department. The price tag had been removed and the customer didn't have a receipt so Tanisha had to page someone for a price check. Tanisha grabbed the microphone and turned on the paging system. "Attention Save Mart associates, an associate from ladies apparel to the service desk for a code seven. An associate from ladies apparel to the service desk for a code seven, please," she sang into the mike.

Tanisha loved to make announcements on the store loud speaker. She felt like a broadcaster announcing the codes. Save Mart had a code for everything, and Tanisha had memorized most of the codes and seldom had to refer to the code cheat sheet taped to the glass overlay covering the service desk counter. A price check was code seven. She hoped Vicky would be the associate on call for price checks so that they could chat. As Tanisha waited for the ladies' apparel associate to appear, she looked up and the well dressed white male was standing at the service desk waiting to get her attention.

"While we wait for your price check, I'm going to help this gentleman," Tanisha explained politely. The customer responded that she wanted to grab something from the Cosmetics department and would be right back. Tanisha smiled at the well dressed man that she'd named "Bob."

"Hello, how may I help you?" Tanisha offered.

A serious look on his face, the well dressed customer stared intently at Tanisha. "Was that your voice on the loud speaker just now?" he asked.

Tanisha looked puzzled, "Yes. I just needed a price check. Was the speaker jarbled or something?" she asked.

"No, it was loud and clear. You have a nice voice," he smiled. "I see your name tag reads Tanisha. Hello Tanisha, my name is Tom. How old are you?" Tom asked.

"Fourteen," she replied naturally. "I mean fifteen," she corrected. "I'm fifteen now," she lied. Her heart rate increased. *Is this guy going to bust me for being too young to work here?*

"Fifteen?" he repeated, staring at her intensely. "I thought you were older than that when I noticed you on my way in," he shared. "But now that I look at you closer I can see that you're younger than I thought at first."

"Is there something that I can help you with?" Tanisha asked quickly.

Tom continued to stare at Tanisha's face, examining her like a painting. Intense and purposeful, his gaze paused on every crevice of her face before methodically roaming her body. She felt uneasy and exposed, powerless to stop his eyes from staring at her so boldly.

Her posture stiffened and she locked on his eyes. "Sir, is there something that I can do for you?" she repeated, her tone peppered with agitation.

Ignoring her question, Tom continued to study Tanisha closely. "Do you have on any makeup?" Tom asked.

"Excuse me? Did you say 'do I have on any make-up' or 'where is the make-up?'" she asked.

"Do you **have** on any make-up?" he repeated, slanting his eyes and studying Tanisha's frame.

"No. Well, I have on strawberry lip gloss. Why do you ask?" Tanisha shifted her weight again.

"What size jeans do you wear, a three or a five?" he asked quickly.

"Excuse me! I don't know what's going on here, but that is none of your business," she blurted. "Why do you need to know that?" she asked angrily.

Ignoring her question, Tom then turned his gaze to her reddish brown hair and studied it intently. "Tanisha, is that your natural hair color?" he asked.

"You're making me very uncomfortable and if you don't tell me what's going on, I'm going to call security," she stated confidently. "Why are you asking me such personal questions?" she stated, casually fingering her hair and folding her arms across her chest.

Tom locked eyes with her, smiled and opened his mouth to respond, but before Tom could answer, Alvin, the ladies apparel manager, appeared for the price check. "What do you need, Tanisha?" Alvin asked. "I'm sorry for interrupting, but I'm in a hurry, I have a customer in the changing room."

Tanisha excused herself from Tom and showed Alvin the jeans, explaining that the customer didn't have a receipt. Alvin studied the jeans and wrote down the label information. "Make sure you look up the woman's name and confirm that she's not in the chronic return file," he reminded. "I'll call you from my office with the pricing information," he finished.

Tanisha had already asked the customer to complete a return slip and had compared her name with her driver's license. The woman approached the service desk as Alvin walked away.

Grateful that she was no longer at the service desk alone with Tom, Tanisha took the return slip and proceeded to look in the small file box again. Any Save Mart customers who returned more than three items without a receipt got placed in the chronic return box. Tanisha had profiled the woman and was confident that her name wouldn't be in the box. She was white, she lived in Homer, wore a sizable diamond ring on her hand and her nails were neat and perfectly manicured. Nonetheless, Tanisha looked in the box again, Bob's security training tips ringing in her ears: *You can't stereotype shoplifters, Tanisha. Thieves come in all shapes, sizes, and colors.*

"I tried the jeans on in the store and they fit fine," the woman explained. "So I popped the tags off and hung them in my closet," she continued. "And forgot they were there, until recently, and then when I tried to wear them for the first time, they were too tight," she ended. "I really just want to exchange them for a bigger size," she clarified.

The service desk phone rang. While Tanisha took the call, the well dressed woman who'd come in with Tom walked briskly up to the counter, tapping her watch and speaking in a hurried voice. "Let's go, Tom. We're going to be late!"

"But I'm not finished here. I didn't get the information that I needed," Tom pleaded.

"We can't be late, Tom," she repeated adamantly.

At the sound of "Kate's" voice, Tanisha looked up in time to see Tom being led out of the store by his elbow. Tom walked backwards waving wildly at Tanisha as he exited.

"If you'd just like to do an even exchange then you can go back and pick out another pair of jeans, and we'll give you a credit for these," Tanisha explained. "I thought you wanted a refund."

Tanisha's eyes followed Tom through the parking lot and watched as he climbed into the passenger seat of a new Cadillac. *I wanted Vicky to see this weirdo creep! Why was he trying to guess what size I am? I guess all kinds of nut cases shop at Save Mart.*

Chapter 5

Big Brother to the Rescue

In the lunchtime selection pageant, the tuna melt had been crowned the winner with first runner up honors going to the cheeseburger. A close third place bronze finish tossed to the chicken fingers. In Tanisha's weight conscious and clear complexion quest to reduce her fried food intake, she'd also substituted carrot and celery sticks for the French fries that came with the special, paying slightly more for the healthier choice and wondering why carrot and celery sticks cost more than the fried side option. The grilled tuna salad with melted Swiss cheese was probably just as caloric as the second and third place options, but she enjoyed it nonetheless. She was even beginning to enjoy the crunchy taste of carrots that had become a regular substitute for the potato chips that she adored. With no customers or team members in sight, Tanisha quickly took a bite from the carrot stick that she'd tucked in a napkin in her smock pocket and chewed furiously. She'd just seen the manager on duty leave the store, so she picked up the phone to call her house again.

It was now 3:30. She'd called home on her lunch break and learned that Jack still wasn't home from the bank, which was odd because every Saturday afternoon he usually came right home to eat lunch, take a nap and recharge his battery for his Saturday night shenanigans.

Tanisha dialed the family's number. The phone rang four times before Allen answered.

"Hey, Tanisha, yeah he's home. He just walked in the door. Hold on for a second. Jack!" Allen bellowed. "Thunder Thighs is on the phone," he laughed.

"Don't call me that!" Tanisha whispered into the receiver. Byron and Allen had turned into her worst enemies, taunting her mercilessly about every little pimple and blemish in her skin. One day, they overheard a phone conversation where she discussed her commitment to eat healthier by eliminating fried foods, and from that day forward they teased her about her figure and started calling her thunder thighs. She frowned into the receiver. *I'm going to kill him when I get home!*

"That's not funny, Allen," she heard Jack say. "Tanisha is thin and you know it. You're going to give her a complex about her weight. Now stop teasing her like that," he scolded. "And tell Byron that I told him to knock it off too," her brother ordered.

"I was just kidding around," Allen replied softly. Tanisha smiled at how quickly Jack had come to her rescue.

Only twenty months apart, they were very close. Billie Mae referred to them as Irish twins. There was nothing that Jack wouldn't do for Tanisha and vice versa. About the only thing that they didn't see eye to eye on was their parents.

Even before learning about Billie's mental illness, Jack felt that Tanisha was too hard on their mother, and would often defend her when Tanisha complained about Billie Mae. He was the classic mama's boy, the apron strings held firmly in his grip. Conversely, Tanisha's opinion of her mother was one of tolerance and indifference. And at almost fifteen, with the new information shared by Jackie on Billie's mental illness and refusal to take her medication regularly, Tanisha's tolerance of Billie Mae was vapor thin. When Tanisha attacked Billie, Jack was quick to remind her that their dad was not Mike Brady, from the Brady Bunch, preferring poker nights to family movie night with his children. Jack also reminded Tanisha about the 'family outings' to the racetrack instead of the zoo. Deep down, she knew that her brother was right, that it was wrong to vilify Billie Mae and forgive Jackie his many parental blunders, but she did nonetheless. Not one to concede an argument quickly, she rationalized her behavior to Jack by stating that at least Jackie was nice to her and didn't treat her like the evil step mother treated Cinderella. Jack didn't have a comeback for that response so the two would just agree to disagree.

After the divorce, Jack and Tanisha had been old enough to choose with which parent they would live. One night, the two teenagers had gone out to dinner with Jackie and he explained that they could decide if they wanted to stay with Billie Mae or move to Chicago where he had rented a small, three, bedroom apartment near Grandma Bootsy's house. Jack and Tanisha had met privately that evening and discussed it. Tanisha was leaning toward moving in with Jackie and longed to live near Grandma Bootsy and finally escape Billie Mae, but her brother was leaning toward staying with Billie Mae so that he could complete high school at River North. In the end, they both agreed that since Byron and Allen were too young to choose, that it would be better if they stayed together.

"Hey, Tanisha, what's up? Do you need me to pick you up from work?" Jack offered quickly.

"No. I rode my bike. Where've you been all afternoon, planning your bank heist?" Tanisha joked.

"Naw, I wish. I came home after I finished work and started doing my laundry, and the pilot light for the dryer went out again so I had to take my clothes to the laundromat to dry so my shirt would be clean. I don't know where Byron and Allen were when I came home, but Billie Mae was still asleep," Jack finished.

"That stupid dryer never works right," Tanisha agreed. "Byron and Allen were probably running around outside playing soccer with Lou and his brothers."

"You're probably right," he agreed. "Do you want me to pick you up and put your bike in the trunk? What time do you get off?" Jack offered.

"That's okay, I could use the exercise after the tuna melt that I chowed on at lunch," she offered. "Maybe then Byron and Allen will stop calling me thunder thighs," she groaned.

"Don't listen to them. They're knuckleheads, sis," Jack assured. "You are thin and you know it. Younger brothers always pick on something to tease their big sisters about," he reminded. "And they usually know exactly what button to push. I'm picking you up," he stated flatly. "End of discussion."

"Okay," she smiled. "I get off at 5:00."

"No problem. I'll be there. I need to iron my clothes. Is that what you wanted?" Jack asked.

"Well, not exactly. I was planning to ride my bike home but I was calling to see if you could drive me and some of my friends to the movies tonight. If you can drive one way, Lori's mom can pick us up. We want to get there by 7:00. I'll put gas in the Blue Goose since I know the car doesn't run on water!" Tanisha spoke in a hurried tone as she saw a customer in the parking lot retrieving a bag from her trunk and walking toward the door.

"Oh, don't worry about the gas, sis, it's just that I have to be at a party tonight at 7:00, but I guess I could be a few minutes late." Jack coughed into the receiver. "No problem. I'll take you and your friends to the movies tonight."

"Oh, thanks Jack," she whispered. "I have a customer now so I'll see you at 5:00," Tanisha said quickly.

She handled the return and quickly called Lori to start the phone tree. Lori would call Maria and Maria would call Rashanda to let them know that Jack would drive them to the movie theatre. Grace wasn't feeling well and Justine was visiting her grandmother for the weekend.

Whew! Two crises averted! My thighs really don't roar like thunder, and Jack can tote us to the movies. Jack is my hero! Even if he has crossed over into the enemy camp.

Chapter 6

Chances Are

David Barton awakened with a new attitude. *I am one of the most popular boys at Homer Glen High School. I'm handsome, athletic, smart, and I drive a Corvette. I will not be flustered by a fourteen year old girl that I barely know. Snap out of it man! You got it going on. You know there will be some fine girls at the John & Judy party tonight, so it's time to stop dreaming about that Tanisha Carlson girl and move on!*

It hadn't worked. At breakfast, he wondered what Tanisha ate for breakfast. By lunchtime, he wondered how she spent her Saturday afternoons. He'd still been unable to come up with a valid reason for calling her. He decided to wash his car on the driveway. He had just soaped up his hubcaps and needed to power wash them to prevent soap streaks. David pulled the garden hose and pressed the silver handle to force pressurized air onto his tires. He squeezed the lever as tight as he could, but the jet spray would not turn to the pressurized setting necessary to blast the grime from his dirty hubcaps. He was meticulous about his new Corvette and hand washed it every Saturday without fail. His parents hated that he washed his car on the driveway and gave him money every week to take the car to the car wash, but David enjoyed washing his car himself and believed that he did a better job than the soft cloth car wash.

He squeezed the handle as tight as he could, but the water pressure refused to change. Frustrated, he unscrewed the nozzle and used his fingers to spray Belvedere. The big dog ran for cover in the garage, shaking his fur wildly. Using the same technique, he aimed the hose at the hubcaps, but the pressure wasn't strong enough to rinse the tires.

"Damn!" David groaned aloud. He rinsed the tires as best he could with the spray nozzle but there was still a stream of soap stuck in the chrome crevices.

He rubbed the silver Swiss Army watch on his sweatpants to wipe away the suds. It was almost 5:00. David planned to meet his pal Todd at the Glen Country Club to squeeze in nine holes of twilight golf at 6:00. David smiled as he thought about how excited his father had been when he noticed that his son had a natural golf swing. David enjoyed being a member of the exclusive private club, but sometimes he was reminded that his family's membership was still an anomaly and not well received by all members.

೮೦೦೫

With weekly excursions to the public golf courses in the area, David's dad introduced him to the game of golf when he was five years old. Dr. Barton's status as an accomplished gynecologist, coupled with his wife's successful medical practice as well as their involvement in civic and community groups notwithstanding, the Barton doctors could not find a member of the Glen Country Club willing to sponsor them. Rumor had it that the Glen Country Club still honored a restrictive covenant whereby Jews and persons of color were not granted membership into the eighty year old club. Although the restrictive covenant had been removed from the club's written by-laws, and a few Jewish families gained membership, there were no black families who held membership in the club.

The practice was finally abolished when a white medical colleague of the Barton's moved his family to their subdivision from San Francisco. Dr. and Mrs. Charles Stokes were aghast at the blatant segregation that existed in Illinois. Compared to the liberal life that they led in San Francisco, with a network circle of same sex partnerships and interracial couples, Illinois was a throwback to the Jim Crow era. The Stokes' family's liberalism was fueled by the fact that Mrs. Stokes was a fair skinned black woman who could pass for white in most circles. She often found herself privy to derogatory comments about persons of color by people who mistook her for white. Never one to deny her heritage, she would use this chameleon quality to discern a person's true character. She reveled in the embarrassment that ensued once she shared her heritage.

An avid golfer, Dr. Stokes was invited to join the exclusive Glen Country Club immediately, and sponsored the Barton family for membership soon after joining.

David's golf game improved each season, and he was the best golfer on the Homer Glen High School Boys Golf team, boasting a four handicap. As a member of the Glen Country Club, David competed and won the teen boys club championship and had been the reigning champion three years running.

Although the Barton family and Mrs. Stokes were the only black members of the country club, the caddy program consisted of several black caddies. David's father always chose the same caddy whenever he played a round of golf at the club. The caddy's name was Michael and he was David's age. David always felt bad that Michael was forced to run beside the cart in the sweltering heat. He usually tried to discourage his dad from using a caddy when they played together. "Dad, I can spot your ball for you. We don't need a caddy," he would whisper. "Son, it's our duty to support the caddy program. Besides, Michael reminds me of myself when I was his age. I know he needs the tip money, and I've seen some of the white golfers mistreat some of the black caddies. At least I know Michael will be treated respectfully when he's with us during our round." David didn't understand his father's comment until weeks later.

One afternoon, as he approached the club house to work on his golf swing at the driving range, an elder white club member stared David in his face and shouted.

"Hey, boy! Where is my bag? I have to meet my foursome in five minutes! Go get my bag, boy!"

David pushed his chest out and stared squarely at the old man. "Who are you calling, boy?" David shouted. He balled his fist ready to fight.

As if out of nowhere, the starter appeared and intervened. "I'm terribly sorry, Mr. Barton. Your golf attire today is identical to the caddy uniform, so he mistook you for a caddy," he whispered. "I'm terribly sorry." He turned his attention to the older white gentleman. "Mr. Ford, this is David Barton. He's Dr. Barton's son, and he's a member of the club. David Barton is the junior club champion, and he's the number one golfer at Homer Glen High School, sir," the starter explained.

The older golfer slanted his eyes and stared at David. "It was easier when all of the darkies were the caddies," he grumbled. "I can't tell them apart now that some of them are members. Tell him not to dress like a caddy if he doesn't want to be mistaken for one."

He never shared this experience with his dad, but he now understood why his father requested Michael as a caddy. David continued to deliberately dress in the Glen Country Club caddy uniform (khaki shorts and a white golf shirt) and was usually mistaken as a caddy by another member at least weekly. When it happened, he would stare at the offender and give the following response. "I am not a caddy. I am a member here just like you. Why don't you have the starter call the caddy shack if you need a caddy?"

⁞⁞

David shook his head at the memory. The following season, the caddy uniform was formalized to include bright orange golf shirts with the Glen Country Club logo emblazoned on their back and the word CADDY embroidered in large letters on the front of the shirt. David wondered if the new caddy uniform had anything to do with Mr. Ford's comments and the slight increase in black golf members at the club.

"Well, Belvedere, it looks like I have to make a run. I'll just trek to the store and pick up a new nozzle. If Mom and Dad get home, tell them where I went okay?" David joked. The dog stared blankly at David and settled into his doggie bed for his afternoon snooze.

David nuzzled Belvedere's head, grabbed his wallet from the kitchen island and jumped into his soapy car to head to the Steiffer Save Mart.

Chapter 7

Checks and Balances

Tanisha completed her count and signed the verification slip. She'd counted the drawer twice before Cathy arrived and smiled confidently as she confirmed that the register balance matched what Cathy, her replacement, had counted. She held the pad as Cathy signed the hand off slip.

To Tanisha, Cathy resembled Farrah Fawcett with her long, blonde, feathered hair, and blue eyes. The resemblance was so uncanny that Tanisha had nicknamed her Farrah. With a cleft in her chin, Cathy was strikingly beautiful on the inside and out. Athletically fit, smart, fun, and nice, Cathy was practically perfect in every way, until she opened her mouth. Her pouty smile hid teeth that were permanently stained a light gray that no amount of brushing or whitening could alter. Her teeth were a daily reminder of the power of tetracycline, an antibiotic that her mother had taken when she was pregnant with her. When Cathy opened her mouth, most people stared shockingly when they saw her green gray colored teeth against her perfect, pink lips and pale white skin. She'd grown accustomed to their reaction and learned to smile confidently. Cathy didn't appear the least bit self conscious about her teeth the way that Tanisha was self conscious about her cavity. Tanisha envied how confidently

Cathy reacted to the stunned expressions of strangers and without prompting would quickly explain why her teeth were permanently discolored. She always said the same thing. *"My teeth are this color because my mother had to take tetracycline when she was pregnant with me. I wish they weren't this color, but I'm lucky to be alive and so is my mother."* Cathy had learned to address the elephant in the room and move on.

When they'd first met at Save Mart, Tanisha had made a face when she saw Cathy's teeth. Unfazed, Cathy had given Tanisha her standard tooth 'stump speech' as she called it. Tanisha had timidly asked if anything could be done to change the color of her teeth, and without a hint of irritation, Cathy had just smiled and responded, *"No. The dentist said that I would have to have all of my teeth capped, which would be expensive, and my family can't afford that right now. One day I'll be able to get them capped, but it's not in my immediate future. I'm just glad that my mother didn't die. Her infection was so severe that she or I could have died. To me, my teeth are a reminder that she loved me enough to take medicine to save my life and hers. My mother is my best friend, I love her so much. I can chew fine with them, and one day I'll get them capped, but right now it is what it is."*

Tanisha had run her tongue along the decayed surface of her front tooth, and contemplated sharing her dental shame with Cathy, but quickly changed her mind. She didn't have the self confidence that Cathy had. She'd never shared her tooth secret with her best girl friends, how could she share such an intimate secret with a girl at work that she barely knew?

Whenever Tanisha looked at Cathy, she was reminded of that statement and wished that she could say that about her mother. *"My mother is my best friend."* Even thinking it silently felt like a lie. She longed for that type of relationship with her mother

Tanisha quickly updated Cathy on the few outstanding service desk activities. The wall clock read 5:00. She glanced out the window and could see her brother, Jack, leaning against the car parked parallel to the curb and tossing his car keys into the air. Tanisha waved and raced to her locker.

As Tanisha sped down the aisle, she was tempted to remove her smock so that she wouldn't be stopped by a customer looking for an item, but she knew that would be a violation of the Save Mart Customer Service Policy. Employees were not allowed to remove their smocks until they swiped out on the time clock. Tanisha picked up her pace and prayed that she wouldn't be stopped by any customers.

I hope my Calvin Klein jeans are clean enough to wear again. I think I'll wear my multi-colored hoodie with my white tee-shirt or maybe my yellow turtleneck in case it gets chilly later. That way if it's hot in the arcade, I can take off my jacket and not be cold. I should have time to roll my hair and take a quick shower before it's time to head out.

Tanisha's thoughts were consumed with her wardrobe as she rounded the corner and zipped into the employee only section of Save Mart.

She swiped the time clock, threw her smock into her locker and grabbed her back pack. She walked quickly through the store, and paused as she heard her employee clock number being paged. "Clock ninety two, please call the service desk. Clock ninety two, please call the service desk," Cathy repeated.

Tanisha approached just as Cathy was hanging up the loud speaker.

"Hey, Farrah Fawcett, what's up? Were you paging me to call the service desk?" she asked, her brow creased with curiosity.

"I did," Cathy admitted. "You have a phone call. But you'd better make it quick because I just saw the assistant manager walking the floor." Cathy handed Tanisha the phone.

Tanisha raised both eyebrows. Jack was in front waiting for her, and her friends knew to never call her at Save Mart unless it was an absolute emergency. On slow nights at the service desk, Tanisha would sometimes sneak and call them, but they never called her unless they were returning a call and she'd given them the all clear to call her right back.

"Hello, this is Tanisha," she answered quickly.

"Hello, Tanisha, this is Tom. I met you earlier today. I was the guy wearing the dark blue suit. We made eye contact and I asked you about your hair."

"Oh, I remember. Did you forget something at the service desk?" Tanisha raised her eyebrows and panned her eyes around the service desk.

"No, I didn't forget anything. I had to rush out of the store because we were late for a wedding."

Bingo! I knew they were headed to a wedding.

"Anyway, I think you're very attractive. Have you ever thought about becoming a model?" Tom asked.

"Excuse me?" Tanisha stated.

"A model. Have you ever thought about modeling? I'm a principal owner with Talent Plus Modeling Agency in Chicago, and I think you have a great look and could be a model."

Tanisha squirmed as Cathy stared down her throat. "Well, I've never given that any thought," she stated.

"Well, you should. I am the new talent scout for teens and I'd love to have you come in and talk to us," Tom said.

As Tanisha digested Tom's message, the service desk phone rang and Cathy raised both eyebrows at Tanisha.

"Tom, we're not supposed to get personal phone calls here, and the phone is ringing, so I'm going to have to let you go." Tanisha spoke quickly.

"I understand," he said. "Can I have your number at home to call you and talk to you about it?"

Tanisha's spider senses were tingling now. *Oh, now I get it, he likes teenage girls and he tells them that he can make them models. What a wacko!*

"I don't think so, Tom. I've got to catch this call so I don't lose my job. Have a nice day." Tanisha pressed the button for line two and transferred the call to the camera department.

"What was that about, Tanisha? You were making some funny faces," Cathy said.

"Girl, it was some weirdo guy that was in the store earlier who was trying to flirt. First of all, he was white, and he had to be at least twenty-five! I'm so sure I'm going to hang out with a twenty-five year old dinosaur!" she laughed. "He told me that I should be a model. How lame is that?"

Tanisha and Cathy giggled before Tanisha raced outside to unlock her bike. Jack lifted the bike and easily slid it into the large trunk.

As she jumped into the front seat, she remembered that she'd placed her backpack on the service desk counter. Tanisha raced back into the store, grabbed her backpack and waved at Cathy who was on the phone.

Waiting in line at the Save Mart checkouts to buy his new sprinkler nozzle, David's eyes casually panned the front of the store. He stopped and did a double take when he saw Tanisha grab something from the service desk and wave at the girl behind the counter. His eyes followed her out the store as she jumped into a waiting car.

Chapter 8

Blonde and Blue

I can't believe that I just saw Tanisha. Was that a mirage like in the desert? Was that Tanisha or was it my imagination? David's thoughts wandered as he paid the clerk for his sprinkler nozzle. David grabbed his change and smiled weakly at the teenage cashier who was grinning widely at him. He grabbed his bag and walked through the exit doors and turned left to reenter through the main Save Mart doors.

He stood in front of the service desk and waited for Cathy to complete her telephone call before speaking.

"Excuse me, Cathy." David smiled, glancing approvingly at her nametag. "Did you know the girl who just grabbed that backpack about thirty seconds ago?" he asked.

Cathy smiled widely at David hoping he was flirting with her. David's expression didn't change as he glanced quickly at her discolored teeth before locking his gaze on her blue eyes.

"Yes, but she's gone for the day. Is there something that I can help you with?" Cathy asked. She quickly remembered the comment that Tanisha had just made about an older customer trying to flirt with her and eyed David cautiously, hesitant to offer any information. *But this guy isn't white, and he doesn't look anywhere near twenty-five so he couldn't be the weirdo that just hung up the phone with Tanisha.*

"Was her name, Tanisha? Tanisha Carlson?" David offered.

Oh, he must know her since our nametags only have our first names on them. "Yes, it was. She just finished her shift. Her brother just picked her up. Do you know Tanisha?" Cathy asked.

She works here? "Yes, I do. Thanks, Cathy! By the way, has anyone ever told you that you have the most beautiful blue eyes and you look like Farrah Fawcett?" David asked.

"That's so funny. Tanisha always calls me Farrah Fawcett. I don't see the resemblance, but thanks for the compliment," Cathy smiled.

With a grin that would rival the Cheshire Cat in Alice in Wonderland, David winked and strolled slowly to his car.

∞∟

Jack pulled the Blue Goose in front of the town house, and Tanisha bolted out of the car before he had time to place the car in park.

"What's the rush, Tanisha?" Jack asked as he walked to the door, tossing his keys from his left hand to his right.

"I have to roll my hair, shower and change, and I don't want you to be late for your party. I can be ready in thirty minutes!" she explained.

"No biggee! Who am I picking up again?" Jack asked.

"We need to scoop Lori, Rashanda and Maria. Before we leave, I'll call them and make sure they're ready so we're not waiting for anyone," Tanisha assured.

"Okay, I'm picking up Kerri to take her to Mr. Licht's party with me tonight. Kerri lives on the same street as Maria," Jack said. "Turn on the iron for me so I can iron my shirt, Tanisha," he instructed. "I fell asleep as soon as I hung up with you, and barely woke up in time to scoop you at five o'clock," he yawned. "By the way, who's bringing you guys home?" Jack asked.

"Lori's mom is going to let Charlotte pick us up since she just got her license." *He's always hanging out with that Kerri babe. She's nice and everything, but if he picks her up then she's going to have to ride with us all the way to the mall. I wonder why Jack is always picking her up and why he is always dressing like he's going to work at the bank?*

A sophomore at River North High School, and a member of Sir Camelot, River North's award winning swing choir group, Jack had inherited his melodic tenor wind pipes from Jackie. He wasn't just a member of Sir Camelot, he was the star. He performed solos and duets at every performance and provided choreography assistance to Mr. Licht, the Sir Camelot director and high school music instructor.

Mr. Licht was a single white male and lived with his brother in Newberry West, the suburb adjacent to Newberry East. An accomplished vocalist and an immaculate dresser, Mr. Licht believed that the teachers at River North were role models, and that one way to command respect from the students was to dress to impress: "If I'm dressed like a student, the students will confuse me as their peer. That will never do," Mr. Licht would say.

Jack idolized Mr. Licht and wanted to be just like him, so he began dressing to impress at school, mixing his standard uniform of jeans and tee-shirts with corduroys and cotton button down oxfords. Jackie didn't understand Jack's artistic side and didn't like how Jack idolized Mr. Licht. Their father was quick to share his opinion about his son's friendship with a male teacher.

"I don't know about him, Jack. He's a grown man living with his brother? And neither one of them has ever been married? That just doesn't sound right to me," Jackie would grumble.

Her brother's newfound fashion sense didn't go unnoticed by the women of Sir Camelot, known as the Sir Camelot Dames, and Jack soon found himself becoming friends with Kerri Peck, the lead soloist of the Dames, and a natural blonde.

Tanisha hung her jacket in the foyer closet and dropped her backpack on the floor. When they'd driven up, Tanisha noticed that Billie Mae's car was not in front of the house. She'd seen her brothers, Byron and Allen, playing soccer in the front with Lou and his brothers. She glanced around the room and briefly wondered where Billie Mae was.

Tanisha walked into the kitchen and studied the yellow wall clock that hung crooked on the wall. The clock was shaped in the form of a sunflower with a bright yellow face and black petals. The center of the clock was a smiley face. When they'd moved to Newberry East, Grandma Bootsy had given the family the clock as a housewarming gift. Whenever Tanisha glanced at the clock, it made her think of Grandma Bootsy and made her smile. The cord from the electric clock hung down the wall to the outlet. Tanisha walked over and straightened the clock face and read the time: 5:45. She had told her friends that she would pick them up by 6:30, so she had more than enough time to eat a snack, shower and change.

After ironing his shirt, Jack laid across the sofa to take another quick nap. Tanisha opened the refrigerator and pulled out the bologna and mayonnaise. She looked inside the bread box and grabbed the near empty bread wrapper. She counted six slices of bread including the heel. She decided to make herself a half sandwich using the heel of the bread, her favorite part. Her brothers hated the thick, crusted heel of the bread, but she loved it. She smeared a glob of mayonnaise on the bread, reached into the jar with her spoon, scooped another glob, and ate it. She loved mayonnaise. When she was younger she loved eating mayonnaise and jelly sandwiches, an acquired taste that she'd outgrown. She slapped a slice of bologna on the mayonnaise mattress covering the bread and bit into her open face sandwich. As she stared in the refrigerator, she picked up a pitcher and wasn't surprised that it contained less than eight ounces of Kool-aid, not enough to fill even a small glass. She debated if she had time to make a new pitcher when she heard the front door open. Tanisha peered around the corner prepared to scold Byron or Allen for leaving such a small amount of Kool-aid in the pitcher when she locked eyes with Billie Mae.

"Hey, Mom," Tanisha forced herself to utter.

"Hello," Billie replied blandly.

Tanisha decided to wash her sandwich down with water so that she could sneak up to her room. She grabbed a glass from above the sink, turned on the cold water, and shoved the bologna sandwich into her mouth. She chewed furiously, praying that Billie Mae would just retreat to her room. As she gulped down her water, Tanisha heard footsteps coming toward the kitchen. For the second time that day, she felt uncomfortable under someone's intense gaze.

Chapter 9

Plan B

The grin was almost as wide as the four lane highway that led him home. Pulling into the driveway, he hit the garage door opener and strolled triumphantly inside. After he turned on the water, he pumped his fist several times like he'd just sunk a thirty foot putt to clench a tournament win.

The wide grin replaced by a whimsical whistle, his hands rubbed together like a Batman villain. *Tanisha works at Save Mart! At least now I have a way to see her. I just need to figure out when she works. I don't know how she's working since she's only fourteen, but Cathy said it was Tanisha Carlson and she worked there and I saw her with my very own eyes, so who cares. She can't work during the day since she's in school so she must work on weekends and in the evenings. I'll call up there every night this week until I hear her voice. And if she answers, I'll jump in my car and go up there and casually bump into her!*

The unrecognizable whistle tune escaped from his lips like a jazz fusion piece, haphazard and difficult to follow by anyone except true jazz aficionados. Too lazy to walk over to the spigot to turn off the water, David bent the garden hose to stop the flow before screwing on the new nozzle. He carefully rinsed his soap streaked hubcaps, rubbing them gently with the lamb cloth that his father suggested he use to protect the car's finish. The car drying in the sun, he cleaned his leather seats, the adrenaline still pumping through his veins. His whistle solo now accompanied by the blaring radio. The concert was interrupted by the ringing telephone, barely audible above the noise.

David walked briskly into the garage toward the extension that his dad insisted be installed in the garage. He was glad that his dad had won that battle. David stepped over the sleeping Belvedere who snored on the garage floor. He grabbed the extension before the answering machine clicked on.

"Hello, speak now or forever hold your peace." David loved answering the phone with different sayings. It always threw off the callers and it drove his parents crazy.

"Hey dude, it's Todd."

"Hey, whas'up man? Perfect timing, I just finished buffing my ride. I was just about to call you. I can meet you there in ten minutes, we can probably get in at least twelve holes if we tee off in twenty minutes," he rambled quickly. "In fact, when we hang up, I'll call the pro shop and have our clubs sent up," he continued. "And I'm starving so I'll call the nineteenth hole and have the waitress leave a turkey sandwich in the cart for me. You want me to have them make something for you?" he finished.

"Slow down, dude," Todd said. "That's what I'm calling you about. I'm gonna have to fake. You're not going to believe this, but I broke my arm playing baseball this afternoon so I can't make it. I'm still at the emergency room with my parents waiting to get a cast," he explained.

"Are you serious? That's messed up," David frowned. "What happened?"

"I was goofing around with my cousins at a family picnic, and they dared me to slide into second base," he explained. "So you know I can't turn down a dare," he continued.

"Tell me you didn't slide into second base," David laughed. "You haven't played baseball since we were in little league together," he teased. "And even then you couldn't slide properly, tubby."

"Bite me!" Todd shot back. "Anyway, I slid perfectly but somehow my left arm slammed into the bag and snapped," he explained. "It's a bad break too. You could see the bone poking through the skin. It was cool," he finished.

Although both of David's parents were doctors, he didn't enjoy hearing about blood and broken bones. "That's way too much information for me, so you can spare me the gory details," he groaned. "I think I just lost my appetite," he said. "How long are you going to be in a cast?" he asked.

"I'm not exactly sure. They're putting on a temporary cast to stabilize it for now because my dad wants his orthopedic surgeon friend to look at it before they put a final cast on. I'll know more when I visit my dad's guy on Monday," Todd explained. "But my dad says that it usually takes at least six weeks for a bone to set and heal properly."

"Your old man is a dermatologist. What does he know about setting a bone? He hasn't done an orthopedic rotation since medical school. Put Max on the phone so I can straighten him out!" David laughed.

"Yeah right. He would rip your head off and feed it to you," he whispered. "Sorry I can't take your money on the golf course today, buddy. Are you still going to drive into the city for the John & Judy party?"

"I don't know. I was looking forward to swinging my sticks," he admitted. "I may just go on over to the club and play a quick nine before it gets dark. But then again, it's almost six o'clock, I'm starving and I could really use a shower," he paused. "So I may just blow it off and play with my old man in the morning. I don't know if I feel like hanging out at the John & Judy party solo, but I did just wax my ride, so I may cruise through there. We'll see." David rubbed Belvedere's head.

"My parents are attending an event tonight, so I'll be at the crib by myself if you want to swing by and play video games," Todd suggested. "Or I may surprise Maria and show up at the Jefferson Mall movie theatre," he whispered. "I know she and her girls are going up there to see some tear jerker chick flick. Once she sees this cast, I know I'll get some serious sympathy from her," he groaned. "But my arm is seriously throbbing so I may just chill," Todd admitted.

"Aaaight man, you take it easy. I'll check on you tomorrow, Shleprock!" David teased.

Maria and her girls are going to be at the Jefferson Mall movie theatre tonight? I wonder if Tanisha will be with her. Maybe Belvedere and I will have to just make a run.

৪৩

Her petite frame hovered in the narrow doorway, like a garden variety bumble bee, planning its nectar raid. To Tanisha, she appeared twice as large as her one hundred and ten pound weight suggested. Tanisha decided to fill her glass with water again, nervously filling the glass half way and forcing herself to slowly drink the tepid water. Her mother's presence loomed larger with each gulp. She could feel Billie's eyes staring, her courage fortified with Jack's presence in the next room.

Gently placing the glass in the sink, she raised her eyebrows, the smile forced and fake. "Did you need something, Mom?" Tanisha asked nervously. *Calm down, Tanisha. Jack is in the living room. If she acts crazy, he'll hear her and get involved.* Tanisha took a deep, cleansing breath like she'd seen the television yoga instructor do.

Billie Mae shook her head as though snapping out of a trance. "No, I was just noticing how much you resemble your Aunt Helen. You look just like her," Billie said. "And as you get older, you seem to look more and more like her," she paused. "You're going to be as pretty as your Aunt Helen is," she finished.

Startled by the flattering comparison, Tanisha forced a thank you, eyeing her mother suspiciously. She'd never heard Billie Mae compliment one of Jackie's relatives before, only complain about them. For as long as Tanisha could remember, Billie Mae had referred to Jackie's sisters as high yellow and funny looking. She'd branded Aunt Helen's brief modeling career a waste of time, gleefully rejecting her request for Tanisha to be photographed with her as the young child in her young mother photo shoot. Aunt Helen's gentle plea to use Tanisha in the shoot because of their resemblance as well as their close bond which would transfer naturally on film was ignored by Billie with no explanation provided other than the terse reply: 'I'm her mother, and I don't want her to do it. I don't have to explain myself to you.' Billie Mae preferred to pretend as though Jackie's sisters didn't exist and when forced to acknowledge them, her speech was generally peppered with derogatory terms including: professional students, fakes, phonies, bourgeoisie, skinny, high yellow bananas. These were the adjectives that had been most used to describe Tanisha's aunts. To hear her mother refer to one of them as pretty was cause for concern. *Did Billie Mae just describe Aunt Helen as pretty?*

When Aunt Helen was appointed as Assistant Provost at Northwestern University, Billie's joy could have been mistaken for mourning. Still married to Jackie, Billie Mae refused to attend the celebratory luncheon to honor Aunt Helen's most recent accomplishment. She'd also boycotted the dinner hosted by Grandma Bootsy to celebrate the successful defense of Aunt Helen's Ph.D. dissertation and the conferring of her doctorate in biology. Billie Mae cheered when Aunt Helen divorced her first husband, but refused to attend the wedding to her second husband, claiming that as a Catholic, she couldn't attend the wedding of a divorced woman because it was viewed as a sin in God's eyes. Billie Mae tried to forbid six year old Tanisha from serving as flower girl, but Jackie insisted that she be allowed to participate in her godmother's wedding ceremony. A kind and successful architect, Aunt Helen's new husband surprised her with a new car as a wedding gift, a needle in the eye for Billie Mae.

Tanisha wrinkled her eyebrows and stared at her mother carefully. "Yeah. Everybody always tells me that I look just like Aunt Helen when she was a teenager," she agreed. "Excuse me, I need to squeeze by you so I can change," she said lightly.

"I was going to make peppered steak for dinner. Where are you going tonight?" Billie asked quickly.

"Jack is taking me to the movies to meet my friends so I'm going to eat there," Tanisha said, her hands in her pockets.

"What movie are you going to see?" Billie smiled.

"I'm not sure. We're going to decide when we get there. Or we may just play video games for a couple of hours. Lori's mother is going to pick us up," Tanisha fibbed. *What's with the third degree?*

No sense telling her that Charlotte is picking us up or she'll ask me twenty questions about how long Charlotte has been driving, blah, blah, blah.

A soft smile on her face, Billie Mae stepped out of the doorway into the tiny dining room to allow Tanisha to pass. As she walked by, Tanisha exhaled. She raced up the stairs two at a time and could hear her mother in the kitchen unloading the dishwasher, a task she seldom performed. At the top of the stairs, Tanisha shook her head in bewilderment. *She's acting concerned about what I'm doing and where I'm going and she's actually going to cook. Is she back on her meds? I can't figure her out.*

Opening her closet door, Tanisha stared at her clothes. She decided to call Maria first.

"Hi, Maria! It's Tanisha," she said.

"Hey, girl. Don't worry I'm going to be on time tonight," Maria said quickly. "I will be ready at six thirty sharp," she promised. Maria was notorious for stepping out of the shower as the carpool pulled into her driveway.

"You better be ready, because Jack has to be at a party at 7:00, and he'll leave your butt if you're not ready! But that's not why I'm calling," Tanisha explained. "What are you wearing?"

"Oh. I just bought these new jeans and a tie dyed tank top with a pink hoodie to match. It's too cute!"

I knew she'd have a new outfit. "Cool. I'll wear my hoodie too then," Tanisha said softly. "Now finish getting ready so we're not waiting for you," Tanisha ordered as she pulled out her stand by Calvin Klein jeans and her favorite hoodie, black with large yellow, red, blue and green patches dispersed in an art deco pattern on the front. She decided to wear a yellow, cotton turtleneck under the hoodie and her yellow socks with her penny loafers.

She turned on the shower and placed eight sponge rollers in her hair. Tanisha carefully placed the pink shower cap over her curlers, brushing her teeth while the shower heated. Pressing her molars together tightly, the grin exaggerated and wide, her tongue instinctively traced the decayed tooth.

A few months earlier, at her insistence, Jackie had taken Tanisha to the dentist. The dentist's prognosis was the same as the previous year. The primary tooth had presented with decay, and would fall out eventually. Again, Tanisha pleaded with the dentist to just pull the tooth. His white hair glistened in the fluorescent light, appearing almost silver against his pale skin, the dentist gently reminded her that the permanent tooth would eventually push the primary tooth out and that to pull it prematurely could potentially alter the structure of her face and jaw line. Smiling, a perfect grin behind his pink lips, the dentist patted Tanisha's hand. "Be patient, pretty lady. The permanent tooth is up there. I can see it in the x-ray. It'll push its way down when it's ready," he assured. Almost three years since his first assurance, the tooth hadn't budged and wasn't loose to the touch.

She wiggled the tooth and prayed aloud. "God, please make this tooth come out. I look like a hillbilly!" she said, the shower water serving as background noise. As was her custom, Tanisha practiced her closed mouth smile in the mirror and rehearsed aloud.

"Hi. My name is Tanisha, Tanisha Carlson. Thank you. I'll be a freshman at River North. Where do you go to school? My friends are over there. No, we're just playing video games. Sure, do you have a pen?"

She usually rehearsed replies to the general questions that she might have to answer if a boy came up and talked to her. What's your name? You're pretty. Where do you go to school? Who are you here with? Did you see a movie tonight? Can I have your phone number?

She practiced her responses until she was confident that she could answer each question without even a hint of her decayed tooth showing. Satisfied with her responses, she jumped in the steamy shower and lathered quickly. Less than five minutes later, she applied baby oil before carefully patting her dewy skin dry and slipping into her clothes. She pulled out her curlers and finger combed her loose curls, spraying herself with her Love's Baby Soft cologne. She dialed the phone to let Rashanda know that she and Jack would be at her house in seven minutes. The girls had established a car pool phone tree. If Tanisha was leading the car pool, she called Rashanda, Rashanda would call Lori and then Lori would call Maria so that everyone was on red alert.

Inhaling deeply, she smelled the peppered steak that Billie Mae prepared. Tanisha shook Jack's shoulder to wake him, envying how easily her brother could fall asleep in the middle of the day. She needed darkness to fall asleep. Jack yawned and stretched, his freshly ironed shirt now covered in small wrinkles.

"The food is almost ready, if you want to eat a quick bite before you leave," Billie Mae offered. "I know how much you like peppered steak, Jack," she reminded.

"I'll eat it tomorrow," Jack announced. "Mr. Licht always has food at his parties," he finished.

"Well, have fun," Billie offered softly, the disappointment in her voice intensified by the melancholy look in her eyes. Tanisha quickly looked away and walked to the car.

Chapter 10

Ready When You Are

Watching from the window, Rashanda bounded down the stairs as Jack arrived, meeting Tanisha on the steps.

"Hey girl!" Rashanda was wearing jeans and a red and blue rugby shirt. Her small, square purse was draped diagonally across her body and she wore her new Sperry Topsider deck shoes with white socks. Her hair was styled in a short bob that barely skimmed the tops of her ears.

"You look cute, but we need to fix your hair," Tanisha offered. "Here, let's tuck your hair behind your ears," she suggested, tucking Rashanda's short hair behind her ears and smoothing her bangs. "And lose the socks."

"But you have on socks," Rashanda protested.

Glancing at her feet, Tanisha nodded. "But I'm wearing penny loafers and my socks match my outfit," she explained. "When I wear my Sperry Topsiders I don't wear socks. Just take them off in the car and stuff them in your purse."

"My purse is too small. I'll just run them back in the house." Rashanda raced back up the stairs two at a time and threw her socks into the foyer. "How do I look now?" she asked hopefully. Rashanda relied on her friends for fashion tips, and between Maria, Tanisha and Lori she always received styling advice whether she asked for it or not.

"Better. Here tuck your shirt in," Tanisha suggested, loosening Rashanda's thin belt and tucking the bulky shirt that she wore into her slim jeans. "Thanks for being on time. Let's hope Maria is on time too."

As if on cue, Jack laid on the horn and yelled out the window, "Tanisha, let's go. I'm late as it is," he barked. "Hurry up!"

The girls skipped to the car and Tanisha jumped into the back seat with Rashanda.

"You know Maria is going to have us waiting," Rashanda whispered.

"Jack has to pick up Kerri from Sir Camelot to take her to Mr. Licht's party, so he will leave Maria's tail if she's not ready. Watch," Tanisha whispered.

"That would be too funny." Rashanda glanced into the front seat and watched as Jack pressed the radio buttons.

Jack drove the two blocks to Lori's house. Lori was waiting on her driveway.

Gotta love her! That girl is always on time! Lori jumped into the back seat.

"Hey, girls! Hi, Jack," Lori squealed. "I called Maria 10 minutes ago and told her that you guys were at my house so she should definitely be ready now," Lori explained. "Your hair looks cute, Rashanda."

"Thank you. I re-styled it for her," Tanisha boasted. "She came out of the house looking like Moe from the Three Stooges!" Tanisha teased.

"I did not!" Rashanda glanced at the front seat to see if Jack overheard Tanisha's comment. As best she could tell, he wasn't paying them any attention as he maneuvered the large sedan down the street singing softly to the radio station.

"You go girl!" Lori gave Tanisha a high five.

"Thank you very much! I got skills!" Tanisha bragged.

"Tanisha, I'm going to pick up Kerri first since we have to pass her house to get to Maria's," he explained.

Tanisha rolled her eyes in the back seat as Jack steered the Chevy Caprice into Kerri's driveway and walked inside. Kerri's family never locked their front door and they adored Jack, so he never rang the doorbell. Once Jack was inside Kerri's house, the girls took open season on him.

"Why does Jack always hang out with Kerri, Tanisha? What's up with that?" Lori wrinkled her nose showing several layers of skin. Her face looked like a pug when she did that.

"They're in Sir Camelot together. She's a lead soloist and so is he so they just hang out." Tanisha shrugged her shoulders.

"LaTonja Miller is also a lead soloist but Jack doesn't hang out with her? Why does he only hang out with that white girl? Is Jack kicking it with Kerri?" Lori asked.

"Naw! They're just friends." Tanisha dismissed Lori's remarks.

"Lori, how come someone has to be kicking it with someone just because they hang out? Can't people just be friends anymore?" Rashanda asked.

"I'm just saying that they spend a lot of time together. Charlotte was telling me that they're always walking down the hall together and stuff," Lori explained.

"It doesn't bother me," Tanisha shrugged. "The fact that Kerri's white isn't a big deal to me, why does it bother you?" Tanisha asked.

"My grandfather said that about twenty-five years ago, a black man would have been lynched for even speaking to a white woman in Mississippi, so he told my brothers that they cannot date white girls because he's afraid that some of their parents might still be prejudiced," Lori paused. "I know you guys remember the story about Emmett Till," she said slowly looking at her friends knowingly. The girls all nodded their heads affirmatively. "Emmett Till was hung and thrown in the river for supposedly whistling at a white woman," she continued. "And later his friends said that he didn't whistle at her, he just asked her a question about something in the store, but she didn't like the way that he was looking at her so she lied and told her husband that he whistled at her."

"I remember that story," Tanisha admitted. "His friends said that he looked her in the eye when he asked her a question instead of looking down when he spoke to her," she paused. "He was from the North and didn't know the rule that Negroes weren't supposed to look white people in the eye," she added.

Rashanda shook her head in disbelief. "It's hard to believe that happened," she said. "They show his picture in *Jet* magazine every year. The one with his head all bloated in that casket," Rashanda shivered. "It freaks me out every time I see it. Do you remember how old he was?"

"I don't remember," Tanisha replied. "I know he wasn't older than fourteen. He may have been as young as twelve," she groaned. "I don't remember exactly. They usually show that picture in *Jet* on the anniversary of his death."

"They do. That picture is so scary looking, but his mother didn't want a closed casket service. She wanted the world to see what those racist monsters had done to her baby," Lori continued. "And the worst part of the story is that the white men who killed Emmett Till ran around town bragging about what they'd done, but they were found innocent by an all white jury. Can you believe that?" Lori asked flatly. "My mother said that she's glad that *Jet* still runs that picture so that the world will never forget the hatred and savagery that racist whites were allowed to inflict on blacks in certain parts of this country."

"My parents are from the south," Rashanda explained. "But my dad only goes back home for funerals because the racism memories are too painful," she shared.

"This is getting depressing," Tanisha groaned. "We all know that story, Lori, but times have changed, and we're not in Mississippi," Tanisha defended.

"We may not be in Mississippi, but times haven't changed that much, Tanisha," Lori reminded. "In my opinion, Jack shouldn't be dating a white girl," she stated boldly. "I think blacks should date blacks, and whites should date whites. Period."

Tanisha glared at Lori blankly. "I don't think anyone asked your opinion, little Miss Segregationist, and for all I know they're not dating. He's just giving Kerri a ride to a party. Let's just drop it. Here they come," Tanisha said quickly.

In all truthfulness, Tanisha was worried about her brother dating Kerri. Afraid that he might get hurt dating a girl outside of his race, she still harbored a slight distrust of white girls.

৪৩ও৪

In elementary school, Tanisha had been shunned by her white classmates, all of whom were unaccustomed to having a black girl in their class, let alone a black girl who was smarter than they were. Feeling like an outsider, Tanisha eagerly tried to befriend the girls, helping them with their school assignments, complimenting their hair and clothes and trying desperately to join their girl chatter. Her efforts were always rebuffed or ignored. The nicer girls would thank her for the answers but never invite her to join in their play. The meaner girls would roll their eyes in her face and walk away. She felt like Rudolph the Red Nosed Reindeer. She learned to sit on the playground at recess and read a book. She cringed each time one of the girls had a birthday party. The girls would boldly pass out invitations in class and skip her desk like she was invisible. As the birthday girl pranced down the aisle distributing the party invitations, Tanisha kept her head down and read a book. Once, Tanisha raised her head and extended her hand when a classmate paused at her desk hoping that perhaps this time things would be different. One of the nicer girls, she looked Tanisha squarely in the eye, snickered and said, "Nothing personal, but you're not invited to my party. My dad would die if I invited a black girl to visit my house. I'm sure you understand, Tanisha." Tanisha lowered her head, embarrassed beyond belief. She prayed that the teacher would not allow invitations to be distributed in class, or at least notice that she never received one, but nothing changed. Month after month, the exclusionary ritual continued. Her Mahala school experience was a lonely one and left her with a belief that white girls were mean and cruel to people who weren't white. Years later, she was friendly with Cathy from Save Mart, but they weren't friends outside of work. And she didn't have any white friends at Battle Creek Junior High School so her impression of white girls was limited to her bad experience at Mahala. She didn't trust white girls, and she didn't want her brother to be hurt by Kerri Peck.

‟‣

Before anyone could respond, Jack and Kerri appeared. Kerri was wearing tight white jeans and a pink halter top with gold open toe sandals, her toes painted a bubblegum pink. She carried a gold metallic purse. Her long blonde hair was feathered in the same cut and style as Farrah Fawcett from Charlie's Angels. Tanisha smiled at her resemblance to Cathy from work. As she approached the car, Kerri grinned widely, showing perfect, white teeth. Jack opened the passenger door for her and she climbed in.

"Hi, Tanisha. Don't you look cute!" Kerri beamed. Her perfectly straight teeth glistened under her shiny lip gloss. "Introduce me to your friends, girlfriend," she grinned.

Girlfriend? Since when did white girls start saying girlfriend? I missed that memo. "Hi Kerri. This is Rashanda and this is Lori. They go to Battle Creek with me," Tanisha smiled warmly. Tanisha actually liked Kerri and thought she was cool. But try as she might, she just couldn't shake her perception that white girls were exclusionary and mean, or at least to black girls.

Jack drove four doors down the street and pulled into Maria's driveway. Lori jumped out to ring the bell. Maria's mom came to the door and waved at the car motioning for Lori to come inside.

"Oh no. That's not a good sign!" Tanisha whispered to Rashanda who nodded in agreement. From past experience they knew that when Mrs. Wesley invited someone to come inside it meant that Maria was not ready. Sometimes it meant that she was just applying her make-up but other times it meant that she was in a robe blow drying her long, thick hair. Tanisha prayed that she was at least dressed.

Clearly preoccupied with one another, Jack and Kerri chatted animatedly. Tanisha exhaled loudly and decided that she would give Maria five minutes before ringing the bell. She glanced at her watch to track the time and noticed that the date on her watch was off by a day. As Tanisha pulled the watch knob out to change the date forward, she realized that she only had three more weeks before she left for student government leadership camp. Her thoughts drifted to the Battle Creek student council election.

Chapter 11

Here She Comes, Miss America!

Like a robot, Tanisha methodically walked to Mr. Smith's office, her anger and disappointment simmering on a low boil. The passage of time had moved the simmering pot from the front burner to the back burner, and now her humiliation was replaced by a quiet state of shock. She absentmindedly kicked a crumpled piece of paper through the quiet hallway. It was twenty five minutes after two, and the dismissal bell had rung ten minutes ago. The hallway was eerily silent. Tanisha kicked her balled up piece of paper harder this time, and paused to listen to the unmistakable whir of the vacuum cleaner coming from the English department. She bent down and quickly tossed the crumpled paper in the trash.

Ordinarily, Tanisha looked forward to her Monday afternoon meetings with Mr. Smith. She enjoyed walking through the empty school without the distraction and banter of the students who were not allowed in the classroom area once the dismissal bell rang. But as a student council representative, Tanisha was allowed to roam the hallways at any time. She relished this special privilege with pride. But today was different. Today, Tanisha was distracted and did not look forward to her meeting. This meeting would signal the beginning of the end for Tanisha.

Tanisha had lost the recent student council election to Tracy Jones. And although it was against school policy to share election results, Mr. Smith shared that she had only lost by a few votes. As far as Tanisha was concerned, she felt like a first class loser. Whether she lost by five votes or fifty votes, the result remained unchanged, she had lost. And losing to her nemesis, Tracy Jones, added insult to injury.

Mr. boiled-egg-breath himself, Darrell Hunter, ran for ninth grade student council president and had chosen his girlfriend Tracy Jones as his unofficial running mate. The students ran on individual tickets, but Tanisha knew that students had voted for Tracy because of Darrell's popularity and endorsement. Tanisha paused to study the campaign poster with their photo. Darrell had gotten his braces removed and his teeth were perfectly straight and pearly white. He was handsome, but Tanisha knew that his good looks were clouded by the boiled-egg-breath lurking behind his pearly whites. Tracy's long hair hung past her shoulders like a brown shawl. Her smile was demure and confident like a toothpaste advertisement. Tanisha removed the poster from the wall, stopping short of tearing it in half. *The election is over. This needs to come down.*

She'd learned to look the other way whenever she spotted Darrell and Tracy in the school corridor. Their public displays of affection always intensified for her benefit. Although she wasn't jealous, like nails on a chalkboard, it irritated her to watch them together. Now part of a couple, Tracy had started inviting small groups of friends over on the first Friday of every month for pizza and dancing, an invitation to her unofficial parties coveted like a ticket to an inaugural ball. Occasionally Maria or Lori received an invitation, but never Tanisha.

Gripping the poster tightly in her hand she trudged to Mr. Smith's office. When Darrell announced Tracy Jones as his running mate, she'd considered pulling out of the race, but Mr. Smith encouraged her to campaign. He practically assured Tanisha of a landslide victory over the inexperienced newcomer. But he'd been wrong.

Tanisha's campaign platform was a recommendation to improve the food in the cafeteria. She drafted a speech proposing that the students be allowed to vote for at least two menu items each month. Tracy ran on a platform to change the school mascot from a Dolphin to a Pirate. Tanisha was shocked when she learned that Tracy had won the election. Mr. Smith had been shocked too and had demanded a recount of the votes, but the recount confirmed that Tracy Jones had won by a slim margin.

As she approached Mr. Smith's office, a sly grin slowly crept across her face like the Grinch from the Dr. Seuss classic. The election experience hadn't been all bad. Tracy had won, but Darrell hadn't. He underestimated his opponent's popularity and lost by a narrow margin. Although embarrassed and angry that Tracy Jones had defeated her, Tanisha felt slightly vindicated in Darrell's defeat. At least she would be spared the Darrell – Tracy first couple hoopla.

As the student council representative for her home room, Tanisha worked with Mr. Smith on the program for the eighth grade year-end dinner. Although her heart wasn't in it, she knew that she had to fulfill this obligation to ensure that the dinner was nice.

Tanisha entered the social studies office and tapped lightly on the window pane. Mr. Smith's back was to the door. He was hunched over his desk writing furiously. Tanisha took a deep breath and knocked harder this time. Mr. Smith took off his large, black plastic reading glasses and jumped from his chair to greet her. He was bursting at the seams.

"Tanisha, I'm so glad you're here!" Mr. Smith grabbed Tanisha's hand and squeezed it firmly before continuing. "Come in and have a seat. I'm not supposed to announce this yet, but I've got to tell you."

Tanisha sat in the empty chair nearest Mr. Smith's desk. "Tell me what, Mr. Smith?" Tanisha stared at him with a raised eyebrow and found herself distracted by the snowflakes on his shoulders. She really liked him as a teacher, and wanted desperately to tell him that he should either get his dandruff under control by shampooing with a serious dandruff shampoo like Head & Shoulders or he should stop wearing the dark colored sweater vests which had become his trademark. His shoulders resembled the top of Mount Everest. Her thoughts consumed with dandruff, Tanisha managed to smile curiously at Mr. Smith as she folded her hands in her lap.

"I just left the principal's office a few minutes ago, and he told me that Tracy Jones' family is moving this summer. She's moving back to St. Louis which means that you will become the student council vice president! Isn't that great?"

Tanisha stared at Mr. Smith and repeated his statement. "Tracy Jones is moving to St. Louis, so I become the vice president?" she repeated.

"Exactly! She only beat you by six votes so it wasn't a landslide. I'm not supposed to tell you what the actual voting margin was, but I trust that you won't repeat it to anyone," he cautioned. "In our by-laws for the student council organization, it reads that if the elected candidate is unable to fulfill his or her obligations for whatever reason, and the first runner up candidate has lost by less than twenty votes, it is not necessary to hold another election," he recited from memory. "You were the first runner up, and you didn't lose by more than twenty votes, so you'll become the student council vice president! Isn't that great? Aren't you excited?"

Tanisha inhaled deeply and smiled at Mr. Smith. "So it's like the Miss America pageant where the first runner up gets to wear the crown if Miss America can't fulfill her duties," she stated.

Mr. Smith chuckled. "That's exactly right. You were the first runner up," he stated. "And now you get to wear the crown."

Staring at the poster in her hands, she quietly placed it on Mr. Smith's desk. "Since the campaign is over, I thought this should come down," she explained. "So even though I didn't win the popular vote, I get to wear the crown. That works for me!" she grinned. "But Mr. Smith, will I have to implement her platform and work to change the mascot? I certainly hope not, because I like our mascot and thought her platform was dumb," she shared.

Mr. Smith chuckled, "No Tanisha, you won't have to implement her platform. I'm drafting the announcement to be read in the morning."

Mr. Smith patted Tanisha on her shoulder. "Isn't it funny how things work out?" he continued. "This news has made my day! I don't know how you lost that election, Tanisha, but it doesn't matter. We have to finalize the announcement for tomorrow, firm up the particulars for the eighth grade dinner and talk about the leadership camp. We have so much to review. I know you usually catch the 3:15 activity bus, but I need you to catch the 4:15 bus today. Is that okay?" he asked.

"No problem. I finished most of my homework in study hall. What's the leadership camp?" Tanisha asked.

Mr. Smith ran his hand through his thick, gray hair. Tanisha shuddered slightly as a fresh coating of dandruff landed on his shoulders. "As the student council vice president, you are invited to attend a government leadership camp in Springfield, Illinois. The two week overnight camp is in June, and it's attended by student government leaders from all across the state of Illinois. We usually cover the camp fee for the student council president, but Roberta Flowers' family will be on vacation that week, so she can't go, so we'll cover your camp fee. Your parents will just have to pay for the Amtrak ticket to get you to Springfield."

Tanisha's heart skipped a bit. "I have a part-time job at Save Mart, so I'll have to miss two weeks of work," she stated.

Removing his glasses, Mr. Smith rubbed his eyes. "You work, Tanisha?" he asked.

"Yes," she stammered. "I work at Save Mart after school and on the weekends," she explained. "I'm sure that I can get the time off," she replied quickly. "I'll just miss the money from taking two weeks off," she continued. "But I'll plan to sign up for overtime and extra shifts now so I can make extra money to make up for it," she paused. "I'm not really saving for anything in particular," she clarified. "I just like building my bank account. Do you know how much an Amtrak ticket will cost?" Tanisha asked.

Mr. Smith studied Tanisha's face. He noticed that her eyebrows were furrowed tightly. "I took the train to Springfield a few weeks ago, and my round trip ticket was fifty two dollars," Mr. Smith replied. He laid his pen on top of his notepad. "Tell you what, Tanisha. I can arrange for the school to buy the Amtrak ticket for you so your family doesn't have to worry about it. I almost forgot that we have a discretionary fund that we can use for special occasions such as this. I'm glad you asked me about the ticket, or I would have forgotten that I can get the school to pay for it," Mr. Smith smiled, planning to pay for the ticket himself. "I'm just so glad that you won!" he beamed. "Take a look at the announcement that I drafted and tell me what you think, kiddo," he finished.

Tanisha skimmed the announcement and grinned. She'd won by default and Tracy Jones was moving. Her summer was off to a great start.

Chapter 12

Bloodhounds & Belvedere

"Tanisha, earth calling, Tanisha. Do you want me to ring the bell or are you going to ring it?" Rashanda gently tapped Tanisha's shoulder to get her attention.

Tanisha snapped out of her student government daydream and was preparing to respond to Rashanda just as Maria and Lori bounced up to the car.

The girls opened the back door and jumped inside.

"Hey, Jack!" Maria glanced at Kerri curiously. Her eyes grew wide as saucers as she stared at Kerri. "Hi, I'm Maria," she smiled like a cheerleader.

Kerri beamed as Maria climbed into the back seat of the car. "Hi, Maria, I'm Kerri. Did you just wash your hair with Pantene shampoo? I can smell it."

"In fact, I did use Pantene. What are you, a bloodhound?" Maria stared at Kerri inquisitively.

The girls burst into laughter at Maria's joke. Tanisha glanced at Kerri who threw Jack a puzzled look, shrugging her shoulders. "I don't get it. What's so funny?"

"She was just kidding, Kerri. She's a jokester. It's a *black* thing," Tanisha said.

"Oh." Kerri shrugged her shoulders again, turned around in her seat and pulled out her compact to powder her nose. "Jack, you'll have to give me more inside information on the *black* thing," Kerri laughed.

"Kerri, it's not a *black* thing!" Jack patted Kerri's thigh. "Tanisha and her friends are just silly. They're laughing at your keen sense of smell, comparing you to a bloodhound. Don't mind them, Kerri," Jack said. "They're young and silly," he repeated. He narrowed his eyes at Tanisha in the rearview mirror.

Tanisha slumped in her seat, ashamed that she had disappointed her brother. She was glad that her friends' animated chatter served as a protective shield from Jack's frosty glare.

A few moments later, Jack pulled into the movie theatre parking lot. "Do you need any money, Tanisha?" he asked.

"Nope. I'm all set big brother, but thanks, and thanks for the ride." Tanisha offered sweetly as her friends jumped out of the car. "Good to see you again, Kerri," she continued. Tanisha climbed out of the backseat ashamed that she and her friends had mocked Kerri.

"Take care, Tanisha. Have fun tonight!" Kerri flipped her long blonde hair as she reapplied her lip gloss.

"You guys have fun," Jack said as he pulled out of the parking lot, narrowly missing a shiny black Corvette that was pulling in.

The girls studied the movie theatre marquee to decide if they wanted to see a movie or just spend their money on arcade games and snacks.

Tanisha was the first to speak, "We've all seen *Fame*, and I really don't want to see *Fame* again, so let's just play games."

"I wouldn't mind seeing *Terms of Endearment*," Lori offered.

"That's supposed to be a tear jerker, and I don't want to spend money to cry. Plus my make-up will smear," Maria explained. "I'm starving, so let's go get some food and then go to the arcade."

The Cineplex had three movie screens and a small food court. The fourth movie theatre had been converted to an arcade complete with pin ball machines and carnival type games.

The girls headed to the food court and ordered slices of pizza and sodas.

"Let's hurry up and eat because I just saw some cute guys going into the arcade area! They were wearing Pillcrest High School jackets. There were like five of them, and they were all fine!" Lori squealed.

"Pillcrest does have some fine men. I'm game," Maria said.

"Lori, aren't you still going with CJ? And Maria I thought you were still kicking it with Todd!" Rashanda stared at the girls in disbelief.

"Of course I'm still with Todd, but girl, it don't hurt to look at the menu. Besides, I like flirting. It keeps my skills sharp," Maria giggled.

"For real! Plus CJ is getting on my nerves lately so I may be looking to pitch him to the curb!" Lori took a bite of her pizza.

"I know that's right! He and his boiled egg breath friend!" Tanisha took a big bite of her pizza and slurped down the rest of her soda, getting a brain freeze from the cold drink.

The girls threw their food scraps in the trash, and walked toward the bathroom. As they approached the bathroom, Maria noticed David Barton standing in the theatre lobby as though he were waiting for someone to join him.

"Rashanda, isn't that Todd's boy David?" she asked. "You met him at the skating rink." Maria elbowed Rashanda in the ribs and pointed.

Rashanda squinted, "I can't tell. I took off my glasses. In fact, I left my purse at the table. I'll be right back. Come with me, Lori." Rashanda and Lori walked back into the food court area.

"Yeah, that's him. I wonder what he's doing here," Tanisha confirmed.

"I forgot you know him from the John & Judy ski trip," Maria remembered. "Let's go say hi!" Maria walked away before Tanisha could respond. Tanisha shrugged and followed her friend.

"David! Remember me? I'm Todd's girlfriend, Maria," she sang.

"Hey, of course I remember you. How are you doing?" David smiled.

"What are you doing here? Which movie are you seeing?" Maria wore her cheerleader smile.

"Hey, Tanisha. Long time no see. How've you been?" David stared directly into Tanisha's eyes as he spoke.

"Hi, David. I'm fine. Did you turn off your hearing aide? Maria asked you a question," Tanisha said.

David slanted his eyes playfully and smiled, "I see you're still as funny as ever. I heard her. I was just trying to be polite and speak to you before I answered her question, smarty pants!" David turned to address Maria directly, "I'm not seeing a movie tonight. I just ran in to get a slice of pizza. I was at the mall and I thought I'd grab a slice of Aurelio's." He turned back to stare squarely at Tanisha. "Is that all right with you, Miss Carlson?"

"Much better. Manners do matter, and I know your mother raised you better than that." Tanisha nodded her head in approval. "But you were standing there like a statue. Were you trying to will the pizza to come to you by just standing there?"

"That's exactly what I was doing. You're too funny!" David had watched the girls walk into the food court. He correctly assumed that they would head to the restroom to freshen up after they finished eating, so he'd strategically placed himself between the food court and the restrooms.

"Isn't the main Aurelio's pizzeria close to where you live?" Tanisha asked.

"Yes, but they don't sell pizza by the slice. And I didn't want to buy a whole pizza, and since I was at the mall anyway I just thought I'd grab a quick slice," David shared. "You ask a lot of questions," he laughed. "You'd make a great attorney."

"Tanisha is planning to go to law school," Maria shared.

David nodded approvingly. "So am I, so when I become a federal judge, I'll let you clerk for me," he said gently ribbing Tanisha in the side.

Tanisha playfully swatted his hand away, "Whatever blows your skirt up!" she giggled.

"Do I look like I wear a skirt?" David thumped Tanisha's forehead gently.

Maria watched the chemistry between David and Tanisha and grinned.

Lori and Rashanda walked up and joined the group. "David, these are our friends Lori and Rashanda. You've met Rashanda already," Tanisha introduced.

David waved his hand in the air. "It's nice to meet you, Lori. How've you been, Rashanda?" he smiled.

"I'm good," Rashanda nodded. "Lori, you want to go get some quarters?" Rashanda asked.

"First, I want to go to the bathroom," she said leaning into Rashanda's ear. "And you need to brush the food out of your braces," she whispered gripping Rashanda's elbow lightly. "We'll meet you guys in the arcade," Lori winked at Tanisha. Tanisha winked back, knowing that Lori was anxious to trail the boys that she spotted going into the arcade.

"Do you guys come here every Saturday?" David directed his question at Tanisha but Maria answered it.

"Not really. I usually try to see Todd on Saturday, but he had to visit his grandmother tonight," Maria offered. "Let's go Tanisha. I really want to play Ms. Pac Man. Good to see you, David. Enjoy your pizza." Maria winked her eye at Tanisha.

"Okay. It was good to see you, David," Tanisha offered casually. *I don't want Lori to get first dibs on the cute boys.*

"Maria, is Todd's arm still in a lot of pain from his cast?" David asked.

Maria turned slowly and eyed David curiously. "What did you say?" she asked. "Did you say cast?" she repeated, glancing at Tanisha for clarification. Tanisha shrugged and frowned, her hands in the surrender pose.

Rubbing his chin, David continued. "Yea, Todd and I were supposed to play golf this afternoon before he went by his, uh grandmother's house," David stammered, his eyes shifted from Maria to Tanisha. He knew that Todd often told Maria various fables concerning his weekend whereabouts so that he could go on dates with other girls. "But I just talked to him about an hour ago, and he told me that he broke his arm playing baseball," he said quickly. "You haven't talked to him today?" David asked.

Maria grabbed David's arm and squeezed, squinting her eyes for clarity. "I knew he was going to a family picnic and then to his grandmother's house," she paused. "But I haven't talked to him since last night," she shared. "He broke his arm?" she squealed. "He's in the hospital? Oh my, God! Was he in a car accident? What happened? Where is he now?" she asked dramatically, her voice in panic mode, her left hand covered her mouth as though she might faint.

"I'm sorry I thought you knew," David said. "He broke his arm playing baseball." Now David's eyes darted from Maria to Tanisha, like an inexperienced chess player searching for his next move. "Calm down, Maria. When he called me, he was at the hospital with his parents, but he should be home now," David said.

"I need to talk to him right now." The tears flowed freely down Maria's cheeks.

Tanisha looked at David with wide doe eyes and shrugged her shoulders.

David reached in his pocket and gave Maria a fist full of change. "Here. There's a pay phone right there. Why don't you call him?" he suggested.

"Good idea," Tanisha agreed. "I'm sure he's fine, Maria," she comforted.

Maria grabbed the change and raced to the pay phone.

"Maybe I shouldn't have mentioned Todd's broken arm to her. She seems pretty upset," David offered.

"She'll be fine. She lives for high drama. Is he going to be okay?" Tanisha asked.

"Oh yeah, he'll be in a cast for six weeks, but he should be okay."

"That's good," Tanisha smiled. "Well, I'm going to catch up with Lori and Rashanda. Enjoy your pizza, David!" Tanisha turned to walk away.

"So where's your boyfriend?" David asked.

Tanisha stopped and turned around to face him. "Where's my what?" she asked.

"The boyfriend you were telling me about on the John & Judy ski trip. Where is he tonight?" David asked.

"Oh, we broke up after the spring Turnabout Dance. It wasn't that serious," Tanisha shrugged.

David twirled his car keys and grinned. "So what do you do, just love them and leave them?"

"Yeah, that's right. I'm a regular heart breaker. I'm too young to date, remember. What are you doing flying solo on a Saturday night?" she quizzed.

"I was supposed to hang with Todd tonight, but since he broke his arm I just decided to take my dog for a ride and thought I'd grab a slice."

Tanisha scowled knowingly at David. "I thought you told Maria that Todd was going to visit his grandmother tonight," she reminded suspiciously.

"He was," David laughed. "But I was going to go with him to see his grandmother and then we were going to hang out," David corrected.

"Save it," Tanisha laughed. "Did you say that you have a dog? How cute! What's his name?" Tanisha asked.

"His name is Belvedere. He's in the car. Come see him. Maria keeps putting money in the phone so she'll be talking to Todd for a while." David grabbed Tanisha's hand and gently led her outside. He held the door open for her to walk ahead of him and guided her through the parking lot to his car. Belvedere was perched in the passenger seat licking the inside of the partially open window.

As they approached the car, Tanisha squealed, "You have a Bouvier! I love those dogs. That's my favorite breed! I've never seen one in person!"

David stopped dead in his tracks and stared at her. "I'm impressed. Most people don't know what kind of dog he is. How did you know he was a Bouvier?"

"I'm not most people. Can I pet him? What's his name again?" Tanisha made funny faces through the window.

"Sure! His name is Belvedere!" David unlocked the passenger door and opened it.

"Belvedere, I'm Tanisha!" Tanisha extended the back of her hand and waited while he sniffed her scent. After he smelled her hand, she rubbed the top of his head and behind his ears and then under his chin.

"I love dogs! We had a sheltie mix breed mutt, but he ran away in December and got lost in that big blizzard," she explained.

"Oh, I'm sorry to hear that," David offered.

"How old is Belvedere?" she asked.

"He's two. I've had him since he was twelve weeks old. My parents bought him the year that my brother went off to college so I wouldn't be lonely."

"He's gorgeous!" Belvedere nuzzled Tanisha's hand encouraging her to keep petting him.

"He likes you." David rubbed Belvedere's head.

"I love dogs. My grandmother had a big German Shepherd named Duke and I used to kiss him and take naps with him when I was little." Tanisha pulled her hand away.

"How do you know so much about dogs?" David asked.

"In a past life I was a dog. No, seriously. Ever since I can remember I would read the dog section of my grandmother's encyclopedia and always loved the Bouvier and Old English Sheep Dog breeds. I've never met anyone who has a Bouvier," she finished.

"My mom picked him out," David said.

"Your mom must be a pretty cool lady," Tanisha replied.

"She is. You'd like her," David continued. "And she'd like you," he added.

Tanisha smiled at David and pointed to the movie theatre. "Listen, I'd better get back inside in case Maria is looking for me. Besides, you didn't get your slice of pizza! Bye, Belvedere." Tanisha patted the dog's head one more time.

She waited as David locked the Corvette. When they returned inside, Maria was still on the phone, twirling the cord in her hand. Tanisha walked over to her and rubbed her back pointing to the Arcade and her watch. Maria held up one finger as she wiped the tears from her eyes.

David walked over to Tanisha and whispered. "Why don't you come with me to get my pizza so I don't have to eat alone? We'll see Maria when she hangs up. Come on." David gently grabbed Tanisha by the arm and led her to the food court.

"You're always pulling me around!" Tanisha quickly thought back to their first meeting on the John & Judy ski trip when he pulled her from his party and insisted that she take a walk around the resort with him. "You don't give me a chance to say no," Tanisha giggled.

"That's because I'm so charming that it's almost impossible to say no to me. And I'm a take charge type of guy," he continued. "But don't worry, I won't lead you into trouble," David winked.

Is he flirting with me or just teasing me? Tanisha slanted her eyes and followed him to the food court. "I can smell trouble a mile away and you smell like trouble."

"Is that right?" David asked.

David ordered a slice of sausage and mushroom pizza with a large cup of lemonade. He offered to buy something for Tanisha, but she declined since she'd already eaten.

As she sat face to face with David, she became conscious of her decayed tooth, realizing that he now had a straight on view of her face. She was very careful to speak while biting the right side of her upper lip so that the tooth decay was not visible.

"So, what's new at Battleship Junior High?" David asked.

"It's called Battle Creek Junior High, genius," she corrected. "And not much. School ends in three weeks," Tanisha shared.

"That's cool. What are you doing for the summer?" he asked.

"I have to go to a student government leadership camp for two weeks in June."

David took a bite from his pizza, "What's leadership camp?"

"I was elected vice president of the student council, so I have to go to camp to learn how to lead. It's in Springfield, Illinois."

"That's cool." David wanted to ask her about working at Save Mart but he didn't want to let on that he knew that she worked there. He decided to keep that to himself.

"What are you going to do for the summer?" Tanisha asked.

"I have to take an advanced placement biology class this summer and then I'm going to teach junior tennis at the Glen Park district in the afternoons. I'm also going to work at my dad's medical office to help him do some research."

"Sounds like you'll be busy," Tanisha said.

"Maybe I can help you with your tennis this summer?" David suggested.

"My tennis game is about as bad as my skiing." Tanisha played with a napkin, twirling it tightly.

"You're being too hard on yourself," he smiled. "You're athletic, and you caught on to the skiing technique pretty quickly, so your tennis is probably better than you think," he assured. "Did you ski the green runs after I left?"

"I did. I skied two runs. They were really icy just like you said they would be, and I started getting cold," she remembered. "It was fun, but I don't think I'll be a professional skier!" Tanisha laughed.

"Skiing in the Midwest is icy. The first time you ski in Lake Tahoe, Utah or Colorado you'll be hooked, trust me!" David took another bite from his pizza and offered Tanisha a bite, waving the gooey pizza in her face, inches from her lips. Without thinking, she chomped it, chewing slyly.

Instinctively, he handed her his lemonade. Tanisha twirled the cup a few inches like she'd seen the priests do for communion and took a small sip, just enough to moisten the pizza bite in her cheeks. Their eyes met as she returned his drink to him. "Listen. I better join my friends and you shouldn't leave Mr. Belvedere in the car too long," Tanisha said as she stood. "It's pretty warm outside today, and he's so cute someone might take him."

"Well if he comes up missing I know how to find you!" David took one last bite of his pizza and grabbed his scraps. He tossed the paper plate into the trash. His napkin slid off and landed on the floor. Tanisha smiled as he bent down to pick up the napkin and toss it in the trash. *He may be a spoiled little rich boy, but at least he's not a litter bug!* They walked toward Maria who was still on the pay phone.

Maria leaned into the phone, "But Todd, if you were hurt why didn't you call me? I wouldn't have come to the movies with my friends. I would have figured out a way to come see you."

"She's been on the phone for over twenty minutes already," Tanisha groaned. "This can go on all night. How much change did you give her?" Tanisha glanced at her watch.

"I don't know. But I have an idea. Maria, can I talk to Todd?"

Maria handed David the phone.

"I can't believe he has a broken arm. I really need to see him," Maria whined to Tanisha. Her eyes were misty.

After speaking briefly with Todd, David covered the mouthpiece of the phone with his hand. "Todd's parents are at a black tie event. Do you want me to take you over there so you can see him?" he suggested.

"Yes! Please, I really want to see him!" Maria squeezed David's arm.

Tanisha shook her head in disagreement. "Maria, why don't you just wait? You can see Todd in a few days. We're hanging with the girls tonight, remember?" Tanisha reminded.

"Tanisha, you don't understand. If I don't see him tonight, I won't be able to see him until next Friday. David, please take me over there. Tanisha, you come too!" Maria directed.

"Yeah, I can drop you both off at home later," David offered. *This is better than I'd hoped.*

Gripping Maria's shoulders, Tanisha spoke firmly. "Maria, you know your mom would have a fit if she saw you getting out of a car with a boy and so would mine. Besides, Mrs. Perkins is expecting to pick us up from here at 10:00," Tanisha explained.

"Well, I could bring you guys back here by nine thirty. It's only 7:00, and Todd lives ten minutes away."

"Groovy! Let's go tell Rashanda and Lori what we're doing. I know they'll understand." Maria wiped her eyes with the back of her hand.

Tanisha wasn't thrilled about riding in David's car on a sneaky mission to visit Todd, but he had just broken his arm and Maria was upset. Her gaze drifted from Maria to David. Tanisha exhaled deeply and thought for a second about just joining Lori and Rashanda in the arcade and letting Maria go alone. But she knew that she wouldn't have a good time worrying about Maria and couldn't believe that her friend would so willingly climb in the car with a boy she hardly knew. And then Tanisha reminded herself that Maria would accept a lift from Satan if it meant she could see her beloved Todd. No, she had to go with her friend to check on Todd.

Before Tanisha could agree that she would go with them, Maria raced into the arcade to talk to Lori and Rashanda. Tanisha trailed behind her, walking swiftly in an effort to keep pace. David shouted behind them that he would wait in the lobby.

Tanisha panned the arcade and saw Rashanda giggling and playing video games with two of the Pillcrest High School boys that had come in. She pointed but Maria had already spotted her and was headed that way. Tanisha looked for Lori.

She saw Lori talking to a tall boy. Walking toward her friend, she stood off to the side and waited for her to finish her sentence. Tanisha could tell by the body language that Lori was flirting. Her eye batting increased and she gripped his bicep when she giggled. The boy looked to be at least six feet tall and had a thin mustache. His skin was the color of tea and he wore gold framed wire rim glasses. His hair was faded short on the sides and tapered into a short box cut on top. At first glance, Tanisha thought it was Byron Bird. But as she got closer, she realized that he was taller than Byron Bird. He wore a red letterman's jacket with red leather sleeves. There was a large basketball in the center of the jacket. Lori stood five feet four inches tall and was tilting her head back to chat with her new friend. Tanisha hated to interrupt Lori's flirtation, but she needed to explain where they were going and why. She tugged on Lori's shoulder and smiled sweetly.

Lori turned on her heels and grinned. "Hey, Tanisha! This is Doug. Doug, this is my friend, Tanisha."

"How you doing, Tanisha?" Doug smiled. He had a dimple in his left cheek. He was fine.

"Hi, Doug. I need to borrow Lori for a minute," she explained, holding her index finger up for emphasis. "I'll bring her right back. I promise." Tanisha pulled Lori aside.

"What's up girl? Isn't he fine?" Lori whispered.

"Truth. Brother is too fine! But listen, David just told us that Todd broke his arm playing baseball this afternoon and Maria has been on the phone talking to him for the past twenty minutes. She's begging to see him so David is offering to drive us over there so she can see him. He says he'll bring us back here by nine thirty so your mom can pick us up at 10:00."

"Speaking of fine, David Barton is too fine! And he was totally flirting with you. I think he likes you." Lori spoke in a loud whisper.

"Keep your voice down," Tanisha said. "He is cute, but he doesn't like me. He was just goofing around with me like he did on the ski trip. That's just his personality."

"You are so clueless. That brother is flirting with you." Lori spoke to Tanisha, but her eyes studied Doug.

"He likes to tease me like a little sister. Anyway, do you think we should go with him to Todd's house? I don't want to go, but I don't want Maria to go by herself and you know she's going whether I go or not."

Lori was staring over Tanisha's shoulder admiring Doug from afar. "Lori, did you hear what I said?" Tanisha repeated.

"Uh huh. Why don't you just have David take you home?" Lori asked.

"I don't want to get busted getting out of his car by Billie. Plus, your mom will probably wonder where we are when she comes to pick us up at 10:00," Tanisha reminded.

"Charlotte is picking us up, remember? And she won't care. I'll just tell her that your brother picked you and Maria up or something. You know your mother probably won't even be home, but just in case, just have him drop you off at the club house behind your house and walk around to the front of the house," Lori explained.

"That's right. I forgot that Charlotte was picking us up. Good point. I could just have him drop me off behind the hill in case Billie is looking out the window," she repeated, imagining the scene in her head. "Okay, I'll just have him take us home. I'll call you tonight when we get home. Go back to your tall drink of water!"

"Girl, if he doesn't ask for my number I'm going to ask for his!" Lori popped a tic tac in her mouth.

"What about CJ?" Tanisha whispered.

"What about him? CJ is played out! I was planning to give him his walking papers this weekend anyway," Lori winked and walked back over to Doug.

A kilowatt grin was plastered on Maria's face as she gripped Tanisha's arm. "Are you ready, Tanisha? Rashanda is totally cool with it. I need to go to the bathroom to freshen up for my man!" Maria tugged Tanisha's arm and led her to the bathroom. *Why is everyone tugging me around today?*

Maria brushed her long black hair and wiped off her lip gloss with a paper towel and water, exfoliating her lips with a fierce intensity. She reapplied her lip gloss and spritzed her neck with the trial size cologne spray that she carried in her Gucci purse. Her Beverly Hills aunt had taken her to Rodeo Drive for her birthday and allowed her to buy the expensive bag. Finger combing her hair, her head nodded disapprovingly as Maria carelessly placed the designer bag on the wet bathroom counter. She borrowed some of

Maria's Vaseline and applied it on top of her own lip gloss. She used the bathroom and went to the sink to wash her hands. Maria was still primping in the mirror when she finished washing her hands.

"Let's go, Maria. You look fine," Tanisha groaned. "You're taking time away from Todd prancing in the mirror. By the way, Lori suggested that we have David drop us off like a half block away from our houses so we don't get busted. She reminded me that Charlotte is picking them up so we don't have to worry about Mrs. Perkins asking questions."

"Groovy! This is working out perfectly! Let's go!" Maria squealed.

When they returned to the lobby, David was waiting patiently, tossing his keys, a wide grin on his boyish face. He held the door open for the girls and guided them through the parking lot. As they approached his freshly waxed Corvette, Maria squealed. "Todd told me that you had a Corvette! Nice car! I've always wanted to ride in a Vette!" she grinned. Accustomed to girls showing excitement about the shiny black sports car, David beamed proudly.

"Is this your car or your dad's car?" Maria asked excitedly.

"It's mine. My parents bought it for me as a present for my sixteenth birthday," David explained proudly.

Maria whistled. "Must be nice," she said. "Do you get pulled over by the police for driving such a nice car? My dad said that black men always get pulled over for bogus DWB violations," she finished. "Young black men always get harassed by the police, especially if they're driving a nice car."

"I've been pulled over for Driving While Black," David admitted. "But only when I'm in different cities. When I got my license, my dad took me to the local police station in Morning Side and introduced me to all of the patrol officers on each shift," he paused. "He described the types of cars that are in our family and explained that I might be driving any one of the cars," he continued. "Basically, he told them that he didn't want to get a call that his son was pulled over for any suspicious reason," he finished. "Now when the Morning Side police officers see me, they wave," David chuckled. "And I wave back. I've been pulled over in Homer and Glen for no apparent reason," he admitted. "But I just show them my license and registration and cooperate. They usually mumble something under their breath, and let me go. I'm sure it hurts their pride to see a young black kid driving a brand new sports car that probably costs as much as they make in six months," he shrugged.

Tanisha listened quietly. She had also heard stories about DWB violations. Even though her brother hadn't had his license for very long, Jack had already been pulled over for Driving While Black. She thought about Emmett Till. *Maybe Lori was right. Things haven't really changed all that much.*

David unlocked the passenger door and pulled on the door handle, pausing briefly as he realized that in Tanisha's excitement to meet Belvedere, she hadn't shown any emotion about his freshly waxed Corvette. *She had been impressed with Belvedere, but hadn't reacted at all to my car.* David stared at Tanisha curiously.

Tanisha's eyes glanced upward, and she caught him staring at her. She stuck out her tongue at him.

"Why are you staring at me?" Tanisha asked self consciously. *I hope he didn't notice my rotten tooth. I don't feel like explaining my dental drama right now.*

"I was just looking at your hair. I didn't realize that your hair had red highlights. It's pretty," David stammered quickly.

"Thanks," Tanisha shrugged. "All of the women on my Dad's side of the family have reddish brown hair."

"Is that a dog? I'm allergic to dogs!" Maria shrieked. "And he's so big! Does he bite?" Maria screamed.

"Only if you bite him first," David joked.

"What? That's not funny. I hate dogs!" Maria barked. "They trigger my allergies."

"You ride in the front, Maria, and I'll ride in the back with Belvedere." Although Tanisha was four inches taller than Maria, she climbed into the back seat of the tiny sports car. "Fasten your seat belt, Maria," Tanisha ordered.

Maria fastened her seat belt. "You have to excuse my friend, Tanisha. She's a seat belt Nazi! Atchoo! Do you have a tissue?" Maria sneezed again.

"I don't have a tissue, but there might be some napkins in the glove compartment," David said.

Maria pressed open the glove compartment and fumbled around until she found a yellow napkin. She wiped her nose, complaining about the harshness of the napkin against her face.

David peeled out of the parking lot and headed to Todd's house. He was glad that Tanisha was sitting on the rear passenger side which allowed him to see her in his rearview mirror. As he drove, he glanced in the rearview mirror and admired how she stroked Belvedere's head which lay squarely in her lap.

As Tanisha patted Belvedere's head, she watched David expertly maneuver the gear stick, shifting effortlessly from second to third gear. Her thoughts swirled around in her head. *It must be nice to get a new sports car for your sixteenth birthday. Even Aunt Helen's kids aren't that spoiled, and they're the richest people I know. I'm not impressed. He's probably a jerk like Todd. What am I doing riding in the car with a boy that I barely know? Am I crazy? No, I'm just going to keep Maria out of trouble. Was he flirting with me? Not likely. Lori thinks every boy that talks to you is flirting. I don't think David likes me, why would he? He's a spoiled, rich, pretty boy who probably has a girlfriend. Besides, he's too old for me. And if he is flirting, he's probably just trying to chase young girls like his sick friend Todd. He better not try anything, I'm not like Maria. I'll kick him in the giblets if he touches me. He won't try anything with me. He was a perfect gentleman on the ski trip. He's actually kind of nice. He just thinks I'm funny and likes to tease me like a little sister. Please God, get us to Todd's safely and in one piece.*

David turned on the radio and the Hot Mix Five disc jockey was playing a dance mix by dee jay Kenny Jamming Jason. Tanisha giggled as David sang along to Blondie's song *Rapture*.

"Oh, you think that's funny? Let's hear you sing then!" David laughed.

"I'll take the zero. At least I know my limitations. You should keep your day job!" Tanisha laughed.

"Bite her, Belvedere!" David whispered.

"As if! Belvedere loves me. He's ready to trade *you* in for me. Now you just keep your little eyes on the road and stop trying to croon," she instructed. "Before you put this tiny death trap in a ditch and kill us all, Mario Andretti!"

"Maria, is your friend always this bossy?" David asked.

"She's not bossy. She's just an old soul," Maria wiped her nose with the napkin.

"An old soul," David repeated. "I like that."

"That's what my mom calls her. She says that Tanisha has been here before because she's too mature to only be fourteen."

"I can hear you, Maria. And I'll be fifteen this year," Tanisha corrected.

"Is that right? Do I need to put my hands on the steering wheel in the ten and two clock face position or three and nine Miss Carlson?"

"I'll let you choose where to place your hands on the wheel," Tanisha giggled. "Just focus on the road, Mario! You're carrying precious cargo!"

David laughed as he turned into the subdivision. He made a series of left and right turns and Tanisha wondered how the residents found their way around at night since the streets appeared to be circular. Even in the twilight, Tanisha could see how large and grand the homes were. All appeared to sit on estate sized lots complete with circular driveways and three car garages. Tanisha dreamed of living in an area as fine as this one day. She exhaled as David pulled in front of a large English Tudor with Todd's black Toyota Supra parked out front. *Do all of the spoiled rich boys get cars for their sixteenth birthday present? It must be nice.*

David placed the car in neutral and reached to engage the parking brake as Maria jumped out to ring the bell.

"Are you going to leave Belvedere in the car?" Tanisha asked.

"No. Todd has a cat but he always hides when people come over. Todd's parents are cool and always let me bring Belvedere inside. He just plops in the laundry room near the washer and dryer so he won't trigger Maria's allergies too much."

As they approached the front door, Todd appeared wearing a fresh white cast. Maria reached out to give him a hug, careful not to touch his cast.

As Todd embraced Maria with his good arm, he noticed Tanisha. "Hey! I'm Todd."

"I'm Tanisha. I've met you a few times at the skating rink, Todd," she reminded. *He is such a knucklehead! I can't believe that he doesn't remember me. I've met him at least ten different times! What a self absorbed loser. I don't know what Maria sees in him.*

"Oh, yeah, yeah, that's right. I remember your face now. Come on in." Todd led them into the foyer. "David knows where everything is. You two can do whatever you want except smoke. My mom will have a fit if she comes back and smells smoke," Todd chuckled.

"Tanisha quit smoking yesterday so we're in good shape," David said.

Tanisha gave David a sideways glance and a closed mouth smirk. As Todd and Maria chatted in the foyer, Tanisha quickly scanned the house.

The foyer was ornately adorned with a marble tiled floor. To the right of the foyer was a grand living room that was completely white. The carpet was snowflake white and the furniture was white on white damask. There were gold accents throughout the room, the lamps were gold plated and the knick knacks were gold. In one corner of the room was a gold harp that stood three feet tall. The centerpiece of the room was a large golden Cherub fountain prominently displayed in the front bay window next to a white baby grand piano. The cherub held a gold vase that poured water into the fountain in a steady stream. Tanisha felt like she was in a museum. *This room is so tacky and ornate. It screams nouveau riche. I wonder what Todd's mother is like that she would decorate her house like this. It looks like a cheap Las Vegas hotel lobby.* To the left of the foyer was a white dining room. The furniture was a washed white French provincial style with white cushions. The china cabinet displayed white china and crystal stemware. The table was set for a formal dinner complete with white placemats and white napkins with gold napkin rings. The dining room led to a small butler's pantry that led into the kitchen.

As Tanisha quickly surveyed her surroundings she heard Todd whisper to Maria, "Let's go downstairs."

"Todd, may I use your bathroom?" Tanisha asked.

"Sure. David will show you where it is." Todd led Maria to the back of the house and down the basement stairs. David walked three feet and opened a door in the hallway that led to the powder room.

Tanisha entered the small powder room and was not surprised by its grandeur. The powder room was wall papered in an opulent green and gold velvet fabric. The toilet and sink were black and the faucet fixtures were gold. A crystal chandelier hung over the sink.

Her Aunt Helen lived in an elegant sixteen room house in the Berber section of Chicago that was tastefully appointed. Aunt Helen had hired a professional decorator to help her select the perfect pieces for each room. Tanisha loved visiting her Aunt Helen's home. It was expensively decorated and grand, complete with a maid's quarters, butler's stairwell and safe room, but Aunt Helen's home had a lived-in feeling that Todd's house lacked.

Tanisha used the restroom and washed her hands, careful not to muss the white towels that hung as though for display only. Tanisha peeked at the back of the towel, curious as to which designer it was, and was surprised that the towel was a Canon brand and still had a defect and clearance price tag attached to it. Tanisha smiled. *That's a shocker! From the looks of this house, I would have never guessed that Todd's mom shopped at a discount outlet. But then again, all types of people shop at Save Mart too. You can't judge a book by its cover.*

Tanisha opened the door to step into the foyer. She looked around, but David was nowhere in sight. She stood for a moment not sure where to go. She walked over to the living room and peered into the white palace but didn't see any footprints on the plush white carpeting. As she turned around, David appeared.

"Boo! I thought I'd give you some privacy to handle your business. Don't step on that white carpet or Todd's mother will have a hissy fit," he shouted. "I'm just kidding. In fact, I usually walk on it so she knows I've been here. Hold on, let me make my mark." Tanisha watched as David paraded around the freshly vacuumed carpet walking from the white sofa to the white love seat and moon walking to the Cherub fountain.

"That was cute. Where are Todd and Maria?" she asked.

"They went downstairs to watch television. So you're stuck with me," he smiled. "We can watch TV up here if you want. Follow me." He walked down the hall and led her to a room adjacent to the living room but separated by white French doors. This room was decorated in green and pink. The carpet was a plush pink and the furniture was green leather. "Todd's mother is an AKA," he paused. "Actually, she's not just a member of Alpha Kappa Alpha Sorority, she's the president or grand poo-bah of her alumnae chapter," he corrected. "She's quite the sorority diva!"

Tanisha groaned, "I should have guessed."

"You have something against AKA's?"

"Not really, but the women in my family pledge Delta Sigma Theta," she explained.

"My mom is a Delta. Is your mom a Delta too?"

"No. My mom isn't but my dad's three sisters are," Tanisha said.

"That's cool. My sister is pledging this year. My mom is psyched! My old man is an Alpha, so I'll probably pledge Alpha Phi Alpha."

David kicked off his shoes and plopped down on the green leather sofa and patted the seat next to him for Tanisha to join him. Tanisha sat in the arm chair facing the sofa.

"I'm not going to bite you, Tanisha," David said softly.

"That's good, because Belvedere told me in the car that you haven't had your rabies shot."

"Oh he did? What else did he tell you?"

"That's privileged information. I could tell you, but then I'd have to kill you," she joked.

"You crack me up! You are an old soul! Are you sure you're only fourteen?" David asked.

"I am only fourteen. I'll be fifteen in December and gifts are welcome!" Tanisha glanced at her watch. It was seven forty five. David was channel surfing and stopped at the *Love Boat.* She glanced around the room and saw a backgammon board and a chess set. "Do you wanna play chess or backgammon?"

"Sure! You play chess? Most girls don't play chess," David stated.

"How many times must I tell you? I'm not most girls," Tanisha smiled. "Since we're making ourselves at home, do you think Todd would mind if we popped some popcorn? Smelling that popcorn at the movie theatre made me want some." She kicked off her penny loafers and tossed her hoodie on the chair.

"Now you're talking! I'm sure they have microwave popcorn." David hopped up and pulled Tanisha into the kitchen.

"Microwave popcorn? I like the old fashioned popcorn better. See if they have some non-microwave popcorn."

David came out of the pantry with a large unopened bag of popcorn and a small bag of microwave popcorn. "I found both, but this one will be a lot quicker," he suggested, waving the microwave bag in her face.

Her eyes rested on the natural kernels. "Great! I need a large pot." Tanisha's eyes scanned the kitchen.

"It'll be quicker if we just use the microwave popcorn," David encouraged again.

"But it won't taste as good. Just shush and get me a pot before I sick Belvedere on you!" Tanisha ordered.

David gave Tanisha a military salute and reached into a cupboard and pulled out a large two handled pan and handed it to Tanisha.

"This pan looks brand new! I usually make popcorn in an older pot in case the bottom gets scorched. Don't they have something that isn't so new looking?"

"Doubt it. This one will be fine," David said.

"Okay. I need vegetable oil and butter or margarine."

"Yes ma'am, boss lady!" David searched in the walk-in pantry and surfaced with a bottle of oil. He pulled open the refrigerator and pulled out a stick of butter and handed it to Tanisha. Tanisha opened the drawer nearest the sink and correctly guessed that it was the silverware drawer. She pulled out a knife and sliced the butter in half. She layered the bottom of the pan with popcorn and covered the top with Wesson oil and dropped the butter into the pan before placing the lid securely on top.

"You're putting the butter in the popcorn now? Whenever my mother makes fresh popcorn, she always melts it separately in the microwave and then drizzles it on top." David settled onto a stool at the breakfast bar.

"Well, we don't have a microwave at home so this is how I make it. It'll be delicious! Just watch and learn."

David helped Tanisha turn on the burner to the electric range that looked brand new. David stepped back and watched as Tanisha gently shook the popcorn over the stove. Once the kernels started popping she stepped back to search for a bowl.

"Are you looking for a bowl? I know where everything is," he explained.

"It's fun trying to see if I can guess how Todd's mom set up her kitchen," Tanisha explained as she opened the cabinets.

"Trust me. Todd's mom probably doesn't know where a bowl is in here. She rarely cooks. They eat out almost every night or eat take out. But when I come over, I usually dirty up their kitchen so they know I've been here."

Tanisha opened the cupboard over the sink and was disappointed to see that it was filled with cleaning supplies. "Okay, I give up, where are the bowls?"

"They're under the sink. I know it's the weirdest place, but that's where they are," David shrugged.

Tanisha reached down and grabbed a large ceramic bowl as the last few kernels were popping. She'd seen oven mitts in one of the drawers and had placed them on the counter. She turned off the burner and grabbed the pot handle with the oven mitt and poured the golden popcorn into the bowl.

As she filled the large bowl, David grabbed a handful, and shoved it into his mouth. "This is so good! I would have never thought to add the butter while the popcorn is cooking. You can make popcorn for me anytime!"

"Take a number," Tanisha teased. "Do you think they have any sodas?" Tanisha asked.

"Sodas? You mean pop?" David quizzed.

"Soda pop, you say pop, I say soda," Tanisha shrugged.

"Okay 'Old Soul'. They have a pantry full of "soda." What kind would you like?"

"If they have any cream soda that would be great, but if not 7-Up or ginger ale would be cool too."

"Coming up." He grabbed two cans of 7-Up and pulled down two large glasses and filled them with ice.

When he returned to the den, Tanisha was sitting on the floor facing the sofa with her legs dangling through the coffee table. Tanisha had found the coasters and had placed two on the coffee table. She munched on the warm popcorn and set up the chess board.

As David approached and stared at the back of her head, he didn't want the night to end.

Tanisha sensed his presence and turned around, "Ready for me to beat you like you stole something?"

"In your dreams! They didn't have cream soda, but I found some 7-Up." He set the drinks down on the table and sat on the floor with his back against the sofa.

Tanisha smiled at him. *This is actually kind of fun. He's cool, and he seems completely different than Todd. Maybe he does like me. Would that be such a bad thing?*

Chapter 13

Fashionista

Tanisha was not a great chess player. She knew all of the moves but did not have a chess strategy, so she lost two games to David before he agreed to give her some pointers.

They were mid way through their third game of chess when Tanisha glanced at her watch. It was nine forty five.

"David, we need to get going. I have to be home by ten thirty," she explained. "I didn't realize it was this late."

"Okay. I'll yell down and tell Maria and Todd to come up for air." He laughed out loud and Tanisha found herself giggling at his joke.

David stood and stretched as Maria and Todd came up the stairs. Todd was the first to speak, "I'll be right back. I need to take my pain medication."

Maria yawned loudly. "We fell asleep watching television," she explained wiping her eyes, her hair matted on one side. "I thought I smelled popcorn. You guys should have brought some downstairs for us. Is there any left?" Maria reached toward the bowl.

"Girl, we popped that popcorn over two hours ago. It's cold now, but there's a little left. Here." Tanisha handed her friend the bowl of now cold popcorn and stood up to stretch. "What were you guys watching downstairs?"

Maria grabbed a handful of popcorn. "Girl, we were watching a James Bond movie that Todd has seen fifty times," she explained between chews. "And then he fell asleep because his medication makes him drowsy. Were you guys playing chess the whole time?" she groaned. "I didn't know you knew how to play chess, Tanisha. Chess looks so boring," she yawned.

Tanisha scowled at her friend, shook her head and stared, her comeback comment tangled in her throat. Squinting, she leaned in closer to Maria.

"What are you staring at?" Maria grumbled, still groggy from her nap.

"Maria, come with me for a second. I have to use the bathroom." Tanisha took the popcorn bowl and placed it on the table. She grabbed her friend's hand and led her into the hallway before she could protest.

Maria was choking on popcorn and could barely speak, "Tanisha, you almost made me choke. What's up?"

Tanisha shoved her into the powder room and pointed at the mirror.

Maria's eyes got big as saucers as she saw the strawberry mark on her neck. The hickey was so high on her neck that her hoodie didn't cover it.

"Oh my goodness! What am I going to do? How am I going to sneak past my parents with this thing on my neck?" Maria whined.

Tanisha just stared at her friend and shook her head. "Maria, I thought you said that you fell asleep watching a James Bond movie?" she asked.

"We did, but of course we kissed before that," she explained sheepishly. "Don't look at me like that, Tanisha. He's my boyfriend, he just broke his arm and I hadn't seen him in a week," she defended.

"But normally he only gives you hickeys on the back of your neck so your hair can cover it and your parents won't see it," Tanisha reminded. "This one is in the front of your neck, Maria."

Maria fussed in the mirror. Her attempts to cascade her long hair over the hickey were futile. "He usually does, but he was in a lot of pain with his arm, and I was just so glad to see him that I wasn't paying attention."

Maria hopped around the bathroom shaking her hands. "What am I going to do, Tanisha? I'll be so busted." She stared at Tanisha. "Tanisha, take off your turtle neck. We'll just have to switch outfits!"

Tanisha looked down and realized that she was wearing a yellow cotton turtleneck that would cover Maria's hickey. Maria had already peeled off her tank top. Tanisha exhaled and took off her shirt. She grabbed the turtleneck and handed Tanisha her tie dyed tank top. Even though it was May, Tanisha still sometimes wore cotton turtlenecks. She hated to be cold in air conditioned places and liked the feel of cotton against her skin. Her friends usually teased her about her turtleneck fetish, but tonight her turtleneck fetish would save Maria's butt.

Maria pulled the turtleneck over her head as Tanisha squeezed into the tiny tank top. She stared at herself in the mirror. Maria always bought her shirts at least one size too small in an effort to emphasize her small thirty A chest size. Tanisha knew without peaking at the tag that the tank top was an extra small. Tanisha's bust line was a small thirty two A so the tank top was extremely tight against her flat chest. She was afraid that if she sneezed or coughed she would bust a seam. She put on Maria's tight hoodie but was unable to zip it.

"Maria, what size is this thing? I can't even zip it up!"

"It's an extra small. You're not supposed to zip it up. It's supposed to stay open so that you can see the tank top, silly," Maria explained. "I am so glad you wore this ugly turtleneck or I'd be so busted." Maria tucked the loose turtleneck into her shorts.

Tanisha stared at her reflection in the mirror and had to admit that the tight tank top gave the illusion of cleavage, especially with the tight hoodie squeezing against her small breasts. The sleeves were too short so Tanisha pushed them up to her elbow. As she admired herself in the mirror, she remembered that she'd left her hoodie in the den.

Maria was sitting on the toilet about to pee, oblivious to Tanisha's presence in the bathroom. Maria continued her banter about how glad she was that they'd bumped into David at the movie theatre and how pretty Todd's house was. Tanisha decided to give Maria some privacy and went back to the den to retrieve her hoodie.

David was the first to notice. "Hey! That's not what you had on. Oh, I get it. Is that why girls always go to the bathroom together, so they can trade clothes? What's that about?"

Tanisha scowled at David and grabbed her multi-colored hoodie. "You don't want to know. We're ready to go whenever you are. Don't forget Belvedere." Tanisha took off Maria's hoodie and put her own jacket on.

Todd walked the group to the door and gave Maria a long lingering kiss. Tanisha rolled her eyes and followed David into the laundry room to retrieve Belvedere.

Once outside, Maria played fashion diva. "Tanisha, take my hoodie since my pink hoodie doesn't match this yellow turtleneck.

I can't believe you wore a turtleneck today, and it's like sixty five degrees out right now! But I'm glad you did. Just take my hoodie, and I'll take yours, otherwise my mom is going to know something is up because I'll be clashing too badly." Tanisha exhaled loudly but unzipped her hoodie and took it off, a chill running up her spine in the cool night air.

"Your mom answered the door when we picked you up, Maria. Won't she remember what you had on today?" Tanisha quizzed.

"She won't remember. I'll just tell her that you and I traded outfits once we got to the movie theatre. I'll tell her that I was cold in the theatre. She'll believe that. She knows we swap clothes sometimes." The girls exchanged jackets. Shivering slightly, Tanisha quickly put on the hoodie and watched as Maria tossed her jacket into the back seat and ran back to give Todd another hug.

David walked toward the car with Belvedere and placed him in the back seat. Tanisha climbed into the backseat as Maria waved frantically at Todd, blowing him kisses like he was going off to the war. *She really likes this guy. I don't get it, because as far as I can tell, he has the personality of a pencil.*

Tanisha giggled loudly.

"What's so funny back there?" David asked.

"It's a private joke," Tanisha replied.

David turned the car around in the circular driveway and asked for directions. Maria had decided that she wanted to be dropped off first and gave him directions to her house. As David drove, Maria bombarded him with questions about Todd asking him if he was seeing any other girls and if he ever talked to him about her. Tanisha smiled as she watched David answer all of her questions. His answers were very general and Tanisha could tell that he was trying not to lie to Maria, but his loyalty was with his friend.

Ten minutes later, David turned onto Maria's street.

"You live closer than I thought," he said. As planned, David dropped Maria off six driveways away from her house.

Maria pulled the front seat up. "Get in the front now, Tanisha. I'll flash my front porch light so you know I got in safely. I'll call you tomorrow."

She leaned into the front seat and said goodbye to David. "Thanks so much for taking me to see Todd. I'm so glad we bumped into you tonight."

"No problem. Funny how things work out," David smiled at Maria.

Tanisha sat in the front seat and watched her friend walk swiftly down the block. As they waited for Maria's signal, David spoke.

"Since you've been bossing me around all night, I thought you might sit in the back like a princess and make me chauffeur you home," he teased.

"I thought about it, but my legs were getting cramped sitting in this death trap that you call a car!" Tanisha smiled broadly, confident that David could not see her decayed tooth in the darkness and since it was on the passenger window side.

"Death trap? Most people love this car. I get much play because of this car!" David explained.

"I bet you do, but I'm not..." Tanisha's voice trailed.

David finished her sentence. "Most people. I know I know." He smiled at Tanisha as she watched her friend walking swiftly down the street. "Tanisha, I had fun with you tonight."

"Duh! Of course you did! Who wouldn't?" Tanisha turned to look at David and noticed that he was staring at her intently, a soft twinkle in his eye. She smiled softly at him and felt an electric charge run through her body. Confused by what she was feeling, she quickly looked away and watched Maria walk down the street. Uncomfortable with the silence, Tanisha struggled for words to speak. Her thoughts raced as she remembered that she was now in the car alone with a teenage boy that she barely knew. She swallowed hard and sat up straight. She'd had a really good time with David at Todd's house and hadn't felt intimidated being alone with him even though he was two years older than she was. They had had a good time playing chess and she felt comfortable with him, like she'd known him for a long time. But now that she was in his car alone, Tanisha became slightly fearful. Her experience with boys had been limited to dancing at the John & Judy teen mixers and her recent turnabout dance experience with Darrell Hunter. She had never been alone with a sixteen year old boy other than her brother Jack and her cousins. She thought he was attractive and enjoyed teasing with him, but now that she was alone with him, she was nervous. Four or five seconds passed that felt like minutes. Tanisha decided to break the awkward silence by changing the subject. "I had fun with you too. Thanks for the chess pointers. You're really good, David."

"No problem. You're a good chess player, too. You just need to develop some strategies which will only come from playing more often and with people who are better than you are. How long have you been playing?" David asked.

Tanisha saw the light flicker on Maria's porch. "Maria's in safely now so we can take off," she continued glancing at her watch. "My dad taught me how to play chess when I was five or six years old, and we used to play a lot, but now that my parents are divorced, I only play with my younger brothers every now and then. I beat them pretty easily."

Tanisha and David chatted casually about chess and backgammon and occasionally Tanisha would give him directions to her house. Tanisha was glad that she only lived five minutes away from Maria.

What will he think when he sees where I live? When they turned into the complex, Tanisha studied David's profile to see if his expression changed once he saw the gray six story apartment buildings and tiny town houses lined four in a row. She was glad that the lushness of the entrance with its manicured lawns and clusters of large trees gave the appearance of a condominium complex instead of a moderate income housing development. Tanisha noticed that David's expression remained constant as he talked about how he developed chess strategies.

"Is this where you grew up?" David asked casually as he shifted the gears of the Corvette.

"Not really. We've lived here since I was nine. We lived in the city before we moved to Newberry East. We were planning to move to Plum Creek and were only supposed to be in Cedar Grove temporarily, but my parents divorced so here we are," Tanisha offered apologetically.

"I'm sorry about your parents. I have a lot of friends whose parents have split up. My grandparents recently split up after forty-five years of marriage," David offered. "Can you believe that? My mom was devastated."

Tanisha listened to David but her thoughts drifted back to visions of the Plum Creek house that would never be.

߷

Plum Creek was considered the nicest section of Newberry East and had a small creek running through the subdivision. She sometimes rode her bike the half mile from Cedar Grove to the Plum Creek area and stared longingly at the chocolate brown split-level four bedroom house that her parents had found. They had taken Tanisha and her brothers to tour the house and Tanisha had picked out which bedroom she wanted. The sellers had asked for a one hundred twenty day close date so that their children could complete the school semester. Billie and Jackie had agreed to the extended closing. Tanisha had been excited about moving into a larger home and out of the Cedar Grove complex. She'd shared her news with her friends, and was devastated when she learned that Billie and Jackie were splitting up. She was sadder that the family would not be moving out of Cedar Grove than she was when she learned that her parents would be getting a divorce and her dad would be moving out of the house. She was ashamed of herself for feeling this way. She loved her dad and missed him terribly, but she saw him regularly. She hated being poor more than she missed her father, and she missed her dad a lot.

‎ℬℭ

Tanisha gestured out the window, "I live in the third townhouse over there, but I don't want my mom to see me getting out of your car, so just drop me off behind this hill, and I'll flash the back porch light so you know I made it in safely."

David pulled up to where Tanisha pointed and shifted the car into neutral gear. Tanisha opened the door and got out of the car. Before closing the door, she reached into the backseat and patted Belvedere's head.

"Goodnight Belvedere, nice to meet you!" She grinned at David with her closed mouth smile. "Thanks for the ride, Mario! Last tag you're it!" She teased as she tapped him on the shoulder.

Before David could respond, she had closed the door and was halfway up the small incline. At the top of the hill, she turned around and waved at David. He waved back. Seconds later a light flickered from the porch.

He turned the car around in the circular entrance in front of a fenced in area that housed a swimming pool near a small clubhouse. He shifted into second gear and drove out of the Cedar Grove complex.

"Well, Mr. Belvedere, now you've met Miss Tanisha Carlson. She's something else isn't she? I still can't believe that she's only fourteen because she's as mature as some of the girls my age at Homer Glen. She'll be fifteen in six months, but she really is an "old soul" like her friend said," he rambled. "I told you that you'd like her! I knew she'd like dogs too! She just seemed like a dog person. I saw you back there with your head in her lap. At least one of us got to touch her," he continued.

Cruising down the empty streets, David casually shifted into third gear. With his free hand, he reached back to pat Belvedere's head. His hand rested on soft cotton. Startled, David tugged on the material and pulled it towards him, ignoring Belvedere's moan of irritation. Placing the garment on the passenger seat, he lifted it quickly and inhaled the fabric. It was Tanisha's hoodie. He smiled as Tanisha's scent mixed with Belvedere's warmth.

Chapter 14

The Play by Play

Tanisha closed the back door and walked through the kitchen. Billie was sitting at her typewriter in the dining room, her fingers flying across the keyboard as she hummed along to the Gladys Knight & the Pips *Claudine* Soundtrack. Billie loved the Motown sound. In order to supplement her income from the cable company, which paid slightly less than she'd made at Eden State College, Billie had started typing term papers for the students that attended the local university.

Billie had a lit cigarette perched in the ashtray near the typewriter and stopped to take a pull as Tanisha walked through the kitchen.

She turned around and smiled at Tanisha. "Hey baby girl! Why'd you come through the back door?" Billie exhaled the smoke through her nostrils.

Baby girl? She only calls me baby girl when she's in a good mood. "Hi Mom!" Tanisha replied nervously. "I forgot my key and didn't want to ring the bell and wake anyone up since it's after 10:00." The Carlson family always kept the back door unlocked.

Billie Mae took another pull from her Virginia Slims menthol, as she glanced at the kitchen wall clock. "Oh. It's that late already?

I didn't realize it was that late. I've been typing this paper for a student. Did you see a movie?"

"No. We just ate pizza and played video games. I have to use the bathroom really bad."

Tanisha was glad that Billie hadn't watched her when she'd left the house because she hadn't thought of a lie for why she had on different clothes.

Billie Mae turned around and continued her typing.

Byron and Allen were sprawled on the living room floor watching wrestling with a half eaten bowl of popcorn in between them.

"Hey guys!" Tanisha shouted as she ran up the stairs two at a time.

"Hey, Tanisha!" Byron and Allen shared a passion for wrestling and studied the television guide circling the wrestling matches so that they could plan to watch them. Tanisha couldn't understand why anyone would watch wrestling. As Tanisha walked upstairs, she heard her telephone ringing. Scurrying up the stairs, she fell across the bed and reached for the telephone.

"Hellooooo!" She shouted into the receiver, out of breath from her sprint.

It was Lori Perkins. "Hey girl! I just wanted to make sure that you guys made it home okay. Since it's after ten, I knew I couldn't call Maria since she can't take calls after 9:30. I'm so glad you have your own line. Why are you out of breath?" Lori asked.

"I was racing up here trying to catch the phone. How many times did it ring?" Tanisha took a deep breath.

"It only rang eight times, but I always let it ring at least ten times before I hang up since I know you're sometimes downstairs and don't hear it."

"I literally just walked in the door and was about to call you. Hold on for two seconds. I have to use the bathroom," Tanisha said.

"I can't talk long so just take the phone with you. I know the cord reaches," Lori suggested. "Girl, Doug asked for my digits. He is too fine! He plays on the varsity basketball team and he's only a sophomore. He said he's going to call me tomorrow," Lori spoke quickly.

Tanisha flushed the toilet and washed her hands. "He is a cutie! If I hadn't been hanging out with Maria and David, I might have snagged his tall tail first! What are you going to tell CJ?"

"I'm not worrying about CJ. CJ is old news. School ends in a few weeks anyway, so I'm going to break up with him and hang out with Doug this summer. By the way, I hate to point out the obvious, but Mr. little black Corvette likes you!" Lori whispered.

"He does not! He's just a jokester, and he likes teasing me," Tanisha said.

"You need to get a quarter and buy a clue, Tanisha. That boy likes you. I could tell by the way he was teasing you. What did you and David do while Maria and Todd were making out? Because I know that's what they did," Lori giggled. "Talk fast, because Charlotte wants to use the phone." Tanisha gave Lori the play by play on her evening with David.

Hanging up the phone, she folded Maria's tank top and hoodie and tucked them neatly in her backpack. She wouldn't be able to wash the items since the family's dryer wasn't working again.

She stared at her reflection in the mirror? *I wonder what it would be like to live in a house like Todd's, drive a sports car and be able to get anything you wanted anytime you wanted it? I wouldn't know how to act if I had privileges like that. Would I still act the same or would I be arrogant and conceited like Todd, forgetting the face of my girlfriend's best friend whom I've met several times before?* Tanisha brushed her hair and inserted her curlers. *Aunt Helen's kids have money, and they seem normal, but they're family. Do my cousins act like Todd with people who aren't related to them? I hope not. Aunt Helen wouldn't allow that. If I had money, I'd be the same Tanisha Denise Carlson that I am now. I'd just dress better, drive a nicer car, and live in a better house in a better neighborhood. I'd be the same me, just better.*

Chapter 15

Fish in the Net

The last few weeks of school breezed by quickly, a flurry of final exams and yearbook signings. True to her word, Lori ended her relationship with CJ the Monday after she met Doug. Although lacking the dramatics of Tanisha's driveway dump of Darrell Hunter, Lori's break up with CJ was far more intense. As was her nature, Lori gently explained to CJ that she needed space and that they should see other people over the summer, assuring him that he was a great guy, but her feelings had changed and she no longer wanted to date him. CJ didn't take the break up well. He pleaded with her to give him another chance and met with her parents to find out how he could win her back. Flowers were sent to her home and notes placed in her locker in a desperate plea to convince her to change her mind. His persistence didn't cease until Lori's new beau, Doug, answered the door at Lori's home one day and threatened to harm CJ if he didn't stop harassing Lori. His exact words were, "Man, she's not into you anymore so why don't you build a bridge and get over it!"

It was Monday morning and Tanisha stood at the service desk wiping her brow from her bike ride to Save Mart. The early June temperatures had reached eighty-five degrees with an expected high of ninety-two. Tanisha was glad that Pat, the full time service desk worker, was on vacation, and she was filling in for her. She wanted to work as many hours as she could before she left for leadership camp next week. By working Pat's full time schedule, she'd more than made up for the loss of two week's pay that she'd miss while at camp. She was also glad that she wouldn't have to see Pat for a few days since Pat had tried to get her in trouble.

For the past several weeks, at least one or two calls came into the service desk for Tanisha almost daily. Pat complained to management, and Deanna, the personnel manager, called Tanisha down to the office for an explanation. Afraid for her job, and not knowing who the caller could be, Tanisha shared that a Save Mart customer had approached her to convince her to start a modeling career. Her friend Cathy had taken two messages from Tom. When questioned, Pat reluctantly confirmed that it was a male caller and the voice did sound more mature than someone who would be a boyfriend Tanisha's age. Pat also admitted that once the caller had identified himself as Tom from Talent Plus Modeling Agency.

Tanisha glared at Pat with a defiant expression, wishing Pat could read the intent in her stare. *Pat, you're such a witch! You were just trying to get me in trouble because you're jealous that this lame, dead end job is your life! I wish I could stick my tongue out at you, but that would be childish! I'm young and cute, and you're not, so you need to build a bridge and get over it!*

So far, the calls hadn't come in on a day when Tanisha was working at the service desk. The person had called on Saturday a couple of times, but both times Tanisha had been working as the checkout supervisor and had been too swamped to take the call. Other times, the caller would just ask to speak with Tanisha, and when Pat said she wasn't working, he would hang up. Tanisha assured Deanna that when she'd spoken to Tom, she'd explained to him that she wasn't interested in a modeling career. And now she feared that Tom was just interested in her. Deanna called Talent Plus Modeling and asked Tom to stop calling Tanisha at Save Mart, and he agreed that he would.

The frequency diminished, but the calls continued. Months later, the Save Mart management team had become concerned for Tanisha's safety. Deanna decided that it was time to involve Bob, the security guard. Bob instructed each of the service desk workers to page a code thirteen over the intercom if a male called for Tanisha.

Another slow morning, Tanisha busied herself by rearranging the supply drawer. She was glad when the service desk phone rang. "Thank you for calling Save Mart, how may I help you?" she sang.

"Hello. May I speak to Tanisha?" the male voice asked.

Tanisha's heart skipped a beat. "This is Tanisha. Can you hold for a moment, please?" Tanisha's hand trembled as she placed the call on hold and reached for the intercom. As she announced the page, the hold button went out. The caller had hung up.

Bob the security guard was at the service desk within fifteen seconds. "Tanisha, which line is he on?" he panted.

"He hung up, Bob. Just as I was making the page, he hung up," she explained.

"Did it sound like the same guy?" Bob asked.

"I'm not sure. He just said, 'may I speak to Tanisha,' but it must have been him because only my brothers would call me at work," she explained.

"Well, if he calls back, try to keep him talking and see if it's the same guy."

"Will do." Tanisha couldn't believe that Tom was still calling her. When she customer profiled him, she'd pegged him as a successful business man, not a weirdo. She crossed her arms over her chest glad that she'd worn a long sleeve tee-shirt under her smock. She knew that once she cooled off from her bike ride, she would be chilly standing in the Save Mart air conditioning all day.

❧❧❧

David grabbed his keys from the hook in the laundry room and jumped into his car. He'd been calling the store every day since school let out trying to catch Tanisha at work so he could casually bump into her. He'd left her jacket in the backseat of his car and periodically hugged it to his chest and inhaled her scent. He knew he could have given the jacket to Todd to give to Maria, but he wanted to deliver the jacket to her himself. Since he'd seen her two weeks before, the weather had been so warm that Tanisha hadn't missed the hoodie. He decided to bring Belvedere and ran back inside to get him. He shoved Belvedere into the car and drove quickly, glancing at the clock on his dashboard.

It's only 10:00 a.m. so she probably just started work, and it's too early for lunch or a break so I'll definitely see her today! I better slow down. I've heard that the Steiffer police love pulling over black men driving fancy cars.

Slowing his speed, David beamed mischievously as he guided the Corvette to Save Mart.

Chapter 16

Duds & Suds Confession

Tanisha had only handled two returns all morning and yawned as she glanced at her watch. She stared at the round wall clock above the door for verification. It was only 10:15. It was going to be a long shift. Mondays at Save Mart were usually slow return days, since most customers shopped on Saturday and Sunday. Tanisha noticed that senior citizens seemed to return items on Monday to avoid the weekend return rush. She usually smiled to herself as she watched the gray haired ladies lined up outside, waiting expectantly for the store to open at nine in the morning. *How sad when the highlight of your day is waking up and heading to Save Mart to wait for it to open. Or maybe their day is so filled with so many other exciting things to do, that they just want to get the Save Mart errand crossed off their ' to do' list.*

She decided to review the list of camp supplies that she would need. She pulled the tattered list out of her pocket and noticed that she had three items left to purchase: flip flops for the shower, bug spray and a spiral notebook.

Tanisha decided that she would buy these things on Friday when she got paid. She'd purchased most of the other items and was looking forward to the leadership camp. This would be her first away camp experience since she was in sixth grade. She thought back to that experience.

෮෬

When she was eleven years old, she'd attended St. Mary's camp for girls in Wisconsin. Tanisha had been scheduled to attend the camp with four of her cousins, but she had developed a kidney infection and had to attend a later session. Her parents had sacrificed and saved for her to attend the expensive, private camp. Because the camp fee was not refundable, she fearlessly agreed to attend the session by herself.

Tanisha watched her dad's car drive out of the camp grounds after her parents dropped her off. She was terrified about being at the camp alone. The only black girl registered for her two week session, her stomach churned as she watched the white campers pair up. She felt invisible. The other campers were not welcoming of her eager attempts to join into their conversations. Her French braided hair and golden brown skin made her different from the other girls. The harder she tried to fit in, the more excluded she felt. She found herself becoming physically ill as she participated in the camp activities: tennis, archery, and swimming by herself.

Tanisha was not excited when she learned that she was part of the Polar Bear Camp group. She remembered that this was the same camp group that her cousins were in each summer. She idolized her older cousins and sought their acceptance. But even knowing that she was in the same camp group as they, hadn't altered her mood. She hated St. Mary's camp. She hadn't made one single friend.

The counselors didn't seem to notice that Tanisha was all alone. She wanted to go home, and so she staged a hunger strike. She refused to eat and told the camp director, Sister Therese, that she was feeling sick. They placed her in the infirmary. She still refused to eat, claiming that she couldn't keep anything down. She was on extended antibiotics for the kidney infection, so the nurse believed her when she said that she wasn't feeling well. They allowed her to stay in the infirmary for two days before calling her parents to come and get her. She'd only eaten saltine crackers and water during her time in the infirmary. She really was feeling sick now. She was weak from hunger.

೫೦೪೫

Tanisha smiled as she remembered how happy she was when her dad arrived to pick her up. She'd felt like a princess being rescued from a tower by her knight in shining armor.

She folded the tattered list back into her pocket and decided to wipe down the service desk counter to kill some time. *What if the leadership camp is no different than my St. Mary's camp experience? Will I meet a friend this time? Will I be the only black girl at camp again?*

The telephone startled her out of her daydream. She transferred the call and grabbed the bottle of Windex and roll of paper towels to wipe off the counter. As she wiped, David Barton walked into the store.

He hadn't seemed to notice her as his eyes panned the store. Startled to see him, Tanisha spoke. "Hello sir, may I help you find something?" she said cheerily.

David's eyes turned towards her voice and his eyebrows perched up as he spotted Tanisha. He walked towards her.

"Hey, Tanisha! I didn't see you. What are you doing here? Do you work here?" David asked.

"No, I just wear this smock and wipe down the counter as a hobby. Are you always this quick, or is this something new?" Tanisha laughed. "I work here. I've worked here for about six months. What are you doing here? Casing the joint for a heist?" Tanisha teased.

"That's very funny. I came to pick up some leather cleaner for my car." He leaned into the service desk and whispered. "I thought you said that you were only fourteen. How can you work here?"

Tanisha blushed. "I am, but since my parents are divorced, I qualified for this special work program arrangement so I just didn't list my dad's employment status and told them that I was fifteen." Tanisha glanced over her shoulder and whispered, "Don't bust me out!"

"Oh, you lied about your age? Now I have something on you! What's it worth to you?" David whispered.

"Could you please lower your voice? I need this job. I'm serious," Tanisha pleaded.

"I am too. I won't bust you out, but keeping your little secret is going to cost you." David rubbed his palms together.

"You expect me to pay you to keep quiet? That's blackmail!" Tanisha wrinkled her eyebrows and glared angrily at David. "You are really psycho!"

"Calm down. I'm kidding. What time can you go to lunch?" David asked.

"I can ask someone to relieve me at 12:00 or 12:15. Why?" Tanisha studied David's face.

"Groovy! I'll take you out to lunch," David offered.

"That's okay. I brought lunch from home," Tanisha replied.

"Well, take it back home or eat it tomorrow. I want to take you out to lunch. And you better not say no or I'm going to tell your little secret." David pointed his finger at Tanisha.

"Is that your price?" Tanisha asked.

"Yes. If you have lunch with me, I won't tell your secret. I have a taste for a burger, and Duds & Suds is right around the corner."

Tanisha shook her head from side to side. "Don't you work? I thought you were giving tennis lessons this summer."

"You have a good memory. I am giving lessons this summer, but I don't give lessons on Mondays. I work in my dad's office today but not until 2:00, so let me buy you lunch. Plus, I have Belvedere in the car and he wants to see you."

"How did Belvedere know that I worked here?" Tanisha asked.

"He didn't know that you worked here, but he was asking about you the other day and I told him that I didn't know when he would get to see you again," David stammered. "He'll be excited that I bumped into you, and he'll want to see you once I tell him that you work here," he finished.

"You talk to your dog about me?" Tanisha giggled.

"Belvedere is not a dog," he corrected. "Mr. Belvedere is a human trapped in a dog's body, and he's my best friend. We talk about everything," David replied.

"Well, isn't that special," Tanisha smirked. "But it's only 10:30 now. What are you going to do for ninety minutes?" Tanisha asked.

"I saw a park a few blocks away, so I'll just take Belvedere to the park and play catch or something and then come back at 12:00. Does that work for you?" David asked.

"This is blackmail, but okay. I haven't had Duds & Suds in a while, and I love their burgers," she said.

"Fantastic! I'll see you at noon." David turned around to leave the store.

"Hey, genius!" Tanisha yelled softly. "Don't forget your leather cleaner. Automotive is in aisle twenty three," she pointed over her shoulder.

David turned around, snapped his finger and walked toward aisle twenty three, grinning from ear to ear.

Tanisha smiled softly. *I have a lunch date! Maybe Lori was right. I think he likes me!*

Chapter 17

I'll Wait For You

At 11:52, David came back into Save Mart and announced to Tanisha that he was parked outside. She called Ellen and asked her if she could fill in for her lunch break. A few minutes later, Tanisha updated Ellen on the service desk activity, before racing to the employee lounge to use the bathroom, hang up her smock and punch out. She sprayed perfume on her wrist and applied Vaseline to her lips. She punched out at exactly 12:00, which meant that she needed to punch back in by 12:45.

As she walked through the store, she ran her fingers through her hair and quickly crunched the mint that she'd popped in her mouth. Outside, the hot sun shone brightly and gleamed on the shiny black car. The heat from the pavement greeted Tanisha as she walked into the sunlight. She squinted and raised her hand to create an awning. David leaned against the passenger door and stood straight up as she walked toward him. Belvedere was asleep in the backseat.

"Hey, there you are. Are you hungry?" David asked.

"Actually, I am. I have to be back to punch in by 12:45 so we better hurry," she explained.

"No sweat. I haven't been to Duds & Suds in a while, but their service is usually pretty quick," he offered.

David opened the passenger door and Tanisha sat down and reached in the back seat to pat Belvedere. The windows were rolled down and a warm breeze rolled through the car. Belvedere woke up when the car shifted and tried to bite at the warm air that wafted through the car. Tanisha was glad for the warm breeze.

"This is a really nice car, little rich boy," Tanisha teased.

Shocked by her comment, David smiled sheepishly. *She's not a cyborg! She does like my car!* "Thanks, but I'm not a rich boy," he explained. "Rich people don't have to work for their money. My parents go to work every day to earn money. When I was very young, I remember my parents explaining to my brother and sister and me that we were blessed. They used to tell us that even though we may have more money than some people, we're certainly not rich. We're just very blessed," he continued. "Fortunately, my parents are generous, and they like to share their blessings with their children. Who am I to complain?" He shifted the gear stick effortlessly.

Tanisha was shocked by his humility.

The black Corvette pulled into the Duds & Suds parking lot at 12:10 and David and Tanisha walked inside. There were two registers open and at least four customers in each line. Tanisha panicked. She didn't want to get written up for returning late for lunch. She shifted her weight as she read the menu.

"I love their burgers. I know this is kind of lame for a first date, but it's close to your job," David said.

"A first date? This is a date?" Tanisha asked.

"Well,...you know what I mean. Whenever two people get food together, it counts as a date. But if that makes you uncomfortable, then we're just two hungry people having lunch," David replied nervously.

"Oh, okay. I'm only fourteen so I don't have any dating experience, but I don't remember you asking me on a date. What I remember is you threatening to bust me at work if I didn't have lunch with you. Do you get most of your dates by threatening people to go out with you?" Tanisha giggled.

David smirked at Tanisha. "Okay, smarty pants. What would you like to eat?"

Tanisha ordered a cheeseburger with everything and a vanilla milkshake. David ordered a double cheeseburger with onion rings and a vanilla milkshake. The server invited them to sit at a booth and offered to bring their food out to them when it was ready.

"Do you need to get something for Belvedere?" she asked.

"He's on a strict diet and can't eat Duds & Suds," David said.

"I hope he's okay in this heat." Tanisha glanced at her watch again and noticed it was a quarter past twelve.

"Relax. The food should be ready in about five minutes and we can eat in fifteen minutes and I'll have you back at work. They're not going to fire you for being a few minutes late are they?" he asked.

"No, but the lady who is covering for me at the service desk has a lot of work to do. If I'm late getting back then she's late doing the stuff she needs to do. Plus, I don't need to give the personnel manager another reason to call me down to her office," Tanisha paused. "It's a long story."

"That's very responsible of you. You won't be late. Trust me."

"Okay. If I get fired, your dad can hire me to work in his office," she suggested.

"No can do. You're only fourteen, remember?" David shook his finger in Tanisha's face and smiled.

Tanisha playfully kicked David under the table as the server brought out the tray. When Tanisha smelled the grilled burger, her stomach gurgled with anticipation. She had only eaten a small bowl of raisin bran that morning and the cheeseburger looked delicious. She ate her burger hungrily, careful to not talk with food in her mouth. She demurely covered her mouth with her paper napkin before speaking; both to hide the decayed tooth as much as the food in her mouth. When David invited her to share in his onion rings, she gladly obliged, savoring the crispy casings and chewy onion centers. As they ate, they chatted about their siblings, and David again tried to encourage her to let him give her a few tennis pointers. She told him more about the two week leadership camp that she was attending in a week. As she finished her last bite of the cheeseburger, she glanced at her watch again. It was 12:40.

"Will you send me a postcard from camp?" David asked.

"Sure. David, we've got to go or I'm going to be late, and you need to get Belvedere out of that hot car," Tanisha reminded.

"Let's hit it!" David popped the last bite of his burger in his mouth, grabbed the tray and tossed the contents into the trash can.

Their seat belts fastened, David casually draped his arm over the passenger seat to steer in reverse, his fingers lightly touching her shoulder. He drove with confidence, careening through yellow lights like a professional race car driver. Tanisha didn't remember the seats being so low to the ground. She tried not to let her body jerk each time he shifted gears.

"Tanisha, I want to ask you something. When can you date for real?" David's fingers nervously drummed on the steering wheel.

She looked at him with a puzzled expression. *Lori was right after all.*

"Well, when I'm fifteen, my parents said that I can go out on double dates. Why do you ask?"

"When is your birthday?" David asked.

"It's in December. What's with all the questions, Sherlock?" she teased.

"Since you seem to be a little slow on the uptake, I like you. You make me laugh, and you're fun and I want to get to know you better." His palms were sweating and his heart was racing, but he'd laid his cards on the table. He gripped the steering wheel with both hands, exhaled and waited for her response.

Tanisha studied his profile and bit her top lip. "Well, what does that mean exactly? Are you trying to get to know me like Todd is getting to know Maria?"

David stared at Tanisha with a furrowed brow. He slapped his right hand on the steering wheel and spoke in a steely monotone. "Tanisha, have I ever tried anything with you? I just want to spend time with you, is that so hard to believe? Why do you get so defensive all of the time?" David turned into the Save Mart parking lot.

She took a deep breath and spoke slowly and softly. "David, I'm only fourteen. I've never been on a real date before. You're sixteen, you have your own car, and we don't really have that much in common."

David's tone softened, "What are you talking about? We have a lot in common. We both like chess, tennis, the same movies, we share the same sense of humor and wit, you like basketball and football. How can you say that we don't have that much in common, Tanisha?"

Tanisha took another deep breath and faced David. "You live in Morning Side, and I live in Cedar Grove. My parents are divorced. I'm lying about my age so I can work at Save Mart because I need the money," she said softly. "Your parents are doctors. You got a Corvette for your sixteenth birthday. Be honest, what would your parents think if you brought me over to meet them?" Tanisha asked.

David stared at Tanisha. "They would think that I'd met a nice girl that I like. My parents don't trip on stuff like where people live. They weren't born doctors, and they worked hard to get where they are."

David pulled the Corvette in front of the store and turned off the ignition. He turned to face Tanisha. "Tanisha, why are you so hard on yourself? On the one hand you act really cocky, but then when it comes down to it, it's like you don't have any self confidence at all," he said softly.

Tanisha looked away from David. *He's on to me. Wait until he sees my decayed tooth. Let's see how much he likes me then.* She looked out the window, unsure what to say, completely oblivious to the time.

David spoke again and gently turned Tanisha's face toward his. "I really like you Tanisha, and I want to get to know you better. I feel like there's chemistry between us. I'm willing to wait for you so we can date on the up and up, if you're interested of course. Now since I know where you work, I could arrange to kidnap you for lunch a few times each week by threatening to tell your secret, but I don't want to force you to go out with me."

Tanisha giggled. "Bob the security guard is my buddy and would like nothing better than to call the police and have you arrested for stalking!"

David smiled and gently grabbed both of her hands. His hands felt soft and warm in hers. She felt a natural ease with him.

"Be serious for a minute, Tanisha. I want to get to know you better. Does that work for you?" David stared into Tanisha's eyes.

She was at a loss for words. "Okay. I think I could stomach getting to know you, as long as you bring Belvedere to chaperone. And bring some mints too because your breath is kicking from those onion rings!"

"Back with the jokes! Well, yours doesn't smell too great either, Miss Lady!" He reached into the console and pulled out a pack of gum and popped a piece in his mouth. He offered Tanisha a stick of gum, and she folded it in her mouth too. "Now that our breath is minty fresh, stop changing the subject. I already know that you can take calls from boys since you gave your number to Byron Bird, so can I at least have your phone number so I can call you to find out when you're working so I can see you at work?"

She bit her lip and smiled. "By the way, did you even bother to give my number to Byron Bird?" Tanisha asked. "He never called me."

David bit his bottom lip and looked sheepishly at Tanisha as he gently rubbed her hands in his hands, the look of guilt plastered on his face.

Tanisha pointed her finger at David. "You still have my number, don't you? And you never gave it to Byron Bird, did you? Did you call me a few weeks ago? My brother told me that a boy called, and I called Byron Bird thinking it was him, but it wasn't. Was it you?"

"Guilty as charged. I wanted to talk to you, but then never got the nerve to call you back. You're too good for Byron Bird. He's my boy, but he's a jerk with girls, so I didn't give him your number. I did you a favor. Trust me," he confessed.

"Well, I called him back thinking that he had called me, and I kind of figured that out for myself. He didn't have much to talk about on the phone. Why didn't you ever call me back?" Tanisha asked.

Belvedere shifted in the back seat and yawned. "Remember, on the John & Judy ski trip, you mentioned that you thought that Todd was too old to be dating Maria, and since I'm older than Todd, I figured that you probably wouldn't want to be bothered with me," David explained.

"That's true. But Todd treats Maria like a child, and he uses the fact that he's older to his advantage. You're so childlike sometimes I feel like I'm older than you," she laughed. "But seriously, thanks for not giving my number to him. I appreciate that."

"Don't mention it. I still have your number so I'm going to call you tonight," he said excitedly.

"Okay. I have my own line so you can call whenever. By the way, don't call me at work, because there's a psycho guy calling Save Mart trying to get me to go into modeling, but we think he just likes young girls. It's a long story, and I'll tell you about it later. But sometimes he calls twice a day to see if I'm there, and the full time service desk lady is ready to have me fired because we're not allowed to have personal calls at work. So if you call Save Mart and I don't answer, just hang up so I don't get in trouble," Tanisha explained.

David opened his mouth to confess to making some of those calls too, but thought better of it. *I'll just keep this one to myself.* "No problem!" he said. "I'll try not to call you at work unless it's urgent," he agreed.

Tanisha reached back to nuzzle Belvedere's head. As she got out of the car, she waved at David and offered. "Thanks for lunch, David!"

"You're welcome. I'll call you tonight and give you my address so that you can send me a postcard from camp. Now scoot, you're late! It's ten minutes to one!"

"Oh fudge!" Tanisha raced past the service desk and assured Mary Ellen that she would be back in two minutes. She unlocked her locker and threw her smock on quickly. She punched in at 12:52.

I'm going to get a red circle on my time card for punching in late from lunch, and I'll probably have to meet with the personnel manager, but I do not care. David Barton likes me! David Barton is the most popular boy at Homer Glen High School and drives a black Corvette. He's nice, tall and fine and could have any girl that he wants, and he just told me that he wants to get to know me! I can't wait to tell my girlfriends! God is good! Tanisha walked quickly to the service desk.

She apologized for being late, and felt better when Mary Ellen assured her that the service desk activity had been very slow, and she enjoyed the break from the linen department. Over one hour later, Tanisha had only had one service desk return. The afternoon was dragging on. Tanisha really wanted to call Lori and tell her that she'd been right about David Barton, but the store manager was in the store, and she didn't want to risk getting caught on a personal phone call. She cleaned and straightened and doodled on a notepad. As the afternoon dragged on, her delight in learning that David wanted to get to know her better turned to suspicion. *Why would David Barton want to get to know someone like me? He's sixteen going on seventeen, why is he interested in a girl my age?*

Chapter 18

Camp Colorblind

Billie Mae fumbled through her purse and pulled out a small nail file. She slowly filed her chipped fingernail as Tanisha watched in agony. Billie took a long pull from the cigarette that hung delicately from her orange lips and continued to meticulously file her nail. She rubbed her thumb across the chipped nail and carefully reapplied a layer of nail polish to the single nail. Using her opposite hand, she expertly dropped the nail file in her purse and forcefully mashed the tiny cigarette butt in the gold ashtray.

Tanisha counted the cigarette butts in the ashtray. Thirteen, fourteen, fifteen, sixteen. There were sixteen cigarette butts in the ashtray, two days worth of cigarettes for Billie. Tanisha studied the butts and could tell when Billie had smoked them. The butts without lipstick were smoked in the morning while Billie sipped her black coffee. The butts with heavy lipstick were smoked while she put on her make-up. The butts with trace amounts of her orange Revlon lipstick were smoked in the evening.

Arms stretched above her head, Billie yawned like a lion. She had been out partying with Aunt Shanay the night before and Tanisha had to awaken her three times for the ride to the train. She'd pleaded with Billie Mae to get up or she would miss the train to Springfield.

Tanisha shifted her weight from her left foot to her right foot, as she stood in the foyer, holding her large duffel bag with two hands. She glanced nervously at her watch. She would miss the train to Springfield if they didn't leave in exactly two minutes. She counted backwards from sixty. When she reached thirty eight, Billie stirred.

"Are you ready to go?" Billie asked.

"Yes. I'm ready." Tanisha offered quickly. She watched as Billie grabbed her keys and purse and walked toward the door, blowing on her wet nail.

"Do you have everything?" Billie asked.

"Yes. The camp fact sheet said that we could only bring one duffel bag, so everything is in here." Tanisha patted the green army duffel bag that she'd purchased from Save Mart. As they walked to the car together, Tanisha prayed that Billie would not have to stop for gas. If they stopped for gas, she would most definitely miss the train.

"The train leaves in twenty minutes, so we should just make it," Tanisha said cheerily.

"I'd better stop for gas after I drop you off then." The Chrysler New Yorker was stopped by every stop light on the fifteen minute ride to the train depot in Homer. The ride to the Amtrak station was eerily silent interrupted only by Billie's yawns and her uttering of "My head is killing me."

Billie pulled into the parking lot and parked the car. Tanisha had already pushed the trunk button in the glove compartment and jumped out of the car.

"You have your train ticket, right?" Billie asked as she met Tanisha at the back of the car.

Tanisha reached into her small pouch and pulled out her ticket.

"Have a good time at camp," Billie Mae yawned. She gave Tanisha a hug and managed a smile as Tanisha grabbed her duffel bag out of the trunk.

Tanisha could see the other passengers standing to leave the small waiting area. She knew the train was due to arrive in less than five minutes as she watched them walk toward the platform.

"I'd better go, Mom. I think the train is coming. Thanks for the ride," Tanisha offered.

As Tanisha approached the train platform, she noticed a girl wearing the identical bright yellow leadership camp tee-shirt that she wore. They'd received the yellow shirts in their camp confirmation packets and were instructed to wear them as they traveled to camp. Her spirits brightened, Tanisha walked toward the girl, made eye contact and smiled encouragingly. Like an eclipse, her sunny disposition shaded as the girl grimaced, rolled her eyes, and quickly turned away, her long blonde hair flapping like a wing. Disgusted, Tanisha sighed, dropped her eyes and fumbled with the strap of her duffle bag, her stomach twisting into familiar knots. She blew the air from her lungs loudly and noticed Billie standing by the car smoking a cigarette and watching the train platform. Her mother waved and smiled. *I've never been away from home for two weeks. Am I going to be able to get through two weeks of camp?* Staring at her mother, Tanisha waved back just seconds before the large Amtrak pulled into the station, shielding her mother from view.

Tanisha boarded the crowded train and counted five other students wearing the yellow tee-shirts. The blonde from the train platform was invited to join the yellow tee-shirt group. Tanisha watched as she hugged her friends and settled into her seat. Walking through the aisle, she noticed an empty seat and was pleased when the boy sitting near the window made eye contact with her and invited her to sit next to him. Like Superman revealing the S on his chest, he slowly unzipped his sweat jacket giving her a glimpse of the bright yellow camp issued tee-shirt. Tanisha greeted him with her closed mouth smile and accepted his invitation to sit next to him. She glanced out the window and saw her mother driving out of the parking lot.

"Hi. I saw your tee-shirt. You must be going to the Leadership camp too. I'm Brian Kraft," he introduced.

"Hi, my name is Tanisha. Tanisha Carlson," she offered.

"Hi, Tanisha. Let me help you with your duffel. I have the same duffel, and it will fit nicely above your seat," Brian said grabbing the overstuffed duffel and effortlessly slinging it above her seat. "I covered up my tee-shirt because I was sleepy and wanted to take a nap," he explained. "But I'm well rested now," he finished.

Settling into their seats, Brian and Tanisha chatted and compared their camp registration packets. Tanisha was relieved to learn that Brian would also be in the same Apache section of camp as she was. A returning camper, she listened intently as Brian described his leadership camp experience from last year.

Three hours later, the trained pulled into the Springfield station, and a long white van greeted the campers, easily spotted wearing their yellow camp tee shirts. Tanisha sat next to Brian for the ten minute ride to the camp grounds.

"Tanisha, why don't you get settled and then I'll see you at dinner," he suggested. I can introduce you to some of my friends from last year."

"Okay. I'll see you later," she waved. *Well, he's certainly being overly friendly. Maybe this camp experience will be better than the St. Mary's fiasco!* Tanisha grabbed her heavy duffel bag and slowly walked toward the cluster of girls' cabins that formed a semicircle. She studied her registration sheet and stopped when she found her cabin name - Chipmunks. She knocked on the wooden screen door. There was no answer. She knocked again before slowly pushing open the door. The cabin was empty. She surveyed the room.

There were four sets of bunk beds lining the cabin and a single twin nearest the door. There were two dressers in the corner of the cabin. Each bunk was covered with a military gray wool blanket tucked with a white sheet creating a neat border on top. A white pillow crowned each blanket. A large round rug covered the middle of the floor and touched each of the frames. She saw duffel bags and personal belongings on two of the bunks in the room. She also noticed a clipboard and papers on the counselor's desk. She chose the bottom bunk on the first set of beds to the left of the door. Tanisha decided to unpack her bag.

She unzipped the duffel and pulled out her clothes. She held the clothes up to her nose and inhaled a sour smell. She patted everything in the duffel bag and could feel dampness. *Oh no! My clothes smell like mildew!* The Carlson family's clothes dryer was on the brink again and only blew out cold air. By the time Tanisha realized that the dryer wasn't working properly, it was too late to take her clothes to a neighbor's to dry so she was forced to pack the damp clothes in the bag hoping that they would air dry on the three hour train ride.

Tanisha decided to hang the damp clothes on the small hooks in the cabin meant for rain slickers and bathrobes. By the four bunk beds lining the room, Tanisha assumed that she was sharing the cabin with seven other girls plus the single twin bed reserved for the camp counselor. She was glad that she was the only person in the cabin and quickly pulled her damp clothes from the duffle bag and hung them on the hooks, even her underwear. She unlatched the wooden windows in the cabin and was grateful when a breeze blew in. She also hung a few things on the bed post of the top bunk bed that she'd chosen. As she pulled the damp clothes from the bag, she felt her Love's Baby Soft cologne and decided that she would try to mask the mildew smell on the clothes by spraying them with Love's Baby Soft. She hated to sacrifice her precious cologne but was desperate to mask the sour smell.

She walked outside and checked her watch. It was after 5:00, and according to the camp agenda, Tanisha had thirty minutes before it was time to report to dinner at the mess hall. She decided to explore the camp grounds.

The camp was a flurry of activity as students in shorts and camp tee shirts walked in and out of the small log cabins. Tanisha observed that the boys' cabins were approximately one hundred yards to the north of the girls' cabins. She counted twenty small cabins on the girls' side and just as many on the boys' side. A large cabin near the camp administration building had a sign that read GIRLS' BATH in big bold letters. Tanisha peered inside and was surprised that the bathroom stalls were without doors. Similarly, the shower area was one large open shower with ten shower heads.

This would be a new experience for Tanisha. She was accustomed to taking quick "group" showers in physical education at school, but had never used the toilet without the privacy of a stall door. Tanisha had to use the bathroom. She walked into the stall farthest from the door and squatted. As she peed, she heard girls walking into the bathroom chatting animatedly. *More repeat campers who know each other from last summer.* The girls continued to chat as they used the bathroom. Tanisha washed her hands quickly and walked outside.

She smoothed out her camp tee-shirt and decided to take a walk. She noticed weathered wooden signs nailed to trees. She followed a sign that read LAKE in black letters. She walked about fifty yards through a cluster of trees and a gravel path and saw another LAKE sign that led to a wildflower meadow. Tanisha paused to inhale the familiar scent of wild onions from the wooded areas that surrounded her home in Cedar Grove. She bent down and picked a few of the small wild onions. As she stood, she noticed a girl sitting on a small hill near the lake. She squinted into the sun and realized that the girl was black. The girl was writing in a small notebook. Excited to see another person of color, Tanisha quickened her pace and walked over to the hill.

"Hi! My name is Tanisha. Tanisha Carlson," she said cheerily.

The girl slowly lifted her head and stared at Tanisha as though she'd spoken a foreign language.

"What's your name?" Tanisha asked.

The girl stared coldly at Tanisha. "My name is Julie." Julie continued to write in her notebook.

"I'm so glad to meet you. I thought I was the only black girl at this camp," Tanisha shared excitedly. "All of the other kids here seem to know someone from last year. Is this your first time here too?" Tanisha was distracted by a small bird hovering three feet in front of her. "Look! I've never seen a bird like that, have you?"

Julie exhaled loudly and lifted her head. "It's a hummingbird. And I was here last year. For the record, I am African American, but just because we're both African American that does not mean that we're going to be friends. So don't try to hang around me, okay? I came here to get the leadership experience, not make new friends. So if you don't mind, I'd like to get back to my poem." Julie put her head down and continued to write.

Tanisha's eyes bugged and her jaw dropped open. The hummingbird hung in the air for a few seconds, flapping its wings as though mocking Tanisha before taking off and flying over the lake. Tanisha was speechless. She couldn't believe it. She'd assumed that Julie would at least be friendly, but she'd been ice cold.

Tanisha had a flashback to how she'd treated Dawn at Mahala Elementary. *This is bad karma! I should have been nicer to that weird Dawn with her tub of Vaseline. She tried to bond with me as the only other African American, and I treated her almost as badly as this Julie babe is treating me!*

Her head hung low, Tanisha slowly walked away, glad that no one had witnessed her humiliating encounter. Fighting back tears, she walked toward the water. The small lake connected to an adjacent pier near a sandy pathway that spiraled into the woods. Tanisha could see smoke billowing through the trees and smelled barbeque. She correctly guessed that the path from the lake led back to the mess hall and the center of the camp grounds. She absentmindedly tossed pebbles into the water, trying to make the pebbles skip like she'd seen on television.

As she continued down the path to complete her circular tour of the camp grounds, two male campers walked toward her, one of whom was black. She smiled softly as she passed the boys, overhearing the white camper's comment. "Hey, Derrick," he said. "That girl that just walked past was cute. Why didn't you talk to her?"

Tanisha slowed her pace to hear Derrick's response. "She looks all right, but you know I like blondes." And on that note Tanisha scurried to the open stall bath house to wash her hands before dinner.

The mess hall was a large cedar pavilion with wooden picnic benches connected in six rows. Open on all four sides, a tiny canopy connected the mess hall to the food buffet line adjacent to the industrial prep kitchen. A breeze blew, carrying the smell of the night's meal. When Tanisha entered, she noticed Brian Kraft's eyes subtly darting back and forth between his conversation and the main mess hall pathway. Seeing her, his eyebrows arched animatedly. She watched in amazement as he excused himself and walked toward her. Inhaling deeply, she was relieved that their Amtrak train friendship had at least lasted through dinner.

"Hey Tanisha," he smiled. "I just got my food, so why don't you go through the mess line and get your food and then join us. I saved a seat for you at our table."

"Okay," she agreed. Tanisha walked through the cafeteria style line and helped herself to the bar-b-que chicken that she'd smelled on the pier, corn on the cob, steak fries and lemonade. As she approached, Brian nudged one of his buddies who'd temporarily sat in the spot reserved for her. The boy smiled and stood as Tanisha reached the table. Tanisha noticed that Brian hadn't started to eat his food. Brian introduced her to the other campers at the table and after bowing her head to silently bless her food, Tanisha enjoyed her dinner. Her efforts to join the table's discussion about their school's student council structure were welcomed and encouraged. Like Tanisha, the other campers were either the president or vice president of the student council. Brian was the president of the student council and had attended the leadership camp the summer before as the vice president, so he knew many of the counselors and some of the campers.

Tanisha enjoyed the meal and was shocked when one of the campers that she'd just met started clearing the trays from the table. "Let me help you," she offered.

"It's cool, Tanisha," Brian whispered. "We all take turns clearing the trays," he explained. "Don't worry, you'll get your turn to clear," he winked. After dinner, the campers were treated to a brief welcome from the head counselor and introductions of the camp leadership staff. Tanisha joined her new friends for the mandatory campfire ritual. The bonfire roared in the open air pit positioned between the boys and girls' cabins. The pit appeared to be six feet in diameter and Tanisha wondered how she hadn't noticed it before. Following Brian's lead, she sat in the circle that was forming, her legs crossed like a pretzel.

"When I first came to leadership camp I thought this was hokey," Brian whispered. "But after a few days it started to grow on me," he continued. "Besides, it's a thirty year tradition," he shrugged. As a returning camper, Brian knew the songs, and Tanisha caught on quickly and sang along:

D-A-V-E-N-P, -O-R-T spells davenport, (davenport)
It's the only decent kind of love seat, (love seat)
The guy who made it must have had a fun streak (fun streak)
D-A-V-E-N-P-O-R-T you see,
It's a seat with some feet guaranteed to make you squeak,
It's a davenport for me!

L-O-double L—I-P-O-P spells lollipop, (lollipop)
It's the only decent kind of candy, (candy)
The guy who made it must have been a dandy, (dandy)
L-O-double L—I-P-O-P you see, it's a sweet
That's a treat guaranteed to make you keep,
It's a lollipop for me!

Initially, Tanisha stared at the campers in dismay and thought the songs were goofy and hokey, but when she looked around and saw all of the campers and counselors swaying and singing, she found herself joining in.

"You have a pretty voice, Tanisha," Brian complimented as the campfire ritual ended. "You're a second soprano, huh?" he asked.

"I am. How'd you know that?" she quizzed.

"I have an ear for music and tonality," he explained. "Even though you weren't singing very loud, I could hear you and you have perfect pitch," he offered.

Embarrassed, Tanisha grinned and wiped the dust from her back side.

"You wanna join us for breakfast tomorrow?" he asked. "I'll save a seat for you," he offered.

Tanisha stared at him curiously. "Sure," she shrugged.

"Okay, I'll see you at eight o'clock," he said. "Good night," he smiled.

"Good night," she returned.

As she walked back to her cabin, she remembered that she'd left her damp clothes hanging on the hooks. A panic ensued. Tanisha prayed that the fresh, lake air had removed the sour smell from her damp clothes. She picked up her pace and practically ran back to the cabin. When she returned, she noticed that her clothes were neatly folded and piled on top of her bed. She picked up a stack of clothes and held them to her nose. Puzzled by the scent of fabric softener, the thud from the screen door slam startled her.

"Hi, I'm Liz," she grinned. "You must be Tanisha." Liz extended her hand. Her grip was firm and strong.

Liz was short and stocky with well defined calves that protruded from her legs like small cantaloupes. Tanisha had never seen calves as large as Liz's calves and couldn't help but lower her eyes to take another peek.

Liz smiled. "I know. I have really muscular calves," she laughed. "I'm a cheerleader, and I run cross country and my mom has really muscular calves too. My dad calls us his little stallions!" Liz neighed like a horse, which made Tanisha laugh.

"Tanisha, I hope you don't mind, but I saw that your things were damp and hanging on hooks so I took them over to the main cabin and tossed them in the laundry to freshen them up," Liz continued. "Welcome to Leadership Camp, Tanisha."

Tanisha smiled at Liz. Her head bowed, her face turned red with shame. "Thank you, Liz. Our dryer wasn't working properly, and I didn't want to miss the train," she explained meekly.

Liz smiled knowingly at Tanisha. "No explanation necessary," she waved with her hand. "That's what leadership camp is all about. As leaders, if we see an issue that needs to be addressed, we address it," she offered. "If there's a problem, we find a solution. I'm glad I could help. I just bundled everything up and had the cleaning staff wash it all in cold water so nothing would run or bleed," she continued. "If you need anything, just let me know, this is my fourth year as a camp counselor and I know how to navigate through the labyrinth pretty well. Have you met any of the girls in our cabin?"

"Not yet. Or at least I don't think so," Tanisha replied. "I met Brian Kraft on the train and had dinner with him, and I met a few of his friends, but I haven't met any of the girls who are in this cabin yet," Tanisha said. *As far as I'm concerned, I did not meet Julie. If Julie is one of my cabin mates, I will die!*

"I met two of them earlier today," Liz offered. "They're awesome!" she assured. Liz smiled warmly at Tanisha, listening as she shared how her day had been so far. Liz had returned to the cabin moments after Tanisha arrived and was overcome by the sour smell of the damp clothes. She touched the hanging garments and felt their wetness. She knew from Tanisha's profile and photograph that she was the only black girl in the cabin. When she saw Tanisha's name written on the tags of the clothes, she knew that she had to act swiftly. She worked hard to make all campers feel welcome and make a good first impression. She knew that even if the clothes dried they would carry a sour odor. Afraid that the other girls might ostracize Tanisha if they knew that the sour smell in the cabin came from her clothes, she decided to remedy the situation before it became an issue. She quickly gathered all of the damp clothes (including the clothes that were still in Tanisha's duffel bag) and took them to the laundry.

Liz rubbed her chin and wrinkled her forehead. "Brian Kraft," she repeated. "That name sounds so familiar. I think I remember him from last year! He's a great guy!" Liz replied. "Well, the other girls should be heading back any minute so you'll meet everyone tonight. There are only four girls in our cabin, instead of eight, because four of the girls had to cancel camp due to family vacations. The two that I met seem very nice," she assured plopping on her bed. "Tell me about your home town, Teenie," Liz paused. "Do you mind if I call you Teenie? It's such a perfect nickname for Tanisha. Do your friends at school call you Teenie?"

Tanisha exhaled, grateful for Liz's kindness. "My friends don't call me Teenie," she replied. "But I don't mind if you do. It's cute," she shrugged. Tanisha flashed Liz her tight lipped smile and proceeded to tell her about Newberry East and Battle Creek Junior High School as the other campers came in together: Laura, Monica and Sharon.

Laura, a blonde cheerleader from Lake Forest, was a pageant participant and had placed first runner up in the Miss Teen Illinois pageant. Monica lived in Springfield. With her black framed glasses and short black hair, Tanisha thought she looked like a cuter version of Velma from Scooby Doo. Sharon was a short blonde from O'Fallon, Illinois. A gymnast, her thin frame was chiseled muscle. Tanisha learned that Sharon was also on the pom pon squad so they agreed to show each other pom pon moves to share with their squads. She was relieved when her cabin mates invited her to join them as they walked to the bathroom to brush their teeth and get ready for bed.

"Teenie, I saw you having dinner with a cute boy and then sitting next to him at the campfire. Who was he?" Laura gushed.

Tanisha laughed to herself at how quickly her new nickname had caught on. "His name is Brian Kraft," she shared. "We met on the train. He's a really nice guy, and he's gone out of his way to make sure that I feel welcome since this is my first time here," Tanisha offered.

"Brian Kraft?" Monica repeated. "I met him last year. He is a nice guy," Monica agreed as she wiped the cleanser from her face in a slow circular motion.

"He's also gorgeous! I don't remember him from last year! Introduce him to me will you, Teenie?" Laura pleaded.

"Sure. He invited me to join him for breakfast since we're in the Apache section together. I'll introduce you to him tomorrow," Tanisha shrugged.

Tanisha had been so grateful to have a friend at camp, that she'd overlooked Brian's physical appearance. But seeing him through the eyes of her cabin mates, she had to admit that he was very attractive. He stood about five feet eleven inches tall and had thick wavy black hair, bushy eyebrows and blue eyes.

Settling into her bed, Tanisha smiled as she inhaled the sweet scent of her pajamas, ecstatic that she'd made friends with her cabin mates. She drifted off to sleep silently humming the d-a-v-e-n-p-o-r-t melody to herself. *Looks like this camp experience will be very different from my first away camp experience. Thank God for that!*

Chapter 19

The Winning Ticket

The next morning, the campers were awakened by a bugle that startled Tanisha from a deep sleep. Like zombies, the girls slowly crawled from their bunks, their late night chat fest replaced by yawns. The girl chatter had continued well past midnight, and had intensified when Liz left the cabin for what she described as a mandatory meeting at the lake with the other counselors. When Liz departed, Monica shared with Teenie that the camp counselors often swam in the lake after lights out, the veteran counselors tossing the new counselors into the lake fully clothed. Everybody knew of this long standing camp counselor rite of passage, including the Camp Director who played possum.

On their way to the bathroom, the girls bumped into Liz who looked chipper and perky. She had already run a 5K and showered, with no hint of the late night swim in her demeanor. The girls trudged to the showers with their camp buckets filled with shampoo, conditioner, toothpaste and other toiletries. Tanisha was glad that she'd recently gotten her hair straightened with a chemical relaxer. She knew that she would be swimming a lot at camp and she was grateful that at least her hair wouldn't puff out after each round with the unforgiving lake water. She put on her shower cap and walked into the community shower corral. The other girls all shampooed their hair. Tanisha didn't mind when her cabin mates asked her why she wore a shower cap in the shower. She was glad to explain that black hair only needed washing once every week or else it would dry out. The girls watched with brief curiosity as Tanisha applied a small dab of pink hair oil to the palm of her hand and rubbed it through her hair explaining that black hair needed oil to remain healthy and shiny. The girls dressed and rushed to the mess hall for breakfast.

Inside the mess hall, Tanisha's eyes searched for Brian Kraft who waved and pointed to an empty seat next to his. Tanisha returned his wave and motioned to her three cabin mates. She held up four fingers and Brian shrugged. He held up one finger and quickly whispered something to his two friends. Brian and his friends got up and walked over to an empty table near the edge of the mess hall. Brian motioned to Tanisha with the OK sign. The girls grabbed cereal and powdered eggs, sausage and sweet rolls. Monica showed Tanisha how to use the milk lever that dispensed ice cold milk. She explained that everyone called it "the cow." Filling one glass with milk and another with orange juice, Tanisha and her new friends joined Brian's table.

"Good morning, Brian," Tanisha smiled. "These are my cabin mates: Laura, Monica and Sharon. Is there room for all four of us?" Tanisha asked.

"Of course, that's why we moved to this table," Brian replied. "Hey ladies! I'm Brian Kraft and this is Bob. My friend Mike is eating with us too, but he went to get another glass of milk. Have a seat," he offered.

The girls placed their trays on the table and slid into the picnic table seats. Brian patted the seat next to his and motioned for Tanisha to sit next to him.

Monica spoke directly to Brian. "Hey, Brian, I met you last year. We were in the same section."

"That's right. I remember you. You wore Secret deodorant. Which section are you in this year?" Brian asked.

"Wow! What a great memory! I'm in Adobe again," Monica shared.

"My boy Mike is in Adobe this year. Tanisha and I are in Apache," Brian said.

"Teenie told us last night," Monica mentioned.

Tanisha glanced at Brian with a puzzled look. "What gives? How do you know and remember what type of deodorant she wears?" Tanisha asked.

"You'll find out soon enough, *Teenie*. You didn't tell me your nickname was Teenie," he repeated. "I like that." Brian elbowed Tanisha in the ribs.

"Thank you for your support," Tanisha giggled.

Laura was seated directly across from Brian and casually flipped her long blonde hair over her shoulders.

"I was in Apache last year, but this year I'm in Adobe too. Brian, where do you go to school?" Laura asked.

"I go to Old Trier," Brian smiled. "I live in Lake Forest, but we have a home in Wilmette too, so I go to Old Trier."

"I live in Lake Forest too," Laura gushed.

"Where do you live in Lake Forest," she quizzed.

"We're east of Greenbay Road, not far from Lake Forest College's campus," he paused. "We're down the road from Barat College."

"Oh my God," Laura grinned. "We live less than five minutes away from each other," she squealed. "I took riding lessons at Barat College."

Brian smiled kindly and focused his attention on Tanisha. "Teenie, we elect officers today, and I am running for president of our section. Why don't you run for vice president?" Brian rubbed his palms together.

"Are you sure? Shouldn't you pick someone that has been here before? No one knows me. I don't want you to lose because of me," Tanisha said.

"It's not like that. Each election is individual, but since a lot of people know me, if I nominate you as my running mate, they'll know you're cool and they'll vote for you. Trust me. It'll be fine." Brian patted Tanisha's hand.

"I'm planning to run for president of my section too," Laura offered, her eyelashes working overtime.

"That's great, Lauren," Brian smiled.

"It's Laura," Laura corrected.

"I'm terribly sorry, Laura," Brian offered. "I thought I heard Lauren when we were introduced. Here comes my friend Mike now," he motioned. Laura shrugged her shoulders and took a bite of her bran muffin as Mike returned with another glass of milk. Laura's eyes widened as the six foot tall, blonde, blue eyed Mike approached the table.

"Hi Mike." Laura shifted her shoulders to face Mike and batted her long eyelashes. She smiled as she noticed his broad shoulders. Mike returned her grin and with a tilt of his head, he motioned for Bob to slide over so that he could sit next to her.

Tanisha frowned at her watery scrambled eggs, covering them with a napkin. She ate her frosted mini wheat cereal and sausage.

Taking one last chug from both her milk and her juice glass, she watched as Brian rose to throw her tray away, grabbing two other trays from the table.

Engaged in an animated chat with Mike, Laura winked and waved at Tanisha as she walked to the Adobe section with Mike, her gaze locked on his chiseled profile. Tanisha followed as Brian led her to the Apache leadership section with Bob bringing up the rear reading the newspaper. The meeting section was fifty paces from the mess hall and was also an open air pavilion with a partial view of the lake. When they arrived, Brian was treated like a celebrity. Tanisha was impressed at how well regarded he was by everyone. He shook hands with the section leader and hugged or high fived many of the other campers like old friends, always stopping to introduce Tanisha to anyone that he greeted. Tanisha was flattered when he introduced her as his "running mate." It was clear that Brian took leadership camp very seriously, and he reminded Tanisha of a politician.

After a brief introduction by Tim, the section leader, the campers played an icebreaker game where each camper said his first name and the type of deodorant that he wore. The next person then had to say the name and deodorant brand of each person in the circle until it got all the way around.

> *My name is Tanisha and I wear Secret.*
> *This is Lucy and she wears Sure.*
> *This is Bob and he wears Right Guard.*
> *This is Tom and he wears Sure.*

And on and on around the circle. By the time it was her turn, Tanisha had sixteen names and deodorants to recant. She flubbed five of them. Sitting to her left, Brian got all of the names and deodorants correct. By the time the game was finished, Tanisha remembered all of the names and the deodorant brands.

The election process was the next agenda item. Tim, the camp counselor, explained the election process as he handed out ballots and pencils. Each camper was allowed to nominate someone for one of the officer positions: president, vice president and secretary. Each nomination had to be seconded. The candidate being nominated would be given an opportunity to accept or decline the nomination by stating: "I accept the nomination or I decline the nomination." The nomination process would continue until a candidate for each position had been identified.

"Do we have any nominations for president?" Tim asked.

Tanisha was taken aback when almost every hand in the group went into the air. Tim pointed to Bob who wore Right Guard.

"Bob has the floor," Tim said.

"I nominate Brian Kraft for president," Bob stated.

"Is there a second?" Tim asked.

"I second it," Lucy said.

"Brian, do you accept the nomination for president?"

"Yes. I accept."

"Are there any other nominations for president?" Tim asked.

No hands went up. It looked like Brian would run unopposed.

"Okay. The nominations for president are now closed. Is there a nomination for vice president?"

"I nominate Tanisha Carlson for vice president," Brian said.

"I second it," Bob offered loudly. Tanisha blushed from embarrassment.

"Tanisha, do you accept the nomination for vice president?" Tim asked.

Tanisha was nervous but tried to speak with confidence. "Yes. I accept."

"Are there any other nominations for vice president?"

Tanisha studied her sneakers, afraid to make eye contact with a possible opponent. She was still stunned by her electoral defeat at the hands of Tracy Jones and was shy about competing in another election.

"Okay. Looks like Tanisha is also running unopposed. Is there a nomination for secretary?"

"I nominate Bob for secretary," Brian said confidently. He leaned over and whispered in Tanisha's ear, "Second it for me, Teenie."

"I second it," Tanisha said softly.

"Bob, do you accept the nomination for secretary?" Tim asked.

Bob jumped to his feet. "But of course. It would be an honor and a privilege to serve as secretary of this esteemed tribe," Bob bowed.

The other campers giggled at Bob's display. "And the academy award goes to Bob," Tim teased. "That'll be enough of that. Sit down Tom Cruise!" he laughed. "Are there any other nominations for secretary?"

The group of twenty student council leaders sat silent and again no hands went up.

"Okay. Since these three are running unopposed, we don't really need to have a vote, but for the record, let's write down your choices to ensure that the slate receives at least a quorum vote which, as you all know, is one more than half. If for some reason a candidate doesn't receive at least quorum, then we'll open the floor again for secret nominations. For president, it's Brian Kraft, vice president it's Tanisha Carlson and secretary it's Bob Dunn," Tim explained.

"Tanisha, I heard Bob and Brian calling you Teenie, which do you prefer?" he asked.

"You can call me Tanisha or Teenie," she replied meekly. "I like them both."

"Alright, I'll call you Teenie since that's what I hear Brian and Bob calling you," Tim said scribbling on his notepad.

Tanisha's heart raced and her confidence waned as her thoughts spun. *Okay, this is where they'll ding me. They'll probably write in the name of one of the white girls and then I'll be embarrassed and have to smile and pretend that I'm okay. This group isn't going to vote for me, watch. She could feel her palms getting sweaty.*

Tanisha filled out her ballot and dropped it into the plastic bowl that Tim passed around. As Tim tallied the ballots, Tanisha pulled at a hang nail.

"Are you nervous, Teenie? You shouldn't be. You're on the winning ticket," Brian offered confidently.

"That's easy for you to say since they all know you from last year. No one knows me," Tanisha whispered.

"But I nominated you and they trust me," he comforted. "Besides, I could tell from our train ride that you have intrinsic leadership skills. You're a born leader. You won the vice president election at your school didn't you?" Brian asked.

Tanisha was intrigued. She didn't know too many teenage boys who could use the word intrinsic in proper context. She didn't have the heart to tell Brian the truth about how she'd "won" her school's election by a technicality.

"True. But I'm still nervous. What if they write in Minnie Mouse or the 'black girl' as a joke?"

Brian stared at Tanisha with a puzzled expression. "Teenie, why would anyone do that?" he whispered. "This is leadership camp.

Most of the kids down here don't think like that, at least I haven't encountered any who do. They're leaders at their schools and see potential in others, not color. You shouldn't limit yourself and box yourself in just because you're black. You need to build your self confidence," Brian coached softly. "By the way, there are only three African American kids at my school, but they don't refer to themselves as black. They prefer African American. Do you prefer black?" Brian asked.

Tanisha stared at Brian. If she was an old soul, he was an older soul wise beyond his years. "It doesn't matter to me. I'm not really used to African American, but I think it's growing on me," she said softly.

"Cool. You're a smart, funny, beautiful girl," Brian whispered. "And you happen to be African American. Don't sell yourself short."

"Someone else just told me the same thing last week," she said. "But he said that I was beautiful, smart and funny. You think I'm smarter and funnier than I am beautiful?"

"See what I mean? I think you're gorgeous. That's why I invited you to sit next to me on the train. I noticed you on the train platform, and when I saw the leadership camp shirt, I made sure to motion you over. Now if you had been a knucklehead unable to conjugate a verb correctly, I would have pretended that I wanted to take a nap and fallen asleep on you," he teased.

"Is that right?" Tanisha ribbed Brian in the side.

Their playfulness was interrupted by the sound of Tim's voice. "OK, no surprises here. Brian, Teenie and Bob are the elected officers for the Apache tribe with a triple unanimous vote. Congratulations you three. I need my leadership officers to stick around after we dismiss, and we'll talk about what our agenda is for the camp," Tim announced.

Brian winked knowingly at Tanisha, grabbed her hand and squeezed it tightly. He then jumped up and gave Bob an animated high five.

Several campers approached Tanisha to offer congratulations. Tanisha blushed and humbly accepted their well wishes with pride, her confidence increasing with each handshake.

Chapter 20

The Postcard

Tim spent the next thirty minutes reviewing the Apache leadership camp agenda with Brian, Tanisha and Bob. The group learned that their primary objective for the summer would be to help Tim coordinate the various leadership activities and competitions for their section. At dinner every night, the section leaders were responsible for preparing and presenting a report to the camp on the Apache section's daily activities. The leadership group would also serve as captains at the daily physical challenge competitions including swimming relay races, kayak races and a treasure hunt hike. The daily Apache meetings would occur in the morning after breakfast and the shorter meeting would occur after lunch before the physical challenge games. The meetings would be run in student government fashion following parliamentary procedure and standard Roberts' Rules of Order with regard to process and protocol. All of the students invited to the leadership camp attended schools whose student governments were run under the same governance.

Brian recommended that the three alternate responsibility for giving the Apache report at dinner. He shared that last year as the vice president of his tribe, the president had made the same suggestion with his leadership team, and it provided an opportunity for the leadership team to hone their public speaking skills in front of the entire camp. Bob and Tanisha agreed to Brian's proposal. Brian reminded Bob that his responsibility was to note points of interest in the Apache tribe and draft talking points that Brian or Tanisha could share with the rest of the campers.

Bob had a spiral notebook tucked into the pocket of his shorts with a black pen protruding from the spiral. He pulled it out and tapped it in his hand. "I'm way ahead of you, Mr. President! A good reporter always travels with his tools of the trade!" Bob planned to pursue a career in journalism and enjoyed the roving reporter aspect of his secretary duties.

"Aren't you a prepared little cub scout? What if someone else had run against you and you hadn't won?" Brian teased.

"I don't think in terms of "what if." I wanted to be secretary again this year, and I came prepared to begin my duties immediately." Bob winked at Tanisha and grinned. "It's all about confidence," Bob grinned. "There's nothing wrong with being prepared is there, Newbie?"

Tanisha shook her head and smiled, "No, Rockford. There's nothing wrong with being prepared." She could tell that Bob was a good guy. He was from Rockford, Illinois and had never heard of Tanisha's home town of Newberry East. He nicknamed her Newbie on the brief walk from breakfast so she'd decided to call him Rockford. She laughed at how quickly her white camp friends had given her two different nicknames in less than twenty-four hours. "I don't know how I'm going to keep track of all of these nicknames that I now have," she laughed.

Since the officers of the Apache tribe had run unopposed, the Apaches had not had to hear campaign speeches or conduct run-off elections resulting in a one hour break in their schedule before lunch and the afternoon sessions. Tim dismissed the group, instructing them to meet in the mess hall at twelve hundred hours so the Apache section could have lunch together. Brian and Bob decided to go for a quick swim in the lake to cool off from the ninety degree heat. Brian had tried to persuade Tanisha to join them, but she declined. She decided to run an errand at the camp store.

Tanisha had tucked money into her denim shorts and raced to the camp store. She studied the meager postcard selection, disappointed by the limited choices: the Springfield, Illinois state capital stairs, fields of corn, and three designs of Abraham Lincoln. She checked her watch and realized that she had fifty minutes before lunch. She decided on a postcard with a picture of Abraham Lincoln's face on it. He was her favorite president. She bought one postcard stamp and raced back to her cabin to get a pen. With her pen, she plopped down on her bunk but could barely breathe from the heat and humidity that was hovering in the cabin like a thick cloud. At breakfast, the head counselor announced that the day's high temperature was slated to reach ninety-eight degrees, and reminded the campers to drink plenty of fluids throughout the day. It felt like it was one hundred degrees in the stuffy cabin. Tanisha gathered her postcard and pen and decided to sit outside where the air wasn't as thick.

She searched for a tree that would provide shade. Her eyes scanned the cabin area quickly, and rested on a large tree near the boys' cabin area. Tanisha wiped sweat from her brow and walked toward the tree. The temperature felt a few degrees cooler in the shade. She was glad that she'd worn denim shorts as she settled into the cool green moss under the tree. She hoped the green moss wouldn't stain her shorts. She crossed her legs pretzel style, leaned her back against the oak tree, and prepared to write a postcard to David Barton.

She blew out her cheeks like a puffer fish and slowly released the air in her mouth like a helium balloon in flight as she thought about her last encounter with David.

⅘⅜

David had called her the night after their Duds & Suds lunch like he said he would and they'd talked for almost two hours. David had shared that he wanted to be a lawyer but his parents wanted him to go into medicine. He talked about his siblings and asked Tanisha about her brothers. Tanisha had heard David's voice on the phone every night since their lunch. He'd stopped by Save Mart the following Friday and brought her a camp goodie bag filled with Hostess Suzy Qs, nacho cheese flavored Doritoes, crunchy Cheetos and Double mint gum. Now she understood why he'd asked her what her favorite junk food was. Tanisha was working the 1:00 to 9:00 shift that day and wasn't scheduled for lunch until five thirty so David stopped by on his way to his dad's office to surprise her with the treats. When he arrived at Save Mart, there were six customers waiting to be serviced. David made eye contact with her, winked and walked over to the camera department where he could watch and wait until the line died down. When Tanisha was down to her last customer, David walked up to the service desk.

"Hey! You were busy earlier," David smiled.

"I know," Tanisha agreed. "Sometimes we get a wave of returns all at once. And three of them didn't have receipts. And then it slows down and you won't get any returns for an hour. Go figure," she smiled. "What are you doing here? This is a nice surprise." Tanisha suspected that David would probably stop by the store so she wore a new white cotton v-neck sweater and light blue bicycle pants with white sailor trim at the cuff. She had on her new navy blue

loafers which gave the outfit a sporty nautical look. She had also lined her eyelids with coal black eye liner and put on a baby pink lipstick. She'd treated herself to a cab ride to Save Mart since Vicky was working the same shift as Tanisha so her mom would pick them up when the store closed.

"I thought I'd stop in to say goodbye before you leave for camp. You look nice by the way. I never noticed how big your eyes are. Wow!" David exclaimed.

"Thanks," Tanisha blushed. "I don't usually wear eye make-up, but I felt like putting some on today."

David smiled at Tanisha. "So I'm wearing you down, huh? You're putting on make-up for me. I like that."

"Slow down sporty! Why did I have to put on make-up for you? Can't a girl just put on a little eye liner? Or maybe I'm hanging with my girls tonight after work. Besides, I didn't know you were coming to the store today," she explained.

"I was just teasing you. You sure do know how to shoot a brotha down! You know I couldn't let you leave for two weeks without stopping in to at least say goodbye. You're not going out after work are you?" David asked quickly.

"No. I have to leave for Springfield tomorrow morning, so I need to finish packing."

"I wish I could take you out to lunch today, but I have to meet my folks for dinner at the club tonight at 6:00."

"No sweat. I'll let you make it up to me when I get back from camp," Tanisha giggled.

"Don't forget to send me a postcard! You wrote down my address, and packed it with your stuff, right?" he asked eagerly.

"Yup. It's in my duffle bag," she assured.

"I better scoot before I'm late. Is that clock right?" David glanced over his shoulder at the large round clock above the doorway.

"It is. I think it might be one minute fast. Look who's sweating the clock now!" Tanisha tapped her watch.

"My old man is a stickler for punctuality. His favorite saying is: 'Life waits for no one. Always be ten minutes early.' He was in the military so he doesn't understand CP time. My mom and I call him the general."

CP or Colored People time was the phrase coined to suggest that if an event was scheduled to start at 7:00, and it started at 7:30, then it was starting on "colored people or CP" time suggesting that blacks are always late for everything.

"My dad was in the military too! But he's always late. He's the king of CP time!" Tanisha laughed.

"Which branch of the service was your dad in?" David asked.

"He was in the army," Tanisha replied.

"So was my old man! See, we have something else in common. The army paid for my dad to go to medical school and my mom too. That's where they met."

"That's cool." Tanisha puffed out her cheeks and bit her top lip.

"You're going to love my parents. They're real cool," David smiled.

Tanisha's thoughts shifted to Billie Mae. If he wanted her to meet his parents when they were able to date, then she would have to introduce him to Billie Mae. David was accepting of Tanisha, but what would he think of Billie Mae? When she turned fifteen and he came by to pick her up for a date, how could she introduce him to Billie Mae? What if Billie Mae was in one of her "moods" and hadn't taken her bipolar medication? How is he going to take Billie Mae?

Tanisha snapped out of her daydream. "My dad's cool, but my mom and I don't really click," she offered.

"Yeah, a lot of girls have mama drama at this age. Okay, I better go. Have fun at camp. And share your junk food stash with your cabin mates," he paused. "Don't fall out of your canoe and remember to write me a postcard. And call me when you get back." David saluted Tanisha before leaving Save Mart.

"Aye, aye, captain," she smiled as she saluted him back. "He got the theme of my outfit, the whole nautical look thing! Mama drama? If he only knew."

ഏരു

Tanisha smiled thinking about David Barton. She watched a squirrel scurry up the branch of the tree in front of her. When he got to the top branch, he twitched his nose and scampered back down the trunk of the tree and disappeared into the woods. She glanced at her watch and panicked as she realized that she'd spent almost forty minutes daydreaming about her most recent David encounter. She wiped beads of sweat from her nose and chewed on the cap of her pen and wrote on the postcard:

> *Hey Belvedere! Leadership camp is great.*
> *I was elected VP of the Apache tribe. Go figure!*
> *I've met some nice people, and it looks like it's*
> *going to be a fun couple of weeks! Make sure*
> *your owner brushes your fur daily and*
> *plays catch with you. And make*
> *sure he reads this to you.*
> *Gotta run - outta room! Ruff Ruff! Teenie*

Tanisha laughed out loud as she wrote David's address and affixed the stamp. She raced back to the camp store and mailed the postcard. On her way back, she bumped into Brian Kraft coming out of his cabin.

Chapter 21

The Doctor is In

Billie Mae had been seeing a psychiatrist for the past few weeks. Sonja, the personnel director at the cable company where Billie worked, confronted her about her erratic behavior and mood swings after receiving a complaint from her supervisor. Billie Mae had not been playing nicely in the sandbox with some of her co-workers. The specific behaviors sited in her personnel file write-up included: an attitude problem, mood swings, and an apparent dislike for authority.

"Sonja, this is bullshit and you know it! I do my job well," Billie Mae growled. "So what if I don't get along with some of the other people in the group. You don't pay me to like people. I get paid to be a secretary, and I'm a good secretary. I'm the best typist you have!" Billie screamed.

Sonja was a petite white woman with short red hair cut in a pixie style. She wore wide rimmed glasses that teetered on the edge of her nose. The thick plastic frames on the glasses contrasted sharply with the fire red hair. Sonja pushed her glasses up out of habit and necessity before speaking,

"Billie, you're a good worker, but it's important that everyone get along. Dick really likes you and likes the work that you do for him, but he's tired of getting complaints from the others in the group. You need to try to get along with the others a little bit. Are you trying?"

"I have a lot going on. I don't have time to be friends with people at work," Billie glared at Sonja.

"No one is asking you to be *friends* with them, just get along with them. For instance, is it necessary to snatch the papers that they bring you to type? Or when someone points out a mistake that they need you to correct, more than one person has said that you often roll your eyes and glare at them when it was your typed mistake that caused the correction."

"I'm not the only person who makes mistakes. I'm not perfect," Billie defended.

"No one expects you to be perfect, Billie." Sonja removed her glasses and walked around to the edge of her desk and leaned against it. "Is everything okay at home? I know you just went through a divorce and sometimes when people are going through major life changes it impacts their work performance. How are you handling your divorce?"

Billie exhaled deeply. "Fine. My kids and I are doing fine."

"How are your kids handling it? You have four children, right?"

"I just told you that they're handling it just fine."

Sonja took a deep breath. "Billie, we've decided that you need to spend some time with the company doctor. I like you and I'm going to give you the straight talk. Dick insists that you speak with the company doctor to ensure that you're fit to return to work. Some of your teammates are afraid that you're going to go off on them." Billie glared at her with slanted eyes as Sonja stammered on. "We've set-up appointments for you to meet with Dr. Benson every day next week during your lunch hour. He's only going to chat with you for thirty minutes so you'll still have thirty minutes to eat your lunch. He's going to write an assessment for us to review so we can determine next steps."

"Next steps? What's that supposed to mean?" Billie asked.

"Based on Dr. Benson's recommendation, we'll determine if this is the right job for you or not. Like I said, you're a good worker, but we need to ensure that you're a good fit for Dick's department."

"Do I have a choice?" Billie asked.

"You really don't. We're making this a condition of your employment, which means that if you refuse to see Dr. Benson or follow his recommendation, we can terminate you."

Sonja placed her thick glasses on her face and walked around to her desk and retrieved a slip of paper.

"Here's Dr. Benson's extension and his office address. His office is expecting you on Monday."

Billie Mae snatched the paper from Sonja without looking at her.

Sonja touched Billie's shoulder softly. "Billie, I'm trying to help you. Was it necessary to snatch the paper from me? If this is what Dick and the others on the team experience, I have to admit that it's inappropriate behavior. I hope you agree to follow Dr. Benson's recommendations."

"Are you done? I need a cigarette." Billie's hands shook.

"I'm finished. Have a good day."

Billie Mae needed her job at the cable company. She was already one month behind on her car payment and feared that she might lose her beloved vehicle if she lost her job, so she agreed to meet with Dr. Benson. After just one visit, Dr. Benson contacted Sonja and shared that further psychological evaluation was necessary.

Dr. Benson referred Billie to Dr. Elliot Dudley, a psychiatrist who specialized in bipolar disorders.

Dr. Dudley had a full patient load so the cable company agreed to allow Billie Mae to meet with the psychiatrist during the only available appointment on Wednesdays at 4:00. They allowed Billie to leave at three forty five to get to her appointment on time and didn't dock her pay for the early dismissal.

Dr. Dudley was a very fair skinned African American woman in her late forties. Her hair was reddish brown and wavy, and she wore it pulled back in a tight bun. She wore no make-up with the exception of a little eye liner and lipstick. She wore loafers without socks and khaki pants and a cardigan. On Wednesdays, she alternated between a navy blue and forest green cardigan sweater atop a simple white oxford shirt. She smelled like Chanel No. 5 perfume. Chanel No. 5 was Billie's favorite perfume when she could afford it. The familiar scent comforted Billie. Dr. Dudley motioned for Billie to have a seat on the leather sofa.

"With a name like Elliot, I expected you to be a man," Billie said.

Dr. Dudley reached in her desk and pulled out a pack of cigarettes. "I get that a lot. It's a family name. What type of cigarettes do you smoke?"

"I smoke Virginia Slims Menthol. How'd you know I smoke?" Billie studied Dr. Dudley cautiously.

"I can smell it in your clothes and on your breath. Can I bum a cigarette off of you? I've always wanted to try that brand. I've smoked these for so long that it's time for a change." Billie Mae handed Dr. Dudley a cigarette and settled into the sofa.

Dr. Dudley lit her cigarette, took a quick pull and placed it in the ashtray. She picked up the ashtray and sat in a small arm chair facing the sofa.

"Thanks. These are really smooth. So Billie, tell me about your mother," Dr. Dudley said.

Billie Mae's eyebrows crinkled. "My mother? Why do you want to know about my mother?"

"In order to help you, I need to get to know you. I want to learn about your mother and father, how they met, what they were like and then we can work our way to the present. When is your birthday?"

Billie Mae placed her cigarette in the ashtray on the coffee table and leaned back against the sofa. "October 16th," she said quizzically.

"You're a Scorpio. My mother was a Scorpio, a lovely woman. So tell me about your mother," Dr. Dudley encouraged.

"I don't know where to begin." Billie's voice was softer, and she subconsciously rubbed her thumb along her fingers.

"How did your parents meet? Tell me the story of Billie Mae Peterson or as much as you can tell in the forty seven minutes that we have remaining in this visit. I'm just going to listen and take notes."

This is what Dr. Dudley learned about Billie Mae in their first office visit.

⁍⁎

Billie Mae Peterson was born on the sixteenth of October in nineteen forty four. She was the oldest child of EJ and Hattie Pearl Peterson. As the story goes, Hattie Pearl was quite a looker and had been married before to Willie Boxdale. Willie died and left Hattie Pearl widowed with four children to rear. Consumed with grief, Hattie Pearl spent her nights partying at the local Veterans of Foreign

War (VFW) Post and came home expecting her fifth child just months after she buried her husband. Since she was playing the role of the grieving widow, she conveniently assigned parental rights to the deceased Willie.

A few years later, Hattie Pearl met EJ Peterson at the VFW post and soon became pregnant with Billie Mae. EJ made an honest woman of Hattie Pearl before shipping off to WWII. While EJ was off defending the country in a segregated unit, Hattie Pearl arranged to have her older children shipped off to live with relatives or foster care to avoid the inconvenience of six children. Two went to live with her sister in Michigan, one enlisted in the army and her last stray lived with a white woman that gave her free room and board in exchange for domestic work. Billie was sent to live with EJ's sister Aunt Jane to keep their only child company. When EJ returned from the war, he was furious with Hattie Pearl for breaking up her family and insisted that she get them back. She did, but she continued to party at night while EJ was on the road as a truck driver, so she shipped the children off to foster care and relatives time and time again. Hattie Pearl's mother was a full blooded Cherokee Indian and her father was a fair skinned man. Hattie Pearl had an exotic look complete with long flowing tresses that men loved. She also had big legs and a passion for scotch.

Hattie Pearl hadn't been prepared for motherhood. She was sixteen when she first saw Willie Boxdale in the colored section of a Pullman train. She was headed south to Tuscaloosa, Mississippi to visit her aunt for the summer. Willie Boxdale was a porter in training and Hattie Pearl was smitten by his smooth, ebony skin, conked hair and starched white porter jacket. Willie's teeth were bright white and gleamed against the whiteness of his uniform and the blackness of his skin.

Hattie couldn't keep her eyes off of him. She wanted to touch his skin and run her fingers through his thick hair. Her mother Minnie had warned her about 'dark' men saying "never date a man darker than a paper sack, cause they'll break your heart fo' sure!"

Hattie didn't understand how a darker man could break your heart quicker than a lighter skinned man, but she knew better than to question Minnie's wisdom. Hattie's father, Captain Macon, was so fair he could pass for white and sometimes did when it served him well. As Minnie's voice rang through Hattie's head, she couldn't help but steal glimpses at Willie every chance she got. Hattie was shocked at her attraction to the coal black Willie Boxdale. When he looked at her and tipped his porter cap, she flashed her gold tooth at him and deliberately rubbed against him on her way to the colored only restroom.

Willie was sweet on Hattie Pearl with her long straight hair and big legs. Although he wasn't supposed to be overly attentive to the colored passengers on the train, he found himself making excuses to walk past her seat three or four times on the twenty-two hour ride to Tuscaloosa. He watched her leave the train and was glad he recognized the people that greeted her. Lucille and Anthony Fambro attended the same church as his family. He grinned from ear to ear. He decided he would pay a visit by the Fambro house during his stopover in Tuscaloosa.

Willie paid several calls on Hattie Pearl, sitting in her aunt's parlor sipping lemonade as her aunt and uncle looked on. When he wasn't working as a Pullman porter trainee, he attended church every Sunday. He made sure to greet Mr. & Mrs. Fambro and speak to Hattie Pearl. Lucille and Anthony disapproved of Willie's dark skin, but were impressed with his Pullman porter in training status. In 1925, a Pullman porter was as prestigious as a doctor or lawyer in the black community. They knew his kinfolk and knew that his intentions for Hattie Pearl were honorable. As the summer progressed, they felt comfortable leaving Willie and Hattie Pearl unchaperoned for short periods of time.

Hattie Pearl was smitten with Willie and didn't want to return to Illinois. Just two weeks before Hattie Pearl was scheduled to return north to Illinois, she shared with Willie that she was expecting a baby. Her aunt and uncle met with Willie's parents and Hattie Pearl found herself married to Willie Boxdale. She became a bride just two weeks shy of her seventeenth birthday.

Eight months later Hattie Pearl gave birth to a son, Willie, Jr. at her Aunt Lucille's house. Her Aunt Lucille was so glad to have a baby in the house that she stepped in and cared for the baby as though it were her own. Hattie Pearl would nurse the baby when necessary but otherwise her Aunt Lucille performed all of the maternal duties. With her aunt raising her child, and her husband traveling as a Pullman Porter, Hattie Pearl spent her time wandering the streets of Tuscaloosa. Less than one year after the birth of Willie, Jr., Hattie Pearl became pregnant with her second child.

"Chile, now you know I know what's going on." Aunt Lucille was furious with Hattie Pearl. "It just ain't right how you treating that man. He's out on the rails making a good living for you and these here chilluns and you ain't got the good since to keep your tail at home? If you gonna act like a fool and roll around with dogs, at least make sure the dog you rolling around with look like the dog at home. You know I know what's going on. Now you cut it out, you here me? God don't like ugly."

Hattie Pearl's second child was a fair skinned girl that she named Dorothy. Everyone assumed that Dorothy had inherited her grandfather's coloring, but Aunt Lucille knew that Hattie Pearl had been spending time with the fair skinned son of the pastor and suspected that Dorothy favored him more than anyone. But she kept her mouth shut and never said a word.

And so it continued. Hattie Pearl had a child every year for the next four years. Willie continued to work as a Pullman porter and Hattie Pearl continued to have babies that her Aunt Lucille raised. Because Hattie's family was so fair, no one suspected anything when the only baby that looked like Willie Boxdale, was Willie, Jr.

Fifteen years into their marriage, Willie Boxdale suffered a massive heart attack while working on the train. Hattie Pearl was widowed at the age of thirty two.

After the funeral, Hattie Pearl packed up her family and moved back up north to Chicago, Illinois. It was in Illinois that she became pregnant with her fifth child. She conveniently assigned parental rights to the deceased Willie Boxdale.

Three years later, she married EJ Peterson and gave birth to Billie Mae while EJ was serving in WWII. She gave birth to two more children when he returned, another son EJ, Jr. and a daughter Shanay.

Hattie Pearl didn't know how to be a mother. All she knew how to do was flirt, attract men, give birth to children and flirt some more.

೮೦೮೩

Billie Mae found herself crying in the psychiatrist's office sharing the loneliness that she felt as a child, as she watched her mom paint her face and go out dancing at night while her dad was working as an interstate trucker.

"Billie, did Hattie Pearl ever hug you or show you affection?" Dr. Dudley asked as she scribbled in her notebook.

Billie wiped her eyes with a tissue from the box on Dr. Dudley's table. She took a pull from her cigarette before speaking. "No. She wasn't much of a hugger."

"What about your dad, was he affectionate?" Dr. Dudley's tone was soft and concerned.

"Not really. He was always working. And when he was home, he was arguing with Mama and trying to keep her from going out. I liked living at my Aunt Jane's house better than being at home."

"You lived with someone other than your parents growing up? When was that?" Dr. Dudley asked.

"I lived with Aunt Jane when I was in junior high school. Aunt Jane is my father's sister, and she had one daughter, my cousin Laurel. I lived with them for two years so my cousin could have a "play" sister. Aunt Jane's husband Donald was paralyzed in a work accident, and he was in a wheel chair. I enjoyed living with Aunt Jane even though me and Laurel didn't get along that well." Billie exhaled a billow of smoke.

"Why did you move back home?" Dr. Dudley asked.

"Hattie Pearl, I mean Mama, said she needed me at home to help with EJ and Shanay. They were getting older. But she really just wanted to go out at night and needed me at home to watch them," Billie explained.

"As you grew older, your mother continued to go out at night? Where did she go?" Dr. Dudley asked.

"She liked to hang out at the VFW Post in Hixmoor or Carvey," Billie said.

"Did she go alone?"

"Mostly. She never learned how to drive so she would walk. The one in Hixmoor was only two blocks from our house but the VFW in Carvey was almost a mile away."

"So did you take care of your brother and sister?"

"Yeah. I used to get them ready for school in the morning and make their lunches and then fix dinner. I also used to wash and press Shanay's hair once a week."

"Where was Hattie Pearl while you were doing all of these chores?"

"She was usually asleep on the couch. She never did anything except sleep and eat. I did everything else: laundry, shopping, cleaning. She would just recline on the couch listening to the radio and sleeping. She used to take a fly swatter and use the metal end of it to scratch her butt and then she would expect you to use the fly swatter to kill a fly."

Dr. Dudley took a quick puff from her lighted cigarette. "Go on tell me more about Hattie Pearl."

Billie's eyes were wide, and her tone was louder. "I don't know who she thought she was! Why would you scratch your naked butt with something and then expect someone to pick it up and hold it? And then she had this spit bucket that she carried around with her. She would spit into the bucket every ten seconds or so. It was like she was afraid to swallow her own saliva! She never emptied out the spit bucket. It just had this nasty odor all the time. Just thinking about it makes me sick to my stomach."

"Did she chew snuff or tobacco?" Dr. Dudley asked.

"No. She just used to spit into this bucket."

"You're using past tense. Is Hattie Pearl still alive?"

Billie's voice softened, "Yes. Mama's still alive. My dad's in poor health, but he's still alive too. He won't eat her cooking though," she laughed. "When I was a teenager, Mama made him pork chops once and sprinkled the top with Bon Ami cleaning powder instead of flour. You know how the flour used to come in little cans that looked like the Bon Ami or Comet cans? Well, she grabbed what she thought was flour but it was Bon Ami. She fried up those pork chops and fed them to my dad. He thought she was trying to kill him and he stopped eating her cooking that day. I had to start cooking for him after that or Daddy ate at a restaurant. I also cooked for my brother and sister. I think Mama did it on purpose so she wouldn't have to cook anymore."

"Interesting. How is your relationship with your mother now?" Dr. Dudley asked.

"Huh? What do you mean?" Billie asked. Her posture stiffened as she took another pull from her cigarette.

"What type of relationship do you have now?" Dr. Dudley repeated.

"It's close, I guess. She's my mother," Billie said tersely.

"How often do you talk to her?" Dr. Dudley continued to scribble in her notebook.

"I talk to her about once a month and I visit them once or twice a year," Billie replied coarsely.

"Did they move far away? Where do they live now?" Dr. Dudley asked.

"They still live in the house where I grew up in Hixmoor."

"How far is Hixmoor from Newberry East?" Dr. Dudley asked.

Billie stared at Dr. Dudley. "It's about five miles. Why, what's your point?"

"It's interesting that you characterize your relationship with your mother as close, yet she lives less than ten miles away from you, and you only see her once or twice a year and talk to her once a month." Dr. Dudley put the cap on her pen. "Our time is up, Billie. I'll see you next week and we'll continue where we left off."

"I don't see how this is helping me. Why are you so interested in my parents? How often do you see your parents?" Billie asked defensively.

Dr. Dudley's tone was soft and soothing. "This isn't about me, Billie," she reminded gently. "This is about you. I'm going to try to help you, if you'll let me. This is a foundational practice in psychotherapy. In order for me to help you properly, I must learn as much about you as I can, and that means I need to learn about your parents, your life as a child and as much as you can remember and are willing to share. The more detailed and honest you can be with me, the more likely I'll be able to help you. I'm not judging you, Billie. I'm just trying to help you understand what's going on by helping you understand how your past has framed your present." Dr. Dudley stood up and held the office door open. "I'll see you next week," she smiled.

Billie took a pull from her cigarette butt before snuffing it out in the ashtray. She grabbed her overstuffed fake leather purse and stormed out of Dr. Dudley's office.

Chapter 22

Fireworks in June

Brian Kraft was tying his shoelace in front of the camp store when Tanisha raced by. "Hey Teenie! Where's the fire?" he yelled.

"Hey Brian! No fire. I just needed to mail this postcard to a friend, and I didn't want to be late for lunch on my first day as vice president," she gasped.

"Did you send a postcard to your boyfriend?" he teased.

"It's actually to my friend's dog, but that's a long story." The temperature had soared into the high nineties, and Brian was wiping his brow with his swim towel. His hair was still wet from his swim in the lake.

"How was your swim?" Tanisha asked.

"Great! It would have been better had you been there."

Tanisha smiled. "It's so hot I wish we could swim right now, but aren't we swimming later against the Adobe tribe?"

"Yeah. We do our physical challenge at 3:00 against Adobe. So, was your postcard to a boy or girl friend's dog?"

"You sure do ask a lot of questions," Tanisha said. She stared at him suspiciously.

"Well?" he asked.

"It was a boy friend's dog. Two separate words." Tanisha held up two fingers. "Boy – friend."

"So you don't have a boyfriend one word?" Brian asked.

"Nope." Tanisha studied Brian with a quizzical expression. He was cute with his dark hair and olive toned skin, but he was white. She wasn't accustomed to the white boys at Battle Creek Junior High School paying her any attention. Some of her classmates were friendly, but none had ever expressed an interest in her or flirted with her, and Brian Kraft was clearly flirting with her.

"Why do you ask?"

"I'm just curious. We'd better scoot before we're late. You're right, it wouldn't look too good for the president and vice president to be late for the group lunch session. Come with me real quick to drop this towel in my cabin. We still have eight minutes left and my cabin's right there." Brian pointed to the cabin nearest the camp store.

"Okay. So I don't get to ask you any questions?"

"Sure. Shoot." Brian walked swiftly to his cabin.

"Do you have a girlfriend, one word?"

"Can I answer that later?" Brian asked.

Tanisha stared at Brian and wrinkled her nose. "Can you answer that later? It's a simple question."

"You're so cute. You know if you were white, you'd be blonde." Brian ruffled Tanisha's hair.

Tanisha tugged at her reddish brown hair. "I'd be blonde or a red head, I guess. Most of the women on my dad's side of the family have reddish brown hair like mine. But what does my hair color have to do with anything? You didn't answer my question."

Brian was laughing as he opened the door to his cabin. "You didn't get it did you?" he giggled. "You're so funny. Come on in." Brian held the screen door open for Tanisha.

"Girls aren't supposed to be in the boys' cabins, I'll just wait right here," she suggested.

"You're such a goody goody. Don't you ever break the rules? No one's here. It'll just take a second, and if the counselor comes back, I'll take the fall." He pulled her hand and led her inside as the screen door slammed shut.

Tanisha noted that the boys' cabin was similar to the girls with four sets of bunk beds and a single bed for the counselor. Like the girls' cabin, the wooden walls of the cabin were etched with carvings of camper's names and phrases.

"How many cabin mates do you have?" she asked.

Brian hung his wet towel over the edge of the bunk bed headboard and walked toward Tanisha. "We have eight. Bob is in my cabin which is cool."

Tanisha read some of the etchings that were carved into the cabin wall. "Have you etched your initials in the wall yet? My cabin mates told me that we would etch our initials into the walls on the last night of camp." When Brian didn't respond, Tanisha began to turn around to see what he was doing. She was startled when she felt Brian's arms encircle her waist and his breath on her neck. She shivered for a moment as he turned her around to face him. Brian was five feet eleven inches tall, and Tanisha had to tilt her eyes slightly upward to meet his. As his arms encircled her waist, she felt an electric charge run through her body and goose bumps on her arms as his warm breath caressed her face.

"What are you doing, Brian?" she asked.

"Teenie, I won't bite you. I just want to kiss you. But if you don't want me to, I won't. Can I kiss you?"

Tanisha's heart raced as he stared at her. She didn't say a word but nodded her head and softly mumbled, "Okay."

Brian stared into her eyes and gently grabbed her hands and placed them over his shoulder before placing his arms firmly around her waist and pulling her into his chest. He tilted his head to the left and rubbed his cheek against her cheek before gently placing his lips on top of hers. Tanisha closed her eyes and braced herself. His lips were soft and moist as he slowly opened and closed his lips around hers. He gently caressed her mouth with his tongue, slowly parting her lips and running his tongue along the tip of her tongue. His breath tasted like butterscotch candy. Tanisha's heart raced as she inhaled his scent. He smelled of fresh air and shampoo. Brian slowly pulled his lips away as Tanisha opened her eyes. "We'd better go before we're late. I'll answer your question now, Teenie. I think I have a girlfriend. Do I?"

Tanisha smiled with her closed mouth smile. "Sure," she whispered.

Brian peered outside the cabin to ensure the coast was clear. He grabbed Tanisha's hand, and they speed walked back to the Apache Tribe site. Tanisha knew that her face was flush, both from the heat and from her first real kiss.

I can't believe that I just kissed Brian Kraft, and it was so much better than that boiled egg kiss with Darrell Hunter!

Brian's hands were warm and soft. He gripped Tanisha's hand tighter as they approached the Apache Tribe site. She tried to discreetly pull her hand away as Tim, the counselor, walked toward them. But Brian just tightened his grip around her fingers. Tim didn't seem to notice, or didn't seem to care, that Brian and Tanisha held hands as they chatted with him about the afternoon's agenda items.

Trying desperately to listen to Tim and engage in the discussion. Her thoughts were a million miles away. *This cute, white boy actually likes me! He's smart, popular, and he could have paired up with any girl he wanted at camp. But he chose me! This is going to be a fun couple of weeks!*

Chapter 23

Your Fault or Mine?

In the span of less than twenty four hours, Brian Kraft and Tanisha Carlson had become the leadership camp power couple.

"Brian, make sure you and Teenie save me a seat at dinner tonight," Bob requested. "Or should I start calling her, Mrs. Kraft?" Bob teased.

"You guys make a cute couple," gushed Lucy.

Tanisha was shocked that none of the other campers seemed to care that she was black and Brian was white.

As she walked to the lake holding Brian's hand, she thought about the biracial couples that she'd seen in Newberry East.

ℝ℞

Back home, there were two biracial couples at River North High School. In both couples, black football players (Dante and Dion) were openly dating white girls. The teammates were best friends, and so were their girlfriends. The couples held hands in the hallway and stole kisses at their lockers.

Each afternoon, Tanisha was bussed with other honor students to River North from Battle Creek Junior High School for an advanced Algebra class. A few times, Tanisha overheard students in the hallway making derogatory comments about the mixed couples under their breath. She thought it funny that no one ever said anything directly to the football players and their girlfriends, and assumed that the athletes' intimidating physical size was a major factor that contributed to the mumbled comments. That, and the fact that the football superstars had helped propel the school to its first state championship. Dante and Dion were high school royalty at River, and had been nicknamed the Double Ds.

Once, Tanisha overheard some of the upper class black girls at River making comments about the biracial couples.

"I can't believe Dante and Dion are dating those stringy hair white babes," the black girl complained as she rolled her eyes. "You know those white girls are only with them because the Double D's got full scholarships to Notre Dame," she continued.

"Those girls would not be giving them the time of day, if they didn't smell NFL contract on their skin," her friend agreed.

"I don't know what the D's see in them," she continued. "Those girls are pencil thin, and they're not even that cute! They probably barely weigh two hundred pounds combined! I don't know why white girls think it's cute to be so skinny," she groaned. "Dante and Dion are bone crushers. They need to get with the program and date a black girl with some meat on her bones," she finished.

"You know that's right," her friend giggled, shaking her butt playfully. "They need a black girl with some junk in her trunk."

Tanisha giggled quietly, careful not to let the upper class girls know that she had overheard their conversation. "At least they agree with my theory that black girls eat, and white girls don't," she thought.

Tanisha was tempted to share her theory with the girls, but she knew better than to speak to an upper class girl. Since she still attended Battle Creek Junior High, she wasn't considered a high school student by the River North classmates. Some of the sophomores in her Algebra class teased the Battle

Creek Junior High honor students and nicknamed them the "Brainiacs." Tanisha didn't mind the label since there were seven other students who carried the label along with her, including her pals Rashanda and Maria. At the beginning of the semester, a code of conduct was explained to the Brainiacs when the teacher left the room. The code was very simple. Brainiacs did not speak to upper class students unless spoken to first. So Tanisha lowered her head and didn't react to what she'd heard.

₧₨

She smiled as they approached the lake. She was glad that Brian had been chatting with another camper while she day dreamed. Tanisha really hadn't given much thought to biracial couples, and now she was in one. What would her friends think?

The campers pulled off their shorts and tee shirts to reveal their swimsuits. Tanisha wore a yellow one piece that showed off her slim figure. The camp guidelines required that the girls' swimsuits be one piece and the boys wear boxer swim trunks.

"I've only known you for two days, and I've got you taking off your clothes already! I'm the man!" Brian squeezed Tanisha's waist and patted her derriere. She pushed him away glancing around to see if a counselor was watching.

"Cut it out. You're going to get us in trouble," she whispered.

"No one saw that. I'm a smooth operator. I know what I'm doing," Brian teased.

The Apache tribe competed against the Adobe tribe in the afternoon swim challenge event. Brian, Tanisha and Bob had agreed to allow the swim team members to represent the Apache tribe. Brian and Tanisha didn't compete. Brian held Tanisha's hand as they cheered their team on the sidelines. The Apache tribe lost to the Adobe tribe by a length. At the end of the challenge, Brian grabbed Tanisha's hand and plunged into the lake with her. Once under water, Brian pinched her butt with both hands and pecked her on the cheek. Tanisha splashed water in his face and swam away as all of the campers jumped into the water, eager to cool down from the ninety degree heat. Tanisha dunked herself under water and tilted her head back as far as she could to let the lake water smooth back her hair. She'd seen women on television do this before getting out of a pool. Climbing onto the pier, she self consciously pulled her swimsuit from her buttocks and sat on the edge of the pier with her feet dangling in the water. Brian challenged Bob to a race. Tanisha agreed to judge the butterfly race and cheered loudly for Brian as Bob won by three strokes.

"I was distracted by Teenie in that swim suit. I couldn't focus," Brian excused.

"Har har har. Be a good sport and shake his hand, Mr. President," Tanisha commanded.

"No way. He cheated. His girlfriend wasn't here looking cute on the sidelines distracting him," Brian whined.

"I'm going to go and leave you two love birds. I'll see you at dinner at seventeen hundred hours. Bye Newbie!" Bob laughed.

"Don't forget you're giving the report tonight. Make us proud, Bob!" Brian said.

"Bye Rockford." Tanisha glanced around and saw Laura on the shoulders of Mike playing chicken in the shallow end of the lake with two other couples. She'd noticed that Laura and Mike were holding hands as they walked to the challenge event.

Brian sat next to Tanisha on the pier. "So, how are you enjoying leadership camp, Teenie?"

"So far so good. It's not as intense as I expected, but it's only day two."

"This is about as intense as it gets. Once we handle the student government meeting aspect of the camp, they encourage us to have fun."

"Brian, how old are you?" she asked.

"I'm fifteen. I'll be sixteen in September. My birthday is late so I'll be a sophomore at Old Trier next year so this is my last year for leadership camp. If I'm still in student government next year, I'll be a counselor. How old are you?" he asked.

"I'm fourteen. I'll be fifteen in December," Tanisha replied.

"Oh. I thought you were a sophomore like me."

"Is that a problem?" she asked.

"Not for me. I just thought you were older." Brian smoothed Tanisha's hair. "I want to kiss you right now. But the camp has these rules on P.D.A."

"P.D.A.? What's P.D.A.?" she quizzed.

"P.D.A. stands for public displays of affection. They know everyone hooks up down here, but they don't want to see it. Even the counselors hook up. Watch, your counselor probably sneaks out when she thinks you guys are asleep."

Tanisha was glad that he was sitting on her left side so she could more easily conceal her decayed tooth. They cheered loudly for Mike and Laura who were still playing chicken. The sun slowly fell behind the trees taking a few degrees of the sweltering heat with it. Tanisha's thoughts drifted as she studied Brian's profile. Her thoughts were conflicted. She really liked Brian Kraft. When he kissed her, time had stood still. Unlike the kiss that she'd shared with Darrell Hunter at the turnabout dance which was rough and disgusting, she hadn't wanted the kiss with Brian to end. As she played in the water with Brian, her thoughts raced.

Is this how Jack feels about Kerri? What will my friends say when they find out I've been kissing a white boy? What about David Barton? What am I doing?

"Can I ask you something? Am I the first African American girl you've kissed?" she asked quickly.

"No. But you're the prettiest." Brian kicked his feet in the water.

"I'm sure that's true," she laughed. Brian pushed her back into the lake and jumped in beside her. This time she squeezed his butt under water.

℘℧℈

Billie Mae was now ten minutes late for her meeting with Dr. Dudley. She'd left work in plenty of time, but had spent ten minutes smoking in her car, trying to decide if she was going to keep the appointment.

Billie hated the idea of psychotherapy and didn't see how it was helping. She'd been seeing Dr. Dudley for almost two months and didn't feel any different. As far as she was concerned, her weekly meetings with the psychiatrist were only serving to open up childhood wounds that she'd long suppressed. She saw no point in dredging up the past. As her mother always said, "Sometimes it's best to let sleeping dogs sleep."

Dr. Dudley had explained to Billie that she had a bipolar disorder, and Billie had gone to the Newberry East library and done some research on bipolar disorders.

Billie Mae recognized herself in the description, but she knew a lot of people who behaved like she did. Dr. Dudley encouraged her to take lithium to help balance the chemical imbalance that existed, but she resisted when Dr. Dudley told her that she would need to take the medication for the rest of her life in order to be well.

She snuffed out her cigarette and dumped the ashtray on to the asphalt to empty it. She ran her hands along the smooth gray leather seats and decided to make the appointment. She feared that Sonja, the personnel director, would actually terminate her if she didn't meet with Dr. Dudley. She hated the thought of having to give up her beloved car. She grabbed her purse and walked into the medical office.

Dr. Dudley's office was located on the first floor facing the parking lot. She watched Billie from her office window. She saw her dump her ashtray onto the asphalt and waited for her to knock on her office door as was their custom. The office didn't have a waiting area so patients entered into the office from the main corridor. Dr. Dudley always scheduled her patients every forty-five minutes and insisted that patients not knock on the door until their designated appointment time or later so as not to disturb another patient in session. When she was in session with a patient, a sign hung on the doorknob that read IN SESSION. .

"Hello Billie. You're late." Dr. Dudley wore her khaki pants and blue cardigan sweater with her penny loafers and no socks.

"I was in traffic," Billie lied.

"Let's get started since we only have thirty minutes remaining for our session," Dr. Dudley stated.

"But you get paid for forty-five minutes," Billie replied dryly.

"That's true, but when a patient is late, their session is shortened so that my schedule is not conflicted."

Billie plopped down on the small loveseat facing Dr. Dudley's desk. Dr. Dudley sat in the chair against the wall and grabbed her notepad.

"What do you want to know today, doc? What I ate for breakfast when I was ten?" she replied sarcastically.

"If you think that will be helpful, go ahead."

"I was kidding," Billie mumbled.

"We can talk about whatever you'd like to talk about, Billie. I'm here to help you," Dr. Dudley explained.

"But that's just it. I don't think you're helping me. I wasn't caught in traffic. I was sitting in my car thinking about why I have to come see you every week. I'm not crazy! I mean I know I get moody sometimes, but so do a lot of people. I was going to drive off, but I don't want them to fire me, and then I won't be able to afford my car."

"Is that why you're here? So you can keep your car?" Dr. Dudley's tone was soft and soothing.

"I love that car. Sonja in personnel told me that they can fire me if I don't come and see you. I had a little red Omni before I got this car, and I don't want it to get repossessed, so I need my job."

"Tell me about your family," Dr. Dudley suggested.

"You mean my kids?"

"However you define family, Billie," she coached.

"I have four kids: three boys and one girl," Billie sighed. "I'm divorced. I've been divorced for almost a year. I've told you all of this before."

Dr. Dudley fiddled with the cap of her Mont Blanc pen. "So you have four children, and you need your job to afford your car. Interesting."

Unaware of the thinly veiled sarcasm in Dr. Dudley's response, Billie continued. "Yeah. Their father pays child support which covers the rent and buys groceries, but it's not enough for me to afford my car note too so I have to work. You know how it is. I tried to get the judge to make him pay alimony so I wouldn't have to work, but he wouldn't."

"What does your ex-husband do for a living?"

"He's an electrician. He makes good money when he's working," Billie offered.

"But do you think he makes enough to afford alimony?" Dr. Dudley asked.

Billie's tone hardened. "I shouldn't have to work. I had four children."

"What's your home life like? Do you cook meals and clean?" Dr. Dudley continued.

"No. I told you I have four children. I've taught them to take care of themselves. They take turns cooking and cleaning. They do their own laundry."

"You've taught them to take care of themselves the way your mother taught you to take care of yourself."

"Exactly. There's nothing wrong with that. It's how my mama raised us."

"Tell me about your sons," she continued.

Billie described Jack's musical talents, Byron's soccer skills and Allen's artistic abilities with pride.

"So they're good students, and it sounds like they excel in extracurricular activities as well. You must be proud. What about your daughter? What's her name?"

Billie's tone changed. "Her name is Tanisha. She's smart. She is a straight A student, but she and I don't get along. It's hard for women to live in the same house together."

"How old is she?"

"She's fourteen, but she has an attitude. She reminds me of my ex-husband's haughty sisters. He has three sisters and they're real smart. They're hoity toity smart alecks and think they know everything. She's just like them." Billie stared at Dr. Dudley and thought she reminded her of Jackie's sister Helen.

"The teenage years are often difficult for mothers and daughters. But they do pass," Dr. Dudley offered.

"She's been like this her whole life. When Tanisha was born, she looked like a chicken, and I thought she wanted to kill me. I couldn't touch her as a baby, so my husband's mother had to take care of her."

Dr. Dudley shifted in her chair, "Go on."

Billie proceeded to tell Dr. Dudley the story of her severe post partum depression and hospitalizations.

"Were you ever close with Tanisha?" Dr. Dudley asked.

Billie responded without hesitation, "No. I never wanted a girl anyway. They're harder to raise. You have to worry that they'll get pregnant. At least with boys you don't have to worry about that."

"Billie, we're out of time. We can continue where we left off next week."

Dr. Dudley stood up and walked toward the door. "Please try to be on time next week so we will have the full session. By the way, I'd like to speak with your older children, especially your daughter, Tanisha. Would you mind if I called her?"

Billie Mae glared at Dr. Dudley. "Why do you need to speak to my daughter?"

"Sometimes during psychotherapy it's helpful for the therapist to speak with other people in the patient's life to gain a better understanding of the patient," she explained. "I think it might be helpful for me to talk to Tanisha."

"Why don't you want to talk to any of my sons? My oldest son Jack knows me better than Tanisha does."

"I'd like to speak with him as well, but think it would be helpful to talk to your daughter first."

"Well she's not here. She's at some leadership camp until next Saturday. She won some election at school and had to go to this camp for two weeks. I think it's selfish of her to be gone for two weeks, but the school paid for the trip, and her father said I had to let her go."

"That sounds interesting. Okay. I have your number at home, so I'll make a note on my calendar to call Tanisha week after next. Do your children know that you're seeing a psychiatrist?"

"No," Billie shook her head. "I haven't said anything to them about meeting with you."

"I see. Well, I think it would be helpful if you told Jack and Tanisha that you've been meeting with me. And explain to them that I'd like to speak with them on the phone. Once you've done that, I'll call Tanisha." Dr. Dudley walked toward the door and held it open for Billie, removing the in session sign hanging from the doorknob.

"Whatever, you're the so called *expert*." Billie threw her hands up and moved her index and middle fingers up and down like quotation marks. "But I told you we don't really get along so there's no telling what Tanisha will say about me." Billie fumbled in her purse in search of her cigarettes and brushed past Dr. Dudley.

The doctor's phone rang. "I'll see you next week, Billie. Please excuse me, I need to catch this call." Dr. Dudley quietly closed the door to her office. Once in the hallway, Billie fumbled in her purse for her cigarettes as she walked. In desperate need of a cigarette, her head down, she didn't notice when the men's restroom door opened and a tall gentleman stepped into the hallway, Billie careened into his path.

Billie bumped into the man and dropped her purse, spilling its contents on the floor.

"Shit! Why don't you look where you're going?" Billie glared as she crawled on the floor to pick up her things.

"I beg your pardon miss, but you bumped into me." The man studied Billie with a raised eyebrow. "Are you okay? Let me help you with your things," he offered.

"Do I look okay? My things are scattered all over the floor!" Billie stuffed loose tissues and pieces of Dentyne gum into her purse. Her hand shook as she grabbed the pack of cigarettes and picked up the red lighter that had slid under the water fountain. She tossed her car keys into her purse and stood to light her cigarette. Her hands shook uncontrollably from nicotine withdrawal. Determined, she held the cigarette in between the fingers on her left hand and grabbed that hand with her right hand in a futile attempt to light her cigarette and calm her nerves with a nicotine hug. But her right hand was shaking as much as her left, and she couldn't flick the lighter.

"Here, let me help you." The man gently took the lighter from Billie and calmly lit her cigarette for her. Billie's gaze was steely as she studied his face. He handed her the lighter and smiled.

She inhaled deeply and took a long pull from her cigarette. As the nicotine ran through her body, she felt herself relaxing. She smiled and spoke. "Thank you. Sorry about bumping into you. I've had a rough day." Billie pushed open the doors to the medical center and walked down the stairs to the parking lot.

"No problem." He shook his head and proceeded down the hall to the office of Dr. Elliot Dudley. He knocked twice and opened the door.

"Hey Mom!" he bellowed. "I thought I'd surprise you and stop by your office instead of meeting you and dad at the club. I'm not too early am I?" David Barton walked around the desk, grabbed his mother in a large bear squeeze and kissed her on the cheek.

Chapter 24

Another Child's Shame

Dr. Dudley removed her reading glasses and gently stroked David's face with her right hand.

"Hello there, handsome!" she gushed. "What a nice surprise! No, you're not too early. I just finished with my last patient, and I was completing some paperwork!" Dr. Dudley stretched her arms into the air and swiveled around to face her son.

Elliot Ernestine Dudley-Barton, MD was named after her maternal grandparents. She was forty-eight years old and still enjoyed the shock on people's faces when they realized that Dr. Elliot Dudley was a woman. As a child, she'd been teased mercilessly about having a boy's name, but she'd always enjoyed it. She'd loved her grandfather Elliot and felt honored to carry his name. Her nickname had become Elle. As a teenager, she considered legally changing her name to Eleanor or Elle, or switching the order of her first and middle name. But she thought this would dishonor her grandfather's memory and her mother's intent, so she remained Elliot Dudley. When she applied to join the army's medical training program, she was certain that her name helped her gain admission. Her grades were exemplary and she'd marked female on the gender box, but when she appeared for her basic training, there was shock and dismay when they realized that she was a woman. Nonetheless, she completed her basic training, along with one other female recruit, and finished near the top of her medical school graduating class. When she married, they decided that she should use her maiden name professionally in an effort to avoid confusion in a house with two medical doctors. Her husband was a progressive thinker and fully supported his wife's decision.

David walked around the desk and plopped down on the small sofa. "How was your day, Dr. Dudley?" he smiled.

"It was fine. Same old same old. How was yours?" Dr. Dudley shuffled the papers on her desk to clear away the clutter before they left for dinner.

"It was cool. On my way out of the bathroom, this lady bumped into me and looked at me like she wanted to kill me. I thought she was going to curse me out. And then she was so nervous she couldn't even light her cigarette. She barely mumbled thank you when I helped her pick up the stuff from her purse. She calmed down and apologized once she started smoking her cigarette. Was she a patient of yours?" David played with the gadgets on his mother's coffee table. She kept an assortment of gadgets on her table in case her patients needed to do something with their hands. He pulled a tiny rake through a platter full of sand, sorting the tiny seashells and sailboats that lay in the soft white sand.

He must have bumped into Billie. Elle continued to clear off her desk. "David, you know I do not discuss my patients. Besides, there are at least twenty doctors in this medical building. The woman that you bumped into could have been anyone's patient. She could have been a patient of your dads. Did you wash your hands when you left the bathroom?"

"I know, but she looked like she could use some psychiatric help. She was pretty, but she just looked a little agitated. I thought she was one of your patients. And yes, I washed my hands! Mom, I'm almost seventeen years old, do you still need to ask me if I've washed my hands?" David put the rake down and picked up a Rubik's cube and tried to sort the puzzle.

"You're right. I'm sorry, sweetie, force of habit. Is your dad ready to go?" Elle locked the files in her file cabinet and pulled out her purse.

"Naw, I didn't see him in the hall when I came in," David offered.

Elle stared at David and raised her left eyebrow. "Naw? Is that how you talk now?" Elle admonished.

David put the Rubik's cube back on the table and corrected himself. "I mean No. Do you want me to knock on his door and see if he's ready?"

"No. He's probably still with a patient. You know how your dad is. He's a stickler for time, so I'm sure he'll be down here any minute. I'm going to run to the ladies' room. We can wait for him in the hallway so I can lock up my office."

Elle removed her cardigan and hung it in the small closet in her credenza. She kept four cardigans in her closet. All were identical except for the color. She had a navy blue one, a green one, a red one and a yellow one. She alternated the color every day. She felt that it was best to keep her attire simple when meeting with patients so that they would not focus on her clothes but instead focus on themselves and their issues. David often teased her that she was a female Mr. Rogers with her closet full of cardigans. When she met with her patients, she liked to exude a sense of calm, confidence and simplicity in dress, speech and manner.

Elliot Dudley was a highly regarded psychiatrist. Her goal was to get her patients to trust her, and she did whatever she needed to do to accomplish that objective. Elle had a soft spoken voice and would soften her tone even further when a patient became irate or agitated during a session, sometimes lowering her voice to a soft whisper. This technique forced the patient to listen intently in order to hear her, and the patient would unconsciously begin to speak in a softer tone. *A whisper often begets a whisper.*

Elle was not a smoker, but had smoked briefly during medical school. When she met Billie Mae, Elle smelled the smoke in her clothes. She had reviewed Billie Mae's file from Dr. Benson at the cable company and read that he believed she had a bipolar disorder. She also read that Billie was not receptive to treatment and displayed hostile behaviors during his sessions with her. At their first session, in an effort to establish trust with Billie, Elle decided to pull out a stale pack of cigarettes that she kept tucked in her desk. When she asked Billie if she could try one of her cigarettes, she could see Billie's demeanor soften. Dr. Dudley had succeeded in establishing a sense of commonality with Billie through a perceived smoker's bond. She had only taken two quick pulls from the cigarette which lay idle in the ashtray the remainder of the session, but her smoking ploy had succeeded in making Billie feel more comfortable, and she began to speak openly about her past.

Elle slipped into the ladies room as David continued down the hall to wait for his dad. As Elle washed her hands in the sink, her thoughts drifted to when David was eleven years old and he pleaded with her not to tell his friends that she was a psychiatrist when they moved to Morning Side.

⊱⊰

"*Mom, just tell my new friends that you and dad are in practice together. If they think you're a shrink, they won't want to come over. They'll think you're trying to psychoanalyze them or something,*" he pleaded.

"*David, I'm not going to lie about my profession. And don't use the term shrink. I am proud that I'm trained to help people with problems that affect their emotional well being. I can't believe you're ashamed of what I do. I finished in the top of my medical class and was only one of two women in the class. You should be proud of what I do, not ashamed. Your father and I didn't raise you that way.*"

"*Mom, I'm not ashamed of you. I'm glad you're a doctor, and I know you help people with brain illnesses the same way dad helps people with physical illnesses. It's just that I don't want my new friends to know that you're a psychiatrist yet. Just tell them you work with dad, okay?*"

"*Well, technically, we are in the same office building.*"

"*Exactly. When people ask me, I'll just tell them that you and dad share an office and practice together. Thanks mom!*" David gave her a big hug and buried his face into her bosom and didn't retreat when she stroked his hair. Elle was so overwhelmed by the uncharacteristic display of affection from her pre-teen son that she silently agreed to honor his request.

ജ

Elle dried her hands on a paper towel and applied lipstick. She removed her bun and brushed her shoulder length hair. *Funny, sometimes no matter what you do or who you are, parents are often a source of embarrassment or shame to their children.*

She stared at her reflection in the mirror and shook her hair. *I hope I am able to help Billie Mae Peterson. She seems like such a nice woman, and her family sounds nice too. Her children are doing well academically, and don't appear to have any behavioral issues that would increase Billie's stress level. I certainly hope I can get through to her, and make a positive difference in her life. But my skills will only help her if she's willing to examine her behavior and commit to a lifestyle change. It's so sad that people are still ashamed to admit that they have psychological medical issues.*

Elle decided to wear her hair loose and quickly tucked the bobby pins in her purse as the restroom door creaked openly slowly.

"Mom, are you ready?" David asked. "Dad is ready to go to dinner now."

"I'm coming. I'm coming. Tell that man to calm down or I'll take my sweet time," Elle giggled.

"I heard that, Elle Barton," David's father barked. "Come out of that bathroom woman or I'll come in there and carry you out."

"You haven't the strength in your old back to carry me anymore, and you know it, you old goat," Elle teased.

"Don't test me, woman," Dr. Barton laughed. "Now let's go. I'm hungry, and the club is serving tuna melts tonight."

David smiled as his dad held the car door open for his mother. He watched as she playfully kissed his dad on the cheek before he closed the door. He enjoyed watching his parents' playfulness. After twenty two years of marriage, they remained friends, and were very much in love.

He climbed into his Corvette and headed to the country club for dinner. *I hope I can have a relationship as solid as my parent's one day. They're my heroes. I wonder how Tanisha is doing at leadership camp.*

Chapter 25

Why Not You?

Tanisha tilted her head back in the shower and lathered shampoo through her hair. She loved the smell of shampoo and inhaled deeply as the aromatic bubbles drifted into her nostrils. That afternoon she'd splashed around in the lake with Brian for almost twenty minutes after the tribe athletic competitions were complete. She enjoyed his game of playfully dunking her underwater and allowed his hands to slide down her torso squeezing her small waist as he tossed her in the lake. She squealed and swam towards him in an effort to retaliate only to have him hold her at arm's length before slowly lowering his hands down her torso and tickling her. When she attempted to swim away, he swam after her, grabbed her gently around her waist and repeated the maneuver. Each time, Brian was careful not to get caught by the counselors who were only casually watching the campers. Tanisha and Brian cheered as Laura and Mike were crowned the chicken champions after successfully defeating all other competitors in the friendly game of aquatic wrestling. Laura was a muscular girl and stood almost five feet seven inches tall. Atop Mike's broad shoulders, they were an unbeatable force.

As the sun began to slowly set, the temperatures cooled down into the mid eighties. Tanisha and Brian lay on their towels on the small strip of sand and watched as the other campers slowly disappeared to change for dinner. Tanisha noticed that many of the campers seemed to be coupled off. She smiled as she watched Monica sitting under a tree batting her eyelashes at Brian's friend Bob. Tanisha giggled as Bob practiced his Apache tribe overview speech in front of Monica thinking that Monica was probably not listening to a word he was saying as she gazed into his eyes.

"What's so funny, Teenie?" Brian asked. Tanisha pointed to Monica and Bob.

"It looks like Monica is putting the full court press on Bob, and he doesn't have a clue. He's totally into his presentation for tonight," she answered.

"Yeah, that's my boy Bob. He takes his role as secretary very seriously. He plans to be a news journalist some day and wants to be the White House correspondent for a major news network. He's well on his way to achieving his goal. But I hope he stops to have some fun since camp is only two weeks long." Brian arched his back and sat with his legs crossed like a pretzel. He rubbed at a large mosquito bite on his ankle. "I think they look cute together."

"Ditto. I like Rockford and Monica's a sweetheart. I'm glad I got cool cabin mates. My first camp experience three years ago was a bust. I was the only African American girl at camp, and the other girls weren't friendly at all. It was lonely and I was homesick so I just faked sick, and my parents picked me up early," Tanisha explained.

"Get outta here? Didn't they know you were faking?" Brian laughed.

"I don't think so. I think my dad may have suspected that I was faking, but since I'd had a kidney infection a few weeks before, they didn't want to chance it. My dad picked me up and I was outta there. I'm glad I made friends this time."

Brian looked over his shoulder and quickly rubbed Tanisha's thigh. "So am I. Let's hang out after dinner okay?"

Tanisha felt a tingle rush up her spine. She glanced around to make sure a counselor wasn't looking and allowed Brian's hand to linger on her thigh for a few seconds before blushing and removing his hand.

"Okey dokey, whatever you say, Mr. President." Tanisha gave Brian a military salute.

Brian laughed. "I'm starving! I'll meet you at the mess hall at seventeen hundred hours."

Tanisha giggled and saluted Brian again. "Yes sir!"

She wrapped her beach towel around her waist and slipped on her flip flops rushing to catch up to Laura who was heading back to their cabin.

Tanisha and Laura strolled to their cabin to grab their shower buckets and wash the lake water from their hair and dress for dinner. Most of the campers had showered and the shower stall was almost empty. Tanisha had gotten accustomed to the open shower that held eight shower nozzles. That morning, some of the campers had asked her why she wore a shower cap and didn't wash her hair in the morning, and she'd explained again that African American hair didn't need to be washed every day. She was glad that she needed to wash her hair and wouldn't have to answer any questions about her pink shower bonnet. She rinsed her hair straight back one more time before toweling off and wrapping her bath towel around her hair and her beach towel around her body. She'd done her best to shake most of the sand from her towel but could feel a few sand pebbles against her wet skin.

She plugged her curling iron into the socket before getting in the shower. She'd forgotten to bring a blow dryer, but Laura had brought her blow dryer, so Tanisha quickly started blow drying her hair while Laura showered.

Tanisha glanced at her watch and realized that she had thirty minutes before dinner. She blow dried her hair quickly. Laura stepped out of the shower just as Tanisha finished with it.

Laura walked over to the mirrors. "Your hair looks cute like that Teenie. You should just wear it straight," Laura suggested. "Mike is so adorable! I'm so glad we hooked up."

Tanisha crinkled her nose and shook her head. "Thanks, but I don't think so. Besides, I have to put a few curls in my hair, because the heat from the curling iron helps straighten it out more," she explained. "Thanks for letting me use your blow dryer. I can't believe I forgot mine. Mike is cute and you guys look cute together," Tanisha offered.

"Thanks. I'm so glad he won that runoff election. I would have died if that creep George won President! So now Mike and I are a tribal power couple just like you and Brian. Brian totally adores you by the way. I can tell." Laura combed through her wet hair.

"You think?" Tanisha blushed. "I really like him. He's cool. He kissed me," she whispered. "It was so awesome. I guess we're going together."

"You guess? You two are so totally an item. Now we just need to find someone for Monica and Sharon."

"What do you mean?" Tanisha asked innocently.

"Everyone always hooks up at leadership camp, Teenie. It's the thing. I think Monica likes Bob from your section. But I haven't found anyone for Sharon yet."

Everyone always hooks up at camp. It's the thing? What does that mean? "Who did you hook up with last summer?" Tanisha asked. She curled her hair as Laura dried off.

"His name was Ed, but he's not here this summer. I was trying to hook up with Brian this year, but he was so into you that I didn't have a chance. It's cool though because Mike is the bomb!" Laura towel dried her hair and turned on the blow dryer. "Find out if Brian has any friends for Sharon."

Tanisha finished curling her hair and got dressed. She slathered lotion over her legs and arms and smoothed out her curls. The campers weren't required to wear their camp tee shirts to dinner so Tanisha decided to wear a pair of white shorts and a pink halter top.

"Laura, I'm going to head back to the cabin. I'll wait for you over there so we can walk to dinner together." Tanisha spoke loudly over the noise of the blow dryer.

Laura nodded her head and gave Tanisha a thumbs up sign.

When Tanisha returned to the cabin, Monica and Sharon were chatting animatedly. Tanisha placed her shower bucket on the desk in the corner and joined their conversation.

"Sharon, he's so your type," Monica squealed as she brushed her hair.

"What do you think, Teenie?"

"What do I think about what? Who are you guys talking about?" Tanisha sat on her bed.

"Oh, I thought you heard that part," Sharon said. "Monica thinks I should hook up with Derrick. He's the black guy in the Adobe section. He's cute, but I don't know," Sharon explained.

"Do you like him?" Tanisha stood up and grabbed the brush from Monica and continued to gently brush Monica's hair. *Brushing her hair feels like brushing Grace or Maria's hair. It's the same texture.*

"I'm not sure. I just met him yesterday. He seems nice enough, but he seems kind of silly," she shared. "But Monica thinks that he likes me." Sharon played with the shoe laces of her sneakers

"He was totally checking her out today in the lake," Monica said. "He couldn't keep his eyes off of her," she explained. "Teenie, you brush so softly," Monica cooed. "I feel so relaxed. It feels like when my mom brushes my hair. My mother brushes my hair at night before I go to bed," she said softly. "It gives us a chance to talk," she yawned.

"Some of my friends at school have long hair, and I always brush it for them," she explained gently shaking Monica's shoulders. "Wake up there, sleepyhead! No napping! We haven't even had dinner yet!" she laughed. "But Sharon, if you think Derrick is cute, then why don't you get to know him?" Tanisha asked.

Sharon bit her lip. "No offense, Teenie, but I've never hung out with a black guy before. What's it like?" Sharon stared at Teenie curiously.

Tanisha opened her eyes wide. "Well, I don't have that much experience, but it's no different than hanging out with a white guy I guess. I've never hung out with a white guy before, and now I'm hanging out with Brian Kraft."

Monica tilted her head up to stare at Tanisha. "You've never dated a white guy before? You guys seemed so comfortable with each other that I thought you dated white guys all the time."

"Me too," Sharon said.

"Nope. This is the first." Tanisha continued to brush Monica's hair.

"Teenie, if you don't mind my asking, but why weren't you interested in Derrick?" Sharon asked.

"It's not that I wasn't interested in him. I actually saw him on the first day before I met you guys. But he barely spoke to me. And then I heard him say to his friend that I wasn't his type." Tanisha shrugged her shoulders.

"Really? He really said that? But you're so cute." Sharon sat on the floor with her hands under her chin.

"He actually said that he likes blondes, which is fine because he's not my type anyway," Tanisha continued. "He's a little short for my taste."

"But he's black, and he's cute," Sharon said.

"Just because he's black and I'm black doesn't mean we're into each other. By the way, I prefer the term African American," she corrected. "Just because we're both African American doesn't mean that we're attracted to each other. You're not attracted to every white guy that's at camp are you, Sharon?"

"No. I never thought of it that way." Sharon studied Tanisha's face. "I never thought of that. I'm not just attracted to someone because he's white. Good point."

"Sharon, Derrick is totally into you," Monica encouraged.

"I don't know if I would feel comfortable kissing him. I've never kissed a black guy before. I mean an African American guy before," Sharon corrected. "I've kissed a few white guys before and one Japanese guy, but I've never kissed a black guy."

Tanisha finished brushing Monica's hair and sat across from Sharon on the floor. "Well, I'd never kissed a white guy before, and I kissed Brian Kraft today and it was fabulous!" she shrugged.

"Get outta here! It's not even the bewitching hour yet, and you've already kissed Brian?" Monica spritzed her head with hair spray.

"The bewitching hour? What's the bewitching hour?" Tanisha stared at Monica.

"After dinner and before the closing session, everyone disappears for an hour to make out. It's called the bewitching hour. You'll see," Monica explained.

"So what was it like, Teenie? Kissing a white guy for the first time, did it feel weird?" Sharon asked. "And where did you guys kiss and not get caught by the counselors?"

Everyone hooks up at camp. It's the thing. Everyone makes out after dinner. Is this what Laura meant?

"Teenie, did you hear me?" Sharon repeated.

"I'm sorry, I heard you. I was just spacing out. It felt good. I've only kissed one other guy before. A few months ago, I kissed a guy at my school's Turnabout Dance, which is our Sadie Hawkins dance," she paused as Sharon tilted her head and stared at her with a puzzled expression. "It's where the girls ask the boys, and we pay for everything," Tanisha explained. "You've never heard of a Sadie Hawkins dance?" Sharon shook her head no.

"We have that at my school, too," Monica shared. "It's our annual spring dance."

"Anyway, he was African American and it should go down in history as the worst first kiss experience ever recorded! It was a horrible nightmare," Tanisha grimaced. "I don't think it was horrible because he was African American. He was just a bad kisser. He had bad breath and food stuck in his braces." Tanisha tightened her face like she'd just sucked into a sour lemon.

"You're too funny, Teenie," Monica giggled.

"Where did you kiss Brian?" Sharon repeated.

"We kissed in his cabin," Tanisha explained. "It was really quick. He was dropping off his towel, so I walked with him."

"You seem like such a goody goody, and here you are making out with Brian in his cabin!" Sharon cooed. "I'm so jealous! I want to make out with someone!"

"I was afraid to go in there, but he assured me that he would take the blame if we got caught," Tanisha explained. "And for the record, we didn't make out. It was just a quick kiss. I was only in there for about five minutes."

"Maybe I'll sit next to Derrick at dinner." Sharon stood up and walked over to her dresser. "I hope he doesn't have bad breath," she shared casually.

"Sharon! Not all African Americans have bad breath!" Tanisha scolded. "Just because I kissed one black guy with bad breath, don't create a stereotype about African American guys having bad breath, okay?" Tanisha coached.

The screen door slammed as Laura walked into the cabin. "Who has bad breath?"

"We found someone for Sharon to hook up with," Monica offered.

"He has bad breath, and you're still hooking up with him? Gross!" Laura frowned.

The girls were startled by the screen door slamming again. "Hey ladies! How are my favorite campers?" Liz asked.

The girls giggled as Liz grabbed her shower bucket.

"Glad to see you guys getting along so well, but what's so funny?" Liz grinned. "Do I have a bat in the cave?" she asked. She self consciously checked her nose and smiled at Tanisha. "Teenie, do you want to let me in on the joke?"

Tanisha shook her head lightly and shrugged. "It's nothing, Liz. We were just trying to convince Sharon that she should try chocolate milk at dinner. She was saying that she'd never tasted chocolate milk, and we thought that was funny."

"I love chocolate milk. That's why the chocolate milk cow dispenser is always empty." Liz grabbed a change of clothes from her dresser and continued. "Most of the campers prefer chocolate milk although white milk has less sugar."

"That's what we told Sharon," Monica explained. "We told her that she should try the chocolate milk tonight, and if she doesn't like it, she can always go back to white milk." Monica could barely contain the giggles.

"I told her that chocolate milk is usually much sweeter than white milk," Tanisha said seriously. "But today I had white milk and it was pretty sweet." Sharon's face turned beet red.

"Sharon, I can't believe you've never tried chocolate milk. I hate milk, but I'll drink chocolate milk occasionally. It is sweeter." Laura said to the mirror as she brushed her hair.

"I better scurry. I only have ten minutes to shower before dinner. I'll see you ladies at campfire tonight if I don't see you at dinner." Liz hurried out of the cabin and slammed the screen door.

"Laura, we're not really talking about chocolate milk," Monica exhaled in a fit of giggles.

Tanisha and Monica brought Laura up to speed on Derrick and Sharon.

"Oh, I get it. Derrick is the chocolate milk." Laura applied blush to her cheeks.

"You're quick, Laura!" Tanisha winked.

"Har Har, Teenie!" Laura laughed.

"It looks like I like chocolate milk and white milk, but the chocolate milk that I tasted a few months ago was definitely sour," Tanisha laughed loudly.

"I'm so glad we're all getting along," Sharon squealed. "Last year there was a black girl in our cabin named Julie, in fact, she's here this year. She was a total dweeb," Sharon frowned. "She was no fun at all, and she didn't even try to get to know anyone."

"I remember her," Laura agreed. "I really went out of my way to try and be friendly to her because she was in my section last year, and she was the only black girl at camp, and I thought she might feel left out, but she was a downer. Actually, I was hesitant to get to know you, Teenie, because I was afraid that you were going to act like Julie. But you're so not like her," Laura finished. "Have you met her, Teenie?"

"I met her briefly when I arrived, and she was not friendly to me either. So it must not be a black- white thing," Teenie concluded. "She's just antisocial and mean. I introduced myself to her, and she said 'just because we're both African American that does not mean that we're going to be friends at camp,'" Tanisha mocked sarcastically. "I wanted to smack her," Tanisha grimaced.

"I can totally hear her saying something like that," Sharon said, "That's her loss, because you're funny and you fit in so well with us. Are you sure you aren't really a white girl in disguise?" Sharon giggled.

"Come on girls, let's head to dinner, I'm starving!" Monica slipped on her shoes.

"I have a little white in my blood like most African American slave descendants, but not enough to be a white girl," Tanisha laughed. "But you hungry babes might have some black in you. I've never seen skinny white girls eat as much as you do," she laughed. "You're disproving my hypothesis."

"What's your hypothesis, Teenie?" Laura asked.

"It's pretty edgy, but I think you guys can handle it so here goes," she said. "Black girls eat. White girls don't," Tanisha stated. She braced herself for their reaction.

"Teenie! That sounds so racist!" Monica scolded. Laura and Sharon laughed.

"It's not racist, Monica," Laura giggled. "It's funny! Black girls eat, white girls don't," she repeated. "We should have tee-shirts made!" she squealed. "It would be our own private joke to remember our camp experience!"

"We could add a small sentence at the bottom of our shirts that reads: dot, dot, dot, but I eat like a black girl," Sharon continued.

"Works for me," Tanisha said.

The girls primped one last time in front of the small hand mirror strategically tilted between the wall and the scattered toiletries on the dresser before walking to dinner.

Chapter 26

The Poppy Field

The mess hall was a large open air pavilion that was open on three sides and affectionately known as "Camp Slop." Camp Slop was located in the center of the camp grounds adjacent to a small cabin that served as the food preparation and serving house. There were five rows of picnic table benches lined end to end under the pavilion. Perpendicular to the picnic tables stood an elevated platform that ran the width of the pavilion and served as the presentation stage with a small microphone atop a stand. The stage shared the back wall with the doorway leading to the kitchen. When the girls arrived at the mess hall, Sharon saw some of the members of the Adobe tribe at a table with Derrick, so she decided to join them.

Laura spotted Mike and Brian holding a table for them. Mike waved the girls over to join them. The boys had already gotten their plates and were eating burgers, fries and salad. The girls rushed to get their food so that they wouldn't miss the tribe updates. Bob was on the stage preparing to give his update speech. Tanisha sat next to Brian with Laura on her left and Mike next to Laura. Monica sat across from Tanisha next to the notebook and pen that belonged to Bob.

The girls were in the middle of their meal when Bob began his tribal update. He highlighted the day's events in a pithy, humorous fashion. Unexpectedly, he invited Brian and Tanisha to the stage to be introduced.

Stunned at hearing her name being called, Tanisha barely had time to wipe the dripping mayonnaise from her fingers as Brian reached for her hand. They ascended the two stairs and joined Bob on the stage. The campers clapped as Brian and Tanisha approached the podium.

"And to my right is Brian "Mr. President" Kraft," Bob pointed. "Better known to the tribe as 'Right Guard' although some days I think he used the Left Guard instead of the Right Guard," he chuckled. The campers laughed as though on cue. "And to my left is our lovely Vice President, Tanisha "Teenie" Carlson from Newberry East, Illinois," Bob bowed. "I call her Newbie," he continued. "And it's no Secret to the Apache tribe that we're glad she's on our team," he winked.

Tanisha blushed and flashed her famous closed mouth smile at the campers. She was glad she'd worn her cute pink halter top and had curled her hair and put on lip gloss.

"Mr. President, would you like to say a few words. I think we have twenty seconds left," Bob offered.

"Thanks Bob. I think the Apache tribe has a strong leadership team, and I'm excited to work with Bob and my buddy, Teenie. But I'm more excited to work with Teenie than Bob because she's obviously prettier than this guy." Brian playfully ribbed Bob in the chest. "Would you like to say a few words, Teenie?"

Tanisha wasn't prepared to make a speech. She swallowed hard and took a deep breath. "Sure. Thanks for the compliment, Mr. President. But I think if we put Bob in a pink halter, and put some lip gloss on him, he might turn a few heads and give me some serious competition," she teased. To her delight, the mess hall cheered wildly.

The Apache leadership team hi-fived each other and walked back to the table to finish dinner.

"That was awesome, Teenie! We didn't even rehearse that, and you just played right along." He squeezed her thigh under the table and ran his finger to the edge of her shorts.

"Thanks!" Tanisha's heart was racing. "I figured since we were all goofing around, I'd just play along."

Brian used his napkin to wipe barbeque sauce from the corner of Tanisha's mouth.

"Oh, wasn't that cute? You two slay me. But thanks for hamming it up with me. I think the reports are better if they're funny and a little impromptu," Bob offered.

"You did a good job, Rockford," Tanisha said sincerely.

The campers devoured their dinner, and the boys cleared the dinner plates, offering to retrieve dessert for the table which consisted of spice cake and strawberry gelatin.

When the boys disappeared, the girls huddled along one side of the picnic bench and Monica spoke first.

"So do you think Bob likes me?" Monica spoke quickly.

"Sure he does. What's not to like? He's just a little geeky and shy. You're totally hanging out with us during bewitching hour, aren't you?" Laura asked.

"Absolutely, but only if Bob goes," Monica replied. She applied more lip gloss and tucked it back into her pocket.

"Look guys! I think Sharon and Derrick are hitting it off," Tanisha pointed.

The girls glanced in the corner and saw Sharon and Derrick engaged in an animated discussion at their table.

"We're back ladies. Hope you didn't talk about us too badly." Brian placed his dessert on the table.

"We roasted you," Tanisha teased. "There's so much material on you guys, it was easy." Brian cut his eyes at Tanisha and winked.

The boys plopped down on the opposite side of the picnic bench across from the girls. Brian winced and slowly rubbed his thigh where a tiny splinter had lodged. The campers ate strawberry gelatin and spice cake and discussed the community service projects that their tribes were conducting. Traditionally, each tribe was charged with introducing a program or project to enhance the leadership camp or the surrounding community. The Apache tribe had decided to focus on donating leftover food from the camp's three meals to a food pantry in downtown Springfield. The Adobe tribe's goal was water conservation achieved primarily by limiting showers and monitoring the drinking water waste. The discussion was lively and animated as the campers shared their ideas.

"I think it's a good idea to give food to the food pantry, but how will you get it to them?" Laura asked. "You'll be relying on the food pantry to pick it up every day which means you'll have to appoint campers to miss some of the camp activities to wait for the pick-ups."

"Exactly. But we've already designed a schedule that addresses that," Tanisha explained. "We've set it up so the volunteers on that particular day only miss about one hour of activities. You'll see. Now how is Adobe going to monitor showers to conserve water? It's a good idea, but it's a bit ambitious don't you think?"

"I agree. I'd like to be the timekeeper in the girls' shower stall," Bob laughed. But how are you really going to monitor that?" he asked.

"We're working with the head maintenance engineer on a system that automatically adjusts the water temperature after a certain amount of time," Mike offered.

"Mike, don't tell them what we're doing. They're in the enemy tribe! We don't want Apache one upping us on our project," Monica said.

Tanisha noticed as Brian checked his watch and nudged Mike.

"Good point! You'll learn more about our project in due time." Mike stared at Brian agitatedly before winking in agreement. "Hey! Who wants to go see the Indian burial ground on the trail path?"

"No thanks. These mosquitoes are eating me for dinner." Tanisha rubbed a fresh mosquito bite on her bicep. "I can only imagine how bad they are in the woods. I'll pass."

"I'd like to see it!" Laura said excitedly and kneed Tanisha under the table.

"Ouch! Why'd you do that? That hurt, Laura!" Tanisha rubbed her knee. Laura mouthed "Bewitching Hour" and batted her long eyelashes before opening her eyes as wide as saucers. Tanisha squinted her eyes and tried to read Laura's lips. She glanced quickly at Brian who winked at her. "I guess I can spray some bug spray and go too. I've never seen an Indian burial ground."

"That's my girl! We'll just lather on mosquito repellent. There's some on the first aid table by the water. Bob, you and Monica should come too," Brian suggested.

"Works for me. I might get some information for my next report," Bob said.

Once again, the boys grabbed the dishes and dropped them in the dirty dish bin.

Laura waited until the boys were out of earshot before speaking. "Teenie! You almost blew it!" Laura groaned. "They want to take us to see the Indian burial ground, but it's really going to be the bewitching hour."

Teenie rubbed her throbbing knee. "Well, why didn't you just say that? And your boney knee hurt like crazy!"

"I'm sorry, Teenie," Laura said sincerely before continuing. "The boys don't think we know what they're up to. It's silly, but we like to let them think that it's their idea. You know, they're taking us on a walk to show us something," Laura whispered and winked.

"I know. Last year the guy I bewitched with told me he wanted to show me a red tail eagle's nest. Of course I went along with it, but I knew it was bogus because my mother is a wildlife preservationist, and red tail eagles don't nest in Springfield," Monica stated pointedly. "He wasn't the brightest bulb in the chandelier, but he was a good kisser though. He moved to Reading, Pennsylvania last summer."

The girls stopped at the first aid table to apply mosquito repellent. Tanisha looked up and noticed the setting sun casting a purple haze across the camp grounds. She reached for the Deep Woods Off spray and misted her legs and arms as the crickets serenaded the campers who seemed oblivious to the natural concert in their midst.

Tanisha applied mosquito repellent to Monica's back as Brian walked up behind her and whispered. "Teenie, don't spray any on your neck, okay?" he advised.

"Why not?" Tanisha misted her legs and arms again.

"Just don't, okay? I'll explain in a few minutes." Brian lightly traced his finger down Tanisha's back which made her giggle.

"Listen ladies," Brian whispered. "The guys will walk out first, and you guys follow us in five minutes. We don't want the counselors to see all six of us walking into the woods together or they'll get suspicious."

"Good point. We'll hang around the mess hall and get water or something." Laura wiped her hands with a baby wipe and passed around the baby wipe tub for the others to follow suit.

Tanisha watched as Brian, Mike and Bob disappeared down a trail in the woods.

The girls walked back over to the food area and got water.

"Does anyone have a mint?" Monica asked.

"No, but I have some gum in my bag at the cabin." Tanisha thought about the care package that David Barton had packed for her. It was the first time since writing him a postcard that he crossed her mind. *I wonder what David is doing? Am I cheating on David by kissing Brian Kraft? How could I be? David isn't my boyfriend, we're just getting to know each other. Besides, everyone hooks up at camp. It's the thing.*

Laura reached into her shorts and pulled out a pack of mints. "Here you go ladies. I was a girl scout for four years, so I'm always prepared! You have to have mints on you for the bewitching hour. Watch and learn, ladies. Watch and learn." She passed around a packet of white tic tacs.

Tanisha popped three tic tacs in her mouth. "It sounds like you're a bewitching hour expert, Miss Laura."

"You got it, Teenie," Laura smiled. "I'm a bewitching hour veteran. Let's move it. We only have about an hour before we have to check in for campfire. I think it's safe to go now."

As the girls walked out of the mess hall, they bumped into Liz, their cabin counselor.

"Hey roomies! Where are you girls headed?" Liz's posture was perfect, and she looked poised to do a cheerleader A jump. She stared directly at Tanisha awaiting a response. For once, Tanisha was at a loss for words.

Laura spoke first. "We're going to show Teenie some of the campgrounds since this is her first time here."

"Great! Did you spray mosquito repellent?" Liz bent down to tie her shoelace.

"Yup! We're all lathered up." Tanisha said cheerily. "I'm glad I'm rooming with girls who are familiar with the camp grounds."

"I'm so glad my cabin mates are all getting along so well. I'm so proud of you. Don't be late for campfire roll call!" Liz waved and continued bouncing down the path.

"Aye, Aye Skipper!" Monica saluted Liz, and the girls walked along the trail.

"Whew! That was close. I thought she was going to bust us out," Laura exhaled. "She probably knows we're going to hook up with the boys, but we have to cover our tracks anyway."

"These counselors are so clueless. Either that or they know what's going on and just choose to ignore it," Monica continued. "Don't forget, at night when they think we're asleep, they all sneak out to hang out with each other."

The girls walked briskly down the path. They could see the boys lingering by a large rock.

Brian reached for Tanisha's hand, and they continued down the path. Mike and Laura strolled arm in arm. Monica and Bob brought up the rear.

Tanisha whispered to Brian, "So where are we really going?" she asked.

"You'll see," Brian smiled. He gently squeezed Tanisha's hand. "Just trust me."

The trail was concealed from the sky by the treetops whose branches touched, forming an arch of leaves above their heads. The narrow path wound around and up a small incline leading to a hillside. Mike led the group through a small grove of trees and parted the hanging branches.

"Watch out for poison oak," Mike instructed. "There's no poison ivy back here, but there are a few poison oak patches." Tanisha wondered how he knew the difference but instinctively tightened her grip on Brian's hand and walked with her head down trying to avoid rubbing her skin against any of the shrubbery. Seconds later, the group appeared out of the woods and stood in a meadow of wild flowers next to a small pond. The meadow stretched the length of two football fields. In the distance was a farmhouse.

Tanisha was taken aback by the beauty of the meadow. She inhaled the smell of lavender and wild onions. "This place looks like a postcard," she said softly.

"A lot of people don't realize that the leadership camp leases its space from the people who own that farmhouse." He pointed to the small farmhouse that looked like a chess rook in the distance.

"You know what it looks like to me? It looks like that scene in the Wizard of Oz when they fall asleep in the poppy field!" Tanisha bent down to smell a flower. "How did you find this place?"

"Mike and I stumbled upon it last year," Brian continued. "You're right. It does look like that scene in the Wizard of Oz! I never thought about that, but that's exactly what it reminds me of too."

"I'm going to show Laura the ducks at the pond," Mike said. "We'll catch you kids later! In fact, we'll meet back here at this spot in forty-five minutes," he finished.

"Okay," Brian said. "Hey Bob, on the other side of the pond are some cool bird houses. I know you're into the Audubon society, so why don't you show Monica the birdhouses?"

"I've never been here before. Where are they?" Bob adjusted his glasses on his nose and squinted.

"Follow me, Bob. I'll show you." Mike motioned for Bob to join him.

As the foursome walked toward a grove of trees Brian shouted after Bob. "Bob, we need to keep this spot a secret, so don't put this in your next report!" he ordered.

"Yes, sir, Mr. President," Bob saluted.

"I love ducks! Let's go see the ducks." Tanisha pulled Brian's hand toward the pond where a family of ducks swam near the shore. The ducklings swam in a line behind the mother duck.

Brian resisted and pulled her toward him. "I had something else in mind. I'll show you the Indian burial ground."

"There really is an Indian burial ground? Cool! I thought that you just made that up. Let's go see it!" Tanisha squealed.

Brian led her to the edge of a short white fence on the opposite side of the small pond where a large weeping willow tree stood. "There's no burial ground, Teenie," Brian smiled, wiping a bead of sweat from her nose with his thumb. He placed his arms around her waist and gently rubbed his nose against hers. "Can I kiss you again?" he asked softly. Tanisha could feel her heart beating wildly. She swallowed hard and remembered to breathe.

The voice was unrecognizable. "Okay," she squeaked, smiling nervously and rubbing her free palm along the cuff of her shorts. Brian rubbed his nose against hers and smiled as he placed his hands around her waist. His lips were soft and gentle as he pecked her lips and stared into her eyes before pulling back and smiling at her.

Why did he stop? Does my breath stink? I still have a mint in my mouth. Are my lips chapped? She forced herself to smile back. He used his finger and traced a zigzag line from her throat to her left ear and back repeating the motion up to her right ear. He squeezed her palms before placing her arms around his neck. She felt herself holding her breath again. This time, his tongue gently licked from her neck to her chin, before slowly prying her lips apart and exploring her mouth. His breath tasted like strawberry gelatin. Stopping at the small tic tac that she'd tucked under her tongue, Brian used his tongue to transfer the mint from his mouth to hers and back to his. He crunched the mint in his teeth and swallowed it. She giggled shyly. He gently leaned her into the tree and nibbled her neck. Staring into the setting sun, she squinted as he rubbed her back while he kissed her neck with soft bites. *Is he giving me a hickey? No wonder he didn't want me to spray bug spray on my neck. I think he's giving me a hickey.* Tanisha giggled softly. *My first hickey! Tanisha, you can't get a hickey! Your parents will scalp you if you come home with a hickey! Relax! It'll be gone before camp is over. Go for it.* She giggled again.

"What's so funny, Teenie?" he asked. "Does it tickle?" Brian whispered. His voice appeared at least an octave deeper.

"A little," she giggled breathlessly. "Are you giving me a hickey?" Tanisha asked, her gaze piercing his.

"I am, but I'll stop if you don't want me to," Brian nodded. "Have you ever had a hickey before?" he asked.

"Nope," she giggled. "What will people think if I'm walking around camp with a hickey on my neck?" Tanisha asked.

"Teenie, you're so cute. No one will see it at the campfire tonight because it will be dark. But even if someone sees it, they're not going to care. It's not like they're going to call your parents and send you home," he laughed tickling her playfully. He moved her hair back and admired his handiwork. "I can see it already," he beamed. "I didn't think I'd be able to see it yet because you're so tan, but it's as plain as the nose on my face," he laughed. "I do good work," he finished.

Tanisha placed her hand on her neck, wishing she had a mirror so she could see it. "Now it's your turn, Mr. President. Let me give you a hickey," she ordered. "What do I need to do?" she asked.

"Just use your lips and tongue and make a sucking motion," he instructed. "But don't use your teeth like a vampire," he added. "Go for it," he suggested, placing his strong hands around her waist and pulling her body into his as he leaned his head back. It felt like her heart was going to jump out of her chest as she leaned in and gently sucked his neck.

Aside from her brief kiss with Darrell Hunter, and slow dancing a few different times, she'd never been kissed or been this close to a boy. She could feel Brian's heart beat. Her breathing quickened as she nervously kissed the side of his neck, trying desperately to imitate the sucking-biting motion that Brian used. With his eyes closed, his hands gently rubbed her back. Moments later, she looked at his neck and saw a purple bruise that was the size of a quarter against his pale skin. Brian squeezed her waist before opening his eyes.

"I can't believe that was the first time you've ever given a hickey, Teenie," he commented.

"Was it that obvious?" Tanisha bit her upper lip nervously. "Did I bite too hard?"

"No, it felt good. I just think that it's so cute that you've never given a hickey before," he cooed. You're a rookie!" Brian squeezed Tanisha tightly.

"I guess I am." Tanisha shrugged. "Guilty as charged."

"There's nothing wrong with that," he assured, staring into her eyes. "You are absolutely adorable, Teenie! I still can't believe that you don't have a boyfriend at home."

"Well, believe it." Tanisha rubbed her hand along Brian's arm, gently feeling the fine hairs along his bicep. *What about David, Teenie?* "Well, there is this guy who likes me," she corrected quickly. "And we've been talking on the phone a lot, but technically he's not my boyfriend. He's never kissed me," she offered quickly.

"Do you like him?" Brian asked.

"He's a couple of years older than I am, and I'm not allowed to date for a few more months so we've not been on any official dates," she replied.

"But do you like him?" Brian repeated.

She squinted into the haze created by the setting sun, stalling for more time. Teenie pursed her lips together, suddenly self conscious about her decayed fang. "I guess I like him," she admitted. "But we're really just friends right now," Tanisha replied honestly, her hand waving at a mosquito.

"Why do you 'guess' you like him?" he asked.

Her eyes stared into the grass as she pondered his question.

"Did you hear me, Teenie?" Brian nudged.

"Yeah, I heard you," she nodded. "We're just so very different," she admitted. "His life is so different from mine. He drives a Corvette, he plays golf at a private country club, his parents are both doctors," she paused and sighed. "I work at Save Mart on the weekend, and he spends his weekends playing golf," she finished. "We're just too different. Plus he's three years older than I am. It could never work," she said flatly. "I can't believe that I'm telling you all of this," she said softly.

"Is he white?" Brian asked.

"What? No. He's black," Teenie said, scowling slightly. "Why would you assume that he was white, Brian?" she asked.

"It just sounds like the profile of most of the guys at my school," he shrugged. "And based on what you've told me about him, he doesn't sound that much different from me," he said. "I don't drive a Corvette, yet, but I'll be getting the car of my choice for my sixteenth birthday," he offered. "I get chauffeured to school by our grounds keeper. I also take flying lessons so I can co-pilot my dad's plane when I get my pilot's license," he continued. "And I'm white in case you haven't noticed," he teased. "So technically, I'm more different from you than he is," Brian finished. "So why are you here with me?" he asked.

Teenie closed her eyes and squinted into the sun. She nervously played with a blade of grass in her hand.

"Do you like me, Teenie?" he asked. "I hope I know the answer to that one," he said. "You do like me, don't you, Tanisha Carlson who wears Secret deodorant?" he asked.

Teenie giggled. "You're alright," she offered playfully.

"I'm alright?" he repeated. "But do you like me, Teenie?" he asked directly. "I'm being serious now," he said flatly.

"Yes. I like you, Brian Kraft," she said.

"Whew! Good answer," he smiled. "So if you like me, why can't you like him?" he paused.

"It's just different," she stammered. "I didn't know any of that stuff about you until just now," she defended.

"So now that I've shared what my background is like, and because it's different from yours," he said. "Are you going to stop liking me?" he quizzed. "I hope not," he said seriously.

"Of course not," she offered.

"You're not using me as some test case to see what it's like to kiss a white boy from the north shore are you?" he grinned tickling Tanisha's side. "I hope I'm not some sociology experiment for you," he continued. "But since you've never given or received a hickey before, you don't strike me as the kind of girl who just makes out with random guys," he finished. "Or do you?" he asked. "Is this goody-goody image all an act?"

"Oh yeah. I'm such a 'goody-goody' making out with you. Get thee to a nunnery!" Tanisha laughed.

"Look out! Now she's quoting Shakespeare!" he laughed. "I'm having so much fun with you. I'm going to miss you when camp is over, Teenie. I wish my girlfriend at home was as much fun as you are," Brian said.

The mosquito landed on her thigh, she smacked it in one blow, carelessly wiping the blood from her hand onto the grass. She took a giant step back, raised her eyebrow and stared at Brian. "What did you say?" she asked. "I know you did not just say 'your girlfriend' back home?" she barked. Her voice was loud and firm. "I thought you said that you didn't have a girlfriend," she continued before he could reply. "Remember, I asked you earlier today, and you said that you didn't have a girlfriend 'one word.'"

"I thought you meant here at camp. Of course I have a girlfriend at home, Teenie," he said casually. "Her name is Susan."

Stunned, Tanisha stared at him in disbelief. "If you have a girlfriend at home, then why are you fooling around with me?" she squealed. She crossed her arms over her chest and balled her fists. Her breathing was heavy as though she would hyperventilate.

"What do you mean? It's what we do at camp. Everybody hooks up. Monica and Laura know the deal," he shrugged. "I thought they clued you in." Brian reached for Tanisha's hand. She pulled it out of reach and scowled.

Everybody hooks up at camp. It's the thing. "They told me about the bewitching hour, and people hooking up at camp, but I didn't realize that you had a girlfriend, or I wouldn't have been making out with you," she whined. "I feel so stupid!" Tanisha plopped into the grass and covered her face with her hands, fighting back tears.

"Teenie, I really like you," Brian knelt in front of her and reached for her hand again, squeezing tighter as she tried to pull away. With his free hand, he tilted her chin up and stared into her eyes. "I really, really like you, Teenie, and I'm having a blast with you," he admitted. Teenie rolled her eyes and stared at him blankly. "But let's think about it. I live in Lake Forest, and you live in Newberry East. How could we possibly date after camp?" he asked. "It would take me almost two hours to get to your house to take you to a movie." Tanisha rolled her eyes and tried to free her hands, his grip tightened around her fingers. She wanted to cry.

"Come on, Teenie. Don't cry," Brian coaxed softly. "When I saw you on the train, I assumed that you had a boyfriend at home. You're pretty. You're smart. You're funny," he listed. "I'm sure this guy that you were telling me about wants to be your boyfriend," he concluded quickly. "Honestly, I wasn't trying to mislead you. I just thought that you knew the deal," he explained. "Even the counselors hook up at camp."

Tanisha stared out into the poppy field. *I am so gullible. I barely know this guy, and I'm making out with him like a knucklehead. What's wrong with me?* Consumed with her own thoughts, she was barely listening to Brian's explanation.

"My girlfriend Susan is at a camp in Oconomowoc, Wisconsin. I know she's probably hooking up with someone because we talked about it," he shrugged.

Her scowl was deep and serious. "You and your girlfriend talked about hooking up with other people at camp?" Teenie asked incredulously. "It doesn't bother you that your girlfriend could be making out with someone at this very moment?" she quizzed. "I find that hard to believe."

Brian wrinkled his nose and furrowed his thick eyebrows. "I guess if I'm being honest it bothers me a little bit," he admitted softly. "But I'm hanging out with you right now, so I haven't really thought about what she might be doing," he explained. "Truthfully, I've been so busy trying to get to know you that I haven't thought about Susan much at all. Besides, Susan and I agreed that we're not going to talk about anything that we do at camp. We call it the 'don't ask don't tell' agreement," he said.

Tanisha stood up and scowled at him. Brian stood up as well. "The 'don't ask don't tell' agreement?" she repeated. "I have never heard of such a ridiculous arrangement in my whole life. You probably just made that up to justify cheating on your girlfriend with me!" she shrieked. She scowled at him and opened her mouth wide to continue scolding him, but her tongue lashing tangled in her throat as he gently yet swiftly wrapped his arms around her waist. Tanisha's arms hung like noodles at her side. Brian's eyes were soft and sincere as he stared at her. This time he looked like he wanted to cry. She felt her frown relaxing under his gaze.

"I really like you, Teenie. Let's just have a good time during camp and see what happens," he whispered. Teenie stared at him confused. She was having fun with Brian, but he had a girlfriend. This time it was Brian who took a giant step back.

"Earth calling, Teenie," he continued, his hands in the surrender pose. "If you don't want to make out anymore we don't have to. We can just hang out and have a good time," he said. "But I like you, Teenie, and I don't want you to be mad at me. But I'd be lying if I said that I didn't want to kiss you again," he said softly. "Just say something. Anything."

Tanisha stared at Brian's face. He was right. She had not considered the geographic barriers that prevented them from having a relationship post camp. Still, she was disappointed. She really liked Brian. He made her laugh, and he'd made her feel welcome and special at camp. *My cabin mates are all hooked up with somebody, and if I break it off with Brian now, the rest of camp will be horrible. If he and his girlfriend have an agreement, what's the harm? It's not like I know her. I'll probably never see him again after this summer, anyway.* She willed her face to scowl at him. It didn't work. Her face betrayed her and smiled softly at him.

As if in slow motion, Brian slowly pulled Tanisha into an embrace. This time she didn't resist. She breathed deeply as her body relaxed and she leaned her head into his chest. He gently rubbed her back, her arms encircling his waist. "Now where were we?" he whispered.

Everybody hooks up at camp. It's the thing.

Chapter 27

The Closing Banquet

David walked to the edge of the driveway to get the mail, counting his footsteps aloud as he walked. "Twenty-nine, thirty, thirty-one." With his parents' busy schedules, they left mail retrieval to David, which meant that the mailbox was only checked every three or four days. Sometimes, the small roadside box was so full of mail that the postal carrier was forced to ring their bell and hand deliver their mail to them. If they weren't home, he left the mail in the base of the bench that sat on their front porch with a piece of bulk mail poking out to grab their attention. David hadn't checked the mail box in over five days, and he needed both arms to carry the stack of bills and advertisements. He stepped over Belvedere, napping on his doggie bed in the laundry room, and began sorting the bulk mail to lessen the height of the mail stack. He wanted to avoid another lecture from his dad on the importance of checking the mailbox every day. He could just hear his dad now, "Son, you never know what's in the mailbox. Someone could rifle through our mail and steal information that could lead to identity theft. It's important to get the mail every day. Your mother and I are far too busy to tend to the mailbox. The least you could do is bring the mail in every day as you pull into the driveway in that sports car that we bought you!"

His dad was always good for a lecture on responsibility. David smiled as he sorted through the mail. He stacked the household bills in a pile and tossed the advertisements into the recycle bag.

He hummed along to the Hall & Oats song *"Sarah Smile"* as he lessened his mail pile. He stopped when he got to a postcard of Abraham Lincoln. Puzzled, he turned it over in his hand and remembered that he'd asked Tanisha to send him a postcard from camp. It had been over ten days since he'd spoken to her, and he was glad that she was coming back tomorrow. He missed her.

The day before, he'd called Save Mart and pretended that he was her brother and had gotten someone to confirm her schedule for the following week. He knew she would be working on Monday from 9:00 until 5:30.

As instructed, he read the postcard to Belvedere, before heading to the backyard to clean out the pool. David loved having a pool, but with his older brother away at college, the maintenance responsibilities fell squarely on his shoulders. He sighed deeply as he prepared to sweep the bugs and leaves that found their way into the large pool each day. His dad swam laps in the pool every night, and expected the pool to be clean when he came home from the office. As David walked around to the deep end to retrieve the bug net from the pool shed, he bumped his shin on the diving board. As he bent over to grab his shin, something occurred to him. Tanisha had signed the postcard, Teenie.

Teenie? I didn't know Tanisha's nickname was Teenie? I've never heard her friends call her Teenie. But I haven't been around her friends that often. I wonder why she never told me that her nickname was Teenie? David casually flipped on his radio boom box and started cleaning the pool.

෨෬

"Teenie, stop primping in that mirror and hurry or we're going to be late!" Monica said. "You look great!" Monica was anxious to deliver the closing ceremony speech for the Adobe tribe.

Tanisha tucked her pink Lacoste shirt into her white capri pants wishing the cabin had a full length mirror. She carefully waved Laura's hand mirror up and down her frame one last time. She'd saved her cutest outfit for the closing ceremony. The leadership camp brochure had instructed the campers not to wear shorts for the closing ceremony. The brochure text read: "You don't have to dress for church or a wedding, but don't dress for a picnic either." Tanisha decided that Capri pants and her pink shirt with her Sperry Topsiders would be appropriate. Her clothes still held the freshly laundered scent from Liz's recent washing. Tanisha smiled as she was reminded of her counselor's kindness. Running her hands down her slacks, Tanisha was worried about the wrinkles in her clothes.

"You guys, are these wrinkles really noticeable?" Tanisha asked self consciously.

Laura climbed from the top bunk where she'd just etched her initials in the wall above her bunk bed. "They look okay to me," Laura said. She handed the Swiss army knife to Monica.

"You look fine, Teenie," Monica concurred. "No one has an iron here, so all of us are a bit wrinkled, so you'll fit right in," Monica finished. Tanisha had already etched her initials into the wall by her bed.

"Let's go, ladies, I'm starving," Sharon urged. Laura and Sharon also had on white Capri pants with pastel colored tank tops, and Monica wore a white cotton skirt with a green tennis shirt. "We look so cute together," Sharon observed. "It's like we color coordinated our outfits. We blend so well together!" she gushed as the girls walked down the path to the mess hall for the closing dinner.

Tanisha smiled. She really had blended right in with her bunkmates, even down to her closing banquet attire. She felt sad. She would really miss them. They'd welcomed her into their group and treated her like a true friend. Tanisha had thoroughly enjoyed her leadership camp experience and was not looking forward to the end of camp.

The leadership component was informative, and she was getting a lot of good governance ideas to take back to share with the student council. She would miss her new friends a lot, but she would miss Brian Kraft most of all. She was fairly confident that she and her bunkmates would write each other occasionally, but she feared that her friendship and romance with Brian Kraft was just a summer fling. The more time she spent with him, the more she dreaded the closing night ceremony. Tanisha and Brian had exchanged phone numbers and home addresses, but still she feared that she would never hear from him again. Just thinking about saying goodbye to him made her want to cry.

Tanisha decided to smile through her sadness, grinning as she thought about the other romances that had bloomed during the two week camp. Mike and Laura were still a hot item and were inseparable. They lived fifteen minutes from each other and were planning to date once they returned home. Monica and Bob were also a couple, but lived two hundred miles apart, so geography would prevent them from maintaining more than a pen pal relationship. Sharon and Derrick were still enjoying each other's company and lived near each other, but Sharon had already started to distance herself from Derrick in preparation for the end of their summer fling.

"Derrick's cool," Sharon had said to Teenie. "But I'm not trying to get serious about him. I have a boyfriend back home."

"Why are you making out with him if you have a boyfriend," Teenie asked. *Am I the only teenager who still believes that it's cheating on your boyfriend to make out with someone else behind his back? Or is this something that white people just do all the time?*

Sharon stared at Teenie in disbelief. "Duh! I made out with him because he's cute, and I was curious to kiss a black guy," she shrugged. "Besides, he has a girlfriend at home too. Everyone hooks up at camp, Teenie. It's the thing."

Everyone hooks up at camp. It's the thing. There goes that phrase again and there went my theory that this is just something that white people do.

The theory was proven several times over as demonstrated by the visible bright red strawberry marks on most campers' necks. Tanisha was beginning to suspect that those that didn't have visible hickeys had hickeys that couldn't be seen. Leadership camp was one giant make-out festival.

As they settled into their table, Tanisha quickly reviewed her notes for the closing ceremony speech. The Apache Tribe had implemented their food share program with the Springfield Homeless Shelter to rave reviews. The leadership camp director had received publicity in the local paper highlighting the food share program as the best camp idea to date. The newspaper printed a photo of Tanisha, Brian and Bob in the Living section of the newspaper. Startled, Tanisha looked up when she felt soft fingers tracing a line down her spine.

"Hey, cutie," Brian smiled. "Are you ready for your speech, Madame Vice President? You look great by the way," he complimented. "Pink is a good color on you."

Tanisha smiled at Brian who looked handsome in khaki pants and a yellow golf shirt with the words **Lake Forest Country Club** embroidered in white lettering.

"Thanks. You look nice too, Mr. President. I'm all set! Just reviewing my notes one last time," she chirped. *I don't want him to see how sad I am or he'll think I'm being silly. This was just a summer fling, Tanisha. Hold it together, girlfriend!*

Brian clapped his hands together and rubbed Tanisha's back. "Since our project won, we have the honor of giving our farewell speech first," he stated. "Let's rock and roll!" Brian reached for Tanisha's hand, helped her to her feet and escorted her to the stage where Bob was standing off to the side reviewing his notes.

As Tanisha and Brian approached, Brian cued Bob to start. Tanisha smiled at Brian's smooth mannerisms. *He is destined for a very successful career in politics. He is so smooth!*

"Fellow campers, may I have your attention, please." The loud chatter dulled to a quiet whisper, and then silence ensued. "First, I'd like to thank you for your support of our food pantry project," he began. "Although it was truly a team effort, it was led by our brilliant battery: our president Brian Kraft and our vice president Tanisha "Teenie" Carlson." The mess hall erupted into applause and foot stomping as Tanisha and Brian ascended the three steps to the podium and stood alongside Bob. "Brian Kraft will now say a few words." The campers stood and applauded louder as Brian leaned into the microphone, raising his hands to silence the campers.

"Wow! Thank you very much for that ovation and welcome. This leadership experience has been extraordinary," he grinned. "The Apache tribe far exceeded the expectations that we set for ourselves. I'd like to thank all of our campers and especially Tim our counselor. Special thanks to Bob for all of his comprehensive summaries. Even when Teenie and I gave the reports, Bob wrote the script and supplied us with interesting copy." Brian hi-fived Bob and pulled him into a hug as the campers applauded. Brian waited for the applause to subside before continuing. Tanisha was impressed that Brian spoke without a script or notes.

"But I would be remiss if I didn't thank my wing man or wing woman, Teenie Carlson," he said. Brian reached for Tanisha's hand. "I met Teenie on the train down to Springfield, and after chatting with her for about ten minutes, I knew she would make an awesome vice president. She didn't even know it, but I started recruiting her on the train," he winked. "It's been a blast working with Teenie. She's smart, funny, hard working, a great leader, and a special friend. Thanks, Teenie, you're the best!" Brian grabbed Tanisha's hand and kissed it before pulling her into a quick embrace. "Teenie, would you like to say a few words?"

Tanisha could feel the tears welling in her eyes as she pulled away from Brian's embrace. She quickly leaned her head back to stop the tears before she spoke into the microphone.

"Thank you for that flattering introduction, Brian." Tanisha took a deep breath before continuing. "This camp experience has changed my life. I have never felt more accepted and more unencumbered than I've felt at this camp," she spoke slowly. "I felt like I really belonged with this group. My cabin mates Laura, Sharon and Monica were amazing, and I'll really miss them," she smiled.

"We'll miss you too, Teenie," they shouted in unison.

Tanisha took another calming breath. "I'd also like to thank our counselor, Liz for making me feel so welcome on the first day. Of course, I'd like to thank the Apache tribe for giving me the opportunity to serve as vice president." Tanisha cleared her throat. She paused, feeling the tears welling up in her eyes again. Her words were slow and deliberate. "Two weeks ago, when I was nominated, I was nervous and was actually suspicious about being nominated. I thought it was a hoax," she confessed. "I was the new girl at camp and doubted that the other campers would vote for me," she paused. The mess hall was eerily silent. Brian studied her expression, unsure where she was going with her comments. "But I'd like to thank you for believing in me and seeing something in me that I didn't see in myself." Tanisha grabbed her throat and the tears flowed freely as she looked at Brian and Bob.

"I can't believe that I'm crying," she smiled.

"It's okay, Teenie," a camper shouted. "We all cry at the closing banquet. It's tradition."

"Thanks. That makes me feel better," she laughed. "Rockford, I mean Bob. Thank you for everything. But I'd really like to thank you for all of your help with the food pantry project and publicity. We couldn't have done it without you. I can't wait to see you on the six o'clock evening news!"

Bob blew her an air kiss. "No problem, Newbie!" The campers stomped their feet and clapped wildly.

Tanisha wiped her eyes with the back of her hand and took a deep breath as she looked at Brian and continued. "Mr. President, thank you for seeing something in me that I didn't see in myself. You saw the light in me that I was trying to dim based on my fear of being different. Thank you for asking me to be your running mate. I wouldn't have considered running for vice president were it not for you," she paused. "I will miss all of the friends that I've made at leadership camp." She clutched her throat for composure. The campers clapped their hands and whistled. Her carefully prepared remarks were now tear stained and she was too overcome with emotion to continue. Brian grabbed Tanisha's hand and pulled her into his arms as he rocked her gently from side to side. Tanisha tilted her head away from the microphone and whispered, "And thank you for sharing the Wizard of Oz with me. I think I'll miss you most of all, Scarecrow."

Brian gazed into Tanisha's eyes as the campers applauded louder and stomped their feet. Tears streamed down his face now. He pulled a tissue from his pocket and wiped her tears before wiping his own.

"How'd you know that I would need a tissue," Tanisha whispered.

"I knew you'd cry, because I knew that I would cry," he confessed. "I love you, Teenie," he whispered. She stared at him, her jaw frozen open. He held her hand and guided her down the stairs to join the others at their regular bench for dinner.

છ∞ભ

Wiping the tear from her face, she stared out the window of the Amtrak train, entranced by the cornfields. She had hoped that Brian would be on her train for the return trip north, but Brian was flying back to O'Hare airport to meet his parents for their annual pilgrimage to Maine, where his family spent the month of July. At daybreak, a limousine had picked him up to whisk him to the Springfield airport for his flight.

The closing session had lasted two hours, so the bewitching hour had morphed into the campfire hour. Brian and Tanisha sat next to each other at campfire and held hands. He'd given her his home address and telephone number again and had taken hers. "In case you lose the first piece of paper," he'd said. "I'll know that you have another copy." They promised to keep in touch. He'd walked her back to her cabin and given her a big bear hug and a long kiss. Tanisha could feel the distance separating them as he hugged her for the last time. They'd both cried openly as they said goodbye.

She came out of her trance as the train pulled into the Kankakee stop. She only had thirty minutes before the train pulled into the Homer terminal. She slipped into the small on board bathroom to check the status of her hickey. The strawberry mark was still visible although not as purple as it had been the night before. She'd worn a polo shirt and turned the collar up to conceal the mark on her neck. The mark was on the right side of her neck so it wouldn't be obvious to her mother when she picked her up from the train.

When the train pulled into the depot, she saw Jack leaning against Bruce the Blue Goose, absentmindedly tossing a yellow tennis ball in the air. She grabbed her duffle bag and walked out to meet him.

"Boo! Hey Jack!" Tanisha beamed, happy to see her older brother.

"Hey, Tanisha! You look tan!" Jack grabbed her duffle bag and gave her a hug. He threw her duffle bag into the large trunk.

"Thanks! It was over ninety degrees and sunny in Springfield, and we swam in the lake every day."

Tanisha continued to share her camp experience with Jack, careful to leave out mention of Brian Kraft.

"What'd I miss at home?" Tanisha hadn't been the least bit homesick.

"Nothing really. Oh yeah, Mom is seeing a psychiatrist now. She wanted me to tell you when I picked you up from the train," Jack shared.

Tanisha stared at Jack curiously. "Okay, so what brought this on and why does she want me to know this now?" Tanisha asked.

Jack drummed his fingers along the steering wheel. "The cable company is requiring her to talk to a psychiatrist or else she could get fired. And Mom said that the psychiatrist wants to talk to us to try and understand her better. She's going to call you sometime next week."

"Great! I haven't been home twenty minutes, and I'm already caught up in Billie's drama!" Tanisha was not in the mood to deal with Billie. "Have you talked to her yet?"

"No. Mom said that she wants to talk to you first, and then she's going to talk to me." Jack turned into the Cedar Grove complex. "I have no idea why she wants to talk to you first, Tanisha," Jack offered. "I'm just telling you what I know, so don't play Sherlock Holmes with me, sis. I know how you are."

"Jack, why did you share this with me? Why didn't Mom just tell me all of this herself?" Tanisha asked.

"You know how she is. She gets so nervous when she talks to you. It's no big deal, really. I think she just wants to ask us a few questions about Mom. She's trying to help her, I guess," Jack shrugged. "Just cooperate and do it, Tanisha. It sounds like Mom is trying to get better and gain control of her mental health issues," Jack pleaded.

"Jack, did she tell you that? Did Mom actually say that she's trying to get better or did she make it seem like the cable company was forcing her to talk to someone?" Tanisha asked.

Jack hesitated before responding. He stared at his sister as he guided the car into the parking space in front of the town house. "Tanisha, what difference does it make? The doctor wants to talk to you, so just talk to her," Jack groaned.

"I will. But Billie's only going to a doctor now because the cable company is making her go. She's not trying to get better on her own," Tanisha doubted. She climbed out of the car and walked around to the trunk.

Jack had already pulled the duffle bag from the trunk and waved Tanisha away. "Sis, I'll carry this. By the way, you might want to throw on one of your turtlenecks before Mom gets home and sees that hickey on your neck," Jack motioned. "Sounds like you had a good time at camp," he laughed.

Tanisha grabbed her neck and blushed. "Shut up, Jack!" She raced inside and ran to change.

Tanisha quickly slipped on a white cotton turtleneck and grabbed the phone to call Lori. As she dialed, she prayed that Charlotte wasn't on the phone.

"Hello," Lori answered after the first ring.

"Hey, girl! It's Tanisha! You're always snatching that phone up in one ring. Whose call are you trying to catch?" Tanisha heard a soft thud and peered into the hallway. Jack had placed her duffle bag outside her door. She pulled the duffle bag into her room and sat on her bed.

"Hey, Tanisha! Welcome back! Doug is calling me to confirm our date tonight. He is so awesome. I am having so much fun with him this summer. How was camp? I missed you."

"I missed you too," she said. She'd had so much fun with her cabin mates that she hadn't thought about her friends from home. But hearing her friend's voice, she realized that she had missed her. "Girl, I have so much to tell you. But I don't want to be cut off when Doug calls or with Charlotte whining to use the phone. Maybe I can get Jack to drop me off at your house, and then when Doug picks you up for your date, he can just drop me back off at home," she suggested. Tanisha quickly unpacked her duffle bag and tossed the dirty clothes in her laundry basket.

"Good idea. Otherwise Charlotte is going to be pacing the floor trying to get me off the phone. You know how she is. See if Jack can bring you over," Lori coached.

Tanisha threw the phone onto the bed and raced downstairs. She found Jack in the kitchen making a bologna sandwich. "Jack, can you take me to Lori's tonight? Her sister can bring me home."

"No problem, Sis. I'm heading out in a few minutes to go to Kerri's. Just be ready in fifteen minutes."

Tanisha raced up the stairs two at a time and grabbed the phone. "It's cool. Jack can bring me over." Tanisha took a deep breath. "I'll be there in fifteen minutes. By the way, you don't have my black multi-colored hoodie do you? I can't find that thing anywhere."

"Nope. You didn't leave it at camp did you?"

"No. I couldn't find it before camp. It's probably here somewhere. I'll see you in a few." Tanisha hung up the phone.

She decided to take a quick shower to freshen up after her long train ride. She brushed her teeth and inspected her decayed tooth again. She wiggled it to see if the primary tooth was even slightly loose, but it wasn't. She was glad that Brian Kraft had not seen the decayed tooth.

Fifteen minutes later Jack dropped her off at Lori's house. "Jack, tell Kerri I said hi, okay?" Tanisha offered cheerfully.

Jack waved as he pulled out of Lori's driveway. "Will do. Have fun, sis."

Tanisha ran to the front door, knocked once and walked in. The Perkins family never locked their front door. Lori sat on the living room floor painting her nails. Tanisha bounced on the sofa and kicked off her shoes.

"Look at how tan you are! And your hair has blonde highlights. It looks so cute," Lori squealed as she blew on her nail polish.

"Thanks! Girl, I met someone at camp! His name is Brian Kraft. Isn't that a nice name? Brian Kraft," she repeated. Tanisha paused and looked around. "Who's in your house?" Tanisha whispered.

"Just Charlotte and my mother, but Charlotte is taking a nap, and my mother is upstairs watching television," Lori said.

"Okay. I'll whisper then. Camp was awesome. And Brian was so cool. He was the president of my section and I was vice president. And look, he gave me a hickey!"

Lori climbed onto the sofa and sat next to Tanisha. "You got your first hickey! Let me see it." Tanisha pulled down her turtleneck collar and showed Lori her hickey.

"Girl, Doug gave me one too. But you can't really see it." Lori's skin was a deep chocolate brown, and the hickey wasn't visible against her dark skin. "It's a good thing you can't see it, because my parents would peel my head if they saw it."

"I know," Tanisha admitted. "That's why I'm wearing this turtleneck. But it felt so good," Tanisha confessed. "Now I know why Maria lets Todd give her hickeys all the time." Tanisha squeezed one of the sofa pillows into her chest. "But here's the best part. Are you ready for this?" Tanisha asked. "Brian was white," she blurted.

Lori's eyes got big. "Did you say white? You're joking."

Tanisha continued, "Nope. He was white. He was fine too. And he made the first move." Tanisha replayed the entire camp story, from her first encounter with Brian on the Amtrak train to the bewitching hour encounters and the closing ceremony.

"Wow! Did it feel weird kissing a white guy? Did it feel different from kissing Darrell Hunter? I want details," Lori demanded. "Did he really say that he loves you?"

"One question at a time," Tanisha blushed. "Darrell's breath smelled like boiled eggs, and he was a horrible kisser. Brian was a great kisser," Tanisha squeezed the pillow tighter. "And yes, he said he loves me," Tanisha blushed.

"Do you love him?" Lori asked.

"How would I know? I've never said I love you to anybody before," Tanisha said. "I really like him, and I was a teary eyed, cry baby, basket case last night when we said goodbye, but I don't know what love feels like to know if I love him. Do you?" she asked.

"I haven't a clue. But I've never spent two weeks eating every meal and making out with a guy that I like either," Lori said. "I guess it's possible to fall in love in two weeks when you see the person every day all day," Lori offered. "I've never had a boy say he loved me before. Tell me exactly what was going on when he said he loved you."

Tanisha settled into the sofa and crossed her legs. "He whispered it when we were on the stage while he was hugging me after my speech. We were both crying. He said it really softly, so I don't know if he was saying it to himself or what. But when he walked me to my cabin, he didn't say it again."

"What did you say when he said it?" Lori asked.

"I was so shocked to hear it that I didn't say anything. I just smiled through my tears and we walked back to the table for dinner," Tanisha shared.

"Do you think you'll see him again?" Lori asked.

"I doubt it. He lives in Lake Forest. It would take him two hours to drive down here to take me to a movie. It was just a summer fling. We said we would keep in touch, but there's one more thing. He has a girlfriend," Tanisha offered softly.

"What? He has a girlfriend?" Lori asked. "When did you find out that he has a girlfriend? Please tell me that you didn't find out about the girlfriend until the last night," Lori said.

"He told me the first night we did the bewitching hour. But he assured me that he and his girlfriend had an understanding that they could see other people over the summer. They won't even see each other until school starts. He goes to his family's house in Maine for four weeks, and she goes to her family's house in the Hamptons." Tanisha shrugged her shoulders and sighed.

"Where are the Hamptons?" Lori asked.

"It's in New York. A lot of rich people in New York have summer homes in the Hamptons. You remember <u>The Great Gatsby</u> by F. Scott Fitzgerald, don't you? Daisy Buchanan's family had a house in the Hamptons, and Gatsby built a big mansion nearby to impress her," Tanisha continued. "Brian told me that his girlfriend's family used to live in New York. Her dad was the president of some company there before they moved to Illinois. Come to think of it, Brian's family must be pretty wealthy, because a private plane picked him up at the Springfield airport to fly him to O'Hare to meet his parents," Tanisha paused. "But we never talked about his family."

"Now I remember. I loved <u>The Great Gatsby</u>. We read that in Humanities class last year. If his family has a summer house in Maine, they're probably not poor. But I'm surprised you made out with him knowing that he had a girlfriend, Tanisha," Lori said.

"I know. I felt bad at first, but then I told myself that if they had an understanding it was cool," she stammered. "And I just felt like saying, what the hell! I was curious about kissing a white guy. He was the most popular boy at camp. He was fine, he liked me, and I liked him. I felt bad for his girlfriend, but he kept assuring me that she was probably making out with someone at her camp, so I stopped feeling guilty." Tanisha twirled one of the pillow tassels. "It's not like I did anything to hurt her. I wasn't trying to steal her man. I just borrowed him for a couple of weeks. Besides, I don't even know her, and I'll probably never see him again."

"Well, why would he tell you that he loved you if he wasn't planning to keep in touch with you?" Lori asked.

"Who knows?" Tanisha said. "Maybe he was just trying to say something to make me feel better since I was crying. If he doesn't call me, I'm not calling him. And watch, I'll probably never hear from him again," Tanisha groaned. "Besides, if he really meant that he loved me, wouldn't he have said it again when we were alone?"

"That's true. Maybe he thought he was consoling his girlfriend, and he got confused," Lori suggested. "You were both emotional, and he probably said it out of reflex."

"Good point. That's probably exactly what happened," Tanisha agreed. "I hadn't considered that," she admitted. "Let's forget that he even said I love you, okay?" Tanisha said. *He must have said it out of reflex, Tanisha. How could he have possibly fallen in love with you after two weeks? That's absurd! But he said, I love you, Teenie. He didn't just say I love you. That's semantics, Teenie. Besides, he would have said it again when he walked you to your cabin, knucklehead. You should have never told Lori that he said that.*

"Deal. But you're not off the hook, little miss. Once you found out that he had a girlfriend, you could have stopped messing around with him." Lori waved her wet fingernails in the air. "Correction. You **should** have stopped messing around with him," she clarified. "Remember the pact we made? If a boy already has a girlfriend, then he's off limits until they break up. And we have to put ourselves in the girlfriend's shoes, because we wouldn't want someone messing around with our boyfriend if she knew he had a girlfriend," she recited. "I know you remember that pact. It was your idea," Lori raised her eyebrows and stared at Tanisha. "Of course he told you that he and his girlfriend had a 'don't ask, don't tell' agreement for the summer, silly. Boys will say anything to get what they want."

"I knew you would bring up the pact," Tanisha groaned. "You're right. I would want someone to back off from my boyfriend if they knew he already had a girlfriend," she groaned. "And I still want to honor the pact. It's the right thing to do," she agreed. "But I just got caught up in the moment. He was so cute, and all of my cabin mates had hooked up with somebody," she explained. "I'm making excuses, but he was so fun to hang out with, and I really liked him. I really did," she admitted. Tanisha stared squarely at Lori. "Do me a favor and don't mention the girlfriend part to Rashanda, Maria, Justine or Grace. I feel really guilty about that now. And definitely don't mention the part about him saying I love you. I can't believe that I even told you that part," Tanisha confessed. "I feel so foolish and gullible."

"Don't beat yourself up. You're human. Everybody gets to stumble a few times," Lori said. "Your secret is safe with me," Lori pledged. "It's fun hanging out with a boy that you like. Doug and I have had so much fun together this summer. I'll see if Doug has a friend that you can meet." Lori blew on her nails. "By the way, have you talked to David Barton since you've been back?"

Tanisha hadn't thought about David since returning home. On the train ride, she'd thought about Brian Kraft, and then when

Jack picked her up and told her about Billie's psychiatrist she was distracted with that piece of family drama.

"No. I called you as soon as I got home. I sent him a postcard though," Tanisha explained.

Lori sat up straight. "Why don't you call him and see if he wants to hang out? Since you're already at my house, you could sneak and see David for a little while. It would take your mind off of Brian."

Tanisha pondered this suggestion. "I don't know. I feel weird calling him. I was just hanging out with Brian," she said.

"You're not going to make out with him or anything, but at least it's something to do," Lori explained. "Grace is on vacation with her parents. Maria sneaked to the movies to meet Todd. Rashanda is in Alabama at her family reunion, and Justine's hanging out with her dad. What else are you going to do tonight?"

"Good point. Allen and Byron are in the city with my dad. Jack went to Kerri's house, and I certainly don't feel like being at home alone with Billie," she paused. "Let me use your phone." Tanisha dialed David's number from memory.

The phone rang three times before a woman answered. "Hello," the voice said.

Tanisha spoke politely into the phone. "Hello. May I speak to David, please?"

"He's not here right now, sweetie. May I take a message?" the woman asked.

"Can you ask him to call Teenie, please? May I leave my number?"

"Sure sweetie. Hold on and let me get a pen."

Tanisha covered the mouthpiece of the phone and whispered. "I'm going to give him this number so that he can call me at your house," she explained.

"Good idea. This way he can just pick you up over here. And if he doesn't call back before Doug gets here, then I'll just have Doug take you home," Lori whispered.

Tanisha finished the call and sprawled across the sofa.

"You left your name as Teenie. Does David call you, Teenie? That's a cute nickname," Lori asked.

Tanisha sat straight up. "Oh, my goodness! I didn't realize that I'd said, Teenie. My cabin mates started calling me Teenie at camp. And that's what everyone has called me for the past two weeks so I did it out of habit," Tanisha groaned. "He's not going to know that it's me. Should I call back and leave my real name?"

"I wouldn't," Lori said. "You'll look too frantic to his mom. Mothers get agitated when girls call looking for their sons," she explained. "Charlotte taught me that. Besides, 'Teenie' is close enough to Tanisha, so he'll figure out that it's you. And if nothing else, he'll be curious to call back the strange number that you left," Lori paused. "I wouldn't worry about it, Teenie," Lori tested. "I like the way that sounds!"

"Isn't it cute? Nobody called me Tanisha at camp, so I got accustomed to referring to myself as Teenie. I'm going to use Teenie as my new nickname. I hope he calls back. I really would like to see him," Tanisha confessed.

"I'm sure he'll call back." Lori walked into the kitchen. "See, you've moved on already. Brian who?" Lori teased.

"That's enough, smarty pants. What do you have to eat? I'm starving." Tanisha trailed Lori into the kitchen.

"By the way, my cabin mates were all white girls, and they were so cool. And these girls could eat! They were thin, but they had normal appetites like black girls. They destroyed my theory that black girls eat, and white girls don't," Tanisha explained.

"I'm glad to see that not all white girls live on dry lettuce and Diet Pepsi," Lori laughed.

"I actually like Diet Pepsi now," Tanisha confessed.

"Okay, white girl," Lori teased. "Next you're going to tell me that you like country music," Lori laughed.

"Actually, I do," Tanisha shared. "It's romantic and tells a story if you listen to it," she admitted.

Lori stared at her friend curiously.

"I've decided that my new motto is to stop stereotyping and judging, stop gossiping and to give everyone the benefit of the doubt," Tanisha stated confidently. "I'm going to assume the best about people instead of the worst. I'm going to try to live by the good book that you're always quoting," she finished.

"Good for you, Teenie," Lori nodded encouragingly. "You **should** read the Bible more." Lori placed the turkey and bread on the table and reached for the condiments. "You came back with a new name **and** a new attitude! Maybe we should start calling you Sister Teenie," she teased. "Are you going to move into a convent?" Lori joked.

Tanisha grinned at how quickly her friend had caught on to her nickname. "Yes, I'll be the only nun in the convent with a hickey," she laughed as she smeared a liberal slathering of mayonnaise on her turkey sandwich. "But seriously, I don't even know if we have a Bible in the house. Where can I buy one?" she asked.

∞

David had gone to the Glen Country Club to work on his golf swing. He dropped his keys on the counter in the laundry room and reached in the refrigerator for a light beer, bumping into his mother.

"Hey Mom!" David grabbed his mother around the waist and nuzzled his head in her hair.

"David Alexander Barton, you know that I don't like you drinking. You're only sixteen," his mother scolded.

"Chill, Mom. It's just a beer, and I'm almost seventeen. Besides, Dad says it's cool as long as I only do it at home, and don't drive after I've had more than one beer. What's for dinner?"

"Chill Mom?" Elle threw her hands in the air and shook her head. "Well, I don't agree with you drinking, and you are not going to drink in my presence until you are twenty-one," she scolded snatching the beer from his hand. She placed it in the refrigerator and handed him a soda. "And you're on your own for dinner. There's some leftover lasagna in the refrigerator. Your dad and I have to go to that hospital benefit tonight, remember?"

"Oh, yeah. I forgot about that. Where's the old man anyway?" David sipped from the soda and burped loudly.

His mother scowled at him and swatted his butt. "He's in the pool doing laps. By the way, someone called for you. I wrote the number down. It's on the table."

David put the soda on the counter and grabbed the note. "Teenie called! What time did she call? Whose number is this?"

"She just called twenty minutes ago," Elle shrugged. "That's the number that she gave me. Who's Teenie?" his mother asked.

David dialed the number and ignored his mother's question. Elle shrugged and went upstairs to prepare for the hospital benefit.

The phone rang twice, and Charlotte awoke from her nap and grabbed the receiver from the family room telephone.

"Hello. May I speak to Teenie?" David asked.

"Teenie? There's no one here by that name," Charlotte replied sleepily.

"My name is David. She asked me to call her at this number." David repeated the number.

Lori and Tanisha stood in the doorway. "Charlotte, Teenie, I mean Tanisha, is expecting a phone call. Who's on the phone?" Lori grabbed the kitchen receiver.

"Since when does Tanisha get to take phone calls at our house? I didn't even know she was here. And I didn't know her nickname was Teenie." Charlotte yelled up the stairs. "Ma, tell Lori to tell her friends not to give out our number!"

Lori covered the kitchen receiver and handed Tanisha the phone. "Just hang up, Charlotte!"

"Hello?" Tanisha said.

"Hello, Tanisha. It's David. Did you call me?"

Tanisha smiled. "Hey, David. No, I didn't call you. You called me," she teased.

"You're always the funny one. I was just about to hang up, because the girl who answered the phone said there was no Teenie there? Is that your nickname? Where are you, by the way?"

"Slow down, sporty. I can't keep up with all your questions. I'm still in Springfield. That's why I'm at a different number," Tanisha giggled.

"Very funny, smarty pants. 543 is a Newberry East prefix. Even I know that."

"You got me. I'm at my friend Lori's house. Did you get my postcard?" Tanisha asked.

"I just got it a few days ago. Thanks. I'm really bad about checking our mail regularly. And I read it to Belvedere like you instructed. The only reason I knew this phone message my mother wrote down was from you was because you signed the postcard from Teenie. Is that your nickname? It's cute," David asked.

"It looks like it is now. I picked it up at camp, and it stuck. I'm glad you like it, not that your opinion matters," Tanisha giggled into the phone as Lori leaned into the ear piece to hear.

"Ouch! You are such a stinging little bumble bee. But I'm going to let that zinger slide because I missed you and your sarcasm."

Tanisha smiled. Lori held up her thumb and waved it excitedly. "I'm surprised you're home on a Saturday night. You're not hanging out?"

"Actually I didn't have any plans. I was just going to hang out with Belvedere and maybe go for a swim. Why, what are you doing?"

"Why don't you pick me up at my friend Lori's house and we can hang out and do nothing together," Tanisha suggested.

David took a swig from his soda. "Are you serious? Where was this leadership camp, in Oz? Did you see the wizard and get some courage? What's gotten into you, Little Miss 'I can't date until I'm fifteen'? It's July, and I thought you said your birthday was in December?"

"In fact, there was a *Wizard of Oz* type experience there, funny you should ask. And yes, my birthday is in December. December thirteenth actually, and I expect a gift. But since I haven't seen you in two weeks, I thought I'd make your day. Is that a problem?" she rattled.

"No problem at all. It works for me. Give me Lori's address, and I'll be there in thirty minutes. I just need to shower. I've been playing golf at the Club all day," David explained.

"Take your time in the shower. We don't want to rush that process!" Tanisha giggled.

"I see you didn't leave your wisecracks in Springfield," David replied.

Tanisha gave David directions to Lori's house before hanging up the phone.

"You go girl! You sounded so confident on the phone." Lori shook her head and wiggled in her seat. "I could tell at the movie theatre that he's really into you. He seems really nice. You should put on some make-up and let me bump a few curls in your hair."

"Good idea. Do you have a hoodie or sweater or something I can borrow to jazz up this turtleneck? I can't take it off or he'll see the hickey, but this turtleneck by itself doesn't work."

"Sure. You can borrow my peach Members Only jacket," Lori offered. "I'll go plug in my curling iron."

Tanisha fluffed her hair and inspected the small purple hickey on her neck. She put on Lori's jacket and borrowed some of Lori's blush to highlight her cheeks. She applied more eye liner and clear lip gloss and sprayed some of Lori's Ralph Lauren perfume. She sniffed her wrists and enjoyed the sweet floral aroma, a welcome change from the insect repellent spray that she wore every day at camp. Tanisha joined Lori in the living room and waited for David to arrive.

"What was that *Wizard of Oz* experience you were talking about with David?" Lori asked. "Did you guys do the play *The Wizard of Oz* at camp?"

Tanisha giggled and described how the bewitching hour meadow resembled the field of poppies in the *Wizard of Oz*.

"Oh, I get it. But seriously, do you have feelings for David at all? It sounds like you were into this Brian Kraft guy pretty seriously. Did you think of David at all while you were hanging out with Brian? And I'm your girl, so you can tell me the truth!" Lori said.

Tanisha took a deep breath before responding. She hugged a sofa pillow into her chest. "It was weird. I have fun with David, but it's like having a playmate fun," she explained. "We joke around and talk about stupid stuff on the phone, not the romantic stuff that you talk about with Doug," she paused. "And since David and I aren't going together or anything, I didn't feel like I was betraying him or cheating. He said he wants to get to know me better so we can date when I'm fifteen, but for all I know he has a girlfriend right now. Think about it, Brian Kraft put the full court press on me, and he had a girlfriend at home," Tanisha explained. "And Byron Bird asked for my number and he also had a girlfriend," she reminded.

"Good point. You never know when guys are telling you the whole truth," Lori shook her head.

"I think David is a really nice guy, but he's still two years older than I am. I'm not going to let myself fall head over heels for him like Maria has fallen for Todd," she continued. "We can hang out and stuff, but I'm going to proceed with caution so I'm not left feeling like a knucklehead. I still can't believe that I even thought for a second that Brian Kraft meant that he loved me," Tanisha groaned. "But that's in the past. Besides, David will be a senior next year and will leave for college the following year. So where would that leave me? Do you really think he'll come back from college to take me to prom?"

"Girl, slow down. That's several months away. But I hear where you're coming from," she agreed. "Who knows what he's really up to! You're only fourteen. He should be getting to know someone his age," Lori suggested.

"That's my point exactly," Tanisha agreed. "That's why I'm going to proceed with caution like he's a speed bump," she laughed.

Charlotte walked into the living room. "You're going to proceed with caution with who? Who are you guys talking about?"

"Charlotte, mind your own business! Ma, tell Charlotte to stay out of my conversations!" Lori yelled up the stairs.

But I've always read that girls mature faster than boys. Did I read this somewhere or is this just Maria's theory? What if it's true? Think about it, Teenie. Most of the boys at Battle Creek are still playing with Star Wars action figures. What's the appropriate age difference when you like a boy? Is there a rule? As Lori battled Charlotte, Tanisha stared out the window for David's car.

Chapter 28

Prince in a Black Corvette

The black Corvette pulled into the Perkins' driveway thirty-five minutes later. David glanced down at his directions and confirmed the address: 7131 Hawkeye Drive. He stepped out of the car as Lori and Tanisha bounced down the stairs and onto the driveway. David wore jeans with a light blue Glen Country Club golf shirt embroidered in navy lettering. He wore his Sperry Topsiders without socks. He smiled widely when he saw Tanisha.

Tanisha smiled warmly at him. "Hi, David! Did you find the house okay?" Tanisha asked.

"Yup. Your directions were good," he smiled. "Sorry I'm late, but I had to stop and fill up my tank."

"No worries," Tanisha shrugged. "You're not late. We were just catching up. You remember my friend, Lori, don't you? You met her at the movie theatre a few weeks ago," Tanisha explained.

"I remember. Good to see you again, Lori," David smiled.

"Same here, David. How cute! You both have on Sperry Topsiders," Lori observed. "So what are you guys going to do?"

David and Tanisha glanced down at each others feet and shrugged.

"We can do whatever the little princess wants to do. I'm just glad to see her," he grinned. Tanisha bit her lip and blushed.

"But I haven't eaten yet, so I need to get some food first," he continued.

"That's cool. I just ate half of a sandwich, but I could snack on something," Tanisha said.

David stared at Tanisha intensely as she spoke. "Wow! Look how tan you are. And your hair has blonde highlights." David picked up a few long strands of her hair and studied her sun streaked mane.

Tanisha playfully smacked David's hand away and smoothed her hair. "We swam every day," she explained. "And my hair always lightens in the summer sun." She was glad that she'd allowed Lori to freshen up her hair.

"It looks nice. You look nice, but aren't you warm in that turtleneck?" he asked curiously.

Lori interjected before Tanisha could speak. "Teenie is the ice princess. She is always cold and wears turtlenecks year round."

"That's good to know," David laughed. "She was wearing a turtleneck when I saw you guys at the move theatre a few weeks ago."

Lori smiled at Tanisha and winked. Tanisha enjoyed how her buddy had quickly taken to calling her by her new nickname.

"Doug and I are going bowling. You should join us. He'll be here in about twenty minutes."

"Lori, you know I am not sacrificing one of my nails to a bowling ball. It's bad enough that swimming in the lake every day peeled away all of my nail polish. I'm surprised you're going bowling since you just polished your nails." Tanisha flashed her ten fingers at Lori, highlighting her long fingernails.

Lori shrugged. "My nails are nubs. I just like to keep them polished. Doug loves bowling. Even if you guys don't bowl, we can just hang out together."

"Bowling alleys are too smoky for my taste, and I'm not much of a bowler either. What about miniature golf? Isn't there a miniature golf range in River?" David asked.

"Now you're talking! I love miniature golf. I haven't played putt putt golf in ages," Tanisha squealed. "Lori, why don't you and Doug come with us? It'll be fun!"

"We're meeting some of his friends at the bowling alley. But maybe next time we can double date."

David looked at Tanisha. "So this is a date?" he grinned.

"Slow down there, sporty. For the record, you're giving me a putting lesson. This is not a date," Tanisha winked at Lori. "I told you, I can't date until I'm fifteen. Lori won't be fifteen until December either, but her parents aren't tripping that she's dating Doug because Lori's parents know Doug's grandmother."

"Doug's grandmother goes to church with my parents. They let my sister go on car dates when she was fourteen and a half, so they're letting me do the same."

David elbowed Lori and pointed at Tanisha. "Has your friend always been such a stickler for rules?"

"She's been known to bend a rule every now and then. In fact, I think this leadership camp experience was liberating for Teenie," Lori flashed Tanisha a knowing smile.

David shifted his glance from Tanisha to Lori. "Did I miss something?"

"Just ignore her, David. Lori has on too much lip gloss, and it makes her say silly things." She lightly touched David's arm. "I left my purse inside. I'll be right back."

Tanisha raced up the three steps on the front stoop, and opened the screen door. She caught Charlotte peering out the window.

"He is too fine! Who is **that** Tanisha?" Charlotte demanded.

"His name is David. He's a friend. I met him on a John & Judy ski trip. He goes to Homer Glen," she rattled quickly.

"Is that his car or his parents' car?" she asked.

"It's his. He got it for his sixteenth birthday. Why?" Tanisha stared at Charlotte.

"So he's fine and rich! Look at you, little miss goody two shoes. What are you giving out to pull someone as fine as that?"

Tanisha grabbed her purse and scowled at Charlotte. "I'm not 'giving' out anything, idiot." Tanisha walked toward the door. "By the way, shouldn't you be studying for your eighth grade mid terms?"

"Eighth grade midterms? What are you talking about? I'll be a junior in high school in the fall."

Tanisha giggled. "My point exactly." She shook her head and walked back outside. *Lori's sister is so immature! It's almost hard to believe that she's related to Lori!*

Charlotte called after her. "What's so funny, Tanisha?"

"Even if I told you, you wouldn't get it, Charlotte," Tanisha laughed.

"What was that about?" Lori asked.

"Charlotte was just being Charlotte. I'll call you tonight." Tanisha walked over to the passenger side of the car as David reached for the handle.

Chapter 29

Saved By a Blonde

David held the passenger door open and Tanisha climbed into the front seat of the Corvette and immediately buckled her seat belt. She inhaled the scent of David's cologne which lingered in the air and mingled with the scent of leather in the warm car. She'd missed that smell. As David walked around the front of the car to get in on the driver's side, Tanisha smiled to herself. He really was a cute guy. He was at least six feet one and muscular. Brian Kraft had stood about five eleven but had been thin. She settled into her seat and twirled the leather handle of her small Coach bag. She'd treated herself to the expensive caramel colored purse with her first check from Save Mart.

"I'm starving. So where can we grab something to eat?" David buckled his seat belt.

"Sanfratello's pizza is not too far from the River miniature golf center. Their pizza is really good. Or there's also an ice cream parlor in River that has Italian food."

"Let's go to Sanfratellos. I always get Aurelios' pizza so I'm up for trying something new. How do we get there?"

David backed the car out of the driveway, and Tanisha compared Sanfratellos' pizza to Aurelios' pizza.

"It's hard to say which pizza is better. It depends what you like. Aurelios has really good sauce, but I prefer Sanfratello's crust. And Sanfratellos puts more cheese on their pizza. But you can decide for yourself shortly," she said as she gave him directions.

David parked the car, and the two walked into the small family owned pizza parlor.

They sat at a booth and ordered a medium cheese and sausage pizza with half mushroom and a pitcher of root beer. The smell of the pizza made Tanisha hungry.

"So how was camp, Teenie? I love that nickname. It suits you," David smiled.

Tanisha gave David the abbreviated version of the leadership camp highlights, emphasizing the Apache tribe's successful food bank program.

"So you were elected vice president of your group? That's really cool."

"Yeah. It was fun. The girls in my cabin were cool too. I had a good time."

"So was the camp mixed?" David studied Tanisha's face.

"You mean boys and girls?" Tanisha raised her eyebrow.

"Boys and girls and racially mixed?" David filled Tanisha's glass with root beer.

"Both. The campers were all students who hold leadership offices at their school's student council. There was an even split of boys and girls, but there weren't a lot of African Americans. There were over one hundred campers there, but only three African Americans, myself another girl and a guy."

David raised his eyebrow at Tanisha. "So was he trying to push up on you?"

Tanisha blushed. "Was who trying to push up on me?"

"The black guy at the camp, was he trying to push up on you?"

"Derrick? He was so not into me," Tanisha giggled. "In fact, I heard him say that he was into blondes."

"Good." David twisted the paper from his straw tightly.

"Good that he was into blondes?" Tanisha asked coyly.

"Good that he wasn't into you," David winked at Tanisha. "So what did you do during your free time, Miss Teenie?"

Tanisha squirmed in her seat. "Not much really. I just hung out with my cabin mates and worked on my tribe's food bank project. Since I was the vice president of the tribe, I had to coordinate a lot of the logistical stuff with the other officers and our counselor."

"That doesn't surprise me. Camp is all about experimenting and breaking the rules, and you were strictly business. You're such a good girl! Tell me you had a little fun, tell me you skinny dipped in the lake or went on an underwear raid or something!"

Tanisha smiled in her famous closed mouth smile, her left eyebrow raised slightly. "I had fun in my own Tanisha Carlson way. I could tell you what that means, but then I'd have to kill you." Tanisha flashed him a coy smile and took a bite of her pizza.

She savored the butter flavored crust. She bit into a mushroom and enjoyed the gooey treat. Pizza hadn't been served in the mess hall, and she'd missed her favorite food.

When the meal was delivered, David bowed his head and silently said grace. This brief gesture surprised Tanisha. The Carlson family always said grace before every meal, but she seldom performed the ritual outside of her house. Her thoughts drifted back to the many meals she'd recently shared with Brian Kraft. He'd never said grace, or at least not in a visible way. She took another bite of her pizza and thought about their nightly kissing festival in the wildflower meadow. They'd not gone past second base, but the bewitching hour had been one of the camp highlights for Tanisha. She could still remember Brian's scent. She looked up and saw David staring at her with a puzzled expression. She smiled self consciously. *Why is he staring at me? Did he see my tooth?*

"Earth calling, Teenie. The pizza is so good that it has you day dreaming?" David asked playfully.

Thank God! He hasn't seen my tooth. "I was just thinking about something that happened at camp, and Derrick's comment about blondes," she replied.

"A lot of guys like to date girls of different races. You shouldn't take that personally," he explained.

"What about you? Are you into blondes?" she asked.

"No. I'm not into blondes. Don't get me wrong, there are some at my school that are really cute, but it's not my thing," David said casually.

"Your thing? What does that mean?" she asked.

"It means that I don't really date outside my race too much."

"But you have dated outside your race?" Tanisha studied David curiously.

"Well yeah. I dibbled and dabbled a little bit with a few white girls. Everybody experiments to see what it's like, but it really wasn't my thing."

"Everybody experiments? Don't you believe that you can like someone for who they are, regardless of their race?" *Is that what I was to Brian Kraft, an experiment?*

"I totally believe that. If you click with someone, you click. Nothing else matters. I haven't been dating that long, but I find that I'm usually more attracted to girls that remind me of the women in my family that I admire and respect, and those women are black or

African American as you would say. I have to be honest. I get all kinds of girls that push up on me, especially when they see my wheels, but I just shrug it off. Most of them just want a ride in my Vette." David took a swig from his root beer mug. "Why all the questions about blondes? Is it because that Derrick cat at camp made that comment?"

Tanisha swallowed her pizza and took a swig of her root beer before answering. "Yeah, I just thought it was a weird comment to say. But it's no big deal. I just wondered. Let's hurry so we have enough time to play miniature golf. How do you like the pizza?"

"Aye, Aye, captain! You were right by the way. This pizza is delicious. I think I still like Aurelios better, but this is really good. Do you want to take the rest of this home? If not, I'll take it home," David said.

"Thanks, but you take it home." She thought about bringing the pizza home as a treat for Byron and Allen, but didn't want to concoct a tale explaining why she had Sanfratellos' pizza. "I'll be right back. I have to go to the restroom."

She went into a stall and lined the toilet seat with tissue. It was fairly clean. She slowly peed into the toilet. Since as far back as she could remember, she hated using public restrooms and only used them out of absolute necessity. She wasn't a germ freak. She just hated using public restrooms. But she'd had two glasses of root beer and really had to pee. She exhaled loudly as the pressure was slowly released. She wiped herself and stared. Her eyes grew wide. She wiped herself again. She stared closer this time. It was blood. She glanced down at her panties and saw a small red stain. *Shit!* Tanisha hadn't been on her menstrual cycle long enough to anticipate when her period was going to start. She didn't know to carry at least one 'just in case' sanitary napkin in her purse at all times. No one had shared that feminine tip with her. She carefully stacked toilet paper in her panties and thought about her next move. She checked her purse for a quarter. She had six dollars, but no coins. *I'll just go to the cashier and get change or tell David that I need to make a phone call and ask for a quarter. That's what I'll do.*

Tanisha washed her hands in the sink, rinsing and washing twice. She reached for a paper towel and used the damp paper towel to turn off the faucet. She casually fluffed her hair in the mirror and reached in her small purse to search for her lip gloss. She was bumped slightly by the restroom door.

"I'm so sorry," a soft voice said.

Tanisha turned toward the familiar voice. It was Jack's friend Kerri Peck.

"Oh my God, Teenie!" Kerri smiled widely. "I didn't hurt you with the door did I, girlfriend?"

"Hi, Kerri. I'm fine." Tanisha's heart raced with panic.

"This bathroom is so tiny. What a surprise seeing you here," Kerri squealed.

"I'm just having some pizza. What are you doing here?" Tanisha gulped.

"Your brother and I just got here. Jack's at the table now. We're going to play putt putt golf. Teenie, your hair looks cute like that." Kerri patted Tanisha's head.

I am so busted! "Thanks. How did you know my nickname was Teenie?" Tanisha asked. "No one in my family calls me Teenie."

"Teenie is such a cute nickname for Tanisha so I just assumed." Kerri applied powder to her nose.

Is there a handbook for nicknames that all white people study? "Kerri, I need a favor," Tanisha said. "Do you have a quarter? I need to buy a sanitary napkin."

"No problem. I have a tampon in my purse. Do you want that instead?"

"No. Just a quarter please," Tanisha replied.

Tanisha grabbed the quarter and inserted it in the ladies' hygiene machine. A Kotex maxi pad came out. "Thanks, Kerri. Let me take care of this. But don't leave yet." She went into a stall and applied the sanitary pad as Kerri peed in the next stall. Tanisha walked over to the sink and washed her hands again.

Kerri exited the stall and reached in her purse for her hairbrush. She brushed her long blonde hair and applied lipstick.

Gross! She's not going to wash her hands? That's so nasty! My bunk mates always washed their hands after using the bathroom, so I know this isn't a white girl thing. Stop stereotyping and focus, Teenie! What am I going to do? If she tells Jack that she saw me here, he's going to flip out and play big brother and want to take me home! He may even confront David and cause a scene. I don't want him to think that I'm a liar. You are a liar. You're supposed to be at Lori's house.

Tanisha looked at Kerri in the mirror. "Kerri, I need a huge favor. I'm here with a friend of mine, a guy. I'm not supposed to be dating for a few more months, and I don't want Jack to know that I'm here. You know how he is," she laughed. "He'll act all big brother on me and get the wrong idea. Can you do me a favor? Please don't tell Jack that you saw me. I'll just go out the side door and wait for my friend by his car. My friend is paying the check now. His name is David and he has on a light blue golf shirt. He's sitting at the booth by the window. Please just go up to him and quietly tell him that you're my friend and that I'm waiting for him at his car. Please don't mention that you saw me to Jack. Can you do that for me, Kerri?" Tanisha pleaded.

"Sure, Teenie. No problem. Your secret is safe with me, girlfriend. I remember what it was like to have to sneak around when I first started dating Jack. I'm glad Jack and I are out in the open now about our relationship." Kerri winked at Tanisha and left the restroom.

Tanisha slipped out the side door and waited by David's car. Her eyes scanned the small parking lot until she spotted Bruce, the Blue Goose. Her thoughts raced and adrenaline pumped through her body as she crouched near David's car.

I can't believe that Kerri didn't wash her hands! And what is it with white people and nicknames? She just automatically nicknamed me Teenie! And what's up with her saying girlfriend? It doesn't work when white girls say it. I wonder if they say it to each other, or if they just say it to black girls when they're trying to fit in and act cool. My cabin mates were cool, and they never said 'girlfriend' to me. And they always washed their hands after using the bathroom! Tanisha, she just saved your butt, so stop criticizing and crucifying that girl! So Jack and Kerri are in a relationship? I knew they were dating! Kerri's cool. She's pretty. She's smart. She's nice, and she has a lot in common with my brother. If he likes her, then that's all that matters. Who cares if she's white? After my summer fling, I'm okay with it. Now, her not washing her hands after she used the bathroom is another matter. That's just nasty.

Moments later David appeared. "Tanisha?" David called.

"I'm over here," she replied.

"Hey! What's with the secretive behavior?" he asked. "Why are you hiding?"

"Hurry! Unlock the door so I can get in!"

"What was that about?" David asked. "Why'd you sneak out of the restaurant?"

Tanisha got in the car and slouched down in the front seat. "My brother is in there with his girlfriend, and I didn't want him to see me and bust me out."

"The white girl that came up to me was your brother's girlfriend?" David asked.

Tanisha jumped in the front seat and slid down so that her head was below the dashboard. "He hasn't said that it's his girlfriend, but they spend a lot of time together, and she just told me they're in a relationship. By the way, they're going to play miniature golf, so we have to do something else."

"No wonder you were asking me all the questions about blondes. Your brother is dipping in that pool. Does that bother you?" David started the car.

Tanisha swatted David's arm. "Just drive out of the parking lot so I can sit up," she ordered.

David backed the car out and headed down Main Street. "Hey, you want to go to my house? You won't run into anyone you know there. Plus, you can see Belvedere and we can hang out by my pool and play chess or play Atari. My parents are at a black tie event and won't be home until well after midnight. I'll have you home long before then since I know you're not into the meet the parents thing."

"You have a pool? You're like the poster child for the spoiled little rich boy," Tanisha grinned. *He has a pool in his backyard. His parents are both doctors. He got a new Corvette for his sixteenth birthday. He's in another league. What does he see in me?*

"Do you want to go to my house or what, smarty pants?" David teased.

"At least I won't run into anybody. Okay, but I have to be home by ten o'clock," Tanisha explained.

"I'll have you home by nine forty-five," David promised.

They headed toward David's home.

"You didn't answer my question. Does it bother you that your brother is dating a white girl?"

"At first it did, but not any more. Lori was right. Leadership camp opened my mind about a lot of different things," Tanisha grinned.

Chapter 30

Beef Chop Suey

Billie pulled into the New Moon parking lot and parked her car next to Jackie's car. She took another pull from her cigarette and snubbed it in the overflowing ashtray. Out of habit, she opened her door and emptied the ashtray onto the pavement, careful to avoid the cigarette butts as she stepped out of the car. She entered the small Chinese restaurant and spotted Jackie sitting in a booth having a cigarette and drinking a bottle of beer.

She'd worn her red Candies slides and a white polyester pantsuit. The wooden heel of her slides made a clicking noise on the tile floor as she walked over to Jackie.

The restaurant was empty save two tables. It was almost ten o'clock at night, and the restaurant was preparing to close for the evening.

Jackie looked up from the menu when he heard her approaching. "Hey Billie. How you doing?"

"I'm fine." Billie replied sweetly, sitting down across from Jackie.

"I was just about to order some egg rolls. I haven't eaten since I took Byron and Allen to McDonalds for lunch, and it looks like they're about to close."

"Let's go ahead and order. I'm hungry too and I know what I want."

Jackie ordered Szechwan beef with broccoli and an order of egg rolls. Billie ordered beef chop suey and a beer.

"So what did you want to talk to me about that we couldn't discuss over the phone or in front of the kids?" Jackie asked. He took a pull from his cigarette.

Earlier that evening, when Jackie dropped off Byron and Allen, Billie asked him to meet her here so they could talk. During happier times in their marriage, this had been their favorite restaurant.

The young waiter brought Billie's beer quickly, and she drank liberally from the ice cold bottle.

"I need extra money for the child support this week," she said softly.

Jackie raised his bushy eyebrows in unison and slowly lowered his right brow making the mole between his brows dance. "You're kidding, right?"

Billie's tone was soft and seductive. "Things are expensive, and I need more money, Jackie," she purred.

"Billie, the court decided how much money you receive. My pay hasn't increased, so why do you think I can pay more money?" Jackie whispered.

Billie sat up straight in her seat. Her tone hardened. "Things are expensive. I have to pay rent and utilities plus my car note and insurance."

Jackie spoke through his teeth. "Lower your voice! Between my own rent, utilities, and the child support that I'm already paying, plus my own car expenses, I'm barely making it. You're making good money at the cable company. What are you doing with your money?"

Billie scowled at Jackie as the waiter delivered the egg rolls. "That's none of your business," she growled.

Jackie reached for a piping hot egg roll and transferred it to his small saucer. "Oh, I get it. You don't want to account for how you're spending your money, but you want me to just give you money outside of what the court has already told me to pay? What kind of sense does that make? I'm already buying the kids stuff outside of what I'm giving you for child support." Jackie covered his egg roll with the yellow hot mustard sauce on the table and bit into the egg roll, sucking the air in and out of his mouth in an effort to cool the hot food on his tongue.

Billie glared at Jackie and ate in silence. Her plan wasn't working. She'd hoped that her plea would go over better in a face to face encounter. She'd applied make-up and worn her tight white pantsuit in an effort to seduce Jackie with her beauty. She needed a new strategy.

Jackie blew into the egg roll and took another bite. He chewed and swallowed. "Why do you need more money, Billie?"

Billie softened her gaze and exhaled loudly. She twirled a paper napkin in her hand and spoke, lifting her eyes slowly to meet Jackie's. "It's Tanisha. She really wants to get her tooth fixed, and you know she's not covered under my dental insurance yet. The dentist said that if he pulls it, the permanent tooth will fall into place."

Jackie took a swig from his beer. "Why didn't you just say that all along?"

"I know how you feel about getting that tooth pulled after your dentist told you that it might disrupt the structure of her face since it's a primary tooth," Billie continued.

"But I just took her to the dentist a few months ago and he said it shouldn't be pulled," Jackie chewed quickly.

"Well, I took her to another dentist for a second opinion, and this one says we should pull it," Billie countered. "And of course this is the dentist that she wants to listen to."

"She really wants that tooth taken out, huh?" he asked.

Billie spoke with authority. "Uh huh, she talks about it all of the time. She and I were just talking about it the other day, and I want to get it taken care of before school starts. Since she'll be a freshman, I'd like her to start high school with a new outlook," Billie explained.

Jackie furrowed his thick eyebrows and stared at Billie. "I see. How much does it cost?"

"It's two hundred dollars," Billie said firmly.

"Two hundred dollars! To pull a tooth?" Jackie coughed to avoid choking on his food. He took a large sip of water.

"They also have to take x-rays and put a support in place to guide the permanent tooth into the proper slot," she explained. "You know when you see a new dentist the first appointment is always expensive."

"I see. I still don't understand why that job won't let you cover the kids for six months. That is the most ridiculous thing I've ever heard. Well, it'll be six months soon and then you can put her on your dental insurance, and let your insurance pay for most of it, right? When is your six month anniversary?"

"My six month anniversary is September, but they won't let me add the kids until open enrollment in October."

Billie had cancelled her family health and dental coverage so that she could afford the car payment and insurance on her new car. She had told Jackie that the cable company wouldn't allow her to cover the kids until she'd worked there for six months. Since Billie had sole custody of the children, Jackie was not able to add the children to his insurance [without going through a lot of legal red tape] as long as Billie was working.

"Why don't you just wait and have it done in a few months?" he asked, "That way the insurance will pay for most of it," he suggested. "Tanisha can wait a few more months."

Billie shifted in her chair as the waiter brought the steaming Szechwan beef and beef chop suey. She scooped food on her plate immediately. "They'll be on my insurance in October, but school starts in August. I just thought it would be nice for her to have it done sooner than later. That way it will give the permanent tooth more time to fall into place."

"I hadn't thought of that. It's not like when they pull the tooth, the permanent tooth is going to fall down immediately. She's going to have a gap there for a while. How much does the dentist want up front to get started?"

"He wants half now and then the other half one week later when they finish the procedure." Billie needed one hundred dollars to become current on her car payment.

"Whew! One hundred dollars? I won't have that until next week. Maybe I can ask Mama for some money."

"The thing is, he has to do it next week because he's taking off the first week in August to spend the end of the summer in Europe." Billie had to bite her lip to stop from snickering. Her lie was becoming more and more intricate.

"Isn't that something? He's spending the summer in Europe. Dentists and doctors sure know how to take your money. I'll borrow the money from Mama and bring it out early next week."

"By the way, I want to surprise Tanisha with this, so don't mention it to her."

"That's fine." It troubled Jackie that Billie and Tanisha were not close. Growing up, he'd watched as his three older sisters forged distinct loving bonds with their mother. He wanted Tanisha to have a similar relationship with her mother. He knew that Billie had not nurtured Tanisha as a child. Partly because of Billie's bipolar disorder and partly because of her open disdain for his sister Helen and Tanisha's uncanny resemblance to Helen. Billie still became angry when people mistook Helen for Tanisha's mother. Although she was now a young woman, Jackie had not given up hope that his now teenage daughter might some day become close to her mother. If his ex-wife wanted to surprise Tanisha with the tooth extraction, then he wouldn't let two hundred dollars prevent her from making an effort to get close to her only daughter. He smiled contentedly as he finished his Szechwan beef and beer.

The restaurant was now empty, and the waiters rushed about sweeping and mopping. The hostess stood politely at the hostess stand in a bright red kimono, patiently waiting for Jackie and Billie to finish their meal.

Billie grinned. She was quite pleased with herself. She hadn't had a backup plan and had been forced to concoct the Tanisha story on the fly. She knew that he would not refuse anything that Tanisha needed. *When in doubt, claim a need for his precious Tanisha and he'll come through.* Billie dragged her fork through her beef chop suey placing a small forkful into her mouth.

On Monday, I'll call him and tell him that the dentist wants the entire amount up front since Tanisha doesn't have dental insurance. He's borrowing it from his mama anyway, so he may as well just borrow the whole two hundred now. I know Grandma Bootsy has it. And then, I'll just tell him that the dentist left earlier for his trip and can't do it until late August. That should buy me some time before he figures out that I used the money for something else.

"It looks like they're trying to close, Billie. I'm finished. I'll just have them wrap up the rest of my food so I can have it for lunch tomorrow. You barely touched your food. Do you want me to have them wrap yours too?" Jackie asked.

"Sure, why not." As though on cue, the waiter rushed over and grabbed the plates and serving dishes still filled with food, returning seconds later with two, silver handled white boxes. Jackie walked to the cashier to pay the bill.

Billie pulled out her cigarettes and lit one. Jackie returned to the table and left three dollars on the table as tip.

"Billie, why don't you smoke when we get outside? They're trying to close. Let's go," he coaxed.

"You can go if you want to. I need to let my food settle. They can wait for me to finish my cigarette. When are you going to bring the money?"

"I'll bring it to your job on Tuesday. I'll see you later." Jackie grabbed the small white container that was nearest his seat and walked away from the table. He left the restaurant shaking his head and mumbling under his breath.

Billie smoked her cigarette and snubbed the butt in her saucer. She eyed the three dollar tip. *That waiter didn't deserve a three dollar tip, and I need some more cigarettes.* Billie slipped two of the dollars into her purse. Her cigarette smoldering in the makeshift ashtray, the beef chop suey carton abandoned on the table, she slowly sauntered to the parking lot.

Chapter 31

The Beer Bust

David pulled the Corvette into the driveway and hit the garage door opener. Tanisha was impressed. The Barton's English Tudor was sizable but looked small next door to the grand house that sat on two lots. David led the way through the garage and turned on a light in the laundry room, waking Belvedere who was stretched out on an oversized black floor pillow. He hung his keys on a hook and punched in the alarm code to deactivate the security system. Belvedere sat up and walked over to Tanisha.

"He must really like you. He never walks over to me when I come home. He just lays there like a furry slug."

"Hey there, Mr. Belvedere! Good to see you, buddy." Tanisha rubbed his head.

Tanisha followed David through the laundry room that led to a large kitchen.

"Do you want to play Atari? I have Space Invaders and Miss Pac Man. Or we can play chess. We can sit in the family room or hang out by the pool. We have this new bug zapper thing that my dad just got, and it works pretty well so the mosquitoes won't eat us alive. And if you feel like making some more of that delicious popcorn, that'd be cool too," David said rapidly.

"I'm full from the pizza, but if you want popcorn I could make some. I'd like a glass of water though," Tanisha replied.

David reached in the cupboard to the left of the window and retrieved a large glass. As he walked over to the refrigerator water dispenser, Tanisha quickly surveyed her surroundings.

The kitchen was a pale yellow and the appliances were white. There were several stacks of mail spread out on the counter and more mail, magazines and newspapers stacked neatly on a desk next to the refrigerator. There was a table with six chairs in a breakfast nook. A black pepper grinder and salt shaker held center court on the large oak table. A chrome pot rack suspended from the ceiling and centered above an extended counter served as home to a patchwork of well worn pots and pans. The pots were clearly used regularly and many of the bottoms were slightly scorched. *Looks like someone uses this kitchen on a regular basis, unlike Todd's mausoleum of a kitchen where everything was on display.*

A pair of yellow rubber gloves hung over a dish drainer. The window overlooking the sink was covered in soft yellow curtains printed with white daisies. The window looked out into the backyard where the soft underwater lights of the large swimming pool reflected against the clear blue water. Sliding glass doors were positioned near the kitchen table which opened to a concrete patio. A gas grill and large black Weber grill sat side by side on the patio. Tanisha could see that the Barton's backyard was quite large even with the sizable pool. *This is the first time I've seen a pool in someone's backyard, but other than that, this house reminds me a lot of Aunt Helen's house. It's large, but it's homey and comfortable. In fact, Aunt Helen's house is a little larger than this one.*

David walked over and handed Tanisha a glass of water.

"Let's play Atari. I love Ms. Pac Man. If you want me to make some popcorn I'll make it," Tanisha offered as she took a sip of her water.

David put the leftover pizza in the refrigerator. "I'm still full too. But maybe we'll make some later, or I can show you how I make the world's best microwave popcorn."

"I'll pass," Tanisha chuckled.

David walked through the kitchen and crossed a small hallway that led to the family room. The room was painted the same soft yellow as the kitchen with one wall covered in paneling. The room was furnished with a large brown leather sofa and a small loveseat covered in a flower pattern. More newspapers and magazines were stacked on the coffee table. Sliding glass doors led to a cement patio covered with a large attached awning that spread from the kitchen to the exterior wall. The family room patio doors provided an unobstructed view of the pool. A stone fireplace occupied one wall of the rectangular shaped room. Photos adorned the fireplace mantle. A large television sat in the corner between the fireplace and the sliding glass doors. A leather recliner sat next to a brass plated reading lamp opposite the television.

"David, where's your bathroom?" Tanisha asked.

"You must have the world's smallest bladder," he teased. "It's right down the hall on your right."

"I drank a little too much root beer," she lied.

She wanted to make sure that her pad wasn't leaking. The main hallway was adorned with family photos on either side of the wall like an art gallery. The powder room was painted a soft blue with navy blue hand towels hanging lopsided on the towel rack. Tanisha checked her pad, content that her menstrual cycle flow was still light and had not soiled the sanitary napkin. She washed her hands with the English Lavender scented soap. There was a toothbrush dispenser with three toothbrushes and a tube of toothpaste on the sink's counter. *That's practical. They probably brush their teeth before they leave the house, and this way they don't have to run upstairs to the other bathrooms to do it.* She quickly ran her fingers through her hair and popped a tic tac in her mouth.

When she came out of the bathroom, her eyes shifted to the right and she tiptoed four steps to survey the living room. On the left side of the double front door was a small living room that was painted the same soft blue as the powder room. The dark hardwood floors that ran through the family room and hallway continued up the stairwell centered in the middle of the foyer. The living room was carpeted in a soft blue plush carpet. An overstuffed sofa and matching loveseat covered in a cream damask fabric with light blue accents filled the room. A pale blue wing back chair nestled nearest the box bay window in the front of the house. A window seat spanned the width of the window and was covered in the same damask fabric as the sofa and loveseat. Framed photos adorned the sofa and side tables, while a bouquet of fresh daisies sat in a small crystal bowl on the coffee table, a few petals littered the table. An afghan was casually draped over the sofa, and a novel left open on the table near the vase, lent a casual, comfortable elegance to the inviting space.

French doors connected the living room to a smaller room that appeared to serve as an office. Tanisha noticed that the carpeting was covered in soft foot prints indicating that the family spent time in the living room, if for no other reason than to access the office. She noticed built in book cases lined one wall of the office. Across from the living room, and on the right side of the front door, was a dining room that connected to the kitchen. The large mahogany dining table was surrounded by eight chairs. The dark hardwood floors in the dining room were softened by a large oriental rug centered beneath the table. A large dining hutch held china and crystal stemware. A small stack of newspapers was neatly stacked on the dining room table. *This family certainly likes to read a lot!*

Tanisha tiptoed back to the family room as David was setting up the Atari. She tossed Lori's peach colored jacket on the sofa, kicked off her shoes and sat cross legged on the floor with her back against the leather sofa.

Belvedere padded into the room and plopped down next to her, his head inches from her hand, his muzzle inviting her to pet him. She took the bait and casually rubbed his head.

"You're the only person that I know who wears a turtleneck with shorts in July," David quipped.

"Hey, it works for me. I'm always chilly, and the turtleneck provides a ying yang balance for my body temperature. Hand over the joystick. I'm the Ms. Pac Man champion. Prepare to die my friend!"

"Doubtful. Let's see what you got," David challenged.

Tanisha cleared the board with her first Pac Man. She was pleased with her score and handed the joystick to David, blowing on her nails and bowing from the waist.

"Not bad, not bad at all. But let me show you how it's done."

David scored over five thousand points with one Ms. Pac Man remaining. "Shall we continue?" he teased playfully.

Tanisha hit restart on the joystick canceling his score.

"It looks like someone is a sore loser," David laughed.

Tanisha responded by giving David a raspberry, dousing him with her saliva. He repaid the favor and gave her a raspberry. Tanisha squealed and wiped her face. She glanced at her watch. It was almost nine o'clock. She knew that her pad would start leaking in another hour and she needed to get home before she soiled her shorts.

David noticed her glancing nervously at her watch. "Relax," he said. "It's only 9:00, and I can have you home in ten minutes."

"I don't want you to get in trouble if your parents come home," she offered.

"Teenie, I'm sixteen years old. I'll be seventeen in three weeks. They know I date and they know I have company. I won't get in trouble for having a girl here. Now if we were upstairs in my bedroom that might be a different story." David laughed out loud.

"Keep dreaming, buddy," Tanisha laughed.

"Pizza always makes me want a beer. Hell, since I'm at home, I'm going to have a beer. Would you like a crème soda, goody two shoes?" David stood up and stretched.

"Sure." Tanisha was touched that David remembered that she'd requested a crème soda when they were at Todd's house a few weeks ago. "But you have to drive me home so don't get drunk, you lush!" she yelled into the kitchen.

Returning with a can of beer for himself and a can of ice cold strawberry crème soda with two frosty, glass mugs, David opened Tanisha's crème soda, and filled her glass. Plopping next to her, he proceeded to open his beer. The can fizzed and spritzed beer like an erupting volcano, soaking both of them.

"David!" Tanisha squealed gripping her wet shirt as Belvedere scurried out of the room. "I'm soaked," she scowled.

"I'm so sorry, Teenie," he offered. "These cans were in the garage and must have rolled around a little bit before I put them in the refrigerator," he explained. "Tell you what, you can wear one of my tee-shirts," he suggested. "By the way, I have your black jacket.

Maria left it in my car when we went to Todd's house. You can just put that on."

Tanisha stood up. "I've been looking for that thing all over the place," she shared.

David left the room and returned with the black hoodie. "I washed it because Belvedere had been using it as a pillow on the back seat."

"Cool! I'll just put this on." Tanisha took the jacket and went into the bathroom to change. She carefully pulled the wet turtleneck over her head and slipped into the hoodie. She inhaled the sweet smell of fabric softener and returned to the family room.

"I can wash your shirt for you real quick, Teenie. We have a quick cycle on our washing machine. That way your mom won't smell beer in the laundry. It'll only take ten minutes to wash and another fifteen to dry," David said slowly.

Tanisha handed David the wet turtleneck. "Good idea."

David didn't reach to take the turtleneck.

Tanisha tilted her head and extended her hand again. "Here you go, David," she repeated. "It's dripping on the floor."

David's gaze was fixated on the right side of her neck, and his eyes became slits as he leaned in closer to her face.

"What's the matter? Why are you staring at me?" Tanisha backed up.

"You tell me, Tanisha. What's that on your neck?"

Tanisha's eyes opened wide. She blushed and instinctively raised her hand to her neck. *I forgot about my hickey!*

"It's not what it looks like, David," she gasped.

"It looks like a hickey. Who gave you a hickey, Tanisha?"

Tanisha took a deep breath and closed her eyes. When she opened them, David was still scowling at her. She lowered her eyes and stared at the floor. "This guy at camp," she whispered softly.

"This guy at camp?" David repeated harshly. "He must have been more than just some guy at camp. Was it that Derrick guy you were telling me about?"

"No. His name was Brian," Tanisha whispered. She was embarrassed.

"When were you going to tell me about him?" David barked.

Tanisha stared at the floor, watching as tiny drops of beer from her wet turtleneck created a small puddle on the carpet.

"So he must have been white then, since you said there was only one black guy at camp. Or did you lie about that? No wonder you were asking me all those questions about white girls," David growled. "Tell me what's going on, Tanisha!"

Tanisha didn't like how harshly he spoke her name. She wished he'd call her Teenie again. "Yes, he was white. There's nothing to tell really," she shrugged. "We made out a few times and that was it. He lives in Lake Forest, so it's not like we're going together." Tanisha increased her grip on the turtleneck and changed the angle to stop the beer from dripping to the floor.

David stared at Tanisha in disbelief. "You made out a few times?" he repeated. He covered his eyes with his hand. "I don't believe this. I poured my heart out to you before you left, telling you how I wanted to get to know you better and couldn't wait until you turned fifteen. I was willing to hang in there and be your friend until we could date officially. While you were gone, I didn't even go on a date with anyone else, and you were making out with some random white guy at camp?" he barked. "And then you called me to hang out knowing you had a hickey on your neck? No wonder you wore that turtleneck. Get your jacket, let's go," he ordered. He walked out of the family room and down the hall.

Stunned, Tanisha grabbed Lori's jacket and quickly followed David into the kitchen. David grabbed a plastic bag, thrusting it at Tanisha, and continued into the laundry room grabbing his keys from the hook by the door. She stuffed the wet turtleneck inside the plastic bag.

Tanisha called after David once in the garage. "David, at least let me explain. It's not like you and I are going together. We're just getting to know each other, right? You said yourself that camp was all about experimenting."

David stopped at the end of the garage. "Tanisha, I told you that I liked you. I stopped by your job the night before you left with a care package for you. While I'm here missing you, you're at camp getting hickeys. And then when I gave you an opportunity to tell me what happened at camp, you acted like you just worked the whole time. You're not the person I thought you were."

David got into the driver side and started the car. Tanisha climbed into the passenger side gripping the plastic bag with her soiled turtleneck in one hand and Lori's peach jacket slung over her arm. Leaving the garage door open, David peeled out of the driveway without buckling his seatbelt or waiting for her to buckle hers. She buckled in and stared out the window.

What have I done? Have I thrown out a relationship with a great boy for a two week fling with someone that I may never see again?

David turned on the radio and turned the volume up. He drove fast, flooring the pedal to race through street lights as they turned yellow. Singing along to the music, he deliberately ignored Tanisha.

As David sped along quickly approaching Cedar Grove, Tanisha didn't know what to say, but she knew that she had to say something. She put the plastic bag on the floor and gently placed the jacket on top of it. Her heart was beating rapidly. She turned down the volume on the radio and stared at David's profile and started talking.

"David, his name was Brian Kraft, and I met him on the train on my way to Springfield. He had on a yellow camp shirt and invited me to sit next to him, and we talked the whole way. Once we got to camp, he went out of his way to introduce me to all of the people he knew since he'd been there the year before," she paused.

"When I was eleven years old, I went to St. Mary's camp in Wisconsin and was the only black girl there, and the only girl who'd never been to the camp before. I didn't have any friends and it was a miserable experience. I pretended that I was sick so my parents would come and get me early. I didn't want this camp experience to be a repeat of that one where I had no friends and was miserable," Tanisha paused. She took a deep breath. "Brian was popular and made me feel welcome. He was the president of my tribe, and I was the vice president, so we spent a lot of time together. We clicked, and my cabin mates clicked with two of his friends. Everybody was pairing off at camp, and so it seemed like the thing to do," she paused. "He kissed me and I kissed him back. We ate all of our meals together and spent a lot of time together. I'm not going to lie to you. I really liked him. I didn't know it at first, but he told me later that he had a girlfriend at home. I thought about not hanging out with him after that," she admitted. "But I didn't want to be by myself and be miserable. Plus, he told me that he and his girlfriend had an agreement that they could experiment and get to know other people while at camp," she explained. "Even though I don't think you should mess around with someone if you know that they have a girlfriend, I enjoyed his company, so we still hung out," she shared softly. Tanisha tucked her hair behind her ear and breathed. "I'm not proud of what I did, but I did it anyway. He was a really nice guy."

His fingers wound tightly around the steering wheel, David stared blankly out the windshield as Tanisha continued. "We exchanged addresses and phone numbers, but when I saw him last night at the closing banquet, I got a gut feeling that I won't hear from him again because he lives too far for us to date. Plus, he has a girlfriend," Tanisha repeated. "And my cabin mates told me that once camp ends, the fling is over. It's just a summer experience. Anyway, you're probably right. He was just some random, white guy that I kissed at camp. I was probably some experiment for him," she offered. "I'm sorry that I didn't tell you before, but I didn't know how. He asked me if I had a boyfriend at home and I said no," she paused. "I said that there was a guy that I liked and was getting to know, but he wasn't my boyfriend, yet," she stammered softly.

Tanisha looked at David to see if he showed a reaction. His jaws remained clenched, but he'd slowed down his speed. "David, he's only the second boy I've ever kissed. I've never had a hickey before so I wore the turtleneck to hide the hickey from my parents, not from you. I wanted to see you tonight so I called you. I really want to still get to know you, and I hope you and I can still be friends. I really like you and I enjoy spending time with you. I don't know what else to say," she finished. Her voice cracked, and she pushed back the tears that were dancing on her pupils.

David turned into the Cedar Grove complex without saying a word. He pulled up behind the hill and stopped the car.

Tanisha held the door handle and paused. "David, say something."

"Don't forget your jacket," he ordered.

Grabbing Lori's jacket, and the bag with her soiled turtleneck, she trudged numbly up the hill. She tensed as he spun the car around and sped away, not waiting for her to enter the house. Tanisha entered the back door and leaned against it. As usual, Byron and Allen were sprawled across the living room floor watching television. She walked through the kitchen and plopped on the sofa. She wanted to call Lori but knew that she wasn't home yet. She had an 11:00 curfew and it was only 9:30.

Tanisha ran up to her room and threw herself across her bed. She burrowed her head into her pillow and sobbed quietly.

What have I done? Have I just ruined everything?

Chapter 32

Doctors Make Phone Calls

Tanisha finished her shift at Save Mart and rode her bike home. She propped her bike against the front rail and went inside, ignoring her dad's reminder to lock the bike. The house was quiet. Byron and Allen usually swam in the Cedar Grove pool in the afternoons. She had not heard from David all day on Sunday. She'd talked to Lori and told her the whole story. Lori had been sympathetic and told her to let some time pass before calling him.

It had been two weeks and she still hadn't heard from him. Tanisha made herself a peanut butter and jelly sandwich and flipped on the television, pausing to watch a *Gilligan's Island* rerun. As she munched on her sandwich, she heard her telephone ringing. She left the sandwich on the saucer and raced up the stairs two at a time, grabbing the phone on the fourth ring.

"Hello!" Tanisha inhaled deeply to catch her breath from the sprint up the stairs.

"Hello. This is Dr. Dudley. May I speak with Tanisha please?"

"This is Tanisha."

"Hello Tanisha. I'm Dr. Dudley. I'm working with your mother. Did she tell you that I would be calling to speak with you?"

"Yes," Tanisha responded. Jack had told her but Tanisha decided not to get into specifics with her.

"I'm so glad I reached you. I've been calling you for the past three weeks. I only have time to call on Mondays, and every Monday when I've called, I've let the phone ring but I never get an answer. Your mother gave me a different number and suggested that I call you on this number. Is now a good time for you to speak with me? It should only take about ten minutes," she finished.

"I normally work on Mondays, but today I only had to work a half shift so I got home early. I can talk now," Tanisha explained.

"Great. Let's get started. How would you describe your relationship with your mother?"

"You mean how she acts with me?" Tanisha asked.

"However you'd like to describe her," Dr. Dudley said.

"Well, I think she acts like she doesn't like me most of the time. She reminds me of the fast girls at my school who smoke in the bathroom and roll their eyes at me and act like they want to beat me up," she blurted. "She's not like that all the time, sometimes she's nice, but I never know when she's going to be nice or when she's going to be mean so I try to stay away from her as much as I can," she explained.

"I see. And how does that make you feel?" she asked.

"Dr. Dudley, are you going to tell my mother what I say about her?"

"Oh, forgive me, sweetie. I should have told you that what you and I discuss is confidential. I'm not going to share any of this with your mother. This information will help me gain a better understanding of your mother. So you can feel free to be honest with me. I am a psychiatrist, and I have privileges that prevent anyone from seeing my files or records unless required by a court order or subpoena. So it would take a lot for your mother or anyone else to ever see my notes. I'm taking notes on a notepad so that I can review them later," she explained.

There was something comforting and oddly familiar in Dr. Dudley's voice.

Tanisha continued, "Well, it used to make me feel bad when I was little, but now I just ignore her."

"Is she aware of how you feel?"

"I don't know. She and I don't talk. I really try to avoid her as much as possible."

"I see," Dr. Dudley said. "Tanisha, what's your happiest memory of you and your mother?"

"I'd have to think about that," Tanisha replied seriously.

"Take your time. It doesn't have to be a recent memory. Just think back and try to remember one really happy memory of her."

"Well, when I was little we used to get picked up by this babysitting service in a station wagon. The babysitter would take us to her house, but first she would drop my mom off at the train so she could get to work. She worked downtown as a secretary and wore nice clothes, make-up and perfume every day. She would always kiss my brother and me on the forehead when she got out at the train station. There was another girl in the car, and she got jealous that my mom never kissed her, so the next day my mom gave her a kiss too. I remember that I didn't want her to kiss that girl. I felt like Billie was my mom and she shouldn't kiss anyone else."

"Uh huh. How old were you then?" Dr. Dudley asked.

"I was five because I went to a half day kindergarten near the babysitter's house," Tanisha remembered.

"Did you ask your mom not to kiss the other girl the next day?"

"No. I just didn't like it. But I never said anything to anyone about it. She kissed her every day. We left that babysitter in the spring because my mother was pregnant with my youngest brother and stopped working so we stayed home with her."

"Is that the happy memory you remembered?"

"Well, it was a time when I liked her and I was proud of her. I think it was nice of her to include the other girl and kiss her so she felt special," Tanisha admitted. "I remember that time because right after she had my brother, she started acting mean again," she added. "So that's really the last happy memory I have before she went to the hospital," she paused. "Actually, that's not true. When I was nine or ten, she would sometimes surprise me and bring me home plastic tote bags or a new jump rope from the grocery store and that would make me happy," Tanisha continued.

"Do you have any memories of her that occur before you were five?"

"Not really. When my youngest brother was born, she went to the hospital for a long time, and when she got out, I didn't like being around her. I didn't think that she liked me."

"Why not?"

"When I was little, she used to stare at me and make mean faces a lot, so I learned to stay away from her. I liked being around my grandmother more and my dad," Tanisha explained.

"I see. How about now? Do you spend any time with her now?"

"No. I try to avoid her as much as possible. Since my parents divorced, she's usually out with her sister, Aunt Shanay," Tanisha shared. "My dad said that my mom has a bipolar disorder," Tanisha finished.

"Do you know what a bipolar disorder is?" Dr. Dudley asked.

"Sort of. My dad explained it a little. I know that Billie, I mean my mom, is supposed to take medication for the rest of her life. She was taking it a few months ago and was cooking and being nice, but I don't think she's taking her medication anymore because she's being mean again."

"Maybe I can explain it a little better," Dr. Dudley responded. Dr. Dudley gave Tanisha a condensed definition of the medical condition.

"Your mother suffered from psychoses after childbirth. From what I gathered, it's possible that she had delusional thoughts that her newborn infants had special powers and could hurt her. It's not uncommon for women to feel depressed after childbirth. Most women suffer from bouts of the baby blues where the mother is sad and despondent during a time when she should be happy. The baby blues usually only last a few days. In your mother's case, her baby blues spiraled into psychotic features where she thought she was going to be harmed. I can't explain why she only experienced these episodes after three of her four children. In severe cases, less than optimal development of the mother infant relationship may result from the clinical condition itself or from separations from the infant. Individuals with a history of episodes after childbirth have a persistence of depressive episodes that may manifest in mood swings and erratic behavior. Have I gotten too clinical?"

"No. I think I understand. Since my mother didn't nurture me as an infant, it affects our relationship now."

"That's my professional opinion. Now I've not been your mother's doctor for that long, but that's what it appears to me. So your father was right. Your mother has a chemical imbalance that is easily corrected by consistently taking her prescribed medications. But if she doesn't take them, her mood swings are uncontrollable and it's likely that she will suffer another episode as you put it. Do you have any questions, Tanisha?"

"No," Tanisha replied softly.

"Why don't you write down my number, and if you have any questions you can call me at my office okay?" Dr. Dudley advised.

"Okay, I'm ready." Tanisha scribbled the phone number on a strip of paper on her dresser.

"Tanisha, I want you to know that your mother is very proud of you. During one of her sessions, she shared that you receive straight A's and you're helpful with your brothers. I know she loves you in her own special way. I don't think it's violating a patient confidentiality to share that with you. I can tell that you're very mature for your age. Keep getting good grades and thank you for speaking with me. You've been very helpful. Bye."

"Bye." Tanisha hung up the receiver wondering how she'd helped Dr. Dudley. Her thoughts were interrupted by her growling stomach. Tanisha raced downstairs to finish her peanut butter and jelly sandwich. As the *Gilligan's Island* theme song ended and the television announced the *Brady Bunch* would be coming on next, Tanisha took a swig from her now lukewarm milk. She walked into the kitchen and dropped an ice cube in her glass of milk.

Tanisha curled her feet underneath her and settled in to watch television. It was rare that Tanisha got to control the television, and she enjoyed having the house to herself for a change. School would be starting in two weeks, and her days of watching endless reruns would soon be over.

Chapter 33

Birthday Blues

David halfheartedly blew out the candles on his slice of birthday cake. He had been moping around the house for the past few weeks, so his parents decided to give him a surprise birthday party. They'd asked Todd to invite his friends over for a pool party. Everyone had cooperated, and parked their cars near Todd's house and walked the three blocks to David's house. Unbeknownst to David, there were twenty teenagers sitting around the pool eating pizza and drinking lemonade.

His parents had taken David to dinner at the Glen Country Club. They had given him his birthday present, a gift certificate to buy new skis. As he opened his gift, the waiter brought out a large wedge of David's favorite dessert, German chocolate cake with seventeen tiny candles in the center.

David appeared unenthusiastic as he read the generous gift certificate amount. He thanked his parents and continued to pick at his cake before excusing himself to go to the restroom.

Elle nudged her husband. "Why don't you talk to him man to man and find out what's going on with him?"

Dr. Barton whispered back. "I tried, but he won't tell me. I think someone broke his heart."

Elle wrinkled her nose. "I didn't realize that he was seeing anyone in particular. There are so many girls that call the house all the time. But the last person he went out with was Patty, and she called the other day to ask me if she could bring anything to the surprise party."

"I don't know for sure, but that's what I think, Elle. What else could it be?"

David returned as Dr. Barton was signing the country club tab. They walked to the parking lot and climbed into the Mercedes. Elle climbed into the backseat so David could ride in the passenger seat and have more room. Less than five minutes later, Dr. Barton turned into the driveway and pulled the car into the garage.

"David, I know it's your birthday, but you didn't clean the pool today, and I want to take a swim. Son, go out back and fish those bugs out for me, please," Dr. Barton ordered.

David groaned, "But Dad. It's my birthday and I'm hanging out with Todd tonight. I don't have time to clean the pool. I don't know why we don't just hire a pool service to do it anyway. I feel like a pool boy."

"Boy, you're lucky you have a heated pool in your backyard. You should have cleaned it yesterday like I asked you. Now go do what I told you to do. It'll only take a minute!"

David walked through the family room and went outside to the patio.

"Surprise!" his friends yelled. "Happy Birthday!" He was shocked to see many of his classmates and friends standing around the pool, all wearing small cardboard birthday hats with rubber band strings under their chins.

He smiled as his friends patted him on the back. He did a double take when he saw Leslie with Vicky, one of the girls that she'd brought to his party in Lake Geneva, standing beside her. His eyes scanned the crowd hoping that Leslie had also brought Tanisha. His smile dimmed when he didn't see her. Nonetheless, he walked over to Leslie.

"Hey Leslie! Thanks for coming. Cute birthday hat!"

"Happy Birthday, David! You remember Vicky. She came to your party at the ski club," Leslie explained.

"Yeah. How you doing? I remember you. You also had another friend with you too, Tanisha, right?" he asked hopefully.

Leslie smiled at David. "That's right. I haven't seen Tanisha much this summer. Vicky talks to Tanisha more than I do."

"I haven't talked to Tanisha that much this summer either. She was at camp for two weeks, but I talked to her briefly today. I called to see what she was doing tonight, but she told me that she was going on a blind date so I didn't even mention that we were coming to your party," Vicky replied.

Tanisha is on a blind date? "Are you ladies having a nice summer?" David asked softly. His heart sunk into his chest.

"It's been cool! Not long enough. But I'm looking forward to going back since we'll be seniors." Leslie gave David a high five.

"I know that's right," David replied unenthusiastically. "You ladies have a good time, and make yourselves at home. I'm going to go work the room." David walked away and plastered a smile on his face. His thoughts were consumed once again with Tanisha. *Who is she on a blind date with?*

As he walked around the pool, greeting his guests, he saw Patty. "Hi David. Happy Birthday!" Patty sang cheerfully.

David studied Patty and smiled. She looked pretty in a floral sarong skirt and light peach halter top. Her naturally curly hair hung loosely at her shoulders. His parents liked Patty and Patty clearly liked him. He thought Patty was nice, but she never had much to say, and she didn't understand his sense of humor. Still, their dads were in John & Judy together, and her parents had recently joined the Glen Country Club. His mom even encouraged David to work with Patty on her golf game.

"Hey Patty, you look nice," David smiled.

"Thanks," Patty giggled.

David chuckled to himself, missing the wisecrack that Tanisha would have offered to his weak, obligatory compliment. But Tanisha wasn't here, and Patty was. He reached for Patty's hand. "Doesn't the birthday boy get a birthday hug?" *It's time I stopped thinking about Tanisha Carlson.*

Chapter 34

The Blind Date

Tanisha hadn't spoken to David in over three weeks. She missed him. She'd been tempted to call him a few times, but as the days turned into weeks and she hadn't heard from him, Lori convinced her that she needed to move on.

"Teenie, you told him the truth," Lori emphasized. "You apologized for hurting his feelings, but like you said, you guys weren't going together so it's not like you cheated on him or anything when you were at camp kissing Brian."

Tanisha knew that Lori was right. If David was unable to move past what happened, then so be it. Besides, he would be entering his senior year at HG and then heading off to Georgetown or the University of Pennsylvania the following year and would forget about her anyway.

She tied the sundress halter strap around her neck and slipped on her white Capezio sandals. She admired her reflection in the mirror. She'd decided to buy a new outfit to cheer herself up and had chosen a red and white sundress from Marshall Fields. The dress had been on clearance, and she'd paid only twenty dollars for it. The dress was a size four and fit snugly in the bodice which gave

Tanisha's slim figure the illusion of cleavage. She twirled in the mirror and admired her reflection.

She'd finally agreed to meet one of Doug's friends. His name was Andre and he played on the basketball team with Doug. Lori had met him once before and reported that he was very tall and very handsome.

It was Saturday night and Billie was roller skating with Aunt Shanay. The plan was that Charlotte would drop them off at the movie theatre, and they'd meet Doug and his friend there. They'd agreed to pay Charlotte a dollar apiece for driving them. Tanisha applied blush to her cheeks and raced downstairs to wait for Charlotte and Lori. She grabbed her blue jean jacket from the closet and waited on the front porch.

Charlotte pulled the large Impala into the movie theatre parking lot and Tanisha and Lori climbed out of the car. They'd agreed to wear sundresses, and Lori wore a light green sun dress with white daisies on the belt. They were ten minutes early.

"That dress is so cute, Tanisha! I can't believe that you only paid twenty dollars for it!" Lori gushed.

Tanisha twirled around on her tiptoes. "Your dress is cute too! I almost didn't try this dress on because it's a size four and I normally wear a six. But something told me to try it on, and it fit!"

"It looks good. Oh, here comes Doug's car," Lori squealed.

The girls watched as Doug parked. Lori's boyfriend got out of the driver's side and Andre exited the passenger side. Tanisha smiled at Lori when she saw Andre. He stood at least six feet two inches tall and had dark brown skin. His hair was cut low on the sides.

Doug walked over to Lori, grabbed her around the waist and twirled her in the air. "Hey cutie!" he gushed.

"Doug! Put me down!" Lori giggled.

Doug smiled at Tanisha as he lowered Lori to the pavement. "Hey! How you doing, Teenie? This is my boy, Andre."

Andre was studying Tanisha appreciatively. "How you doing, Teenie? I've heard a lot about you. Doug told me that you were pretty, but he lied. You're gorgeous."

Tanisha blushed. "Hi. Nice to meet you too Andre and thanks for the compliment." Andre wore dark blue Levi jeans that hugged his hips tightly and a short sleeve yellow polo shirt that gripped his biceps, emphasizing his strong upper body. Tanisha grinned at Lori and gave a discreet 'thumbs up' sign.

"So, let's do this thing. You remember our strategy right, Dre?" Doug asked.

"I got it, just chill. You're sure *Fame* is playing in theatre two, right?" Andre confirmed.

"Yeah, Kip saw it last night with his girl and told me it was still in theatre two," Doug responded.

Tanisha looked at Lori. She raised her eyebrow and whispered, "What are they doing?"

"You'll see. They have this system so that only one of us has to pay to get into the theatre. Watch," Lori answered.

"But this is the dollar theatre. They can't pay one dollar to take us to a movie?" Tanisha wrinkled her forehead.

"It'll be fine. Doug and I do this all the time," Lori explained.

Andre walked into the theatre to buy the ticket and Doug escorted Lori and Tanisha to the side exit. Five minutes later Andre opened the side fire door and hustled the waiting trio inside.

Tanisha followed reluctantly as Andre whisked her into the dark theatre, grabbing her hand so that she could follow as her eyes adjusted to the dark. His palms were sweaty. *His hands feel like an eel.*

As they walked in the row, Tanisha quickly pulled her hand away and rubbed it on her new sundress.

Doug and Lori decided to sit in the row behind Andre and Tanisha. As Tanisha's eyes adjusted to the movie theatre darkness, she could see that the theatre was practically empty with one other couple huddled in the far back row kissing passionately.

"Doug, I got us in, now you get the popcorn," Andre whispered.

"That's cool. Give me your ticket stub so I can get back in," Doug said.

Tanisha watched as Andre handed Doug his ticket stub and then picked up a discarded popcorn container from the floor and handed it to Doug.

"What are you doing with that?" Tanisha asked.

"Oh. You just take an empty popcorn container and tell them that you just bought the popcorn but you spilled it and you get free popcorn," Andre explained casually. "They'll give him a fresh container. I never pay for popcorn at the movies," he bragged.

Tanisha was mortified. They'd just snuck into the dollar movie theatre, and now her date was running a scam for free popcorn! She crossed her arms and put her jean jacket around her shoulders, bracing herself for a long cold night.

Tanisha shifted in her seat so that she was leaned as far to the left as possible since Andre sat on her right side.

"What's the matter, are you cold, Teenie? I can warm you up," Andre offered. He leaned in next to her.

"That's okay, I'm fine," Tanisha stated. She gently nudged him back into his seat.

She crossed her legs right over left and settled in to watch *Fame* for the third time.

Doug returned with the popcorn container and handed it to Andre who stuffed a handful in his mouth and munched noisily.

Andre thrust the popcorn container at Tanisha. "Want some? It's nice and hot."

"No thank you," Tanisha growled.

"Why are you sitting way over there? I won't bite you," Andre whispered as bits of popcorn fell out of his mouth.

"I'm sure you won't, but I'm fine. Shhh! The movie's starting," Tanisha barked.

"You don't really want to watch the movie do you? This came out over six months ago. I know you've seen it," Andre purred, "I want to get to know you better."

"I've seen it twice, but I want to see it again," Tanisha said sternly.

Andre let out a deep guttural sigh and stood up. "Yo, Doug. Meet me in the lobby, man!"

Doug looked at Lori and followed Andre into the lobby.

Lori leaned into the seat to whisper to Tanisha. "What's up, girl? I told you he was fine."

"He's fine all right, but he's a scam artist. Sneaking into the movies and scamming for free popcorn?"

"It's no big deal, Teenie. They'll buy us pizza or something after the movie," Lori explained.

"And then he's acting like I'm supposed to make out with him, and I just met him. I haven't even known him for five minutes!"

"Did he try to kiss you?" Lori asked.

"No, but he keeps trying to put his hand on my leg or his arm on my shoulder. I don't even know his last name. I'm just irked that he scammed us into the movie theatre," Tanisha sighed.

"Well, do you want me to have Doug take you home?" Lori asked.

"I can hang out and watch the movie. He's fine, but I'm not going to be making out with him when I just met him. You know that's not my style."

"I'll say something to Doug," Lori assured her friend.

The girls were interrupted by Doug.

"Uh, Andre just remembered that he has to go to his cousin's house tonight. He totally forgot," Doug stammered. "I need to drop him off, and then I'll drop you off, Teenie," he finished.

Tanisha looked at Lori knowingly, folded her arms across her chest and stood up to leave the theatre. *Looks like Andre isn't having such a great time with me either. Why is it that most boys are like old fashioned sinks? They have a hot nozzle on one side of the sink, and the cold nozzle on the other side of the sink. There's no middle ground. They're either hot or cold. At least Brian Kraft gave me the option of kissing him or not. If I had told Brian Kraft that I didn't want to make out with him, after learning that he had a girlfriend, I wonder if he would have turned ice cold too? Guess, I'll never know. But at least we'd spent several hours getting to know each other before he tried anything. Hmph! I bet if I'd agreed to let Andre rub my thigh, or kiss me, he wouldn't have had to go to his cousin's house all of a sudden. Some boys are as simple as a one cell organism!*

Her arms still folded across her chest, she quietly followed Doug and Lori to the parking lot, where Andre stood waiting by the car. Andre didn't say a word to Tanisha as she approached. She climbed into the back seat and returned Andre's silence. *Two can play this game. I didn't do anything wrong, and if he wants to act like a three year old, then good riddance. No love lost! I don't care how fine he is! I can't believe I wasted my new dress on this big baby!*

Doug and Lori held hands and whispered as Tanisha and Andre stared out of their respective windows. The silence was occasionally broken by Andre giving directions to Doug.

Tanisha's eyebrows creased as she paid attention to where she was. They were headed to Morning Side. She sat up in her seat as Doug turned into the subdivision. Tanisha's heart raced as he pulled the car into David Barton's driveway. *Was Andre David Barton's cousin?*

Before exiting the car, Andre offered a polite, "Nice to meet you, Teenie." Her response was barely audible. She was stunned by her surroundings. She couldn't believe that she was sitting in front of David Barton's house. Doug got out of the car and walked up the driveway with Andre.

Tanisha leaned into the front seat and whispered. "Lori, this is David Barton's house!"

Lori stared at Tanisha in disbelief. Her jaw hung open. "You're kidding! Are you sure, Teenie?" Lori asked.

"I'm positive. I've been to his house, and this is it," Tanisha gasped. "And that's his car. What date is it?"

"It's August 15th," Lori replied. "Why?"

"August 15th is David's birthday," Tanisha remembered aloud as she shook her head from side to side. "I can't believe that I'm sitting on David Barton's driveway," she exclaimed. "He hasn't bothered to return any of my phone calls, and now I'm sitting outside of his house on his birthday!" she groaned. "I wish Doug would hurry up," she sighed. She could hear dance music and voices coming from the backyard, but she didn't see any cars on the driveway or in the cul de sac. *He must be having a birthday party. But if there's a party here, where are the cars?* She was confused.

"Take a deep breath, Teenie. Try to calm down," Lori encouraged. "I have an idea. Maybe we should go inside so you can at least wish him a happy birthday," Lori suggested. "Confront him and make him talk to you."

Tanisha stared at her friend in disbelief. "Are you serious? And give him the chance to ignore me and embarrass me in public at his own party? I don't think I'm up for that," Tanisha said.

"Well, what do you want to do?" Lori asked.

"I have no idea," Tanisha moaned. "But I'm glad that you're here with me," she admitted. She looked through the back window. Her eyes became narrow slits as she stared intently up the long, driveway. "Is that him standing in front of the garage holding that girl's hand?" she whispered to Lori. "Yup! That's him!" she stated confidently. "He's talking to Doug and Andre, and now they're pointing at the car!"

Chapter 35

The New Deal

David's parents decided to go to a late movie. They knew all of the teenagers at the party and trusted David not to let the festivities get out of hand. They planned to return at midnight to end the merriment.

David had personally spoken to all of his guests. He'd been truly surprised by the party and was glad to see his friends, some of whom he hadn't seen since school let out in May. Patty had been glued to his side the entire evening. As he studied Patty, he decided that he would give her an opportunity to be his girlfriend. She was also entering her senior year, and she hadn't dated anyone all through high school, patiently waiting for David to make a move. He'd taken her to junior prom and been her cotillion escort. They'd even gone on a few dates, but he'd made it clear to her that he was dating a lot of girls. He knew his parents liked Patty and would like nothing better than for him to spend more time with her.

He grabbed her hand and led her into the garage. He leaned her against the back of the BMW and placed his arms around her waist. As he whispered in her ear, he was interrupted by a tap on his shoulder and a slight cough.

David turned around slowly and smiled when he saw his cousin. "Hey, Dre! I was wondering where you were."

"Hey, dude! Happy Birthday, Cuz! Don't let me interrupt," Andre chuckled.

David grabbed Patty's hand and pulled her out to the driveway. "Patty, this is my cousin, Andre."

Patty smoothed her hair and waved softly. "Hello. Nice to meet you. How are you related?" Patty asked.

David and Andre stared at each other and shrugged. "Our grandmothers are sisters," Andre explained.

"Oh, so you're third cousins," Patty offered.

David stared at Patty. "I can never keep all of that straight," he shrugged.

"Me neither," Andre agreed. "This is my boy Doug. We play ball together," Andre said.

"Hey, Doug! Welcome! You two can make yourselves at home. My parents threw me a surprise party. There are about twenty people in the back by the pool. Dre knows where everything is." David shook Doug's hand and waved them into the house through the garage.

"Sorry I'm late," Andre continued. "But I went on this blind date from hell," he groaned. "Doug set me up with his girlfriend's friend."

David's ears perked up when he said blind date.

"Dre, you have to admit that Teenie is a cutie. And she's usually a lot of fun. I don't know what got into her tonight," Doug explained.

"She's fine, but she's too uptight. She wouldn't even let me put my arm around her at the movies," Andre whined.

David stared at the car in his driveway. "Did you say her name was Teenie?"

"Yeah, Teenie is her nickname. Her real name is Tanisha," Doug explained. "In fact, they're in the car right now," he continued. "So I can't stay. I need to drop Teenie off so Lori and I can finish our date," Doug finished, casually tossing his car keys from his left hand to his right.

"They're in the car right now?" David glanced at the car parked at the end of the long driveway. His thoughts raced as he stood in the garage holding Patty's hand.

Tanisha watched from the backseat, wishing she were any place but there.

David dropped Patty's hand. "Doug, why don't you invite them to the party? The night's still young. Dre, there are plenty of honeys by the pool that you can meet. In fact, Patty, why don't you take Andre to the pool and introduce him to Kim?" he suggested. "Doug, I'll walk over to the car with you and personally invite them to my birthday party. They can't turn down the birthday boy," David charged.

"Good idea. He'll like Kim," Patty said

Patty followed Andre through the garage as David and Doug walked down the driveway to the car.

Tanisha slumped down in the backseat.

"Lori, this is David. Today is his birthday, and he's inviting us to his party," Doug explained. "And this is Tanisha," Doug continued. "Or should I introduce you as Teenie, Teenie?" he teased.

"We've met before. Hi David," Lori said.

"Hi, Lori. Good to see you again," David said.

Doug stared at Lori suspiciously. "How do you know David?" he asked.

Lori climbed out of the car. "Let's go inside, and I'll explain," she whispered.

She led Doug away whispering as David peered into the back seat with one hand on the roof of the car.

"Hi, Tanisha." David opened the rear door and extended his hand. Tanisha took his hand and let him guide her out of the car. His fingers felt soft and warm. *At least his hands aren't sweaty like Andre's.* Once out of the car, Tanisha quickly dropped his hand and fiddled with a ring that she wore.

David studied her face. "So you weren't even going to come inside? You know this is my house, and it's my birthday, and you weren't even going to come inside? What's up with that?"

"I didn't remember that it was your birthday. Happy Birthday, David," she said softly. Tanisha stared at her feet. "Honestly, I didn't know where we were going until we pulled into your driveway. Once I realized that we were at your house, I was just sitting here asking Lori what I should do when I saw you in the garage."

David was at a loss for words. He hadn't seen or spoken to Tanisha in several weeks. Seeing her face brought back memories of happier times.

"Is Andre really your cousin?" Tanisha asked. She tilted her head slightly to look at his face.

"Yeah. Our grandmothers are sisters." David nodded his head from side to side several times and studied her face. He hadn't realized how much he'd missed her.

"You didn't look surprised to see me, so how'd you know that I was in the car?" Tanisha asked. "I'm sure your cousin didn't have anything nice to say about me."

"He said your name. Actually he said he'd gone on a blind date with a pretty girl named Teenie who wouldn't even let him put his arm around her, and since your name isn't that common, I assumed it was you."

Tanisha toed a small pebble with her foot.

"Why are you staring at your feet?" David tilted Tanisha's chin up with his hand. The gesture sent chills up Tanisha's spine.

Tanisha's tone softened. "So was that your girlfriend?"

"Was who my girlfriend?" David asked.

"The girl you were just kissing and holding hands with in the garage?" Tanisha asked nervously.

"I wasn't kissing her. She's just a friend. So you saw me in the garage, and you still weren't going to get out of the car and speak? What's that about, Tanisha?"

Tanisha's eyes held David's. "David, I wasn't sure it was you until you came out of the garage. What was I supposed to do? It looked like you two weren't coming up for air."

"It's not even like that. We were just talking," he flushed.

"Don't even try it. I saw you. You had her pressed up against the car!" Tanisha's tone was serious. She folded her arms across her chest and took a deep breath.

"Now look who's jealous." David stared at Tanisha squarely. "Now you see how it feels."

Tanisha stared back. "David, I explained what happened at camp and you didn't say a word to me. I apologized even though I hadn't done anything wrong. I called you three or four times and waited and waited for you to call me so we could talk about it and you never did. And then I happen to come to your house by accident, and I see you making out with some girl, and I'm supposed to get out and run up to you? And you made me feel so guilty about what I did at camp. You have some nerve!" she barked.

"You're right. I should have called you back. But I was mad at you. I don't usually get played," David whispered.

She locked eyes with him. "David, I didn't play you. What I did at camp had nothing to do with you. It was just something that I did for me, and now it's in the past."

David stared at Tanisha, unsure of what to say.

"So is that your girlfriend? You didn't answer my question," Tanisha repeated.

"I wouldn't say all that. Her name is Patty. She's a senior at HG. Our parents are friends." David put his hands in his pocket, shifted his weight and shrugged.

"You two look pretty chummy to me," Tanisha said sarcastically.

"We've hung out a few times. I took her to junior prom last year, and I was her escort at the Links cotillion. We've gone to a few movies." David shrugged his shoulders. "She's definitely not my girlfriend."

"But you're dating?" Tanisha asked.

"I wouldn't say all of that." David took his foot out of his shoe and rubbed it along his calf.

"What would she say?" Tanisha tilted her head to the side and stared at David.

"I don't know," David shrugged.

"I'm a girl. Trust me. She'd probably say that you're dating."

"But she's not my girlfriend. We're not going together," David protested. "She knows that I date other people."

Tanisha shook her head at David. "See, that's the problem. You're thinking one thing, and she's probably thinking something completely different. You have her all pressed up against the car five minutes ago, and now you're acting like she's just some girl from school. She's probably bragging to her friends right now that she's your girlfriend. Why would I want to sign up for that when I'm old enough to date?" Tanisha reasoned.

"Tanisha, Patty knows that she is not my girlfriend. And this isn't about Patty. You're missing the point," David said.

"I'm missing the point? What is the point, David?" Tanisha asked.

"The point is that I missed you, and I still want to get to know you," David said softly.

"The point is that you're busted! You're holding me to a double standard," Tanisha said, pointing her finger at David's nose.

David studied Tanisha's face wanting desperately to kiss her at that moment.

Tanisha tapped her index finger into his chest. "Just admit it. You were about to give her a tonsillectomy."

David laughed at Tanisha's joke. "Well, since I can't give you a tonsillectomy."

Tanisha scrunched her face into a soft scowl and slanted her eyes at David. "So is that what this is about? You're jealous that I kissed that guy at camp and not you?" Tanisha asked. "Is that your point?"

David stuffed both of his hands into his pockets. "Well, I'm a man and I have needs. We'd been getting to know each other and you'd been telling me that you couldn't date until you're fifteen, so I think you're this good girl who doesn't break the rules. Then you come back from camp with a big hickey on your neck! How do you think that made me feel, Tanisha?"

Tanisha counted off on her fingers. "First of all, I never said that I was a good girl, David. You said that. I just said that I couldn't date until I'm fifteen, which is true. Second, you never tried to kiss me so it's not like I rejected you. Third, I'll probably never see that guy from camp again, but you go to school with Patty and she was your prom date. So if you ask me, your crime is worse than mine," she finished.

"You knew I was trying to get to know you better. I told you that before you left for camp. Don't play dumb, Tanisha," David said.

"Well, it looks like you got over me quick, fast and in a hurry!" Tanisha quipped.

"I didn't expect you to be on the driveway." David looked seriously at Tanisha.

Tanisha's gaze was soft but serious. "Just like I didn't expect you to spill beer all over my shirt and see the hickey on my neck," she whispered.

They both looked away. Neither knew what to say. Tanisha twirled the strap on her purse as the music from the party floated down the driveway. She strained her ear to hear what the song was. She recognized the melody but couldn't hear the words clearly. She listened harder.

"*…won't you smile awhile for me Sara? Sara smile awhile for me. Won't you laugh a little?*" Tanisha loved that song. *Hall & Oats' Sara Smile*. She was lost in the song and didn't notice David staring at her intently.

"So now what do we do?" David asked. She could feel his breath on her face.

"I have no idea," Tanisha said. "You want to try to be friends again?" she asked.

"I usually kiss my female friends at some point," David advised. Tanisha raised her eyebrow and pulled her head back indignantly. David studied Tanisha's expression. "I'm just keeping it real," he explained. His breath was warm on her cheek. She could smell his cologne.

"And then what happens?" Tanisha asked. Her heart was beating out of her chest. *Breathe, Tanisha. Breathe!*

"What do you mean?" David furrowed his eyebrows.

"Once you're no longer kissing them, then what happens?" Tanisha tapped her foot lightly awaiting his response.

"Well, we usually do other stuff or we go our separate ways." David slowly grabbed Tanisha's hands and played with her fingers. He used his thumb to trace the ring on her right hand.

"Exactly. And when you go your separate ways, then you're not friends with them anymore. Is that what you want?" Tanisha asked.

David stared at Tanisha, a blank expression on his face.

Tanisha's tone was soft. She stared directly into his eyes as she spoke. "David, you're going to be leaving for college this time next year, and I'll still be in high school. What happens then?" Tanisha continued without waiting for a response. "I'll tell you what happens. You'll be dating college girls, and I'll be here pining away for you like an idiot."

"What are you saying?" David rubbed Tanisha's hands in his hands.

"I'm saying that even if we started dating now, where would it get us? Are you really going to come back and take me to prom? I doubt it." Tanisha took a deep breath. "Wouldn't it be better if you hung out with girls who were able to drive, and I hung out with boys who might be able to take me to my high school dances?"

David slowly dropped Tanisha's hands and placed his hands on her bare shoulders. He lightly rubbed her shoulders and traced his thumb along her collar bone. "You look really nice tonight by the way," David said softly.

Tanisha playfully swatted his hand away. "Duh! Tell me something I don't know! But stop changing the subject. You know I'm right," she scolded.

David laughed and rubbed his hands along Tanisha's forearms. His touch gave her goose bumps. Tanisha playfully pushed his hands away again, and gently cupped his face in her hands.

"Focus, David!" Tanisha ordered. "Even if I wanted to let you use your beer soaked tongue as a tongue depressor in my mouth right now, I wouldn't want to catch Patty's cooties!" she giggled.

"I haven't had a beer in several weeks," David corrected. "Between you and my mom making me feel guilty about it, I haven't had a taste for beer," he said. "Plus, every time I look at a beer, it reminds me of the last time I saw you," his voice trailed. "I missed you," he shared.

Tanisha stared at him softly. "I missed you too, David," she replied, her eyes boring into his. "I really enjoy spending time with you, but you're seventeen now, and I'm scared that if we start messing around, like Todd and Maria, we'll kill our friendship." Tanisha gripped David's hands in her hands. "So my birthday present to you is you have my permission to give your little friend Patty a tonsillectomy, and I'll still be your friend. You can even dance the horizontal hula with her if you want, but spare me the details," she giggled.

"Who said I was going to do all that with her? That's your little imagination run wild," David chuckled.

"Everyone knows that the first step in any reputable twelve step recovery program is admitting that you have a problem," Tanisha giggled.

David laughed out loud. "You're such a trip! How old are you again?"

"I'll be fifteen in less than four months. And now that we're friends again, I expect a big gift! Huge!" Tanisha spread her arms wide like an airplane. "By the way, the tonsillectomy thing works both ways. Once I find someone who's worthy to share saliva with me again, I get to go for it, and you have to promise that you'll be my listening ear if I want to talk to you about any of my little Romeos. Is that okay with you, Mr. Double Standard?"

David narrowed his eyes at Tanisha and crossed his arms over his chest. "What if that doesn't work for me? What if I want to be more than your friend?" David asked.

"That may happen, or it may not, so you can perfect your tonsillectomy technique on Patty or anyone else you choose Mr. 'I'm a Man and I have needs.' But if we're going to be friends, you can't freak out and act like a jealous lunatic if I start dating somebody. Follow my example, I just saw you trying to give Patty a tonsillectomy, and I didn't act crazy."

David rubbed his chin with one hand. "I have to think about that one a little bit."

"What's there to think about, David? Haven't you ever been friends with a girl before?" Tanisha studied David's face.

"Yeah, but I've never been friends with a girl that I'm attracted to. I don't usually mess around with that friendship stuff. If I'm attracted to someone, I usually go in for the kill and seal the deal." David slapped his hands together.

"That's your problem, Casanova! You exchange bodily fluids before you even know someone, and once you get to know them, you don't want to be bothered, while they're pining away looking for the title." Tanisha shook her head from side to side clucking her tongue disapprovingly.

"Exchange bodily fluids? You are too funny, but that's not completely true," David defended. "I don't just mash and dash! I'm a gentleman and try to let them down easy. And for the record I don't exchange bodily fluids," he winked.

"That's way too much information there, big guy. And saliva is a bodily fluid, genius," Tanisha laughed.

"What's the title?" David asked.

"You know, it's the girlfriend title. After you've exchanged bodily fluids, your conquest is expecting to be called your girlfriend, get it? She's expecting to hold 'The Title,'" Tanisha made quotation marks with her fingers.

"You are cracking me up," David laughed.

Tanisha swatted at a mosquito on her leg. "I'm just telling you the truth. But seriously, I know your type. You're a spoiled little rich boy who is accustomed to always getting his way and letting his shiny black sports car do his dirty work. You're probably only interested in me because I didn't bite your Corvette baited hook right away, and I'm a challenge for you," Tanisha suggested.

"Not quite true. When I met you at the ski club in Lake Geneva, my car was in the parking lot, so I wooed you with just my good looks, charm and wit," David boasted.

"Don't flatter yourself. But if that's what you want to believe, psycho, it is your fantasy," Tanisha giggled.

David gently grabbed both of Tanisha's hands. "But seriously, what happens next, Teenie?"

He's using my nickname again! Tanisha stared in David's eyes. "Let's just be friends and see what happens, okay?"

"So, that's it. We're not going to try to hang out when you're able to date officially?" David asked.

"David, I really like spending time with you. I really do. But I don't want to be one of your statistics. Let me get some experiences under my belt and then we'll see," Tanisha explained.

"Oh, I get it, you need to exchange a little bodily fluid of your own, is that it? Sow your wild oats?" David asked seriously.

"Now I've created a monster!" Tanisha laughed. "I didn't say all of that, but I do want to be able to hang out and experience high school without feeling like I'm cheating on you and doing something wrong when you go away to college next year."

David studied Tanisha's face. "Damn! I can't even argue with that one because it makes too much sense!"

"But now I'm going to be comparing these guys my age to you. You'll be like my boyfriend mentor to help me steer clear of losers," she continued.

David smiled at Tanisha. "Good luck. I'm a pretty tough act to follow!"

"Don't flatter yourself, Romeo!" Tanisha poked David in the ribs.

"Okay bossy, you win. But we can be friends under one condition." David held up his index finger.

"What's the condition?" Tanisha asked.

"You can't date or mess around with anyone that's related to me or anyone that I know," David stated firmly.

Tanisha giggled. "You've lost your mind. You know a lot of people. I'm not agreeing to that. Besides, how silly would I look asking someone if they're related to you or if they know you? Am I supposed to stop what I'm doing every time someone asks me for my phone number and call you first? Who has that kind of time?" she laughed. "I'm a man magnet!"

"Well, you better ask them if they know me, little arrogant one." David's look was playful but serious. "And what are you doing going on a blind date when you're not old enough to date yet, Miss Sneaky?"

Tanisha covered her mouth with her hand so she could grin without concern for her decayed tooth. She spoke through her cupped hand, "I know. I'm so busted." She removed her hand and continued. "I was bored and Lori convinced me to meet him. I had no idea Andre was your cousin, I swear! You guys look nothing alike so who would have thought? What are the odds of my blind date being related to you?" she asked. "But Andre is a cutie, and I was attracted to him initially. But he irked me with the free movie & free popcorn scam." Tanisha placed her index finger at her temple as if in deep thought. "But he's fine so I could get over that. Let's go find him so I can make it up to him." She snapped her finger and spun around to head into the house.

David grabbed her elbow and turned her around gently. "What's the free popcorn scam, Teenie?"

She smiled at the playfulness in his tone as he used her nickname so effortlessly once again.

Tanisha shifted her weight from her left foot to her right foot. "I'll tell you later. I have to use the bathroom, and these mosquitoes are eating me alive." Tanisha walked up the long driveway. "Is Mr. Belvedere at the party?"

"You know where the bathroom is, tiny bladder. Belvedere is in my room, but I'll go get him for you. And I'm serious, don't mess around with Andre."

Tanisha rubbed her index fingers together. "Uh, Uh, Uh, that's not your call," she scolded. "He's fair game. Why isn't Belvedere at the party?" she asked.

"Patty's allergic to him," David said.

"She's allergic to Mr. Belvedere? Strike one for Patty!" Tanisha laughed out loud.

David gently grabbed Tanisha's arm as she walked toward the garage and turned her around again. "Can I at least have a birthday kiss?"

Tanisha furrowed her eyebrows together and grimaced. "Gross! You just kissed Patty! Besides, when we exchange bodily fluids, I want the title! Did I not teach you anything?" Tanisha laughed.

"My fault. Force of habit. I just meant a peck on the cheek or something. And for the tenth time, I wasn't kissing Patty!" David placed his arms loosely around Tanisha's waist. "Hey, you said **when** we exchange bodily fluids. There's hope for me yet!"

Tanisha took a deep breath, enjoying David's arms around her waist. *I haven't been hugged like this since I kissed Brian Kraft at camp.* She had to tilt her head back to look into David's eyes. She took another deep breath and felt his arms tighten slightly around her waist. *I wonder if David is a good kisser. It is his birthday. What's the harm in one kiss? No! Be strong, Teenie.*

"You don't miss a trick do you?" Tanisha smiled. "I'll make your day one day, but today is not the day, birthday boy." She placed her hands on his and removed his arms from her waist. "How about a hug instead?" she offered.

"If that's what you're serving up, I'll take what I can get, Miss Teenie with the teenie, tiny bladder!" David teased.

"Groovy! But make it quick, my prom date might be inside your party, and I don't want him to see me make a puddle on your driveway."

David slowly pulled Tanisha into his body and tilted her chin up to look into her eyes. "Let's be serious for a minute," David paused. "I really missed your friendship, Teenie," David whispered. He slowly encircled her in a warm embrace, his fingers gently tracing small circles on her back as he rocked her from side to side. With his soft breath on her neck, she felt herself relaxing in his arms.

"I missed you too, David." Tanisha said seriously. She inhaled deeper and felt David's arms tighten around her body. She squeezed her arms around his waist and leaned her head into his chest. She breathed in his familiar Polo scent, enjoying the warmth of his body, and listening to the beat of his heart. *If he tried to kiss me right now, I would totally let him.*

She took a deep breath and spoke. "I can't breathe," she joked. "Let's go inside before I pee on my new dress," she pleaded as she pulled out of his embrace.

"You and that bladder," David laughed. "You sure know how to kill a moment."

He draped his arm across Tanisha's shoulder and led her through the garage. She casually wrapped both of her arms around his waist as they walked.

Tanisha took a deep breath. *I don't know where this friendship is headed, but I'm glad he's back in my life.*

To be continued...

About the Author

A native Chicagoan, JC Conrad-Ellis lives in Wisconsin with her husband, their three children, and their son's three goldfish; the precursor to getting an allergy free puppy. At printing, the goldfish had not been replaced with understudies, and JC still had no plans to visit the town's barbeque coon festival.

Coming Soon!

<u>Chemistry & Chaos</u>

Book 3 in the Black Diamond Series

In <u>Chemistry & Chaos</u>, the girls are celebrating their sweet sixteen and the stories of Maria, Lori, Rashanda, Grace & Justine are introduced in depth. Tanisha's story line continues and serves as a gossamer thread delicately weaving the teen tales together.

To read a chapter excerpt visit the author's website at
<u>www.blackdiamondseries.com</u>

www.ingramcontent.com/pod-product-compliance
Lightning Source LLC
Chambersburg PA
CBHW070746190726
48292CB00002B/432